HIGH PRAISE FOR THE WORK OF
TERRY C. JOHNSTON

"Based on careful research and field study, [Terry C. Johnston's] novels follow the adventures of Seamus Donegan, sometimes scout, sometimes sergeant . . . Johnston can be considered king of the Indian wars' fiction writers."

—John D. McDermott, retired historian and
administrator for the National Park Service and
the Council on Historic Preservation, author of
*Forlorn Hope: The Battle of White Bird Canyon
and the Beginning of the Nez Perce War*

"Rich and fascinating . . . There is a genuine flavor of the period and of the men who made it what it was."

—*Washington Post Book World*

"Rich in historical lore and dramatic description, this is a first-rate addition to a solid series, a rousing tale of one man's search for independence in the unspoiled beauty of the Old West."

—*Publishers Weekly* on *Buffalo Palace*

"A first-class novel by a talented author."

—*Tulsa World* on *Dream Catcher*

THE PLAINSMEN SERIES BY TERRY C. JOHNSTON

CRIES FROM THE EARTH

The Outbreak of the Nez Perce War
and the
Battle of White Bird Canyon
June 17, 1877

Terry C. Johnston

St. Martin's Paperbacks

CRIES FROM THE EARTH

Copyright © 1999 by Terry C. Johnston.

For information address St. Martin's Press, 175 Fifth Avenue, New York, NY 10010.

ISBN: 0-312-96907-4
EAN: 80312-96907-3

Printed in the United States of America

St. Martin's Paperbacks edition / April 1999

St. Martin's Paperbacks are published by St. Martin's Press, 175 Fifth Avenue, New York, NY 10010.

10 9 8 7 6 5 4

with my deep admiration
and heartfelt respect
for how he breathes such passion
into our common history,
I dedicate this novel on the
outbreak of the Nez Perce War
to my friend,
Paul Andrew Hutton

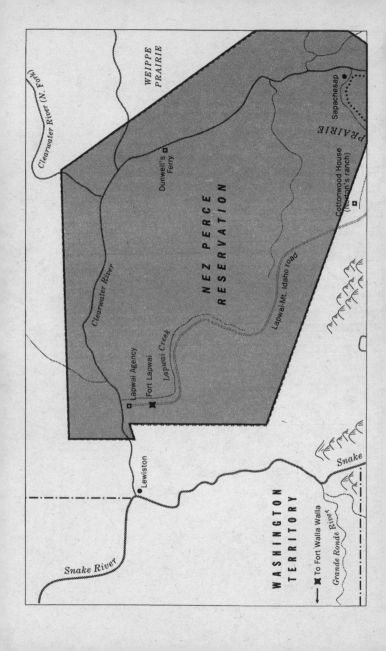

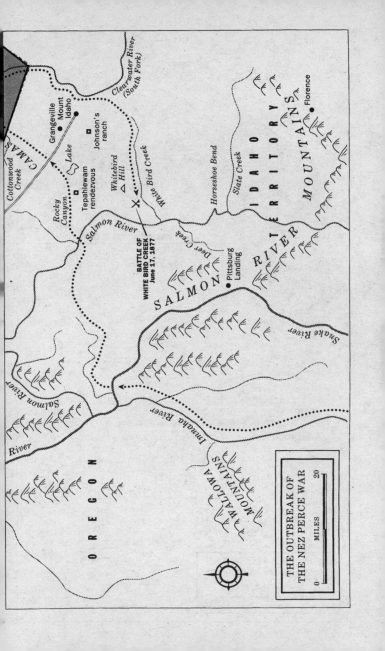

THE OUTBREAK OF
THE NEZ PERCE WAR

0   MILES   20

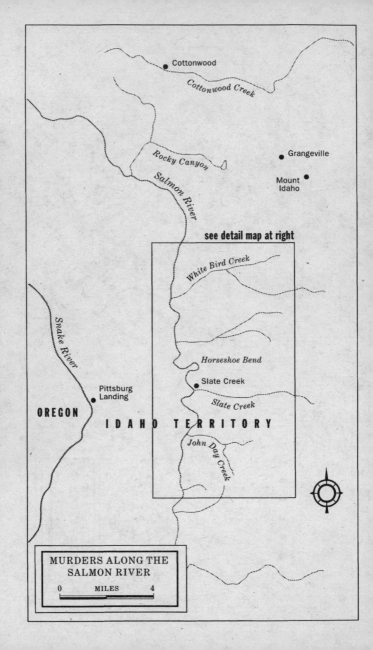

Cottonwood

Cottonwood Creek

Rocky Canyon

Salmon River

Grangeville

Mount
Idaho

see detail map at right

White Bird Creek

Snake River

Horseshoe Bend

Pittsburg
Landing

Slate Creek

Slate Creek

OREGON

IDAHO TERRITORY

John Day Creek

MURDERS ALONG THE
SALMON RIVER

0   MILES   4

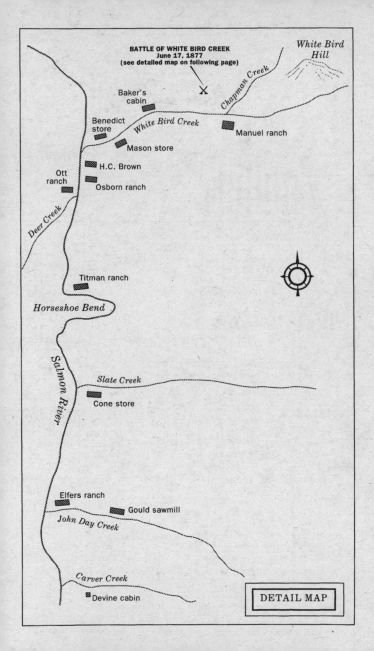

BATTLE OF WHITE BIRD CREEK
June 17, 1877
(see detailed map on following page)

White Bird Hill

Chapman Creek

Baker's cabin

Benedict store

White Bird Creek

Manuel ranch

Mason store

H.C. Brown

Ott ranch

Osborn ranch

Deer Creek

Titman ranch

Horseshoe Bend

Salmon River

Slate Creek

Cone store

Elfers ranch

Gould sawmill

John Day Creek

Carver Creek

Devine cabin

DETAIL MAP

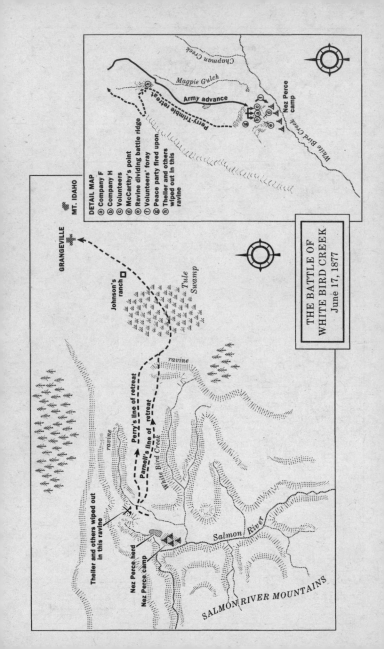

DETAIL MAP

ⓐ Company F
ⓑ Company H
ⓒ Volunteers
ⓓ McCarthy's point
ⓔ Ravine dividing battle ridge
ⓕ Volunteers' foray
ⓖ Peace party fired upon
ⓗ Theller and others wiped out in this ravine

Chapman Creek
Magpie Gulch
Army advance
Perry-Trimble retreat
Nez Perce camp
White Bird Creek

THE BATTLE OF
WHITE BIRD CREEK
June 17, 1877

GRANGEVILLE
MT. IDAHO
Johnson's ranch
Tule Swamp
ravine
Perry's line of retreat
Parnell's line of retreat
White Bird Creek
ravine
Theller and others wiped out in this ravine
Nez Perce herd
Nez Perce camp
Salmon River
SALMON RIVER MOUNTAINS

Cries from the Earth
Cast of Characters

Civilians

Larry Ott
Emily FitzGerald
Elizabeth FitzGerald
Bert FitzGerald
Jennie
Mrs. —— Perry
John B. Monteith
Charles Monteith
Erwin C. Watkins
Perrin B. Whitman
—— West
William Watson
John Wood
Hiram Titman
E. R. Sherwin
—— Van Sickle
Harry Cone

CIVILIANS INVOLVED IN THE FIRST MURDERS

Jurden Henry Elfers	*Emmy Benedict*
Fritz Elfers	*Catherine Elfers*
"Harry" Burn Beckrodge	*Richard Devine*
—— Whitfield	*Robert Bland*
Norman Gould	*Victor ——*
George Greer	*Charles "Charley" P. Cone*
Samuel Benedict	*Isabella Benedict*

CIVILIANS INVOLVED IN THE SECOND RAID

James Baker
George Popham
Conrad Fruth
John J. Manuel
Maggie Manuel
Jennet Manuel
Albert Benson
William Osborn
Annie Osborn
Helen Walsh
William George
"French Frank" /
   "Frenchie" / François
   Chodoze

—— Koon
August Bacon
Patrick Brice
H. C. "Hurdy Gurdy"
   Brown
Harry Mason
Elizabeth Klein Osborn
Edward Walsh
Masi Walsh
"old man" Shoemaker

CIVILIANS INVOLVED IN THE CAMAS PRAIRIE RAIDS

Benjamin B. Norton
Hill Norton
Luther P. "Lew" Wilmot
Lewis "Lew" Day
Mrs. —— Chamberlin
F. Joseph "Joe" Moore
Charles Rice
James Adkison
Doug Adkison
John G. Rowton

Jennie Norton
Lynn Bowers
Pete Ready
John Chamberlin
Hattie Chamberlin
Frank Fenn
George Hashagen
John Adkison
Cash Day
George Shearer

CIVILIANS (CONT'D)

Charles Horton

Herman Faxon

John W. Crooks

John Crooks, Jr.

Delia Theller

William Coram

Theodore Swarts

Loyal P. (L.P.) Brown

Sarah Brown

Charley Crooks

Arthur "Ad" ("Admiral")
   Chapman

Joe Robie

Military

General Oliver Otis Howard— "Cut-Off Arm"

Captain David Perry— Commander, Fort Lapwai,
F Company, First U.S.
Cavalry

Captain William H. Boyle— Commander, G Company,
Twenty-first U.S. Infantry

Captain Joel Graham
Trimble— H Company, First U.S.
Cavalry

First Lieutenant Peter Bomus— Fort Lapwai post
quartermaster

First Lieutenant Edward
Russell Theller— F Company, First U.S.
Cavalry

First Lieutenant Melville C.
Wilkinson— aide-de-camp to General
Howard

Second Lieutenant William
Russell Parnell— H Company, First U.S.
Cavalry

First Sergeant Alexander M.
Baird— F Company, First U.S.
Cavalry

First Sergeant Michael
McCarthy— H Company, First U.S.
Cavalry

Sergeant Patrick Gunn— F Company, First U.S.
Cavalry

Sergeant Patrick Reilly— H Company, First U.S.
Cavalry

Sergeant Isidor Schneider—	H Company, First U.S. Cavalry
Sergeant Henry Arend—	H Company, First U.S. Cavalry
Sergeant John Conroy—	H Company, First U.S. Cavalry
Corporal Charles W. Fuller—	F Company, First U.S. Cavalry
Corporal Joseph F. Lytte—	F Company, First U.S. Cavalry
Corporal Michael Curran—	H Company, First U.S. Cavalry
Corporal Roman D. Lee—	H Company, First U.S. Cavalry
Corporal Frank L. Powers—	H Company, First U.S. Cavalry
Trumpeter John M. Jones ("Jonesy")—	F Company, First U.S. Cavalry
Trumpeter Michael Daly—	F Company, First U.S. Cavalry
Trumpeter Frank A. Marshall—	H Company, First U.S. Cavalry
Farrier John Drugan—	H Company, First U.S. Cavalry
Blacksmith Albert Myers—	H Company, First U.S. Cavalry
Private James Shay—	H Company, First U.S. Cavalry
Private Aman Hartman—	H Company, First U.S. Cavalry
Private Charles E. Fowler—	H Company, First U.S. Cavalry
Private John Schoor—	F Company, First U.S. Cavalry
Private John White—	F Company, First U.S. Cavalry
Surgeon John FitzGerald	

Nez Perce

Abraham Brooks
Abraham Watsinma
Alpowa Jim
Jonah Hayes

Frank Husush
James Reuben
Joe Rabusco
Nat Webb
Putonahloo

———◆———

THREE TREATY SCOUTS CAPTURED AT WHITE BIRD
Robinson Minthon   *Joe Albert (Elaskolatat)*
Yuwishakaikt

———◆———

NEZ PERCE (CONT'D)

Yellow Wolf /
   He-mene Moxmox
   (White Thunder—Heinmot
   Hihhih)

Swan Necklace (Wetyetmas
   Wahyakt)

Five Wounds (Pahkatos
   Owyeen)

Rainbow (Wahchumyus)

Old Rainbow

Old Joseph (Tuekakas /
   Old Grizzly)

Young Joseph
   (Heinmot Tooyalakekt /
   Thunder Traveling to
   Loftier Heights Upon the
   Mountain)

Ta-ma-al-we-non-my (Driven
   Before a Cold Storm)

Ollokot / Frog

Wetatonmi

Hophop Onmi / Sound of
   Running Feet

Welweyas

Half Moon

Three Eagles

John Wilson

Two Moons (Lepeet
  Hessemdooks)

Sun Necklace (Yellow Bull /
  Chuslum Moxmox)

Big Morning (Big Dawn /
  Hemackkis Kaiwon)

Toohoolhoolzote

Bare Feet

Stick-in-the-Mud

Tissaikpee

Red Elk

Geese Three Times Lighting
  on the Water

Red Grizzly Bear (Hahkauts
  Ilppilp)

Black Feather

Two Mornings

Wounded Head (Husis
  Owyeen)

Five Winters (Pahka
  Alyanakt)

Jyeloo

Five Times Looking Up
  (Pahkatos Watyekit)

Going Alone (Kosooyeen)

No Feet (Seeskoomkee)

Hand in Hand (Payenapta)

Vicious Weasel (Wettiwetti
  Haulis)

Red Raven (Koklok Ilppilp)

Going Fast (Henawit)

Fire Body (Otstotpoo)

Strong Eagle (Tipyahlahnah
  Kapskaps)

Looking Glass
  Alalimiatakanin /
  "A Vision")

Yellow Bear

Tucallasasena

*White Bird (Peopeo / White,
    White Goose, White
    Crane, White Pelican)*

*Eagle Robe (Tipyahlanah
    Siskon)—father of
    Wahlitits*

Shore Crossing (Wahlitits)

*Red Moccasin Tops (Sarpsis
    Ilppilp)*

*Yellow Grizzly Bear
    (Heyoom Moxmox)*

Teeweawea

Black Foot

*Tolo / Tula (Tulekats
    Chickchamit)*

Palouse

*Bald Head / Shorn Head
    (Huishuish Kute)*

Red Echo (Hahtalekin)

In thinking about American Indian history, it has become essential to follow the policy of cautious street crossers: Remember to look both ways.

—Patricia Nelson Limerick

If Colonel Perry had not listened to the [Mount Idaho] volunteers, not a man would have been lost, as Perry was ordered to protect the citizens of Mount Idaho and Grangeville ... They urged Perry to hurry before the Indians could escape across the Salmon, for they were "cowardly and would not fight." When too late we found the reverse to be the true facts.

—Private John P. Schorr
F Company, 1st U.S. Cavalry

Although exhaustion of men and horses afforded some measure of explanation, White Bird Canyon was only the first of several episodes of the Nez Perce War that reinforced the First Cavalry's reputation for mediocrity.

—Robert M. Utley
Frontier Regulars

Certainly the Nez Perces['] defeat of Perry's command [at] the Battle of White Bird Canyon created an inducement for the tribesmen of White Bird, Joseph, and Toohoolhoolzote to continue the fight and perhaps raised false hopes among them as to the eventual outcome stemming from this initial victory. For the army, the battle produced a healthy respect for the fighting abilities of the Nez Perces.

—Jerome A. Greene
*The U.S. Army and the
Nee-Mee-Poo Crisis of 1877*

The Battle of White Bird Canyon was one of the worst defeats suffered by the United States Army during the period 1865 to 1890. Perhaps only the Fetterman disaster in Wyoming in 1866 and the Custer disaster in Montana ten years later rival it in ignominy, [but] in both those cases the Indians outnumbered the military units in great proportion.

—John D. McDermott
Forlorn Hope

Introduction

Before you begin, take a moment to consider . . .
   The story you are about to read is entirely true.

I haven't fabricated a single one of the scenes to follow this introduction. Every incident happened when and where and how I have written it. Every one of the characters you will come to know actually lived, perhaps died, during the outbreak of the Nez Perce War.

After my previous thirteen Plainsmen novels, hundreds of thousands of you already have an abiding faith in me, a belief that what you're going to read is accurate and authentic. But for those of you picking up your first Terry C. Johnston book, let me make this one very important vow to you: If I show one of these fascinating characters in a particular scene, then you best believe that character was there, when it happened, where it happened. I promise you, this is how that history of the Nez Perce War was made.

What's more, I want you to know I could have written a book nearly twice as long as this if I had gone back to explore the background of the old treaties and how they were broken, to tell of the discovery of gold deep in Nez Perce country, if I had begun reciting, chapter and verse, all the intrusions by whites where they were not allowed by the treaties, the seductive lure of alcohol and firearms on the young warriors, the firestorm of rapes and murders committed against those Nez Perce bands helplessly watching their old way of life passing away right before their eyes, not to mention the government's feeble efforts to keep a lid on each troubling incident after the fact . . . Suffice it to say that the government's position was that the minority Non-Treaty bands (those who refused to sign) were bound by the vote of the more populous Treaty bands (even though no more a minority of the Treaty males signed the government's land-grab).

But for all that background I'm not going to give, the reader can learn everything he wants to know in the following books:

I Will Fight No More Forever, by Merrill D. Beal

The Flight of the Nez Perce, by Mark H. Brown

The Nez Perce Tribesmen of the Columbia Plateau, by Francis Haines

The Nez Perce Indians and the Opening of the North-west, by Alvin M. Josephy, Jr.

As for my story, I'm going to dispense with all that historical background you can learn elsewhere because I prefer to drop you right down into the middle of the outbreak of this war.

As you are drawn back in time, you may well wonder: what of those brief news stories that appear here and there at the beginning of certain chapters or scenes? Keep in mind that those aren't the fruits of my creative imagination. Instead, they are torn right from the front pages of the newspapers of that day.

Oh, one more thing before you start what will surely be one of the most fascinating rides of your life—the letters that Emily FitzGerald, wife of surgeon John FitzGerald, writes home to her mother from Fort Lapwai are real, too. Transcribed verbatim for you, every last word of those letters makes them simple, heartfelt messages from a woman who finds herself squarely at ground zero, right in the middle of an Indian war. They, and those brief newspaper stories too, I hope will lend an immediacy to this gripping tale that little else could.

As you make your way through this story, page by page, many of you might start to worry when you find this tale missing our intrepid Irishman, Seamus Donegan. But take heart! He, Samantha, and their son, Colin, are at Fort Laramie this spring of 1877, preparing to make their way north to Fort Robinson, where they will be center stage for the last months of Crazy Horse's life . . . a distance that makes it impossible for Donegan to be in Idaho Territory for this start of the Nez Perce War at the very same time he is returning from the end of the Great Sioux War on the Northern Plains.

So please remember as you begin this ride with me: Every scene you are about to read actually happened. Every one of these characters was real—and they were there . . . to live or die in this outbreak of a damned dirty little war.

I don't think I could have made up this tragic story if I'd tried. I'm simply not that good a writer.

Prologue

Autumn, 1874

A jagged shred of lightning split the leaden sky suspended just over his head. On its heels rumbled a peal of autumn thunder so close he felt it clear to his marrow. Clouds hung low, wisps of their shredded underbellies suspended like tatters of the white man's muslin among the heavy branches of the firs towering over him like silent giants.

The rain would not be long behind, Eagle Robe thought as the cabin made of unpeeled logs came into sight. He sucked in a sudden breath, startled to find the crude structure standing there at the edge of the clearing. Even more surprised to see the second, larger, building slowly take shape out of the mist behind the cabin. It was not made out of unchinked logs, but from planks milled from the huge pines that steepled this paradise of the *Nee-Me-Poo,** the people a band of long-ago white explorers first called the *Chopunnish.*†

At that time of first contact, the *Nee-Me-Poo* numbered more than six thousand souls who referred to the light-skinned traders coming among them as "Boston Men." But in the last few generations, as a full half of the *Nee-Me-Poo*

---

*Although this tribal name appears in different spellings throughout the many sources on the Nez Perce, I have chosen to use the spelling subscribed to by the Nez Perce National Historic Trail Advisory Council.
†The Lewis and Clark Corps of Discovery

died off with the rampant diseases brought them by the new-comers, Eagle Robe's people started referring to the white men as Shadows. Dark, soulless creatures, most of whom were cordial, while some took real pleasure in conniving to get their hands on everything they coveted, especially what already belonged to others.

Beyond both structures Eagle Robe saw the first of the cattle grazing in a far pasture. As he got closer, he could hear them lowing. On the far side of the larger building stood a sizable pole corral where a few horses milled.

Another crack of thunder reverberated off the hillside, all the closer now. So close Eagle Robe felt the vibration drag a rusty finger to the base of his spine. The storm would not be long in coming now.

Perhaps this white settler named Larry Ott would give him shelter if the rain came hard, if a strong wind blew. As he got older, Eagle Robe had discovered the cold grew more and more painful, stabbing him all the way to the bone with the approach of winter. He had no reason to suspect that this Shadow would not offer him a place out of the wind and the cold. Larry Ott had been a most pleasant sort early last spring when that white man began to graze his cattle and horses on the fringes of the tribe's land, right beside some of Eagle Robe's garden plots. Then last spring, this Shadow appealed to chief White Bird's band of *Lamtama* to allow him a little more land where he could graze even more cattle.

While everyone else turned away and would not even give the Shadow the courtesy of an answer, Eagle Robe had instead stayed behind while the others walked off just as the sun broke through the high, blue-tinged clouds pregnant with the promise of a heavy spring thunderstorm.

"You know me. I claim a little land right next to the pasture you already are using," Eagle Robe had told the white man and his interpreter, even though the translator did not speak very good Nez Perce at all. "In a few days I am leaving this place for several moons."

"Leaving?" the interpreter had repeated. "Where are you going?"

"I will be among the first of our people who are traveling across the mountains to the buffalo country this season."

The interpreter nodded and grumbled something to the settler next to him. They spoke a moment before Eagle Robe continued.

"Tell this man who comes asking for a little more land to use for his cattle that since my land already lies right against what he has been using, I can let him use my ground for the rest of the spring and summer while the grass grows its tallest."

Both of the Shadows bobbed their heads with eager smiles on their faces.

"My friend says that is a good offer," the interpreter explained, using his hands now and then to make sign for a word. "Are you coming back from the buffalo country at the end of the summer?"

"If the hunting is not so good, we will be back before the last of the hot days," Eagle Robe had told them. "But if the hunting is good, why should I hurry back?"

All three of them chuckled, and both Shadows were grinning constantly now. Eagle Robe found himself very gratified that he had made them happy. *This is the way it must be,* he recalled thinking at that moment. *Our peoples are thrown together and we should find a way to help one another.* It had been that way since the first white men had come among the *Nee-Me-Poo* while on their journey to the great western ocean back in the long-ago time of Eagle Robe's great-grandfather.

"If the buffalo want me to keep shooting them," he had gone on to explain to the Shadows, "I may not return until the first frosts brown the grasses of both trails leading over the mountains."

"Autumn." The interpreter had wanted confirmation.

"Yes," Eagle Robe said. "This man, my new friend, can graze his cattle and horses on my little piece of ground until I return. But do not worry; when I come back, he will not have to rush out of here. I will give him a few days to gather up his belongings, pack them onto his wagons, and herd his cattle to another place before I bring back my horses to that pasture."

"Will you show us this ground of yours that lies next to Larry Ott's?"

"Come now," Eagle Robe had said, shaking the hand that smiling white settler held out to him. "I will take you to the ground where this man can graze his cattle and horses until I return from the buffalo country.''

At that time last spring he had expected the Shadow might erect a crude lean-to with its supports cut from forest saplings, maybe covering it with a large sheet of oiled canvas to make himself some shelter for the grazing seasons, perhaps even improving upon that crude, temporary shelter by raising a wall-tent. But Eagle Robe had not expected to find that the settler had erected not just one of his log lodges, but two! And around them both stood a network of pole fences. Clearly this Shadow had worked hard since Eagle Robe and many others departed for the long journey over the mountains. Why, when he would now have to leave all that hard work behind as he went in search of another place to fatten his cattle?

The first drops began to pelt Eagle Robe as he brought his pony to a halt between the two wooden buildings, sighed, and stared around him at the place that reminded Eagle Robe of when the Shadows' settlement began at Lewiston, or those agency and army buildings at Fort Lapwai up near the Clearwater River.

This wasn't like the *Nee-Me-Poo,* who carried their shelters along with them, the squat lodges made from the hides of those buffalo harvested during their annual treks to the far plains. No, Eagle Robe's people moved their shelters from place to place across their ancient home ground, migrating from season to season as they ranged across a great piece of territory that all the bands had long considered their home in its entirety. But, from what he himself had witnessed over the past thirty-some winters, the Shadows did not live for a time in a pretty spot, then pick up and move on. Instead, when a white man put this much sweat into building a shelter against the rains of spring and summer, against the frosts of an autumn night, then it meant the pale one had every intention of staying put.

Just like those white gold-seekers who had flocked to the mining camps, or those cattle-tenders who had gradually closed a noose around the peaceable bands who had foolishly signed one treaty after another with the Shadows' government.

Eagle Robe discovered he was scared and angry all at the same time, and that bewildering mix of feelings made him all the more scared and a great deal more angry too.

Stay calm, Tipyahlanah Siskon, Eagle Robe reminded himself as the rain began to fall a little harder. Sensing the big, cold drops spilling down his back, he pulled up the wide collar on his thick blanket coat, pushing aside one of his thick braids dusted with the iron of his many winters. He knew he had to have a calm heart and steady hands when he talked to this Shadow. So he took a deep breath and started to swing his leg off the pony.

"Stop right where you are, Injun!"

The strident voice caught him even before his feet were striking the ground. Eagle Robe slowly turned toward its chilling sound, finding the hairy-faced settler emerging from the wide, ill-hung doors of that bigger of the two wooden buildings. The Shadow rested his hand on the butt of the pistol stuffed in the front of his belt.

Eagle Robe wasn't sure, but this Larry Ott's face appeared very different than it had that day back in the spring when the *Nee-Me-Poo* were headed for buffalo country and Eagle Robe had come by to give his farewell to the cattle-tender at the Shadows' camp. Below the misshapen brim of the man's felt hat, the Shadow's eyes glared with a cold fire that caused Eagle Robe to shudder.

"W-what this?" he stammered in the settler's tongue.

Of a sudden Eagle Robe realized now that he had come to talk to a man who knew practically nothing of the *Nee-Me-Poo* language—even worse, that he himself knew so little of the Shadow's tongue. They were bound to have trouble understanding each other if the words flew fast, now that angry fury had gripped the settler. Eagle Robe reminded himself to breathe slow, stay calm. There had to be a good reason why this Larry Ott had decided to raise his permanent lodges here instead of preparing to move on when Eagle Robe returned from the season's hunt.

"What's this?" the Shadow repeated those white man's words. He kept that right hand on the pistol butt as he swung his left arm in an expressive quarter-circle. "This is my home now; cain't you see that?"

"My home," Eagle Robe repeated the words crudely, confused at first. . . . Then suddenly they made sense. He nodded agreeably. "Yes. My home—"

"Mine now," the settler interrupted, as he took another three steps toward the Indian, his left arm waving at

Eagle Robe as if he wanted to shoo the warrior away. "Time you got off *my* land."

"My land. My home. *I* home," he struggled for the words, watching those dark eyes beneath the hat brim, feeling the rain frighteningly cold as it sluiced down his backbone like March thaw, sensing the awakening of a desperation that he had not come here with any weapon, even a belt gun like the one the settler gripped.

"Git!" the white man shouted. "This here's my place now. You run off and left it, Injun. By rights it's mine now, done proper."

"Run off?"

"You gone to buffler country, didn't you? Now this place is mine. G'won and get up the valley away from here. Just don't ever get nowhere near none of my stock."

Eagle Robe gazed around him a long moment, looking at the smaller building. Then at the doorway of the larger building where the settler had emerged. Better to talk about this right now and get things settled, he decided. Another man might ride away, planning to come back with a few of his *tillicums*, friends who would bring their guns, and then there would be trouble. There always was trouble when you mixed guns and white men. Never failed: the *Nee-Me-Poo* always ended up on the poor end of the bargain when it came to how the Shadows abused the *Nee-Me-Poo* women or what they did to steal the land they wanted.

So riding off, then returning to throw the settler off by force would only make things more ticklish. Instead, Eagle Robe decided, he should just get things straightened out here and now.

The warrior turned to his left, stepping across the sodden ground toward the rail fence that cut right through the middle of the garden Eagle Robe had cultivated for many years. The Shadow had turned it into a pasture for his cattle. And the animals had trampled everything they hadn't eaten.

"Whatcha doing, Injun?" the settler demanded sharply.

Eagle Robe laid the pony's rein over the top rail of the fence and loosely looped it once. Then turned back to face the settler. Eagle Robe wanted to show him he didn't have a weapon—so he held up both hands, then slowly began to work at the knot in the sash wrapped around his blanket coat.

Larry Ott angrily shouted something at him, and Eagle

Robe froze the moment that pistol came partway out of the man's belt.

"I am not armed," he said in his language, frustrated that he did not remember the Shadow word for weapon, pistol, firearm—so many words for the same thing.

Again Larry Ott shouted.

But Eagle Robe shook his head and started forward to show him he did not carry a weapon. But he stopped mid-step when the settler shook his head violently, waved his left arm in that manner of someone in great fear, then nonetheless advanced another two steps, hunching his shoulders forward provocatively. Still shouting, louder still. The way a frightened animal blusters when it feels cornered.

"Git ——!"

And that one word was all Eagle Robe understood of so much shouted at him, except for that word *land* Larry Ott kept repeating.

Then Eagle Robe pointed at the buildings, starting to wag his head in befuddlement, ashamed that he had been made a fool by this Shadow. Growing all the more angry that he had been duped, he began to yell back at the settler.

By then the two of them were bellowing at each other, shouting at the same time, their voices rising, each one straining to be heard over the rising wind that whipped Eagle Robe's braids across his cheeks like the lash of a bone-handled quirt. The settler took a step closer and stopped again as Eagle Robe continued to point and shake his arm at the two log buildings, those cattle in the field, that nearby corral, and then Eagle Robe suddenly turned to the settler, balling up his fist.

Slowly, slowly, Eagle Robe raised that brown fist over his head like a club, his arm trembling in anger when the Shadow's sneer turned into a snarling growl.

"*You* go now! Not me!" Eagle Robe hollered at the settler. "Come back later for your belongings, for your cattle and horses. Go now!"

"Go to hell with you, goddammit!"

Eagle Robe understood those words. He fixed on the settler's eyes at that moment, the very instant a flash of lightning lit up the whole valley like the heart of the day in the hottest of the summer moons. The shocking white light made the hairs on his arms crawl, prickled the hair at the back of his neck as it stood on end.

The moment the very air around him seemed to crackle with that celestial explosion, Eagle Robe yelled, "Go now—"

He didn't get to finish because with that next heartbeat a horrific clap of thunder slapped its paw down on them both.

Snarling something unintelligible as the thunder's reverberation faded, trailing off down the valley, the settler turned his back on the warrior and started to slog away as the wind whipped itself into a fury.

That Larry Ott should turn his back on him and stomp away infuriated Eagle Robe. Looking about at the ground, he bent and scooped up a stone that he nestled into the palm of his hand. Crooking his arm, he flung the rock at the impudent Shadow's back. The rock smacked the settler high between the shoulder blades.

Instantly the white man wheeled as the sky about them both turned white-hot with the sizzle of another lightning bolt.

Eagle Robe's eyes widened as he saw the muzzle of the settler's pistol come out of his belt—spewing a tongue of fire like the very lightning that had just brightened the valley with such momentary brilliance, then pitched them into an inky, sodden darkness once more—

He felt a fist slam his chest, hurtling him backward against the rail. Collapsing across the muddy ground, Eagle Robe spilled among his pony's legs.

The pressure inside him grew as he struggled to breathe, the very center of him growing a little colder each time his heart pounded in his ears.

And now his hat was gone. Eagle Robe realized that it had fallen off his head as he blinked his eyes against the pounding rain. Suddenly it was pouring even harder, his face so wet with the drenching it was as if he were standing under a waterfall. He blinked and blinked, trying to clear his eyes, then realized the Shadow was standing directly over him.

Larry Ott cocked the pistol's hammer back again, then held the end of its muzzle inches away from a spot between Eagle Robe's eyes for what felt like an eternity.

Then the Shadow grumbled something low and profane, yanked the pistol aside, and with his free hand reached up for that top rail of the fence directly above Eagle Robe. Larry Ott grabbed the reins to Eagle Robe's pony, then immediately bent to one knee in the rain-soaked grass. Then the white man shoved the braided buffalo-hair rein into the Indian's glistening hand already smeared with his own dark blood.

Bending low over Eagle Robe's face, the settler hissed, "There, you red nigger. That'll serve you. Now take your goddamned horse and get off my land while you still can."

Through the film of rain spilling over his face, Eagle Robe watched the Shadow stand, turn, and walk off toward the smaller log building.

It quickly grew harder and harder to breathe. Another peal of thunder rattled the valley. He looked down at his chest, saw the red oozing from the hole piercing his deerskin shirt, watched the ooze as it was washed off, turned to a pale, translucent pink. In the pelting rain Eagle Robe was reminded of how the missionaries had tried to teach him that if he truly believed in their *Book of Heaven* then the Shadows' savior would wash away their sins with his own blood.

He shivered uncontrollably, wanting so to believe in the white man's *Akunkenekoo,* his everlasting heaven.

Eagle Robe closed his eyes, sensing the autumn rain growing very warm on his cold, cold cheek.

It was dark when he heard approaching footsteps. No, Eagle Robe *felt* them. The post against his shoulder seemed to vibrate with each step. Perhaps the Shadow had decided to return and finish him off, not give him a chance to live.

Funny, he thought. He wasn't going to live anyway. Just taking a long time dying . . . and he recalled the countless times he had tracked wounded game through the hills, following a small drop of blood here, a smear on some leaves there, the animal taking many miles and agonizing hours to die.

Then the earth reverberated with an overwhelming sound, and Eagle Robe thought the cruel thunder had returned to awaken him.

But he quickly recognized it was the pounding of pony hooves.

Eagle Robe looked up, surprised to discover his own pony still standing over him. The animal stood motionless except that it turned its head to the side, its ears perked, poking its muzzle into the wind.

"Father!"

As Shore Crossing slammed onto the ground beside his father's horse, the young man's feet made a dull thud in the sodden grass. Eagle Robe's son knelt in the mud beside his dying father.

"Did the Shadow do this to you?" Shore Crossing asked, his words dripping with fury.

"*Wahlitits* . . . you came—," he sighed, whispering his son's *Nee-Me-Poo* name.

Then Eagle Robe knew he couldn't talk anymore, because his chest was seized with a wet cough. No longer did he have enough breath to force out many words. He blinked his eyes and gazed up into his son's face, realizing evening had come upon this valley, realizing that the storm was passing.

"You should have been back long ago," Shore Crossing explained as he squatted to cradle his father's head in the crook of his arm, hovering over the older man in the last of the rain. "I came to see what delayed you." Then the son looked up, gazed around at the cabin where a lamp flickered dimly behind a window curtain. "The settler decided to stay, didn't he? He has stolen our land."

Eagle Robe felt the young man gently withdraw his arm, positioning his father's upper body back against the post. He looked at Shore Crossing, watching his son pull the long knife from the scabbard at his waist.

"I will go take his scalp for you, Father," vowed the young man of no more than nineteen summers.

With the last of his strength, Eagle Robe reached out and snagged his son's wrist in one hand, stopping the young warrior. "N-no."

Shore Crossing's face hovered over his father's as he said, "What? You cannot be telling me not to kill this man who has shot you!"

"Do not . . . ," and he coughed. "It must end here."

"NO!" Shore Crossing railed against the falling of the light. "I will kill him with my own hands if I have to!"

"Please," Eagle Robe begged. "Promise me . . . promise me you will not take vengeance—"

"I cannot!" the young man shrieked.

He felt the hot blood thicken at the back of his throat, swallowing hard in hopes of speaking more clearly to his son. "Promise me—," and he squeezed his son's wrist.

For a long time the young warrior's face was suspended over his in the fading light. Eagle Robe didn't know if he would live long enough to hear his son answer with his promise. Then, finally, Shore Crossing spoke softly, reluctantly, and very, very sadly.

"I promise you, Father."

Eagle Robe closed his eyes at last, sensing that last breath gushing up in a ball from his punctured lungs, spilling across his tongue and over his lips. His head gently sagged to the side as he felt the release come at long last.

Anguished, Shore Crossing sobbed, pressing his head against his father's bloody breast, "I promise . . . promise not to kill this man who has killed you!"

Chapter 1

May 1, 1877

She scraped the thick sulphur head of the lucifer across one of the rough boards lying beneath her shoe and watched the match leap into life. Emily FitzGerald cautiously inched the wavering flame to that stubby, blackened wick protruding from the top of the half-used beeswax taper and lit the candle she and the Doctor kept atop the tall bureau near their bedside at night. The flame struggled a moment, then caught, spreading a small womb of warm light around her.

Emily peeked over her shoulder at her sleeping husband. He was turned toward the wall, snoring gently. After sliding the candleholder to the side, she quietly removed the glass stopper from the top of the inkwell, dipped her pen, and started scratching the nib across that first small sheet of paper she held in place beneath her reddened left hand.

> *Fort Lapwai*
> *May 1, 1877*

Dear Mamma,

Emily got that far, then caught herself staring at the red knuckles of both hands as she considered how to begin this letter. With those two children of hers, there was so much washing of clothes grown so grimy in their play, doing her best to keep her children scrubbed as much as possible with what seemed to be one bath right after another. While Jennie, their Negress, did lend her efforts with the washing, as well as the cooking and keeping after the house, Emily did not allow the servant girl to assist in bathing Bess or her little brother, Bert. Mending and sweeping the floors, baking and peeling and snapping beans, scrubbing chamber pots, and boiling the doctor's underthings were all tasks Jennie had performed dutifully for the family over the last few years now, ever since the Doctor—that was the name Emily always used for her husband, John—had first shipped north for that assignment in Sitka, Alaska. But bathing these young, precocious, grimy children remained Emily's domain alone.

My brown babies are still the picture of health.
Such solid, round, little brown toads you never saw.

She gazed at the slim hand holding the long pen there in the pulsing candlelight, that tiny flame stirred only by her breath, remembering those vibrant red spots showing up on little Bert's arms just before they left Sitka for the Nez Perce country last spring. The Doctor had vaccinated his son in one arm; then two days later, when it appeared the vaccination wasn't going to take, her husband vaccinated Bert in the other arm. Then both arms took! How sore her little Bert had been, pouting so badly that it really hurt his father.

Emily remembered those first months after coming here to Nez Perce country—a land where the Doctor said he wanted to return once he finished his service to the army. It was undeniably beautiful, she agreed, in spite of the half-wild Non-Treaty bands who came and went past the fort and agency every now and then. She recalled the frightening hubbub of last summer's Indian troubles so many hundreds of miles and many days to the east over in Sioux country and reassured herself again that her little family really was far enough removed from those scenes of such horrid disasters that were on everyone's lips for a time last year. Then she thought of how she had written to her mother giddily celebrating that the Doctor wasn't going to be among those outfits posted to Sitting Bull's country.

The Indians respect no code of warfare, flags of
truce, wounded—nothing is respected! It is like fight-

*ing to exterminate wild animals, horrible beasts. I
hope and pray this is the last Indian war. Don't let
anybody talk of peace until the Indians are taught a
lesson and, if not exterminated, so weakened they will
never molest and butcher again. These Sioux Indians
will give trouble as long as they exist, no matter how
we treat them, "for 'tis their nature to." They will
never stay on their reservations and the lives of settlers
in this entire western country are not safe as long as
the Indian question is unsettled. This is all we talk
about out here.*

But did she want to tell her mamma about what rumors of
trouble loomed on the horizon now?

Best not to worry that gentle Quaker soul, she decided.
Better that she fill her letters home with only news of the
children and the Doctor, reports on the spring flowers car-
peting the hillsides in a brilliant blaze of color despite one
gloomy, rainy day after another.

*The Doctor finally found us another Chinaman to
be our cook. At first I had a soldier, but he was not
nice, and the Doctor sent him off. I don't think I am
very fond of kitchen work. I don't wonder at cooks
asking 30 or 35 dollars a month. I will cheerfully pay
Mr. Sing his thirty dollars in gold a month, though it
does seem awful. All the other officers here, except
Colonel Perry, have Chinese help. Mr. Sing moves
around the house like a mouse in his soft shoes. Bert
calls him a "lady." Mr. Sing's long hair and gown
confuse Mr. Bert! Just think of paying 35 dollars in
greenbacks to a man who does not do nearly as much
as a woman in the East does for 14.*

*My Chinaman, I hope, is going to prove a success.
He made delightful muffins for breakfast and is now
making a cake for dinner. I am going to have a baked
stuffed salmon for dinner tomorrow night. It is such
a comfort to go out and sit down to a nice, full table
and not have to fuss over things before hand.*

*Bertie finally had his turn with the mumps, and he
is getting his big teeth at last. Everything with my Mr.
Bert now is a horse! He insists upon you singing*

*about a horse when you put him to sleep, and every-
thing he gets he sticks between his legs and says, "Get
up, horsie!" Last night John was going out and took
Bert up in front for a few minutes. The horse started
to gallop, and Bert laughed out loud! Bess delights in
her dollies, and, much to my delight, Bertie does, too.
Doctor has an idea boys won't play with girls' things.*

*Yes, Bess and Bertie are brown as berries, so de-
lighted to be out in the sunshine after Sitka. You never
saw such sunburnt little scamps in your life. They get
so dirty that the bath tub is brought in and we scrub
them every night.*

*None of the three ladies here has any children. Al-
ways before, I and my whole set of intimate friends
have been engaged in wondering how to prevent any
more babies coming. Now I get among these people
who would give their heads to have a baby and are
just as busily engaged trying all sorts of means to have
one.*

*Lapwai is a pleasant post, as far-away posts go, but
it is very quiet and lonely here. Doctor thinks we will
be east of the mountains before 1879.*

Then Emily realized that her mother might well hear a
disquieting report from this faraway post, any fragmentary
news item about the Nez Perce that might frighten her
mamma if Emily did not mention it first, preparing that dear
old Quaker soul for the upset. Best for her to mention certain
things in a calm, reassuring way. . . .

*Indians are passing by the post continually, but In-
dians are no novelty to us now. We are all very much
interested in the news from the Black Hills and the
Sioux War as we all have friends with the troops, and
as we are surrounded by Indians here, we are all the
more anxious that victory doesn't crown the Plains
Warriors. You know, two-thirds of the Nez Perces are
Non-Treaty Indians, and they are intimate with the
Sioux and other tribes on the warpath.*

She re-read that part, wondering if she buried the threat of
trouble in a letter her mother would not grow as concerned

as she might if she happened upon it in the papers one day.
Quickly she dipped her nib into the ink bottle and continued
with her flowing hand beneath the flickering candlelight:

> *Certainly these Nez Perce are jealous of what they
> once owned for this is a lovely region, of rich prairie
> land with such pretty wild flowers and such herds of
> fat sheep and cows as it would do you and father
> good to see. Remember that we live in one half of a
> double house. The other side is occupied by the Com-
> manding Officer, Colonel Perry.*

Emily stopped, put the end of the pen between her front
teeth, and chewed thoughtfully on the wood, listening to
nothing but silence seeping through the thin wall that separated their bedchamber from that of Colonel Perry and his
wife. Suddenly struck with a thought, she dipped the pen and
wrote:

> *Already Joseph's band has been driving settlers
> from that valley they claim, Wallowa Valley.*
> *The news makes us all feel worried and anxious
> because it is probable the troops will be sent out to
> try and prevent bloodshed. The Indians have forced
> the settlers to leave, and the settlers, about seventy or
> eighty, have joined together and are armed. The In-
> dians are determined that they shall not settle in the
> Valley, and they are determined that they will, and, of
> course, have the right and must be supported by the
> troops.*
> *Everybody wants to prevent bloodshed, for this lot
> of settlers in the Wallowa are an awful set of men and
> have made all the trouble for themselves.*
> *I am in terror for fear Doctor will have to go out
> with Colonel Perry. Everybody is waiting to see what
> is going to happen. I hope it will all blow over as it
> did last summer, but the gentlemen seem to think it
> means business this time. We are between sixty and
> seventy miles from the Wallowa.*

That really was too close to allow her heart any real comfort. Doctor had seen enough of the horrors of combat during
the Rebellion.

She continued to stare at the flickering, hypnotic flame, hoping her husband, hoping none of the other officers and these young soldiers stationed at Fort Lapwai would be sucked into an Indian war.

Oh, how it weighed on her mind—these matters of the Nez Perce and how trouble was brewing like a foul broth. Too much for a body to take at times. All the way to the core of her she felt such a weariness from the tension of these days that she believed she might just be able to sleep now—

Emily heard one of the children coughing: a harsh, dry hack. She listened for a long moment but heard nothing more. The child must have fallen back to sleep.

> As promised I will write at least once a week. Promise me you will write me once a week too. Doctor sends much love to all. Give my love to all at home.
>
> Your daughter,
> Emily F.

She carefully lifted the blanket and the comforter and slipped beneath them, gently rolling against her husband's back, snuggling against his warmth as she looped an arm over him, pulling herself against his bulk reassuringly. He grunted in his sleep, then resumed breathing deeply.

She reminded herself she must sleep, no matter her fears of his leaving with the troops and not returning to the three of them. Never again walking through that door, calling out in that quiet, reserved way of his, "I'm home, Emily."

She hadn't known him before or during the Rebellion of the Southern States. Hadn't been in love with John FitzGerald back then, hadn't given her heart and soul and every fiber of her being to him in those long-ago times . . . so why did this threat of another Indian war have to hang over their heads like a sword suspended by the thinnest of threads now?

With a sigh, Emily wiped her damp cheek against the back of the Doctor's sleeping gown.

And silently cried herself to sleep.

Chapter 2

Season of *Hillal*
1877

Yesterday's council with the trio of Shadows beneath the canvas awning had not gone well. But this second meeting this morning with the soldier chief his *Nee-Me-Poo* people called Cut-Off Arm was turning all the worse.

Leading his *Wallamwatkin* band here to this fort and agency from their ancient home in the Wallowa Valley, *Hein-mot Tooyalakekt* had arrived a day ago for the first of these talks he had hoped would be a turning point in the relations between his tribe and the "crowned ones," so called because of the tall top hats the white men wore. At first the *Nee-Me-Poo* had referred to these Americans as the "Big Hearts from the East," because they were more liberal in their trading practices than were the stingy and niggardly British traders.

Some thirty-two summers old now, he was a civil leader of these people sometimes called *Iceyeeye Niim Mama'yac,* or People of the Coyote. Simply put, he was a village chief who saw to matters involving the women and children. He did not have much military experience, if any at all.

Through the interpreter, this chief, whose name meant "Thunder Traveling to Loftier Heights Upon the Mountain," had told Cut-Off Arm that fellow chief White Bird would not arrive with his people from their Salmon River country until the next day.

"You must not be in so much of a hurry," he tried to explain to the soldier chief. Some of his people claimed he had the singular gift of oratory. "White Bird's people are already in the Craig Mountains and will be here before morning."

"Mr. Monteith and I," Cut-Off Arm replied, gesturing toward the agent, "have pressing business we must see to."

"We will all be here tomorrow," the chief repeated, smoothing one of the long braids that fell down his chest. Above his smooth, copper-skinned forehead, the black hair was combed in the tall, upswept curl of their traditional "Dreamer" religion. "Then we can talk about this matter of you telling us we must come in to this reservation or you will send the army to drive our women and children to this place."

Cut-Off Arm scratched at his beard with his one hand, then spoke to the interpreter, an agency layabout named James Reuben, one of the chief's own nephews, who sat in a chair translating for the white Boston Men.

Reuben cleared his throat nervously and said, "We have received our orders from Washington City. The President sends us to your people. I want to repeat myself—to underscore the importance of complying at once so your people can get the pick of the land offered you for your new homes."

With the soldier chief's words, this leader of the Wallowa people—who had been born in a cave and was later baptized by the missionary Henry Spalding with the Shadow name Joseph—wagged his head and said, "I am not the only leader of the *Nee-Me-Poo*. The other chiefs must be here to listen to your words, and decide upon them."

The exasperated soldier chief nearly interrupted Reuben's translation when he grumbled, "Very well, Joseph. We can wait another day for White Bird if that is your wish. But my instructions to him will be the same as what I have instructed you."

With Reuben's translation of the soldier's words the squat, muscular chief sitting to Joseph's left bolted to his feet. This leader of a small band of *Nee-Me-Poo* who made their home on Asotin Creek turned from the soldier and directed his ire at Perrin B. Whitman, a nephew of the famous missionary Marcus Whitman, who served as the government's representative to this important council at the army fort beside Lapwai Creek, in the Valley of the Butterflies.

Standing at least a half a foot shorter than Joseph, old Too-hoolhoolzote growled at the young Whitman, "Because of the generations of my people yet to come, for the children's children of both you white people and the *Nee-Me-Poo*, you must interpret correctly."

Whitman blinked, clearly surprised at the scolding, and glanced at the soldier chief's interpreter, James Reuben, before he swallowed and vowed to the old chief, "I promise you I will translate every word to you with complete satisfaction."

"We want to talk a long, long time," Toohoolhoolzote continued, "talk many days about the earth, about our land you want to take from us."

"Please," begged the agent John B. Monteith as he stood and took a step toward the homely, barrel-chested Toohoolhoolzote, "you must understand that the time for debate is over."

As Reuben's translation was given, Joseph saw how the finality of those words struck the rest of the chiefs, especially Toohoolhoolzote, a *tewat*, or shaman, among the *Nee-Me-Poo*. Joseph and the older man shared a belief in the Dreamer religion, rather than have anything at all to do with the Christian agency schools or the nearby Catholic missions—which was the way of the Treaty bands who had agreed to live on the confines of the reservation.

"Your people were given until the first day of April to come here to the reservation, where they will take up your new homes," the agent reminded them sternly.

Joseph felt sorry for Monteith. The two of them first met six winters ago upon the death of Joseph's father, Old Joseph. The following year the agent had exhausted himself attempting to convince his government that the part of the Wallowa Valley Joseph's people wanted most was not really suitable to settlement and cultivation. Better to let the white farmers keep that portion of the valley where they had already been putting down roots following the 1863 treaty that had been signed by a majority of the *Nee-Me-Poo* bands, an agreement that even gave away the land of those who had refused to sign, those who steadfastly refused to recognize the authority of the white man's government.

Then something terrible had gone wrong when the government finally relented and agreed that Joseph's Wallowas could stay in their valley. Just last year Monteith had tried to explain that a grave mistake had been made: The newly drawn boundaries dictated that the *Nee-Me-Poo* had to move to the ground where the white settlers had been grazing their cattle, and the whites were told to move to that part of the

Wallowa where Joseph's people had lived for more generations than any man now alive could count.

Although a terrible error had been committed by his government, Monteith declared that there was nothing anyone could do.

A long descent had brought them to this impasse: season after season they had suffered the crimes of the white men, or repeatedly been threatened with soldiers coming to change things forever . . .

"You must come to the reservation now," Monteith said firmly. "There is no getting around it any longer. You chiefs here, and White Bird too, must return for your cattle and horses, bring your people here."

"I will stay here until your bands are settled on the reservation," vowed Cut-Off Arm sternly.

Ollokot, Joseph's younger brother, stood at his right elbow. While Joseph was a civil chief, Ollokot was a war leader. He was every bit as striking, tall, and imposing as his older brother.

"Know that we will think for ourselves, soldier chief," he warned the army officer. His name meant "Frog," affectionately given him back when this handsome, athletic man had been an exuberant child. "For many summers now we have shown respect to your people, but the white man treats me like a dog. There must be one law for all of us. If I commit a murder, then I should be hung from a tree by a rope. But if I do right, I should not be punished and have what is mine taken from me— my cattle, my horses . . . and not the land of my grandfathers."

"This has been decided by those above us," Cut-Off Arm repeated with growing exasperation.

The muscular Ollokot sternly replied, "Our friends among the White Bird people will be here by tomorrow. At that time I will tell them what I think of giving you what you cannot have."

"We are under the same government," Cut-Off Arm declared, turning to gaze at Joseph, his one hand imploring for understanding. "What our government commands us to do, we must do. Your people must first come to the reservation; then your agent will give you the privileges of hunting and fishing in the Imnaha country. But if your people hesitate in coming, then our government has directed me to use my soldiers to bring you here. Now, Joseph . . . both you and your brother know that I am a friend to your people. And you know that if you comply, there will be no trouble."

Toohoolhoolzote grumbled something to the other old men gathered close by, words that alarmed the even-tempered Joseph.

"What did he say?" the soldier chief demanded of James Reuben, his voice grown shrill with alarm.

The interpreter's eyes darted nervously as he stammered, "Some-something about there not being enough soldiers to . . . to—"

"To *what?*" Cut-Off Arm railed, his cheeks grown red, his neck crimson above the stiff collar of his soldier tunic.

"Enough s-soldiers to make him do what his heart tells him is wrong."

The soldier chief slowly turned toward the Non-Treaty leaders arrayed before him. He took a step closer to the delegation, then briefly let his eyes touch them all before fixing his gaze on Joseph and Ollokot.

"You must give good advice to your people, and White Bird's people, too, when they arrive. If you do not convince them that they must comply and come to the reservation, I shall be forced to come for you. I will arrest you and put you in the guardhouse."

Then Cut-Off Arm turned slightly and stepped right up before the old Dreamer, Toohoolhoolzote. In an even tone he said, "If you continue in making these insults to me, I will arrest you, and send you to Indian Territory. It would be wise for you to remember what happened to Skamiah at the Vancouver post."

Just as the *tewat* was about to snap in reply about that uncooperative Indian chief who had been arrested and sent far away, Joseph laid his hand on the old man's elbow and squeezed. He nodded to the soldier chief as he answered, "When White Bird has arrived, we will meet again tomorrow."

So it was that their second council convened beneath the canvas tent erected with its long ridgepole and the sides tied out so that it made a large awning where the soldiers, other white men, and the *Nee-Me-Poo* sat, joined by *Peopeo,* the one called White Bird, along with the smaller band of Palouse under their chief *Huishuish Kute,* who was known as Shorn, or Bald, Head.

From the moment he greeted that sunny dawn, Joseph remained hopeful that the sun itself was not setting on the ways of his grandfathers. But almost from the moment the white man's prayer was made by the half-breed called Alpowa Jim, followed by Cut-Off Arm repeating the government's orders for all bands to move onto the reservation, Joseph realized matters were steadily deteriorating. There was no discussion and compromise, no room for disagreement. Decisions affecting the lives and futures of the *Nee-Me-Poo* had already been made without them.

Peopeo was a short, heavy-set man of some fifty winters whose name was variously interpreted as White, White Goose, White Crane, even White Pelican—any variation of a large white bird. He stood when Joseph introduced him to the soldier chief, the agent, and the missionary. White Bird politely shook hands with them all, then settled once more upon the ground, again positioning his large eagle-feather fan across the bottom half of his face so that it hid everything below his eyes.

"I have talked with you, Cut-Off Arm, and you, Agent Monteith, many times in past summers," Joseph declared. "But this is the first time White Bird has seen either of you. I have told him what you said to the rest of us."

Cut-Off Arm glanced at the older chief, then brought his eyes back to Joseph, asking, "Does White Bird understand his people must come to live upon this reservation?"

But at the moment Joseph opened his mouth to answer, Toohoolhoolzote leaped to his feet and warned dourly, "What the soldier chief wants . . . I cannot do! Wherever *Tamalait,* my creator, has put me, that is there I am to stay. No earthly man—not any *Nee-Me-Poo,* and certainly not any Shadow—can command me to go anyplace but where *Tamalait* saw fit for me to live!"

"This is true, what Toohoolhoolzote says," Joseph defended. "The Creator made no marks or lines of division on the bosom of the earth."

"It is too late to argue over this now," Cut-Off Arm grumbled impatiently as he glared at the old shaman.

"Don't you see that it is the white man who argues over the Creator?" Joseph instructed the soldier chief. "Your missionaries teach us to quarrel about God. See the fighting between your Catholics and Protestants on the reservation! We do not want to learn any fighting over God. We may sometimes quarrel with men about the things of this earth, but we never quarrel about God."

Cut-Off Arm listened to the entire translation before he countered, "I'm afraid your people do not understand anything more than a primitive concept of the Almighty."

At which point Toohoolhoolzote declared, "Perhaps I should tell the soldier chief how my people were started in long-ago days, and how the Shadows were started, so you will understand why you cannot come move us where the Creator did not intend for us to be."

Joseph saw how the old man's intransigence quickly irritated the soldier chief, how those words about *Tamalait* made the agent, himself the son of a Christian preacher, squirm in his ladder-back chair.

"My people were like a tree the Creator planted in this land a long time ago," Toohoolhoolzote pressed on, not dismayed by the anger apparent on the faces of the white men. "And the Creator planted your people like a tree in a place far, far away to the east. For a long time now these two trees have grown side by side, both becoming large, their branches spreading until their limbs met and eventually intermingled. That is how we have grown as two peoples, and as long as the limbs of our two trees cling together we will be at peace as one people."

Coming from the hard-bitten old chief, these profound words surprised Joseph. It was almost as if, instead of telling the Shadows that fighting was inevitable, the old *tewat* was instructing the soldier chief and others that there remained some tangible hope of averting bloodshed if each side would listen to the other.

"That is all I have to say to you, Cut-Off Arm," Toohoolhoolzote continued. "I say these things so that you will know what we believe. You must see that there are two parties to a disagreement. And the party that is in the right will always prevail in the end, no matter what wrongs are done against them by those who are not in the right."

For a moment the soldier chief remained thoughtful, studying the old *tewat*'s face before he spoke. "Your story is all fine and well, but you must understand that we are all subjects to those who are not here, those above us. You must accept that we are all children of a common government and must obey what that govern—"

Toohoolhoolzote did not wait for any more of the translation. Arching forward suddenly, he interrupted James Reuben the instant the translator interpreted the word *children*. "I am only one man's child! Surely I am no white man's child!"

Cut-Off Arm jerked back in surprise at the suddenness of the *tewat*'s scathing reproach, looking as if he was on the verge of sputtering a response when Toohoolhoolzote pressed on.

"I have heard much of the bargain struck between you white men and the Treaty bands who gave away our land for all of us. But I want you to know that my father's bones are buried in this country and I cannot give it to you. Remember that I am no longer a child. I came from this land. Therefore the land does not belong to me. *I* belong to *it*—"

"Those of your people who did not sign the treaty are in the minority," Cut-Off Arm interrupted the old chief's argument with an impatient wave of his one hand. "Those who did sign live peaceably on the reservation. Only your few bands are making for the trouble we now find ourselves in. Because the majority signed the treaty, your people are bound by that agreement too."

Toohoolhoolzote shook his head violently, flecks of spittle crusted at the side of his mouth as he said, "You have no right to treat me as a child, trying to order me to come here or go there. *Tamalait* made the world as it is, just as He wanted it—without your people coming to change things for everyone else. The Creator made a small part of the world for us a long time ago, and so we have lived here ever since. Neither your government nor all your soldiers have any authority to declare that my people shall not live where the Creator placed us in the beginning of time."

The soldier chief was flexing his one hand into a fist, his jaw jutted, neck flushing red again as he lunged a step toward Toohoolhoolzote—then brought himself up short. The rest of the chiefs clambered to their feet, immediately causing the soldiers and the other Shadows to stand. Behind their leaders, the warriors grew restless and the women murmured anxiously—

"It would be better for us to talk another day," Joseph suggested, worried that the next foolish words would be the spark that could set off this explosive situation.

When Cut-Off Arm turned to him, the soldier chief's eyes were filled with the closest thing to appreciation Joseph had seen on the face of a Shadow.

"Yes, I agree, Joseph," Cut-Off Arm said. "It is Friday. We will adjourn until Monday. These next two days will give your people time to reflect upon the grave choices they face. Two days to deliberate with careful thought on the welfare of your families, on their future."

Chapter 3

May 4–6, 1877

But forty-six-year-old Brigadier General Oliver Otis Howard found himself far too worried by the bellicose display
of that ugly old heathen to sit on his thumbs doing nothing
while he awaited the resumption of peace talks come Monday, the seventh day of May.

After dark that Friday night, the fourth, this commander
of the Military Department of the Columbia, headquartered
at Portland, dispatched a courier to Fort Walla Walla with
his orders for two companies of cavalry to embark for the
Wallowa, where they would be in position when and if trouble erupted.

So if this old Civil War brigade commander, this veteran
of the Apache wars in Arizona, knew anything . . . he knew
trouble was on its way.

Everything that had gone before in his life had prepared
Howard for this critical trial. If Otis, as he had been called
since childhood, ever believed God was testing him before
. . . then surely the Almighty had been doing nothing less than
preparing him for this opportunity of a lifetime. The winding,
bumpy road that had carried him here to this moment had
been a journey that clearly prepared him for this day of redemption.

Born in the tiny farming village of Leeds along the Androscog-
gin River in the south of Maine on the eighth of November

1830—the same day his maternal grandfather turned sixty-two—Oliver Otis had been dutifully named by his mother for her father. Throughout his life he often spoke proudly of how his Howard ancestors reached Massachusetts from England in 1643, not migrating north to Leeds until 1802.

When he was five, his father returned from a trip down to the Hudson River Valley of New York State with a young Negro boy not much older than Otis. Over the next four years they became fast companions—working the farm and playing together—until it came time that his father returned Howard's young friend to that New York farm far away. Still, their fast friendship would indelibly inscribe Howard's future years.

There was winter schooling while the snows lay deep, a little more schooling when the fields were fallow. Every week on the Sabbath there was Scripture class and sermons, most family evenings spent reading by the lamp or listening to his father play the flute, as well as a grandfather with a strong and guiding hand who regaled Otis and his brothers with tales of the Revolutionary War. When Otis was ten his father died and Grandpa moved away to live with another son. The following year his mother remarried a man who would treat his stepsons with such kindness that Howard recalled those years as "a blessing to us all."

After persevering at some of the hardest work of his life while preparing for the daunting entrance exams, he was admitted to the freshman class at Bowdoin College in September of 1846. "I seek not mere money," he wrote home during his tenure at Bowdoin, "but a cultivated and enlightened mind." And later, when some of his closest friends had abandoned college to return home for a "more practical life," Otis would remind his mother that "a general education fits a man for any work."

This opportunity to learn was not an opportunity he would let slip through his fingers. "I am strongly ambitious," he wrote his mother. So it was that throughout his life, this powerful drive to succeed—an ingredient inscribing the character of those who aspired to leadership—would ultimately come to taint this thoughtful and moral man. While he did not drink, he did enjoy his pipe and tobacco, unsuccessfully trying twice to rid himself of the habit.

More than any thought of national politics of the time, the Mexican War, or the Wilmot Proviso, Otis was interested in

Elizabeth Ann Waite, the young but serious fifteen-year-old cousin of his college roommate. It was Otis's deep love for Lizzie that eventually compelled him to give up his tobacco. By the time he was in his junior year, the two of them agreed to an engagement, planning on marriage after his graduation. But in June of his senior year, his uncle suggested Howard seek an appointment to West Point, although that would delay his marriage to Lizzie for another four years.

In the fall of 1850, Howard began his career in the United State Army as a cadet underclassman. How he missed his Lizzie in those early days, and grew extremely homesick, made "sore by the sharp drilling, and a little angry, from having my pride so often touched." But by the next spring, when he began to feel more comfortable at the academy, Otis suffered some ostracism and ridicule because of his regular attendance of Bible classes and for his abolitionist views, becoming despised by no less than Custis Lee, the son of Colonel Robert E. Lee, who became superintendent of the academy in 1852. Nonetheless, one of Howard's fastest friends during his last two years at West Point proved to be Jeb Stuart, soon to become the flower of the Confederate cavalry.

Howard's friendship with Stuart and other Southerners of that day went far to disproving the contention that Howard was an ardent, if not rabid and uncompromising, abolitionist. In fact, during one of his presentations before the Dialectic Society, a cadet literary and debating forum, Howard eloquently advanced the argument that the Constitution actually sanctioned slavery!

Upon graduation in June of '54, while Custis Lee was ranked first in the graduating class, Howard was not far behind: proudly standing fourth in a field of forty-six. He was leaving the academy in success. Feeling a powerful *esprit de corps,* he wrote his mother that "The Professors are without exception my fast friends, and I wish I was half as good a man as I have the reputation of being here."

At the beginning of those years at the academy, he had little idea just what he wanted to become when he would graduate. But in those four intervening years, Oliver Otis Howard had become a soldier. It was the only profession he would ever know.

Still, there was one thing he wanted even more than a career in the army—Otis wanted Elizabeth Ann Waite. They were married on Valentine's Day in 1855, and their first child was born on December 16.

While he had been reading the Scriptures since childhood and attending Bible study at the academy, it was not until two years after the birth of his first child that Howard actually turned his life over to his God. Although he consistently went to church and diligently read his Bible every night in those intervening years, Otis had long been troubled that he hadn't yet experienced his own emotional conversion. Then, just before the birth of his second child, Howard found what he had been seeking. So it came as little surprise to him now that he spent the long spring evenings of this first weekend in May 1877 striding up and down the long vine-covered porch that graced the front of the Fort Lapwai house where the Perry and FitzGerald families lived as he recited Scripture.

Autumn of 1857 had found Howard on the faculty of West Point, where he would remain until the outbreak of hostilities with the rebellious Southern states. Shortly after Lincoln's election, he wrote his mother that he really didn't care if South Carolina did in fact secede from the Union, figuring it would prove a good lesson for "her people to stand alone for a few years."

Although December brought secession, that following spring of 1861 found Howard considering a leave of absence to attend the Bangor Theological Seminary. The notion that the North and South should ever go to war over their political squabbles was hardly worth entertaining. Yet April brought the bombardment and surrender of Fort Sumter.

Oliver Otis Howard stepped forward to do his duty as a professional soldier. But rather than remaining as a lieutenant in the regular army, he instead lobbied for and won a colonelcy of the Third Maine Volunteers. Before the year was out he would win his general's star, and scarcely a year later he would become a major general.

Few men in the nation at that time had the training or experience to assume such lofty positions of grave leadership in either of those two great armies poised to hurl themselves into a bloody maelstrom. Howard was no exception. Yet over the next four years he, like many others, would struggle to learn his bloody profession on-the-job.

Ordered to lead his brigade of 3,000 toward the front at the first Battle of Bull Run, on the way to the battlefield he and his men saw the hundreds of General McDowell's wounded as they were carried to the rear. The nearness of those whistling canisters of shot, the throaty reverberations of the cannon, the incessant rattle of small arms—not to mention the pitiful cries of the maimed, the sight of bloodied, limbless soldiers—suddenly gave the zealous Howard pause.

For the first and only time in his life, his knees began to quake. Nearing McDowell's position with his brigade for that opening battle of the war, Howard pleaded with God to give him the strength to do his duty that day. He later wrote that in an instant his trepidation was lifted from him and the very real prospect of death no longer brought him any fear. From that moment on, Oliver Otis Howard would never again be afraid in battle.

Bull Run was a demoralizing defeat for the untrained Union volunteers. But while others were sickened with despair at the loss, Howard wrote home to Lizzie saying: "I try to rely upon the Arm of Strength."

Not long after George B. McClellan took over the Union Army, Howard was promoted to brigadier general of the Third Maine. In action during the Peninsula Campaign, his brigade found itself sharply engaged on the morning of the second day of the Battle of Fair Oaks as the Confederates launched a determined attack. Ordered to throw his remaining two regiments into the counterattack rather than holding them in reserve, Howard confidently stepped out in front of his men and gave the order to advance. Although Confederate minié balls were hissing through the brush and shredding the trees all around them, Howard continued to conspicuously move among the front ranks of his men on horseback, leading his troops against the enemy's noisy advance.

Less than thirty yards from that glittering line of bayonets and butternut-gray uniforms, a lead .58-caliber bullet struck Oliver Otis Howard in the right elbow. Somehow he remained oblivious to the pain as his men closed on the enemy. Within yards of engaging the Confederates in close-quarters combat, a bullet brought down his horse. When Howard was getting to his feet seconds later, a second ball shattered his right forearm just below the first wound.

With blood gushing from his body, Howard grew faint, stumbled, and collapsed, whereupon he turned over command of the brigade to another officer. Later that morning Howard was removed to a field hospital at the rear, where the surgeons explained the severity of his wounds, as well as the fact that there was little choice between gangrene, which would lead to a certain death, or amputation. By five o'clock that afternoon, the doctors went to work to save Howard's life.

The following morning as Otis was being settled upon a litter for transport to the rear, up rode General Phil Kearny, who himself had lost his left arm during the Mexican War. After Kearny gave the new amputee some reassuring and sympathetic words, Howard—minus his right arm—surprised Kearny with his own courageous sense of humor, proposing that in the future the two of them save money by purchasing their gloves together!

Lying on his stretcher beside the railroad tracks awaiting a freight car that would carry the Union wounded to White House Landing, Howard gripped a pencil in his left hand and clumsily attempted to write his Lizzie. All but impossible to read, his letter said in total: "Dearest I am on my way with only my left arm."

Fair Oaks had been one of Howard's bravest hours.

"What did they do with your arm when they sawed it off?"

He turned now that spring evening in Nez Perce country, gazing down at the little girl who stood right where his missing elbow would have been, finding the FitzGerald child staring at the fold in that empty sleeve, her wide, inquisitive eyes slowly crawling up to his face as her mother swept toward them with red-faced embarrassment and a rustle of crinoline petticoats.

"So, so sorry, General Howard," Emily FitzGerald gushed in apology as she laid her hands on her daughter's shoulders and dragged the girl back a step.

Emily's husband, the post surgeon, was already making his way off the porch railing where he had joined other officers who were relaxing after supper this Sunday evening, smoking their pipes and cheroots, drinking coffee or a delicious port Colonel David Perry had dragged from some hidden corner of his resi-

dence. These soldiers had all been getting to know one another
very nicely this weekend just drawing to a close. Career men,
one and all, along with a few wives and their children, too—the
whole evening made Otis very, very homesick for Lizzie, for
those bygone days when their children were little. But Guy,
their firstborn, would be twenty-seven this December—

"May I touch it, sir?" the girl asked.

"Bessie!" Mrs. FitzGerald shrieked in horror at her daughter, who had her arm out pointing at that sleeve empty from
the elbow down.

For photographs and other formal settings, Howard tucked
the empty coat cuff into the front of his belt just behind his
buckle, but most of the time he kept the useless sleeve folded
and pinned neatly against the upper arm.

Howard flashed Mrs. FitzGerald a quick smile in his beard,
realizing she could not be any older than his own daughter,
Grace Ellen. Then he gazed into the little one's face as he
sank to one knee. One day soon he might well have a child
as curious as this one for a granddaughter.

"Now, what was your name again, young lady?" he asked
her, his eyes crinkling at their corners, bemused.

"Bess—," she began, then thought better of it and took
one big step back, correcting herself very properly, "Elizabeth FitzGerald, sir."

"He's a general, Bessie," Mrs. FitzGerald prompted.

"General," Bess echoed, then surprised everyone on that
long porch in the last of spring's warm twilight as she grabbed
the sides of her long pinafore, dragged one foot quickly behind the other, and dipped into a low curtsy.

When Emily FitzGerald spontaneously clapped her hands
before her face, the tears of motherly pride brimming in her
eyes, Howard himself was overcome by the moment. His eyes
began to sting as he laid his left arm across his belt, smartly
clicked the heels of his muddy boots together, and snapped
his upper body forward stiffly in an elegant bow. And before
he straightened, Howard reached out with his left hand, in-
serting his fingers within Bessie's tiny palm, then raised the
girl's hand to his lips.

He kissed the back of it, lowered the hand, and released
her gently as he said, "I am so honored to meet you, Elizabeth FitzGerald."

Howard glanced up at all the faces of the officers, wives,

and children, at the faces of all those soldiers who had suddenly seemed to halt in mid-stride out on the starlit parade, everyone's attention suddenly turned his way.

Struck by the sudden regard riveted on him, Otis announced, "And I am very honored to meet all of you—"

"He gonna tell you, Bessie?" the FitzGerald boy whispered noisily as he instantly shuffled up beside his older sister, tugging on her free arm.

"Yes," Howard replied with no more prompting, "I'm going to tell your sister all about it, young man."

He held out his hand for Elizabeth, and she placed hers in it without the slightest hesitation. The general led her over to the edge of the porch, where he could sit on the railing as darkness settled down on the Lapwai country.

"Here, Miss Elizabeth FitzGerald," and he tapped the fold in his right sleeve. "You may touch it now, to your heart's content."

"It's all right with you, General?" John FitzGerald asked in that apologetic tone parents of precocious children must take of times.

"Quite all right, Doctor." Then he took hold of the girl's hand and laid it on the end of that upper arm. "There."

He waited a moment while she felt around the blunted stub in a most tentative manner, then turned to her brother.

"Go ahead on, Bertie," she announced. "It won't hurt you a bit."

The little boy stepped up, much braver now, and held up his hand as Howard leaned forward so the young child could reach the amputation.

"Miss FitzGerald," Howard began as the boy was pursuing his examination, "I don't really know what the doctors did with my arm that day so long ago. I only know that outside those surgical tents, there was a pile of arms and legs big enough to fill another tent, all by themselves."

Mrs. FitzGerald and the other wives immediately put their hands to their mouths with gasps of horror and surprise.

"I apologize, ladies," he said, sorry for his candor. "I'm just an old soldier, and I forgot myself there." Howard looked again at the young girl. "I heard that your father was a surgeon in the war, Miss FitzGerald. Perhaps when he believes you are ready to understand, your father can explain to you just what they did with all those people parts that had to come off to save the lives of so many men in that horrible war."

"Yes, one day I will do just that, General," FitzGerald promised, stepping up behind his children, placing a hand on a shoulder of each one.

"Thank you for rescuing me, Doctor," Howard said gratefully, then knelt before the two youngsters. "But as for me, children—I've always wanted to believe my arm just went on to heaven a little bit before I will. Why—do you know that when I came home in 1862 right after losing my arm, my daughter, Grace, was about your age?"

"Did it scare her to see her daddy without his arm on?"

"I really think it did, Miss FitzGerald. But she soon found out I could give her just as good a hug with one arm as I had done with two."

"I want you to thank the general now, Bessie," Mrs. Fitz-Gerald said as she stepped up beside her husband to scoop her children against her. "It's time I took you both inside to get dressed for bed."

"Good night, General," the little girl called as her brother turned shyly into the folds of his mother's dress. "When I say my prayers in my bed tonight, I'll ask God to take good care of your arm for you in heaven till you get there to see it again for yourself."

Suddenly struck with a deep, unexplainable sadness, Howard stood ramrod straight in that spring moonlight. He felt all of his forty-six years. "Thank you, Bessie," he said softly. "But I also want you to pray that we won't have any war with the Indians. I want you to pray that no one will have to lose an arm, or a leg, or their life. Will you pray that for me?"

"Yes, General," she replied before she curtsied again, turned suddenly, and led her brother by the hand toward the far doorway.

Howard watched after the children as their mother hustled them off for the night. He blinked his stinging eyes and looked about at those officers gathered on the porch: his departmental staff and those leaders of Fort Lapwai who would bear the brunt of things if hostilities broke out.

"Gentlemen," he said, "I believe we can all say *amen* to that prayer I asked little Bessie to make on behalf of us, one and all."

In the sudden, still hush of that spring evening, more than a dozen career officers softly whispered as one.

"Amen."

Chapter 4

Season of *Hillal*
1877

"Soldiers have come to the Wallowa?" Joseph echoed that shocking news the courier had just told him in the darkness of their camp here on the edge of the army's fort beside Lapwai Creek.

The breathless rider gasped as he pulled the dripping canteen from his wet lips. "Little more than a day ago. The *suapies* are camped where the valley widens by the point of rocks."

"Yes, I know the place," Ollokot growled as menacingly as a dog with its neck hair ruffled by danger, gazing south toward that faraway valley where their families, their people, were awaiting the outcome of this crucial council with the soldier leaders.

Not surprising to Joseph, the late-night arrival of this messenger from the Wallowa had awakened some of the delegates from the other bands. From all sides the leaders appeared out of the cold, pre-dawn darkness to close in on him and his followers.

"What is this news he brings?" demanded *Alalimiatakanin*, whose name literally meant "A Vision."

Because of that round lens from the white man's far-seeing instrument he wore strapped around his neck in the middle of a thick leather star decorated with tarnished brass tacks, not only for decoration but also as symbol of his venerated status, this veteran war chief of more than forty-six winters was known to the Shadows as Looking Glass.

"Horse soldiers have made a camp in the Wallowa," Ollokot announced.

"Perhaps they are only on their way through and won't be staying," White Bird offered hopefully. He was an attractive older man of more than fifty summers—his hair, once chestnut rather than black, now turning white with the snows of his life.

"No," the courier argued. "Before I left yesterday to hurry here with the news for my chief, it was plain the soldiers intend to stay for some time."

"And keep watch on our village until we are driven onto the reservation," Ollokot growled sourly.

"It is just what they did to the Lakota called Red Cloud some ten summers ago," grumbled the older Toohoolhoolzote as he lumbered to a stop among them. Almost as broad of shoulder as he was tall, this stout and powerful man could easily carry two deer back to camp, one on each shoulder, back in his younger days.

"I do not remember that story of the Lakota," White Bird said.

The thick-necked Toohoolhoolzote took the canteen from the runner, drank a swallow to wash down the night gather from the back of his throat, then handed it back before he explained, "The army said they wanted to talk to Red Cloud about making a treaty for some of the Lakota land over there in buffalo country. But at the same time ... the army was already sending its soldiers into the Lakota's hunting ground to build their forts, making ready to steal it."

Looking Glass, his hair streaked with iron, snarled angrily, "The army means to take our land from us anyway, my friends. All this polite talk from Cut-Off Arm is nothing more than a ruse to convince us we have had our say before they—"

"No, no," Joseph protested sadly, sensing the angry frustration in that circle of leaders. "I cannot believe they would make such fools of us."

"The time for war is coming!" cried Sun Necklace,* a war chief among White Bird's band.

---

*The name of the warrior later called Yellow Bull, *Chuslum Moxmox*—which is the name used for this character in most of the historical literature concerning this 1877 conflict

Joseph whirled on him. "Enough of such talk. That's all the young men think of—fighting and war. It remains for the rest of us to think of our women and our children. What of them, if you go racing off to kill those soldiers in the Wallowa even though you do not know why the army has come to our valley?"

"My hands are ready to fight," Ollokot explained to his brother, "but my heart will go with you, Joseph."

"We know what happened to the Modocs: They are no more," Joseph reminded them. "Their leaders were hanged. All the rest now scattered to the four winds, far from the lands of their forefathers. And now the Lakota, too. Sitting Bull takes his people to the Old Woman's Country* far away, a land where his people have never lived. Meanwhile, reports from the buffalo country say the rest of the Lakota are trickling in to the reservations the white man has established to corral them."

The group fell silent around him until the voice of Looking Glass broke the hush.

"Joseph is right. From all sides the Shadows have pushed in upon us. There are more white men than there are trees in the Imnaha. We chop down a few, like those soldiers invading the Wallowa . . . There will always be more trees than we could ever hope to cut down."

Joseph studied the graying war chief, sensed the pain such an admission caused this veteran of many battles against the Lakota and Blackfoot. "The white man's powerful religion gives him the might to create his weapons and wealth: not just kettles and blankets, but guns and bullets. He possesses his *Book of Heaven,* which contains the knowledge our people once went far to the east to find and bring back."

"The Boston Man's *Book of Heaven* means nothing to our Dreamer religion," snarled Toohoolhoolzote. "It is true the Shadows may have those *things,* but we Dreamers believe that one day the earth will swallow up all the Shadows and everything will be as it was before the first whites ever came among us."

"Until that day," Joseph sighed, "we must somehow protect our people—safeguard our women and our children. For the time being, we must make as good a peace as we can . . .

*Canada

for the sake of those who must survive until the Dreamers' vision comes to pass and the earth finally swallows up the white man."

Later, after breakfast, the leaders dressed in their finest, adorning their ponies with the heavily beaded headstalls and feathered bonnets much like those the headmen themselves wore. Wrapped in blankets and buffalo robes, they paraded onto the fort grounds in a long procession, singing and beating their drums, the women *u-looing* afoot on either side of the chiefs' caravan as they approached the council awning for this last, crucial day of talks with Cut-Off Arm and his soldiers.

As soon as the half-breed interpreter said his Christian prayer to open the ceremonies, the old men started their pipe on its rounds among the chiefs and headmen. For the most part the white men were quiet and respectful until the pipe had finished its path among the leaders of the Non-Treaty bands. Yet Joseph could clearly see that disdain the agent held for the practices of his *Nee-Me-Poo*.

"One of the things I fear most about being forced to come live in this place is that I worry about what will happen next to my people," Joseph explained as he stood before the agent, the missionary, and the soldier chief in the shade of the council tent.

"Only good can come of you bringing your people here," Agent John B. Monteith asserted.

With a wag of his head, Joseph argued, "Once we are here, you will try to make us like the upper bands who are under the spell of your Christian missionaries."

"What do you mean by that?" Perrin Whitman demanded from the side. He knew the language and did not require an interpreter.

"We are afraid you just don't merely want us to abandon our long-held tribal lands," Joseph declared firmly. "We believe that once we have come here, you will do everything in your power to make us into Christian Indians like those you already have here at the agency . . . the ones who have cut their hair like a white man, wearing the white man's clothes, reading and believing the white man's religion."

The agent shook his head, arguing, "You have evidently gotten the wrong impression, Joseph. We do not want to interfere with your religious rites. There will be no restraint of religion here on your reservation while I am in charge." Monteith tore his eyes off the young chief and glanced a moment at the older Toohoolhoolzote. "Only when one of your *tewats* disturbs the peace with too much drumming and too much savage zeal will I forbid those extreme practices."

Cut-Off Arm was already standing in front of his chair, ready to speak his mind as soon as the agent finished. "It makes no difference what church a bad leader belongs to. White or Indian. Dreamer or Christian. If one of your religious men gives bad advice to your people, advice that causes disobedience to the requirements of the agent or the army . . . then that leader will have to be punished and taken away to Indian Territory."

"But what of the women and children?" Joseph asked. "Must they be punished for the sins of the men?"

"No one is going to punish any of your people if you peacefully come to this reservation as my government tells you to."

"I think you are already preparing to punish my people in the Wallowa," Joseph announced, and watched the surprise cross the soldier chief's face.

The hairy-faced Cut-Off Arm asked, "What do you mean?"

"We know they are already in the Wallowa, ready to attack my people."

The soldier chief shook his head, waving his one hand. "No, no. There will be no attack on your camps. My soldiers have gone to the Wallowa only to help bring your people here as soon as you can get them under way. And those soldiers are there to help protect your people from angry settlers if there is trouble."

Bolting to his feet, Toohoolhoolzote grumbled, "There is not a shred of truth in what you say! Already the white man has taken what was not his in the Wallowa. And now the soldiers have come to take away more of what my Creator never intended the white man to have!"

"Don't you understand that the majority of your people signed the treaty?" the agent protested.

Toohoolhoolzote, leader of the small *Pikunan* band that wandered the area between the Salmon and Snake rivers, took a step forward, his thick neck tortoised into those powerful shoulders to give him an even more intimidating appearance. "You must stay off the land *Tamalait* gave us long ago. Take all that belongs to you and go away, now! The earth is my mother, and she must not be disturbed by your plow and hoe. For generations my people have lived just the way our Creator made us, surviving only on what grows in the forest, the animals in these hills. This has always been our land. Soon there will be a great reckoning for those who would use violence to take from us what has always been ours!"

"This matter has been decided," Monteith said as calmly as he could. "The majority of the Nez Perce signed the treaty."

But Toohoolhoolzote shook his head vigorously, loudly protesting, "Lawyer's people had no right to do that! *Tamalait* made us chieftains over the earth, to care for it, protect it. That chieftainship cannot be sold, nor can it be given away. You white leaders must accept that we are all chieftains of the earth."

Cut-Off Arm slapped his left thigh with his one hand, clearly growing agitated at how the arguments of this persuasive orator were stirring up those *Nee-Me-Poo* spectators ringing the council's awning. "I told you already: I do not intend to interfere with your religion. So it is time to stop all this talk and get on to practical matters. Twenty times over you tell me the earth is your mother, and twenty times over you tell me about being a chieftain over the earth. I want to hear no more of such talk! You must come to business at once!"

How the soldier chief's words slapped the old *tewat*, stinging his pride.

Joseph grew saddened, beginning to realize that perhaps the white man and the soldiers did not really want to listen to the complaints of his people in these council talks. Instead, he was coming to believe that Cut-Off Arm and the others were here only to convince Joseph and the others that they were being listened to.

Toohoolhoolzote's eyes were like the slits of a prairie rattler in those moments before it attacked. Flecks of foam collected at the corners of his angry mouth. "What the Treaty bands talk about is born of today. Their Christian beliefs aren't the true law at all! You white people get together, measure the earth back and forth with your ropes and poles, then divide it among yourselves! Yes—I agree with you, Cut-

Off Arm: we should talk about practical matters."

He drew a deep breath, then continued, "So I want you to tell me exactly what you mean for me to do now that you are moving soldiers into my country to frighten my people."

But the agent stepped to the soldier chief's side and spoke first: "The law says that you must come to this reservation. That law is made in Washington. We did not make this law, but we must enforce it."

Jabbing a finger at the agent, Toohoolhoolzote snarled, "We did not make any agreement with you or your government. We made no trade. Only part of the Indians gave up their lands to you. I never did. Joseph didn't either. Not Looking Glass or White Bird, not *Hahtalekin** or *Huishuish Kute* of the Palouse either! The earth is part of my body and I can never give up the earth!"

With his one hand braced against his left thigh, Cut-Off Arm shot to his feet, towering over the squat Toohoolhoolzote. He glared down at the chief and argued fiercely, "You know very well that our government has set aside a reservation for your people and your people must go live upon it. If any of you become a citizen, then that Indian can claim land outside the reservation just like any citizen in accordance with the law. But he has to leave his tribe to do that, and take up the land on his own the way the white man does."

Shaking his head violently, Toohoolhoolzote shouted, "We will never live as the white man lives!"

Angrily the soldier chief snapped, "Then you and your children must live on the reservation my government gives you, where you will prosper in peace among your own kind."

Quaking with fury, the old chief whirled on the other leaders and asked them in a harsh whisper, "Who are these white creatures who stand before our Creator and tell us that they will divide His people and scatter us across the land we alone were given long ago?"

"What was that!" Cut-Off Arm was shouting, stomping one way, then the other, demanding a translation from the half-breed Reuben as well as from the one called Whitman. "What did this old man just tell the others?"

The Christian missionary stood and reported, "He says, 'What person pretends to divide the land and put me on it?' "

*Red Echo

As Toohoolhoolzote took a step closer to confront Cut-Off Arm, the soldier chief stiffened noticeably and clenched that one fist at his waist. "I . . . am . . . that . . . man. I stand here for the President—and there is no spirit, good or bad, that will hinder me. My orders are plain and will be executed. I hoped that your people had good sense enough to make me your friend, and not make me your enemy. But I see I am mistaken."

The nervous half-breed stammered and stuttered through his translation, trying to keep up with the soldier chief's spiteful words as angry feelings flew about the council tent. Joseph and the other chiefs and headmen, not to mention the young warriors surrounding them, were growing more and more upset.

Then White Bird lowered the eagle fan from his face and said in a much calmer tone, "If I had been taught from early life to be governed by the white man, I would be governed by the white man. But, as it is, I have been brought up on this land, and it is this earth that sustains me."

Instead of acknowledging White Bird, the soldier chief turned back to the stocky Toohoolhoolzote and asked, "Then you will not comply with the orders of the government?"

"No," the shaman replied firmly. "As long as the earth keeps me, I want to be left alone. You are trifling with the law of the earth."

Quickly glancing over the other chiefs and headmen, Cut-Off Arm said, "Our friend here does not seem to understand that the grave question before you is: Will your people come peaceably upon this reservation? Or . . . do you want me to put them here by force?"

Of a sudden Toohoolhoolzote was fairly spitting, "I did not give these Christian Indians the right to give away my lands!"

An equally aroused Cut-Off Arm demanded, "Do you speak for yourself alone? Or the rest of these chiefs?"

While the other leaders remained in stunned silence, the old man waited a moment before he eventually answered, "These others may do what they wish. As for me, I am never going onto a reservation."

Joseph watched the crimson fury bring a blush to the soldier chief's neck, that color climbing up his bearded cheeks like a swell of storm clouds.

Cut-Off Arm said, "This is very bad advice you give the

others, old man—so you best shut up. On account of your bad words, I am going to send you to Indian Territory. Look here, Joseph and White Bird appear to have good hearts, but it is plain your heart is very bad. You will be punished in the hot land of the Indian Territory until you have a good heart again, even if it takes years and years—"

"Do not threaten me with your faraway land!" Toohoolhoolzote interrupted the soldier chief that instant a translation was made. "This is my land—where I was born, where I will fight, and where I will die if need be. Not in some hot, faraway—"

"When I heard you were coming, I feared you would make trouble for the rest of these leaders," the soldier chief grumbled peevishly. "You say you are not a medicine man, but you talk strongly on behalf of your religion. I think these people can see no good while you are their spokesman. You are telling them to resist what is law, telling them to fight what will be, to lose their horses and cattle and have unending trouble because of your hard-headed foolishness."

As the interpreter was translating, Howard stepped past Toohoolhoolzote and stopped before the other chiefs to say, "Will Joseph, White Bird, and Looking Glass go with me to pick out their land on the reservation? This old man will not go, so he must stay here with soldier chief Perry."

With the half-breed's translation, Toohoolhoolzote stomped up to the soldier chief's empty sleeve and demanded, "Are you trying to scare me about my physical body?"

Cut-Off Arm glared down at him, turning squarely on the squat chief with his left hand raised into a claw, as if he intended to seize the old man as he growled, "For now I am going to leave your body right here with soldier chief Perry!"

With that threat Toohoolhoolzote lunged backward, bent at the knees, clearly prepared to knock the soldier chief's hand aside should Cut-Off Arm make his advance.

Instead, the bearded white man wheeled around to shout orders to the other soldiers gathered there, most of them getting on their feet, too.

"What did he just say to them?" Joseph demanded of the half-breed Reuben, unable to understand a word of that flurry of English.

Reuben gulped. "He told them to bring a guard, so the

guard can take the old man to the small iron house."

"Small iron house?" Joseph repeated. "What is that?"

"Iron bars cover the windows, bars on the doors," Reuben explained with fear in his eyes as they darted back and forth between Joseph's and Toohoolhoolzote. His fingers started to pantomime the iron bars on the doors and windows. "But, hold on, now the soldier chief won't wait for a guard to come—"

At that instant Cut-Off Arm whirled on his heel and with his one hand clamped a lock on Toohoolhoolzote's elbow, jerking the *tewat* into motion. "I will take you to the guard-house myself!"

The stunned chiefs sat frozen as the other white men and soldiers parted their ranks for Cut-Off Arm and the shaman. A few of the soldiers fell in behind their leader as he dragged the old chief away. A tense, stony silence settled over the council.

Later, by the time Joseph spotted Cut-Off Arm returning across the open meadow that lay between the fort's buildings, some of the women had quietly begun to keen behind their leaders. Closer and closer the soldiers came until Cut-Off Arm stopped once more, directly in front of Joseph and the other chiefs.

Cut-Off Arm quickly glanced over the leaders, then spoke to his interpreter.

"Now, I want you to ask these leaders if they are going to listen to that old troublemaker I took to the guardhouse myself . . . or are they going to accompany me to look for their new homes on the reservation?"

Chapter 5

Season of *Hillal*
1877

BY TELEGRAPH

CHEYENNE.

Indian and Deadwood News.
CHEYENNE, May 19.—General Crook with
Major Randall and Lieutenant Schuyler leave here
in the morning for the agencies, where the final
grand council will be held, which must be simply
a formality, as the disarmament of the Indians
renders their consent to any proposition easily
obtained. A small band of Cheyennes arrived at
Red Cloud Wednesday, bringing in some two
hundred horses. The Indians are convinced that the
government is acting in good faith, and are
evincing a like fidelity to the terms of the
surrender.

Joseph stretched out his arm and tapped his younger
brother on the shoulder. The moment Ollokot turned to
look, Joseph laid a finger against his lips, then pointed that

same finger at the brush more than an arrow-flight away at
the edge of the ravine.

Ollokot nodded and started away cautiously, creeping wide
across the side of the grassy hill. Joseph remained still, watching his brother, then moving only his eyes to watch the brush
below them, and listened. He smiled, feeling confident that
they would bring even more meat into camp before the sun
set beyond the valley.

One by one, the days had been growing longer, allowing
the brothers to leave their wives and lodges earlier every
morning, to return from the high slopes later every evening.
Today's would be their last hunt together in these hills blan-
keted with huckle and gooseberries the women usually harvested in the heat of the *Wa-wa-mai-khal,** hills the two had
roamed as boys.

That melancholy thought stabbed him again in a place well-
protected by his breastbone. Joseph swallowed at the sharp
pain of loss and watched his brother continue across the
breast of the hill above him as they both slowly worked their
way in on the deer that had taken cover in that copse of
timber. Just the way it had been when they were boys, back
when they carried toy bows and tiny knife-sharpened stick
arrows, hoping to kill a ground squirrel or a vole with their
mighty weapons. Because their father, an important chief, did
not often have time to train his youngest son, it was Joseph
who had taken his brother under his wing and helped the
younger one along. So many hunts, so many trips through
these hills, had they shared over countless seasons.

They were truly more than brothers of blood. Joseph and
Ollokot were friends. And that made them brothers of the
heart.

But now, things would never be the same again. These hills
near the lake at the edge of the Camas Prairie,† just like the
hills in the Wallowa where they both were born, would never
again be theirs to hunt. Monteith and Cut-Off Arm had convinced the chiefs that any further resistance, any more stubborn attempts at delay, were nothing less than futile.

The day after Toohoolhoolzote had been locked behind the

---

*The August moon
†The 10,000-year old Tolo Lake near present-day Grangeville,
Idaho, the sole natural lake on Camas Prairie

iron bars inside the white man's log house, Cut-Off Arm had taken the *Nee-Me-Poo* leaders on a day-long ride across Monteith's reservation so each of them could select the sites where their bands would make their new homes, there to live out the rest of their existence the way the Christian bands were living out theirs attempting to be white men.

"This is the land of your father," Old Joseph had instructed his eldest son in those moments before the old man died six winters ago.

Tuekakas was his *Nee-Me-Poo* name, meaning "Old Grizzly." When so many thousands of white people began to flood in upon a few hundred of his people, contrary to the guarantees of the white peace-talkers, Old Joseph tore up his copy of an early treaty he had signed and even burned the Bible he had kept in his lodge for more than thirty years, ever since his Christian baptism.

Nearing his final breath, he clutched the hands of both sons weakly and made them promise, "You must never sell, you must never give away, the land of your father."

Later, as their long-held customs dictated, Young Joseph had laid the skin of his father's favorite horse over the covered grave where they put Old Joseph to rest for all time. Thin, peeled lodgepoles painted red were planted all around the grave. A pair of bells hung from the very top of each pole so that the stirring of the slightest breeze might make a gentle music above this place.

Ever since, Joseph tried time and again to convince himself that he and Ollokot had not given away the land of their father.

Why, the *Nee-Me-Poo* did not even have a word for "enemy" in their language. However, the concept of a "coming force" had been well understood ever since the first hairy-faces had arrived.

So Joseph had long struggled to reconcile the death-watch vow he had given his father with the inevitability of the white man closing in around what had once belonged only to the Wallowa people. By choosing to go to the reservation, by doing as Monteith and the soldiers ordered, chiefs like him had ultimately decided that the lives of their people were more important than the pride of their warriors.

"Rather than kill a white man in a war," Joseph had explained to Cut-Off Arm, "I will bring my people to Lapwai."

All the leaders felt as if they had been shamed by the soldier chief, given no chance to salve their wounded pride. When Cut-Off Arm not only talked about using force in the council but actually used force in dragging old Toohoolhoolzote to the iron-barred house, it was the same as if the soldier chief was showing them the rifle. In peace councils, a man simply did not speak of force, much less use it!

Nonetheless, Joseph bravely asked the soldier chief for more time to reach the reservation than Cut-Off Arm had given the Wallowa band initially. Joseph attempted to explain how his people had to cross both the Salmon and the Snake on their way to Lapwai and at this time of year the snowmelt had swollen those rivers so the mighty waters roared and raged between their steep banks.

Couldn't the Wallowa put off coming in to the reservation until the rivers had quieted?

"No," repeated Cut-Off Arm in a stern reproach that only served as one more serious wound to the *Nee-Me-Poo* pride.

"I think the soldier chief and agent believe that the more time they give us," Joseph explained later to his headmen and warriors, "the less likely we are to comply with their demands. Before we left the agency, Cut-Off Arm told us that any delay on our part might risk a dangerous confrontation with the soldiers already in the Wallowa."

And to further impress his audience of Non-Treaty leaders before they left Fort Lapwai to gather their peoples, the soldier chief had read aloud a petition he recently received from a large number of settlers along the Salmon River: Shadows who accused the Nez Perce of stealing horses, rustling cattle, and destroying the property of industrious white people. That petition, which demanded the immediate removal of the Indians from the river valley, had been signed by fifty-seven settlers who threatened to take matters into their own hands if the army didn't resolve the tensions.

"So it's dangerous for you to stay in the Wallowa any longer, Joseph," Cut-Off Arm had declared. "Surely you don't think you should stay where you're not wanted, do you?"

Even when the chiefs had gone with Cut-Off Arm to select the sites for their new homes, the soldier chief led Joseph and the others to some land that was already occupied by some Treaty Indians and a few white settlers.

Nonetheless, Cut-Off Arm pointed about him and announced, "If you will come on the reservation, I will give you these lands and move these people off."

Even though his own home was being taken from him, Joseph had shaken his head, explaining, "No, that is not right to do. It is wrong to disturb these people. I have no right to take their home. I have never taken what did not belong to me. And I will not start now."

Later that day, Looking Glass rode on one side of Cut-Off Arm and White Bird rode on the other as they traveled from site to site. Agency interpreter Joe Rabusco translated for them.

"Toohoolhoolzote meant no offense to you with his strong words," White Bird did his best to apologize. "We were told to come to Lapwai to speak our minds. That is what the old man was doing."

Looking Glass had nodded in agreement, saying to Cut-Off Arm, "If you free the old man, he will be fine in the days to come."

The soldier chief had meditated on it a few moments without speaking, then shook his head.

So White Bird pleaded more strongly, "He was only speaking his mind, as the men of my people have always done when in council. I know he will not do anything bad—but you can shoot me if he does."

"I agree," Looking Glass emphasized. "If the old man causes you trouble, you can bring me in and shoot me, too."

That's when Cut-Off Arm smiled and told the two chiefs, "I am glad to hear your support for the old man. But I am not going to shoot anyone. Toohoolhoolzote gave some bad advice to the council today. I want him to understand he must not give bad advice ever again. So Colonel Perry is going to keep the old man for a few days until you chiefs have selected your lands and started back to collect your people. Then I will release him, on your promise that I can punish you if he does not act right."

"This is a good thing to do!" Looking Glass cheered. "Now I feel like laughing again!"

But the soldier chief still appeared doubtful that all had been made right. "There are three kinds of laughter: one from fun, another from deceit, and the third from real joy."

"Mine comes from real joy!" Looking Glass exclaimed, laying a hand flat against his breast. "I shall never forget this ride we are taking together, Cut-Off Arm. I shall never forget these moments with you when we talked of our new homes."

Having gone out with the soldier chief to choose their new lands, the chiefs turned homeward for the last time, returning to their ancient haunts to bring in their bands. All told, these Non-Treaty peoples numbered no more than seven hundred.

Satisfied that he had struck a lasting peace, Looking Glass marched southeast for the Clearwater with his forty warriors to rejoin their *Alpowai* band.

Angrily licking his wounded pride, Toohoolhoolzote eventually reached his *Pikunan* band of thirty warriors in that wild country of the Grande Ronde and Asotin Creek, so rugged the Shadows never came to look for the precious yellow rocks or to farm.

Wounded in battle* many summers before by a cannonball that had grazed his head, leaving a large hairless patch, *Huishuish Kute,* the *tewat* called Bald, or Shorn, Head, returned home to that rocky country south of the mining town of Lewiston to bring in his small band of some sixteen Palouse warriors.

White Bird and his fifty sullen warriors made their way back to the country of their *Lamtama* band near the junction of White Bird Creek and the Salmon.

A saddened Joseph and a brooding Ollokot rode south by west, crossing the swollen Snake to the Grande Ronde, then over the next high ridge into the Imnaha. From there they climbed high into the land of the Winding Water, returning home for the final time. Before leaving the Wallowa behind forever, the brothers visited the resting place of Old Joseph. There they raised two freshly painted red-striped poles and laid a fresh horsehide over their father's grave.

Once he and Ollokot had argued down the shrill voices that shouted for war, once those sixty Wallowa warriors had reluctantly crisscrossed their homeland gathering up the last of their horses and cattle, Joseph's *In-an-toin-mu* people began their slow, dispirited march north with what animals they could find and bring in before their time ran short. Down the valley of the Imnaha they began their two-hundred-mile ordeal, pushing their herd of some six thousand ponies and

---

*Wright's Campaign of 1858

about two thousand horned cows toward the first dangerous crossing at a point called Dug Bar—where the mighty Snake plunged north through a narrow canyon. At this long-used ford the Joseph people stood on the west bank,* staring in dismay at the frothy river swollen with the snows melting in the faraway Yellowstone thermal region. The Idaho side of the Snake lay more than ten long arrow-flights away.†

After selecting a quartet of the strongest young men to ride four of their strongest ponies, Ollokot sent the group into the roaring current with a raft made of lodgepoles upon which sat buffalo-robe bundles of their belongings. All four were soon swept off the backs of their ponies as the river foamed about them, shoving each bobbing youth and animal downstream some distance as each struggled just to stay above the strong current. Eventually the young men managed to reach the other side, clambering out of the swirling waters more than three long arrow-flights downstream.

But they had done it! Now the rest could follow.

On more rafts and in bullboats, the men pulled their women and children into the current, one craft making that dangerous crossing at a time. When each boat or raft reached the far shore, those left behind raised a cheer for those who had survived the turbulent journey at the mercy of the furious water spirits.

By the end of that long, exhausting day, no more than half of Joseph's people had reached the far side. But by the time the sun began to set the following afternoon, all of the Wallowa band stood on the north bank, save for those young men who watched over the cattle and pony herds. All that remained was to take their prized horses into the boiling river.

At sunrise the next morning they discovered that during the night some white settlers had sneaked in among their herds sheltered there beside the mouth of the Imnaha and stolen what horses they could lead away. Angry at this treachery, but undeterred in his mission, Ollokot called out to his young pony herders. They formed the vanguard of this attack on the swollen waters, clinging atop their ponies as long as they could, until the strength of the current hurtled them off, when they had to grip a tail or mane, each warrior crying out

---

*May 31, 1877
†At least half a mile

his encouragement to those coming behind, yelping at the ponies battling those waves lapping around them. To hear those hundreds and hundreds of horses scream in terror, snorting with their exertion, eyes wide in fear and nostrils flaring as they struggled to keep their heads above the surface—the Wallowa people watched in horror and held their breath.

A young colt was the first to go down, swept away from its mare in the fury of the snowy runoff. Then a second: this time an old horse too weak to fight the mighty current. And still the warriors cajoled, whistled, and growled at the ponies. A third colt and a fourth were sucked under before the first of the herd reached the far bank. Now more of the younger animals, the weaker horses, were beginning to tire with their exertions, starting to struggle. Where they could, the warriors worked their stronger ponies in among the weaker animals— to encourage, perhaps to blunt some of the water's force as it tumbled against their upstream side, draining the horses of every last shred of endurance they might possess.

Those animals least able to make the hazardous crossing, the first to disappear beneath the turbulent waters, were the fresh cows and brood mares, along with their calves and foals. The little ones birthed just that spring, and their mothers too, were drowned by the hundreds or hurtled with the river's fury against the rocks. Joseph knew he would never forget the frightened screams of the children and the terrified cries of the women, the bawling of the cattle and the screeching horses.

By the time Ollokot's warriors had the last of the great Wallowa herd on the north side of the Snake, the most liberal accounting confirmed they had lost nearly a third of those ponies they had forced into the river earlier that morning. No more than half their cattle had survived the deadly crossing.

"But we have the rest." Joseph did his best to cheer the people. "And we have our families!"

"Joseph is right!" Ollokot had rejoiced as many grumbled sourly. "Look around you and see—not one of us is lost!"

Cold and soaked, their souls troubled by the terrible losses they had just suffered, dogged for years by the insatiable greed of the white man, and constantly reminded of the impatience of Cut-Off Arm's soldiers, the Wallowa people limped up the steep, ages-old trail that took them to the plateau. Despite how the Snake had swallowed up all those horses and cattle, the Wallowa band pushed on, descending to the rain-swollen Salmon, where they made a second, less-costly crossing near the mouth of Rock Creek. Not far beyond, just beyond the cleft of Rocky Canyon, lay the small lake at *Tepahlewam,* meaning "Deep Cuts" or "Split Rocks,"* a sacred, traditional gathering site where the chiefs had agreed to rendezvous for their last few days of freedom. White Bird was already there. *Huishuish Kute* and some other minor chiefs too. Toohoolhoolzote's people came in about the time Joseph's band arrived.†

Of these Non-Treaty peoples, only Looking Glass's band of forty warriors did not come to enjoy this last celebration of freedom, for they were already camped at *Kamiah,* well within the southern reservation boundary.

Here at *Tepahlewam,* Joseph's people and the rest would celebrate life as they had known it for generations beyond count, far back to that long-ago time before the first white faces came among them—a small band of Shadows on their way to the western ocean and back again. It was here near the lake** at the southern edge of those rich camas meadows where the women gathered the *kouse* and camas roots that—when steamed, mashed, and dried—would provide much of their food through the coming winter. As far as the eye could see, the meadows extended toward the far buttes and mountains in all directions, a veritable ocean of blue flowers waving beneath the warm summer breeze.

Even some members of the Treaty bands showed up to spend these last few days, too, eager to listen in on the Dreamers' creation tales, as well as some war stories from the buffalo country. Perhaps even to travel over the White Bird Divide to visit those traditional burial grounds near White Bird Hill where they could pay their respects. So beloved was this ancient gathering ground, that for generations the *Nee-Me-Poo* had reminisced during this time of melting snows:

"My son was born here."

"Our daughter was married beside these waters."

---

*An area about six miles west of Grangeville
†Around June 3, 1877
**Today's Tolo Lake

"My brother's son killed his first deer in that patch of timber over there."

Bone dice rattled in horn cups and wagers were placed on who might have the fastest horse. Yes, here at *Tepahlewam* the young people courted and coupled, old men recounted their war exploits against the Lakota and the Blackfoot, and women gave birth to children who would soon be living in a new world.

Women like his wife, Driven Before a Cold Storm—the one called *Ta-ma-al-we-non-my*—so heavy with child and ready to deliver any day now as their people rested here among the hills and meadows around the lake. As she grew more and more uncomfortable, exclaiming that her time was near, Joseph set up a small lodge for her far away from the circle, by tradition raising it in a secluded spot.

That night after they returned from their deer hunt, Joseph and Ollokot found the chiefs and headmen of the various bands embroiled in a fiery debate: the hotbloods who spoke in favor of taking vengeance against the whites for countless winters of abuses arguing against those who saw nothing short of suicide in making war.

One after another the young warriors stood and recounted for the council how they had a sister or mother shamed by the unspeakable attacks committed by the white men. Or told how an uncle or a father had been murdered in a dispute with a settler, only to have the white man's courts release the guilty Shadow. A growing number argued that now was the time to give blow for blow, shed blood for blood. Especially old Toohoolhoolzote, who stood and ranted that the Shadows must pay for how Cut-Off Arm and his soldiers had humiliated him.

Joseph looked at White Bird's wrinkled face, remembering the promise that older chief had given to Cut-Off Arm if Toohoolhoolzote made any more trouble.

"Why should we be driven like dogs from the land of our birth?" the angry *tewat* ranted.

The young men hooted and screamed for battle, even many among Joseph's band. They noisily shouted out a recitation of injustices at the hands of the Shadows: the unpunished murders and rapes, and those arrogant orders of the soldier chief who had shown them the rifle in a peace council!

With angry pride Toohoolhoolzote raged, "Only blood will

wash away the stain of disgrace Cut-Off Arm has put on us!"

"But if we fight and kill the soldiers who have come upon our land," Joseph stood all but alone against the swelling tide of war, "the Shadows will only send more."

Toohoolhoolzote whirled on the tall chief, his body tensing. "Instead, we will be forced to go out and kill the settlers who have stolen our land from us!"

"That would be wrong," Joseph declared. "The settlers did not steal anything that the government hadn't already taken from us first. Nothing that the reservation treaty signers hadn't already given away."

"You are wrong, Joseph!" Sun Necklace snarled. "It was a settler who killed Eagle Robe, the father of Shore Crossing!"

Joseph's eyes found that war chief standing in the crowd, the flames of the council fire licking shadows across the harsh lines of the man's face, his jaw set and lips a straight line of growing fury.

"One after another," Toohoolhoolzote argued, stepping right in front of Joseph to stab a finger in the air between them, "the settlers have defiled our women, killed our men, or stolen our horses and cattle—even as we crossed the Snake River, on our way to the reservation! They have cheated our people in their stores, and they have whipped us like disobedient dogs. Why do you continue to counsel peace with the Shadows?"

Shadows. Something dark, even evil. Something not altogether human at all. A mere wisp or shape of a human being, but without substance, without heart or soul. Maybe, Joseph thought, they truly were a race of shadows, these white men.

"The settlers . . . those Boston Men," Joseph began as the council hushed, "they are few, but they have many soldiers behind them."

"We will escape into the hills and kill all who come after us!" a shrill voice cried from the outer ring of warriors.

Joseph turned toward that call for war. "We cannot fight the whole government the white man will keep sending against us. Look around you. There are not many of us. We are not that strong. We must make the best peace we can, then live by the peace we have made as men of honor."

"If you wish to be a coward, Joseph," Toohoolhoolzote

hissed, "so be it. But as for me, I will wash away the stain to my honor with the blood of as many soldiers as I can kill before I watch Cut-Off Arm die beneath my knife."

"What you and your people would do, let them do it," Joseph said, wagging his head dolefully. "But do not give your bad advice to my people. I do not want to see any of my band killed because you still lick your wounds from the house with the iron bars. It is better for my women and children to live at peace than to have the magpies and jays pick at their flesh, tear at their lifeless eyes, because they were killed in your fruitless war."

"You surely are a coward—"

"My people!" Joseph interrupted Toohoolhoolzote's slur as he turned away from the shorter man, flinging his stentorian voice over the crowd. "Do not follow those who counsel war with the white man or his soldiers! My people . . . know that I love you far too much that I cannot stand to lose you!"

Old man White Bird stood slowly and walked up to Joseph, laying his hand on Joseph's forearm, then said, "I am for war. Because of all the wrongs done my people, we must fight."

Ollokot stood there between them, gazing into his older brother's eyes. "Joseph, we should fight."

"No, Brother," he answered, not comfortable with that sudden betrayal by his own blood. "Peace is all that will keep our people alive. We are few, and the white men are too many. We have our troubles with them, but fighting is not the answer. War will only bring more trouble, bigger trouble. Toohoolhoolzote and White Bird, all the rest of you chiefs and warriors—you have had your say and spoken in favor of fighting. But what of the women and children? A war will kill those who never had a voice at our council this night."

"I speak for them," White Bird claimed. "It is at times such as these that the strong must speak for the weak."

But Joseph shook his head. "Don't you remember what the Shadow squaw man named Chapman told us when we were at Lapwai to choose our land with Cut-Off Arm? He described what he had seen in a war between Indians and the white men: some of us would be killed; many more would be badly wounded and maimed for the rest of their lives; we would have all our horses and cattle taken from us; and then, the Shadows will force us to go far away to *Eeikish Pah*, the hot country of Indian Territory, where they will make us live apart from one another."

Joseph could see how most of them, old and young, were deep in thought—weighing the consequences of fighting the inevitable. But he knew he had lost their hearts.

With a sigh, he eventually confessed, "We are the few, against the many and the strong. Let us make the best peace we can with the white man."

All those gathered around him had grown so silent that he could hear the crackle of the fire.

"Is there any more talk?" Joseph asked. He slowly looked from one to another.

The war supporters averted their eyes, staring into the flames, a barely suppressed anger darkening their stony faces. So, perhaps he had silenced them—for now.

"Very well then," Joseph finally admitted in little more than a whisper. "We must spend our last few days here among these old places where our people have come for many, many generations. . . . Then we will go onto the reservation to begin a new life meant to save those generations of us yet to come."

Chapter 6

Season of *Hillal*
1877

BY TELEGRAPH

THE INDIANS.

**A Fight That Was Not Reported
in This Direction.**
CHICAGO, May 29.—Lieutenant General
Sheridan has a dispatch from Red Cloud agency
confirming the news of the Indian engagement
reported last night. Two runners have come into
that agency giving the particulars of the location
and the killed and wounded, the same as the
Bismarck dispatch, and saying that Sitting Bull led
the band which was attacked.

Oh, how he wanted the young woman to look his way, to
acknowledge him, to smile as she slowly lowered her
eyes in that woman way.

He was no longer a boy. No longer merely a young man.
In the last three winters, this warrior known as Shore
Crossing had become a man of the *Nee-Me-Poo*, like his fa-

ther, Eagle Robe, had been. Even though this handsome warrior was already married, he found himself eager to seduce a beautiful young woman from Joseph's Wallowa band, to make her his wife, too.

He hoped she would see him riding in today's war parade, the *tel-lik-leen,* a traditional practice of their people when the bands gathered here every summer on these ancient camping grounds in the meadows at *Tepahlewam.* This summer, a new, martial edge had been added to the ancient procession. This year, the young warriors didn't merely sing their songs and strut in their finest before the eligible women. Instead, for the past ten days the young men had been parading through camp shouting curses upon the Shadows, vowing vengeance upon the settlers for taking their lands, death to the army for protecting those white thieves. With each new day the war fervor tension grew around this grand procession, each afternoon's parade more like a declaration of hostilities than the last.

"Do you see her yet?" *Sarpsis Ilppilp,* called Red Moccasin Tops, asked in a whisper, leaning close at Shore Crossing's ear.

Red Moccasin Tops was seated right behind his older cousin. The two of them had grown up together, more like brothers than cousins. Sun Necklace, Red Moccasin Tops's father, had not given his son a pony to ride for this day's parade, so Shore Crossing offered his cousin a place on his old pony. Why not ride two on a horse? After all, this pair of swaggering youngsters had been worked into some cocky strutting with the rest of those older, veteran warriors of many fights against the Lakota and Blackfoot. Yes, why not ride together on a horse? These two were more than cousins; they were best friends in everything.

Shore Crossing shook his head, fearful she would not show up. "No, I can't see her yet."

"Tell me when you do," Red Moccasin Tops suggested. "Then I will keep my eye on her to learn when she looks at you."

His cousin was a good young man, part Cayuse in blood, grandson of Tomahas, one of the murderers of missionary Marcus and Narcissa Whitman many years before. What a terrible, troubled legacy that tragedy was to those Upper bands, those who had signed the treaty with the white man and stayed put on the reservation.

Despite the growing strain between those who advocated going to war and those who counseled peace, Shore Crossing remained hopeful the beautiful one would look up at him and smile beneath those long, black lashes, telling him he should come courting her that night when the sun sank and the fires glowed. None of them had much longer before they would have to go onto the reservation. If he was going to grab another wife by strutting, preening, and crowing in the old way . . . this was the time to do it. The last any of his people would ever know of freedom.

For ten days already the Non-Treaty bands had been celebrating here by the Camas Prairie lake. As it had always been, this time of the earth's warming was a season for the young of their people. Far, far back into any man's memory, this had always been a time for courting and coupling.

Hillal, this "season of melting mountain snow and rising rivers," was more like a time of melting his heart and the rising of his fevered manhood for Shore Crossing. If he could no longer be a fighting warrior for the *Nee-Me-Poo* in the old way, then he was at least eager to take another wife.

Riding here at the tail end of this daily *tel-lik-leen* winding its way through the encampment—here in the traditional position of greatest danger, where those warriors at the rear of the march protected the village from their pursuers—Shore Crossing kept his old horse behind all the rest so that he and his cousin secured this position of honor.

Glancing over the shoulders of those just ahead of them in the parade, Shore Crossing could see that it would be only moments before he himself entered the village where the old men and the women were setting aside their labors of drying meat and the *kouse* roots in the sun to sing and keen as the procession threaded its way among the lodges. Up and down the gauntlet, white men beat on hand-held drums, singing their songs of celebration, while dogs barked, and children ran alongside the horses' legs, everyone laughing. Despite where the bands had been ordered to go, despite what they had been forced to leave behind, despite all the rest . . . this was still a good time in Shore Crossing's life.

Between the lodges, the old ones were rising from pieces of canvas they had spread upon the ground. There they split open the camas roots and lay them to dry in the sun. Those old men and women were waving their arms in joy, laughing and singing as Shore Crossing drew closer to the outlying lodges. He thought he caught a glimpse of her—just enough of her face as she glanced his way, then quickly turned to watch something else. Of course, he told himself, she did not want to seem too eager to be his.

Oh, it was her! He kept staring as he rode closer and closer to the lodges, not daring to take his eyes off her lest she flick those dark, black-cherry eyes at him for but an instant. He must keep watching so he could catch her glancing at him, to let her realize that he knew she wanted him, too.

A sudden shrill screech penetrated his reverie.

Shore Crossing looked down in surprise, finding the old man at his knee, waving his arms wildly and shouting.

"See what you do? See what you do?" shrieked *Heyoom Moxmox,* the one known as Yellow Grizzly Bear.

Jerking back on the reins, Shore Crossing discovered his old pony was trampling on a piece of canvas, its hooves crushing and scattering some camas from the cedar-bark baskets.

Nearly under the pony itself an old woman crouched, Yellow Grizzly Bear's wife. She was frantically scooping up the roots as the frightened horse pranced back and forth. The old man swung his fists at the animal, pounding it on the ribs, yelling at the young rider.

"You fool!" the old man screamed in a reedy voice as he lunged to seize the reins.

Below them, the old woman was sobbing loudly as she flung aside her two-foot-long digging stick and swept up the crushed roots with the side of her hand, gathering them into a fold of her dirty dress.

Shore Crossing pleaded, "I am sorry!"

"You play so brave, don't you, young man?" Yellow Grizzly Bear shouted, trembling with fury. "Like a warrior, you ride right over my woman's hard-worked food!"

Struggling to yank his pony away from the old man, from the sobbing woman, off that torn canvas on the ground where he had made a mess of the roots, Shore Crossing promised, "I will try to make it up to you—"

"If you are so brave," Yellow Grizzly Bear growled, seizing hold of the fringe on the young warrior's legging, "why don't you go kill the Shadow who killed your father?"

Until that moment he had been sorry, truly sorry for the mess he had caused these old people ... but in an instant Shore Crossing was of a different heart. Like a sharpened needle, the man's harsh words had suddenly lanced a festering wound where an evil corruption still poisoned Shore Crossing's heart.

He leaned forward and reached down to grab the old man's wrist, wrenching it from the pony's reins. Glaring with steady eyes into the wrinkled face of Yellow Grizzly Bear, Shore Crossing spoke with a voice tight as a drumhead: "You will be sorry for your words."

By the time he looked up, the rest of the procession was far ahead of him, and the beautiful woman was nowhere to be found among the crowd scattering through the lodges.

The young man wheeled his pony about and crossed the side of the hill to his lodge where he leaped to the ground alone and ducked inside. Shore Crossing snapped at his wife the moment she questioned his sullen face.

After tying off the pony to a tent peg, Red Moccasin Tops drew back the lodge door and entered. He settled near his cousin, but far enough away so that it did not make Shore Crossing angry. When her husband would not explain himself, his wife threw up her hands in exasperation and left, shaking her head in disgust.

It did not matter to Shore Crossing, for here he could sit out the rest of the afternoon away from the accusing glares of those who had been standing near the old man and woman, all of those who had mocked him again because he had not taken his vengeance on the white man who had killed his father.

Didn't they remember that Eagle Robe made his son promise not to harm the white man?

A promise made to his father. A promise given a dying man was a sacred thing! If Shore Crossing had any facet of character, then it was honor, enough honor that he would not break his promise to his dying father.

For three winters he had carried the onus of this failure upon his head. Even though everyone knew of the promise he was forced to make to his father, nonetheless there had been three winters of the cold and unfriendly stares, three winters of the whispered murmurings at his back.

By the time his wife returned to the lodge long after the

finish of the grand war parade this day, Shore Crossing and his cousin had already nursed at the canteen filled with the white man's whiskey acquired from one of the Grangeville and Mount Idaho traders who had come among the *Nee-Me-Poo* while the bands were united there at *Tepahlewam*. He knew that this stinging water sometimes made a man a fool. But he was also certain that at other times the whiskey could give a man the courage to do what he would otherwise not.

So that day had grown old by the time his wife discovered Shore Crossing and Red Moccasin Tops in the lodge beside the dying fire, both of them red-eyed and mumbling thick-tongued to themselves as her husband sharpened his knife on an old whetstone.

"Aren't you going to take me to the Kissing Dance?" she asked.

His knife stopped in his hands. He suddenly thought of the beautiful one he wanted so badly. "Tonight?"

"Yes," his wife answered him. "It begins soon."

Glancing at his cousin, he grumbled, "Do you think—"

"You should be there," Red Moccasin Tops interrupted with a wicked grin. Then he leaned close to Shore Crossing so the wife would not hear of the young woman as he whispered, "If the girl does not kiss you as her husband-to-be tonight, I am sure she will kiss some other young man before the dancing is done!"

After quickly re-braiding his hair, Shore Crossing left the lodge, ordering his wife to stay behind, that he did not want her to attend the grand dance. He promised that he would return and that they would couple—which seemed to satisfy her.

He and Red Moccasin Tops started toward the singing that reached their ears in the darkness. Shore Crossing's head was numb, but his heart was singing. This would be the night he could make his intentions known to all.

Already the drums were throbbing fervently as he neared the grand circle, shouldered his way through the crowd, casting his eyes over every young woman, searching for the one. After he had stumble-footed it halfway around the crescent, someone suddenly grabbed his arm, stopped him—pulling him around. It was the young woman's older brother. *Hahkauts Ilppilp.*

With a sneer, this warrior called Red Grizzly Bear asked, "Who are you looking for, Shore Crossing?"

"Why do you care?" he demanded of the brother.

On either side of Red Grizzly Bear gathered a few of White Bird's young warriors, mockery in their eyes. Red Moccasin Tops stepped up beside Shore Crossing. Together, their breath made a cloud strong with the stench of stale whiskey.

The brother sniffed at their faces, then chortled, "Ho, look at you! A married man, but you come anyway: ready for a dance with my sister, are you? All of you, look at Shore Crossing!" he roared at his companions. "So pretty and handsome in public, isn't he? But everyone knows he is nothing more than a coward."

Shore Crossing crumpled Red Grizzly Bear's hide vest in both hands, spewing his anger: "Do you really mean to call me a coward?"

Seizing Shore Crossing's wrists, the brother flung the hands away from his vest. "I call you that, yes! You are nothing less than a coward. Look—back there on the Salmon—don't you see your father's grave in the country we are being forced to leave behind? He was murdered by a Shadow, but you don't have the manhood to kill the one who took your father's life!"

All around him even more of the young men and women were squeezing closer, drawn to the noisy confrontation, many of them already sniggering behind their hands. Shore Crossing prayed the pretty one was nowhere near to see his shame, but he realized she would hear of it all too soon. The dance drums pounded in his aching head even louder, the shrill keening of the women caused such pain in his ears, and now the brother's burning rebuke coursed a tongue of cold fire to his marrow with a terrible, unquenchable pain.

Then he remembered what he had told the old man who had mocked him in just this way.

"Today I told Yellow Grizzly Bear what I now declare to all of you: you will be sorry for what you have said to me!"

Shore Crossing turned on his heel, pushing his way through the sniggering crowd, hurrying as far away from that shame as he could take himself, realizing that he had just breathed life anew into a fire long smoldering.

Later that night while he sat in his lodge with Red Moccasin Tops, Shore Crossing wept angry, bitter tears as he swilled down more of the whiskey from those two canteens traded from a Boston Man.

"Don't they realize that I never returned to kill the Shadow who murdered my father because I had given him my word?"

"They are silly fools," his wife consoled as she came up to settle next to him.

But Shore Crossing pushed her aside angrily and swilled more of the whiskey before he continued, "Don't these growlers realize that if I had killed the Shadow who murdered my father, it would only have given the white men and their soldiers just the excuse they needed to kill more of our people?"

"Your wife is right," Red Moccasin Tops slurred, thick-tongued himself. "The others are blind fools who cannot see that you have much courage to keep your vow."

"No more!" Shore Crossing snapped, the fiery burn of the whiskey raw at the back of his throat. "I have been a slave to that stupid vow long enough. Don't you see I have been a prisoner of the mistake I made for too many seasons already!"

Fort Lapwai
June 13, 1877

Mamma Dear,

It seems a long time since I wrote to you, as I did not write all last week, but I suppose you will find so many of my letters waiting for you when you get home, you will think I spent all my time writing.

John is in Portland and I am awfully lonely without him. I do hope he won't make many trips of this sort away from us. I know, too, he wants to be back as much as we want him here. He left a week ago today, and I hope he will be home a week from tomorrow, but Major Boyle and Mr. Monteith told me they don't think it possible for him to come so soon. I will be dolefully disappointed if he doesn't.

I hope someplace in your travels you will find some sacks for the children. The evenings and mornings are all too cool for them to play without something, and their present wraps are positively shameful. I wish I had some-

thing real common for their play and then something a little better for Sunday School, but we are feeling awfully poor. I have such a time getting them hats. I got Bess a little brown sundown and trimmed it with my pet necktie (a brown one) as I could not get any brown ribbon. John will bring me a couple of sailor hats for Bert from Portland. The hats they bring to this town, 12 miles from us, are perfectly awful.

Do you know the army will have no pay for practically six months? We heard from some army friends in Portland and they say army people are very blue there.

Major Boyle's family arrived last week and they are nearly fixed. Mrs. Boyle is a very pretty woman and pleasant. They have children, for which I am very glad. They are much older than mine, but it is pleasant to see the young people about this quiet post. They have a pretty girl about twelve, a boy about ten, and a grown-up son.

Our Indian troubles ended in a sort of compromise with the dissatisfied Nez Perce understanding they must come in and be good. They are the ones who always make for the trouble. I wish they would kill them all.

Doctor and I went to some of the councils, but did not stay more than an hour. The Indian smell was awful. This chief of theirs, Joseph, will admit no boundary to his lands but those he chooses to make himself. I wish somebody would kill him before he kills any of us. The last day of the council Agent Monteith leaned over and asked me if my hair felt on tight. It doesn't feel very tightly on when I think of these horrible devils around us.

Mrs. Perry was confident the Indians wouldn't come to terms and that we would have a war this spring but it appears General Howard has been able to settle matters so we will have no more Indian scares.

There was an Indian funeral in sight the other day, and the brave was tied onto his horse and taken that way to the burying ground, his arms, head, and legs hanging over the sides of his horse.

On Sunday mornings we see dozens and dozens of the Treaty Indians, dressed in the brightest combinations of colors, going down to church. The women nearly all *have babies strapped to their backs in those funny things, one of which I sent you.*

During church a few Sundays ago, an Indian came in, and as he came up to his seat, he stood something tied in a pillow case, up in a corner. Mrs. McF. says she thought he had brought a present of a ham to the Agent, but after church he produced a little dead baby out of the pillow case and wanted it buried.

Enough about the Indians at last. I must finish our letter as our first mail for this week is being gathered up. With much love,

Your affectionate daughter,
Emily F.

Chapter 7

Season of *Hillal*
1877

BY TELEGRAPH

All England Waiting to

Welcome General Grant.

Account of the Late Indian

Fight Up North.

DAKOTA.

Lame Deer's Dear Defeat.
CHICAGO, May 30.—General Sheridan has
dispatches confirming the following account of a
battle with the Indians on the 7th: General Miles,
with companies F, H, I and G, of the 2d cavalry,
and twenty-five mounted men of the 5th infantry,
attacked an Indian village on little Muddy creek,

ninety miles from the mouth of the Tongue river, surprising and routing them. They pursued the redskins five miles over a rough country on foot. Fourteen dead Indians were counted upon the field, and many others are known to have been killed and wounded. Some 450 ponies and horses and fifty-four lodges, with their entire contents were taken. The cavalry found many new agency goods, together with the saddles, guns, officers' clothing, etc., taken from the cavalry in the Custer fight. The band were Minnecongous, led by Lame Deer. . . . General Miles had a narrow escape from being shot by two Indians, who, under cover of friendly greeting, came near shooting him just before the engagement.

"Where are you going so late in the morning?" his wife asked Shore Crossing as he flung aside the lodge door and stood in the muted light of that overcast sky.

He turned to look at her with disdain, finding the woman on her knees, bent over the roots she had scattered across a piece of canvas spread upon the ground still damp from last night's rain. The leaden drops had hammered against the lodge skins as he quickly fell asleep near the snoring Red Moccasin Tops.

Shore Crossing squinted at her, his head throbbing with a sharp pain as he heard his cousin follow him from the lodge. Struggling with what to say to her because the *Nee-Me-Poo* language had no profanity, he eventually explained, "We are going off to make these many fools sorry for their sharp words to me."

She stood, her hands balled on her hips accusingly. "I am afraid you will be the fool if you go."

"Leave me be of your words, woman." Shore Crossing turned away from his wife, releasing the knot in the long lead rope that tied his old pony to a lodge peg. "Perhaps you will be singing a different song when I return."

At the lodge of Red Moccasin Tops they stopped to collect a blanket they threw over the sodden back of the pony; then Shore Crossing's cousin collected one of his family's poor travois horses to ride.

Instead of immediately leaping onto the back of his pony, Shore Crossing stood a moment, thoughtfully gazing up at

Red Moccasin Tops. "We need a horse holder."

"Who should we bring?" Red Moccasin Tops asked.

"We'll go get my nephew."

Wetyetmas Wahyakt, Swan Necklace, was sitting alone beneath a tree, watching some young girls assist their mothers and grandmothers drying out rain-soaked bedding, when Shore Crossing and Red Moccasin Tops rode up. He was a little younger than them both, no more than twenty summers.

"Come with us, Nephew."

Swan Necklace stood, dusting his hands off on the front of his leggings, looking one last time at the nearby girls who giggled behind their hands, playing coy with him. "Where are we going?"

"To kill a white man." Shore Crossing held down his hand.

Swan Necklace gazed longingly at the girls, then looked up at his uncle again and shrugged. "All right," he answered. "I will go." He reached out and grabbed his uncle's wrist, swinging himself up behind the warrior.

They turned their ponies away from that camp at *Tepahlewam* and started down the breaks on the north side of White Bird Hill, following the creek of that name west as it descended the slopes for its rendezvous with the Salmon.*

As the trio turned upriver that afternoon, Shore Crossing realized his head no longer hurt as much as it had, the hangover having put him in such a foul humor. Nonetheless, he remained steadfast that those who had ridiculed him would be made the fools by the time he returned to camp bearing the Shadow's scalp. He would find that settler named Larry Ott and, in those moments before he killed the Shadow, remind the white man of what he had done to his father—then take the hair, some horses, and any firearms they could find at the place.

The scalp and all of that plunder would make for a grand entrance into the camp upon their return. No one would laugh behind their hands at Shore Crossing ever again!

He was as handsome as any man, trim and athletic, with a reputation as the unsurpassed long-distance runner and wrestler among the Non-Treaty bands. Shore Crossing had honed his strength by clambering up the Wallowa country's sheer mountain escarpments and swimming the fierce currents of the Snake, the Salmon, and the Imnaha. It was reported his

---

*Sometime around midday Wednesday—June 13, 1877

strength could well be that of two men, because he roped and broke young, fiery colts. Some claimed Shore Crossing's chief amusement was to disrobe and sprint after a band of green, half-wild horses, driving them right into the river, where he would plunge after them—mounting the most spirited of the herd—and swim the pony to the far shore despite its frenzied attempts to throw him off.

It was Shore Crossing who would be the fuse that ignited the powder keg Cut-Off Arm had shoved under Toohoolhoolzote and all those young warriors who had been clamoring for war.

Not all that far down White Bird Creek the trio came upon the homestead of John J. Manuel, who served as postmaster at the tiny settlement of White Bird. The Shadow stood back in the doorway of his store there at the mouth of Chapman Creek as the three reined up in the yard and made signs that they wanted to use the white man's grinding stone for their knives.

Manuel looked them over. Finding they carried no firearms, he pointed them in the direction of the foot-treadle grindstone he had sitting beneath a shady tree where he sharpened plow and hoe blades for nearby settlers. Smiling in a most friendly manner, the three young men nodded and turned away to begin work on their knives.

When they were finished, the trio remounted, waved to Manuel, and left, continuing on down White Bird Creek. After a short distance they came to a store owned by Harry Mason, which stood less than two miles from the Salmon.

"Before the weather grew warm this spring," Shore Crossing explained to the other two as he brought his horse to a halt outside the log building, "this Shadow whipped two of Toohoolhoolzote's men because he thought they were cheating him in a trade."

"Are you wanting to kill him too?" asked Red Moccasin Tops from the other horse.

"No," and Shore Crossing shook his head. "But maybe we can trade him for a weapon."

Inside, the trio offered the store man one of their ponies for a rifle and some bullets. None of the three could speak any of the white man's tongue, so they had to make do with pantomime, struggling to make the stern-eyed Shadow understand.

Throughout the short-lived dickering, Mason remained planted in one spot behind his counter, his suspicious eyes flicking back and forth over his three visitors. Time and again he refused their trade, ordering them to leave. On their way out the door, Shore Crossing asked about the price of a few other items and signed to explain that they might be back later with some money.

Harry Mason did not take his sweaty, trembling hand off the revolver he clutched under the counter until the trio had remounted and were on their way down the creekside trail.

At the mouth of the White Bird the three warriors crossed to the west bank of the Salmon, where they stopped again and dismounted long enough to smear on a little grease and paint Shore Crossing had brought along in a pouch he wore over his shoulder. It wasn't until they stopped at this place that Swan Necklace truly believed that the other two fully intended to kill the man who had murdered Shore Crossing's father.

Wide-eyed and subdued, the youngest quickly painted himself, squatting on the damp ground with the older men. That finished, they turned upriver. The Ott homestead was no more than three of the white man's winding miles away now.

Halting on the hillside overlooking the settler's place, the three gazed down upon the buildings the murdering Shadow had raised on this stolen ground, looking with contempt upon the fences that thieving Shadow had erected across Eagle Robe's garden. For a long moment Shore Crossing stared at that unmarked spot near the smaller of the log houses where he had found his father propped against the fence post, breathing his last.

"Come," he finally said to Red Moccasin Tops as he started his own pony down the hill. "Let's go get this killing started."

Larry Ott was not in the smaller building. Nor did they find him working in the larger. After returning to the smaller log house and pilfering through the Shadow's belongings for firearms or anything of value, Shore Crossing stomped outside.

The other two followed him into the yard, where they stood for a moment until Shore Crossing finally admitted, "He isn't here."

"S-so we go back to camp now?" Swan Necklace asked, his voice quaking a bit in relief.

Shore Crossing shook his head. "There is another."

"Who?" asked Red Moccasin Tops, a grin appearing.

"The one called Devine."

"I know of him. He murdered a crippled Palouse woman last autumn."

"Yes, Devine murdered old *Dakoopin*," Shore Crossing said, turning to Swan Necklace.

"What did the old woman do that he would kill her?" the youngest asked.

With a shrug, Shore Crossing said, "*Dakoopin* chased the man's horse out of her garden—and for that she lost her life."

"Devine has bad dogs, dogs he sets on Indians," Red Moccasin Tops explained. Grinning wickedly, he headed for his pony and said, "Let's go find him instead."

After re-crossing the Salmon they struck the main north–south trail that ran along the river's east bank and continued up the valley. Covering another four of the white man's miles, the trio reached the mouth of Slate Creek, a tributary of the Salmon. By this time the three young men were growing hungry, so they stopped to buy some food from Charles P. Cone, a settler who had always been on good terms with the *Nee-Me-Poo* because he had actually purchased his land from Chief Whistle Knocker back in 1863.

After trading off Swan Necklace's knife for a bit of food, Shore Crossing next offered to trade something else for a handful of bullets. Cone looked the three over suspiciously. When he saw they had no weapon, he refused to trade.*

Another four miles up the Salmon brought them to the ranch of Jurden Henry Elfers on the north bank of John Day Creek. Elfers and his two hired hands were in the barn milking cows when the trio appeared out of the growing gloom of twilight. From where she sat on the front porch, Catherine Elfers thought the horsemen were travelers in need of a bed in their wayside inn, so she disappeared into the house as her

---

*This Shadow was well aware of the large encampment at Split Rock, so he would later remark that he thought it strange that the three young men were traveling upriver away from Rocky Canyon so late in the day. Even more memorable were the three because they were riding two poor horses, when the Nez Perce always rode their finest and strongest animals if they had a long journey to make. And now the sun was rapidly falling.

husband came out to talk to the three young men in their Nez Perce tongue.

"We are looking for some horses that strayed from our camp on Camas Prairie," Shore Crossing explained, his eyes glancing at the fine horses this Shadow kept in the corral against the barn.

Elfers eyed the poor condition of the two animals the trio were riding. "How many?"

Holding up his hands, Red Moccasin Tops showed all fingers.

With a wary shake of his head, Elfers said, "No loose horses around here. Sorry."

Shore Crossing shrugged and turned his horse away, followed by Red Moccasin Tops on the second pony. Elfers watched them move slowly away into the nearly consuming darkness of that summer night.

The stars were out and the moon had nearly risen to midsky by the time the trio worked their way on up the east bank of the Salmon. Near the mouth of Carver Creek, they halted the two horses back in the trees and the shadows looming at the edge of the clearing where a small cabin stood, its black windows like the eye sockets of a grinning buffalo skull.

"Get down," Shore Crossing ordered.

Swan Necklace gulped apprehensively and obediently slipped off the back of the pony. Shore Crossing hit the ground at the same time Red Moccasin Tops dismounted.

"Here," and Shore Crossing dropped the weary pony's reins into his nephew's hand.

Swan Necklace took the rope to the second pony, too.

The leader instructed, "You stay here until we return."

"Y-you going in there?" the youth asked, his eyes flicking back to the log house.

Shore Crossing turned to stare at the cabin, too. He nodded, then turned to Red Moccasin Tops. "Elfers had some good horses, didn't he, brother?"

"Fine horses, yes."

"Are y-you thinking of going back to steal some horses f-from Elfers?" Swan Necklace stammered.

"When we finish here," Shore Crossing declared in a raspy whisper, "in that cabin is a man who needs killing. And I want his gun."

Red Moccasin Tops turned to Swan Necklace, using that

expression harkening back to those early days of first contact between the tribe and white traders: "This Boston Man, he came here from far away across the big ocean. Ever since he arrived, he has been very cruel to our people. I am going to help Shore Crossing kill this Shadow tonight."

After creeping stealthily to the door, Shore Crossing had no trouble finding the latchstring. He pulled it slowly. When Red Moccasin Tops nodded that he was ready, they threw their weight against the planks, bursting into the moonlit interior. Across that darkened room Richard Devine kicked savagely at his blankets, half-rising from his bed as he lunged for a rifle standing against a wall. The three of them reached the carbine at the same time, but the old sailor was no match for the two youngsters.

Wrestling the repeater from the Shadow's hands, Shore Crossing leaped back, worked the lever, and growled a warning to his cousin.

In that breathless heartbeat as Red Moccasin Tops released the white man, Devine spun around in the dark to stare boldly into Shore Crossing's eyes. Cursing his attackers, the Shadow was leaping for the rifle holder when the bullet from his own weapon caught him squarely in the face.

Standing there in those moments that followed, Shore Crossing waited while the echo of the gun's blast faded from his ears, until he felt his eyes grow accustomed to the darkness after the blinding muzzle-flash. Listening, watching for some movement from the white man sprawled on the floor, he finally spoke to his cousin.

"Look for a belt gun. And bullets, too. Anything good we can trade."

They ransacked the tiny cabin, stuffing a few poor items into a carpet satchel; then Shore Crossing knelt over the dead man.

"I like his shirt," he said, rolling the red felt between a thumb and forefinger.

But he did not steal it to wear. Instead, they cut long strips from the shirt and used the red flannel to wrap up their braids.

"It is the color of the blood," Shore Crossing exulted, holding one of his braids out before his eyes to admire what he had done. "The first blood we've taken from the Shadows!"

They crossed the starlit yard to reach the frightened Swan Necklace.

"Is . . . is he . . ."

"Dead?" Shore Crossing finished the question. "Yes. I killed him. With his own gun." And he held it up for the youth's inspection.

Red Moccasin Tops clambered atop his pony, clutching the carpet satchel. "That Boston Man Elfers talks very funny, doesn't he?"

"Yes, he does," Shore Crossing replied. "And he has those fine horses I would like to take back to camp with me."

The younger cousin smiled as Shore Crossing climbed atop his pony and pulled Swan Necklace up behind him. Then Red Moccasin Tops said, "We are going past his place on our way back to *Tepahlewam,* you know."

"Our two old horses are very tired," Shore Crossing observed as he nudged his heels into the weary pony and patted the carbine's gleaming barrel in the moonlight. "I think we should get us some new horses now."

Chapter 8

June 14, 1877

BY TELEGRAPH

WYOMING.

An Indian Canard Contradicted.
CHICAGO, May 31.—A dispatch received this morning at General Sheridan's headquarters from Lieutenant Clark, dated Red Cloud agency, May 29, states that after a careful investigation he considers the part of the Cheyennes' story, relating to Sitting Bull, absolutely false, this chief being north of the Yellowstone and probably north of the Missouri. The rest of the Cheyennes' report appears to be founded on fact, though there is no certainty about it. Probably Lame Deer's village was captured and the version of the affair given correct.

After failing at two careers already, he had come to the new world from Hanover, Germany, eighteen years ago. From the moment Jurden Henry Elfers reached Idaho in 1861, life had begun to turn around for him.

At first Elfers had worked hard for others, trying his hand at the sluice boxes up near the mining town of Lewiston, then grunting and sweating as he plowed fields owned by others. But by the latter part of 1862 he had joined in partnership with Harry Mason and John Wessell, staking out his own claim on John Day Creek.

He paused a moment this cool morning to gaze back at the buildings he had raised with his own hands. Sighing with contentment, Elfers continued toward the high pasture he intended to have mowed before noon. Henry believed his good fortune had really begun the day he met Catherine back in the spring of '71. She was German too, come to America with her parents. Catherine and Henry were married by October that year. And by the next summer Elfers felt confident enough to buy out his two partners.

Henry and Catherine owned the whole place, a good thing when they started having children. In addition to the horses they bred, the Elfers raised milk cows for their dairy business, as well as renting out some tiny rooms nailed against the side of their house to travelers along the Salmon River Road. That, along with the general store Catherine ran and Henry's part-time prospecting, the two of them counted up a handful of blessings here in this young country barely a hundred years old.

It appeared as if their life was destined to get better and better, especially now that the army was herding the Non-Treaty bands onto the reservation and quieting things down. It wasn't as if Henry had ever done a thing to harm any of the Nez Perce. Although he could be a hard-headed businessman, Elfers had never hurt a soul. Only that time last year when he came back to the house to find the dogs barking and Catherine confronted with at least a half-dozen warriors who had come boldly into the yard. Holding no weapon in his hands, Elfers had yelled at the Nez Perce to leave—wishing the hired men weren't so far away in the hay field.

But when those young warriors got haughty and two of them started toward Catherine and the house, Henry got angry enough to step over to the gate and fling it open, freeing his hounds. Out raced the four dogs, snarling and yapping, compelling the two warriors to remount and gallop from the yard. For the rest of that day he and Catherine kept a careful eye trained for any strangers, fearing that the warriors would return—if for nothing else than to kill the dogs.

Weeks and months passed, until Elfers figured all the hard feelings had healed. He eventually felt at ease when this past spring the Non-Treaty Nez Perce permitted Henry to sit on the council of arbitration convened to look into the matter of that whipping Harry Mason gave a couple of warriors at his store. The Indians certainly knew that he and Harry had been partners years ago, so Elfers figured it spoke well of his relations with the tribe that they allowed him to sit in judgment of Mason despite their past business dealings.

Especially since there had never been a peep out of any of the Nez Perce after that council decided Harry Mason was justified in using martial force to drive the unruly warriors from his store. If the tribe was sore about Henry's role in that judgment, then the wounds must surely have healed. Besides, each day could only find things getting better and better now that the Non-Treaty bands were within a few days and miles of settling upon the reservation.

Here at forty-two, Jurden Henry Elfers had fathered three offspring over the last five years, and Catherine was heavy with child again. He stopped on the hillside trail and breathed deep of the cool air pregnant with the damp, heady aromas of fertile earth and those piles of cow dung dotting this narrow path leading to the far pasture that lay on an elevated plateau behind the ranch.

His twenty-one-year-old nephew, "Harry" Burn Beckrodge, had gone ahead with more than a half-dozen cows and their young calves from that spring's drop, driving them up the brushy hillside to spend the day in the high pasture. Hired man Robert Bland was the next to leave the barn, following a half-mile or more behind Beckrodge with the rest of the barren milkers.

Elfers was at least a half-hour behind the two of them, most of that time consumed with pulling his new mowing machine from the barn, laying out the newly oiled harness, and backing the two draft horses into their traces. Now the mower clattered beneath him as the big, powerful haunches of those Belgians dragged the mower up the last steep part of the climb and topped out on the plateau just east of the homestead.

Something caught his attention less than a hundred yards ahead. Something out of place among the trees fully leafed with the green of early summer. Then the Belgians caught wind of the two horses. A pair of them, poor and ill-kept: an easy thing for a sharp-eyed horse breeder like Elfers to tell even at this distance. But they hadn't wandered here, for it appeared they were ground-staked at the side of the trail skirting the edge of Henry's upper pasture, grazing there in that patch of wild oats. *Gott*-damn, if someone had planted their horses in the good feed, for free!

It made Henry's neck burn that anyone would try to steal when all he had come by he had been earned with the sweat of his brow and the muscles in his back. Besides, if someone wanted a little feed for their horses, all he had to do was ask.

Slapping the four long, thick straps down on the backs and yard-wide haunches of the matched Belgians, Elfers picked up their pace a little, finding himself irritated at the freeloaders, especially nettled that neither his nephew nor the hired man had done a thing to run off the impudent squatters.

In a matter of seconds and a few more yards Elfers spotted something else out of place. For the life of him, it looked like a man's knee sticking up above the short grass some twenty-five yards from the two poorly kept horses. A man's knee poking up, just the way a fellow would if he was lying down in the grass, taking himself a nap.

Perhaps this was one of the freeloaders, Henry decided. And it made him all the more angry. He'd wake that fellow up but good and give him a good chunk of his mind.

The off-hand Belgian whickered and tossed its massive head as the freeloader's body came in sight the moment Henry reined the draft horses off the trail at the edge of the high pasture.

"*Gott*-damn!" he growled as he hauled back on the reins with all his might the instant he realized it was the hired man.

A shiny smear blackened Bland's upper chest as if the man had spilled Catherine's molasses syrup all over himself at breakfast.

"Robert! Get up—no time to take a nap, *Gott*-dammit!"

From the corner of his eye Elfers spotted the figure stepping away from the brush, a heartbeat later realizing the man was leveling a rifle at him.

Starting to dive, he felt his boot get entangled in the mower's footboard.

The bullet caught him high in the arm, continuing on to

pierce his chest. With a grunt, Elfers pitched headlong off the mower, dragging his foot from that boot still wedged between the newly varnished boards. With but one good arm now, he couldn't drag himself very well, nor very far, before he felt all his strength was drained from him. Perhaps with every beat of his heart, the way all that blood had seeped from him into this ground he had plowed the last few seasons.

He lay there, trying to catch his breath, deciding at last to look down at the wound. Surprised to find that there was little blood on his upper arm, Henry realized he was bleeding out inside and unless he got help quick—

A moccasin jammed down on the wounded shoulder and shoved Jurden Henry Elfers against the ground with a roaring flame that shot through his whole body.

He blinked through the tears of pain, trying to focus on the figure that stepped over him. His eyes cleared and he saw two of them. His ears heard the *clack-clack* of a carbine's lever and receiver as he glanced at the repeater one of the Indians held against his hip.

Then Henry looked up at the warrior's face, recognizing the young man who had come looking for stray horses yesterday. He and the other one were grinning down at Henry apishly.

Elfers slowly closed his eyes and said good-bye to each of his three children. Struggling to take a breath, Henry uttered one last word as he heard that carbine bark, as he heard his head explode.

"Catherine—"

Shore Crossing had led them up the ridge in the pre-dawn darkness, circling far around the homestead and the buildings, far from the outbuildings and the corral, to eventually reach this overlook where they could gaze down on the ranch as the sky grew pale in the east.

It wasn't long after it got light enough for objects to cast a dim shadow that the first of the white men emerged from the large building, hitching up his suspenders. A second went directly to a tiny board house nearby as he pulled down his suspenders and worked at the flaps on the front of his britches.

The first, a young Shadow who Shore Crossing thought

could be no older than he himself, emerged from a far building a little while later leading a saddled horse. He began to drive some cows and calves from the corral, keeping them in front of his horse with a long willow switch. That white man was putting those animals on a hillside trail Shore Crossing could see would take them up the side of this plateau to where the three young warriors lay watching.

"That is a nice horse," Red Moccasin Tops observed. "Better than mine."

"You can have it," Shore Crossing said. "Come; we'll stake out the horses."

Red Moccasin Tops's eyes narrowed with a glint of mischief. "Set a trap?"

He nodded, seeing Swan Necklace nervously lick his dry lips. "These Shadows are a curious sort. Our horses will draw them to their death."

By the time that first white man was halfway up the plateau trail, Swan Necklace came sprinting over to the patch of wild oats where Shore Crossing and Red Moccasin Tops were setting out the old ponies, announcing that a second Shadow had emerged from the tiny house and was now driving some more cows up the same trail.

"And a third one is busy outside in the corral," Swan Necklace said breathlessly, "hitching up two giant horses to a funny wagon."

Shore Crossing smiled, his eyes gleaming. "Not just one. But we can kill all three."

The young Shadow was first. Shore Crossing knocked him from the saddle with a bullet as the curious white man brought his horse to a halt near the two Nez Perce ponies. Their trap was a good one.

And the older Shadow was next. Evidently he heard the crack of the carbine when Shore Crossing dropped the first man and came hurrying up the last switchback to the top of the plateau, scattering the lumbering cows with their distended udders swaying between their hind legs as the herd reached the grassy pasture. This second Shadow began hollering for the first man in a frantic call.

Shore Crossing stepped out of the brush and shot him from behind with a bullet to the head. The bright red halo exploded in the new day's sunlight as the Shadow pitched onto the ground and his horse took off at a run.

"We'll catch it later," Shore Crossing told Red Moccasin Tops.

The cousin nodded. "I hear the other one coming."

It was good, all that noise from the white man's strange two-wheeled wagon. *Clack-clack. Clack-clack. Clack-clack* . . . probably what kept the wagon man from hearing the gunshots.

But the Shadow spotted him stepping boldly from the brush to fire the stolen rifle. Chiding himself for his brashness after that missed shot, Shore Crossing started toward the spot where the white man fell off the two-wheeled wagon the big horses slowly dragged it away, *clack-clack, clack-clack;* then they came to a stop and started eating in that same patch of wild oats with the two camp ponies.

"It's the same Boston Man who said the store man had a right to whip our friends," Red Moccasin Tops declared as they walked up to the wounded Shadow.

Shore Crossing didn't say anything as he shoved the white man onto his back with the heel of his moccasin. The Shadow gazed up at him and began speaking in that strange Boston Man accent of his. All that *clack-clack* talk like his noisy two-wheeled wagon really irritated Shore Crossing, so he levered another cartridge into the chamber.

This is for all the whippings gone unpunished, he thought as he pulled the trigger, the crack of the carbine blotting out the Shadow's last word the moment the back of his head exploded against the ground.

Swan Necklace was already digging through the pockets of one of the other men, and Red Moccasin Tops claimed what he could find on the second Shadow. So Shore Crossing knelt beside the quivering body and stuffed his hands into the pockets, feeling for anything of curiosity, if not of value. All he found was a folding knife, which he dropped into the pouch under his left arm where he carried a fire steel, along with his vials of grease and paint.

When Shore Crossing stood, he moved over to the giant horses. They were too big. So he decided to leave them here and instead yelled for his companions to bring over the pair of white man horses. He took the one from Swan Necklace, then instructed his nephew to pick which of the old *Nee-Me-Poo* ponies the youngster wanted.

"But I wanted this one," Swan Necklace said with a downcast turn to his lips, patting one of the white man's horses. It was a pretty roan, a glowing reddish-brown with spots of gray across its front shoulders.

"All right, you can have it," Shore Crossing relented. "Besides, I think this Boston Man has far better horses down there."

At the corral, he and Red Moccasin Tops ducked between the fenceposts and moved among the restive horses, choosing at least ten they wanted to take back to *Tepahlewam* as the spoils of their revenge raid.

"Before we go, we should see if the Shadow woman is in there," Shore Crossing suggested.

Red Moccasin Tops dragged the back of his bloodied hand across his lips. "You want her?"

He shook his head. "No. She is too fat for my taste. But I think we should look inside to find guns and bullets."

With a yelp of joy, Red Moccasin Tops clapped in glee. "Now I can have a gun of my own!"

Inside the big wooden house they called out, but no one heeded their calls. The place was empty. Swan Necklace was busy looking at everything, picking up objects, turning them over, then dropping them on the floor. Some broke with a crash; others merely clattered and rolled underfoot. But they discovered a rifle standing near the door. And on a small table nearby Red Moccasin Tops spotted a handful of cartridges.

Stepping back outside, Shore Crossing started toward the corral and the horses. He leaped atop the one he wanted most of all, grabbed its halter, and reined it over close to the gate, where he pulled the pole aside so they could drive the rest of the horses out of the corral.

With Swan Necklace on his own Shadow horse now, the three of them flushed the horses into the yard, whooping with glee.

"*Yi-hell-lis!*"* Shore Crossing screamed, his whole body atingle. "None of those sour-talkers in camp will call me a coward now!"

---

*Scum of the earth!

Chapter 9

June 14, 1877

BY TELEGRAPH

WYOMING.

Starvation Among the Indians.

OMAHA, June 5.—A private telegram from Atlantic City, Wyoming, states that the Shoshone Indians are in almost a starving condition. Their supplies are lying at Green river and Bryan stations by some irresponsible delay. Some fears are entertained by settlers that the Indians will be driven to commit depredations to keep from starvation.

Whitfield listened again as the rifle shot faded just beyond the far hill.

He figured someone else must be out hunting early this morning, same as he was.

It grew quiet for a long time after the echo died, so maybe the hunter had dropped his game. Whitfield started down the long slope toward the bottom where he would have to begin the hard climb up that plateau where the shot had echoed.

But if the other hunter hadn't been lucky enough to drop his target, then Whitfield figured the odds were damned good the animal would soon be heading his way.

If he kept his eyes open, chances were good he would be seeing some deer come busting off that brushy hillside in no time.

Whitfield hadn't yet reached the bottom when he heard another crack of the rifle. Certain now that the hunter had been trailing a wounded animal, he stopped among some clumps of brush and waited a few moments—listening, his eyes raking the far hillside that would lead him to the top of the plateau. He was fully expecting to see something moving down his way, some creature driven over the edge toward the brushy bottom where the deer loved to conceal themselves once they had watered of a morning and were heading back to their feeding grounds before the heat of the day.

Early morning like this was the time to be out hunting, because the deer were up and moving from their beds to water—

By damn, a third shot.

Was that fella a poor marksman or just down on his luck this time out?

Leaping across the narrow rushing stream that circled the base of the plateau on its way to the Salmon just past the Elfers place, Whitfield started trudging up the hill, doing his best to keep his eyes moving across the slope above him for anything that might bust on over. But nothing so much as moved on that hillside during his laborious climb, zigzagging his way up to the top, where he finally stopped, collapsed to one knee, and sucked wind like a swaybacked plow horse.

This was good pasture; that much was for sure. The German had done well with this patch of ground, Whitfield grudgingly conceded. Maybe Henry himself was the hunter this morning, because Whitfield spotted Elfers's two matched Belgians way across the meadow . . . that pair of big brutes still hitched to the new mower Henry had brought out from Portland just last week. Whitfield started toward the draft animals.

"Jesus God!" he gasped when he stumbled across the first body.

It was the youngster, Henry's nephew: lying on his back, his pockets pulled out of his pants like they were droopy mule ears. A black smear across his chest—so dark in contrast to the pasty white of the young man's cheeks. And those lifeless eyes glazing over just the way a deer's eyes would by the time you had it split open from brisket to bunghole—

"Jesus God!" Whitfield exclaimed again, this time cursing himself for standing there, thinking of such stupid, ghastly things when Henry Elfers's nephew lay dead in the hayfield—

Did Henry kill the boy? No, couldn't have, Whitfield thought as he started off toward those Belgians again, this time at a trot, loping along fast enough that he didn't see the second body until he had tripped right over it.

Sprawling into the short grass, Whitfield rolled onto his side and looked back. Just a yard beyond the soles of his dusty boots lay the hired man. The back of his head was a shiny, black, pulpy lump of gore where the flies were already buzzing a swarming clot. Staring dumbfounded at that, Whitfield wanted to curse again . . . but discovered his mouth was too dry to utter a goddamned thing.

He realized he had to tell Henry, had to find Henry. Jesus God.

Dragging himself out of the bloody, dusty grass, he wheeled clumsily, then stumbled forward to scoop up his rifle—

And that's when he spotted Jurden Henry Elfers.

Lying there on his back, a boot missing and his dirty stocking halfway off his foot. A patch of blood on his upper arm and more staining his armpit. Despite the hole in the middle of Henry's face, Whitfield was certain it was Elfers. The graying beard and that big waxed mustache. He'd know that German anywhere.

All three of 'em. Jesus G—Who was there to tell now?

Likely Injuns. Goddamned red-bellies. Probably got to Catherine and had their way with her, too. Cut the throats of the little ones . . .

Whitfield did the best he could to squeeze that image out of his mind as he lunged onto the trail where the milk cows were bunched, chewing away at the grass as if hell weren't falling in all around them—then caught himself, stopping suddenly. Better that he don't go down the trail to the yard and the house. If the bastards were still about their savage business—

Turning slightly, Whitfield dropped over the side of the plateau, plunging almost straight downhill. He figured he could strike the John Day just above the milk house, maybe hide there beside the creek if he caught sight of any skulking redskins in the Elfers yard.

Breathless by the time he reached the creek bank, he peered back through the trees, squinting through the salty drops that dribbled into his eyes, spying the stone wall of the milk house in the midst of the verdant brush. Wheeling, he dropped to one knee, clutching the rifle in his sweaty hands, and peered through the trees in the opposite direction at the distant yard. Nothing moved around the house; no one he could see at the barn or the corral. In fact, he spotted none of the critters at all.

Then Whitfield got back on his feet and turned away from the buildings, this time starting upstream. Realizing his mind had become all the more numb as his breath came short and hard.

Gould. He had to find Gould. Norman would know what to do.

Whitfield was near done in by the time he had loped those two miles between the Elfers place and the sawmill that Norman Gould operated for Henry up at a wide spot in John Day Creek.

"Nor—Norman!" he cried out, pasty-mouthed, as he lurched into the yard between Gould's small cabin and the large shed that housed the steam-driven sawmill that was sitting quiet for the moment.

"What's the bee under your bonnet?"

Whitfield whirled around, finding Gould stepping out the cabin door, George Greer at his elbow. A settler from farther up the Salmon, Greer was there getting some planks sawed for an addition he was nailing onto the side of his barn.

"Henry!" Whitfield gasped, his tongue sticking to the roof of his mouth.

"Good God, man," Greer said as he stepped up. "What's the lather?"

"They killed 'em!" Whitfield gushed. "Injuns killed 'em all!"

"Killed who?"

"Henry. Saw him: shot in the face," he continued, struggling to work up enough saliva so he could get more words out. "The other two. That nephew Harry and the hired fella. All."

"Catherine and the babies?"

Whitfield nodded, even though he admitted, "Didn't see 'em myself. Dared not go to the house. But there wasn't a soul stirring. I'm feared they butchered the whole lot."

Greer and Gould looked at each other for a long moment. Then Norman Gould asked, "You brung you a gun, didn't you, George?"

"Only this," and the settler tapped the pistol stuffed in the front of his belt. "But I got a dozen more bullets on me, too." He patted a britches pocket.

"I don't like thinking on what we're gonna find over to Henry's place," Gould said quietly as he returned from the small cabin with his repeater in one hand, a box of shells rattling in the other. "C'mon—let's go see if there's any of 'em left alive."

"Jesus God," Whitfield groaned quietly as the three of them set off on foot. "Hard to believe them goddamned Nez Perce gone on the warpath."

Catherine Elfers hushed the children the moment she spotted the three young warriors crossing the small patch of open ground that would take them to the back of the house. Little Fritz was the fussiest, always had been; so she slipped free a half-dozen tiny buttons at the front of her dress and pulled out the engorged breast. Guiding the nipple into the infant's mouth, she quieted the child and took another look out the crack she maintained in the milk house door.

The trio of Indians rode past, more than forty yards away, likely unaware of the milk house tucked away in the thick vegetation here beside John Day Creek. Unlike last evening when the three of them showed up in the yard, now they were each mounted on a horse of their own, driving along at least a double-handful of horses.

Seems they found the stray ponies they were searching for, Catherine thought as she watched the trio drive their herd slowly into the distance, heading for the Salmon River Road.

One of the children tugged on her dress. Catherine looked down.

"I need to pee, Mamma."

She pulled back the door with her free hand, feeling safer now that the Indians were out of sight. "Go pee right outside, then get back in here till I get my butter done."

It took less than an hour before Catherine Elfers finished churning and laid little Fritz into the basket made of rived ashwood, then re-covered the infant with his blanket. She took her time scooping the butter out of the churn with a big pewter soupspoon, ladling it in a tinned bucket, then set the top on the bucket and stood to rebutton her dress.

After kneeling for a moment to wash her hands in the shockingly cold creek water that kept this milk house cool, Catherine picked up the bucket and pinned it beneath one arm, then hooked the basket's handle over her other elbow and pushed out the door, the other two little ones in tow. She leaned her shoulder into the door to close it against the jamb and started for the house.

She had the children nearly to the porch when she saw the four horsemen hurrying down the trail from the pasture. Stopping a moment, she squinted a bit, trying to see who the riders were. Henry, Harry, and Mr. Bland only made for three. Catherine watched a moment longer, wondering who the fourth man might be, then shooed the kids into the house before her.

"Mrs. Elfers!"

She had set the butter tin on the sideboard, then nestled the baby's basket onto the cane rocker she kept in the kitchen where she could rock the child to sleep as she prepared meals . . . when she heard the second, stirring call.

"Mrs. Elfers!"

Still wary of the Indians, she went to the window and peered into the yard, able to see only the four horses. Sure as sausage wasn't Henry and the others. When she got to the door, Catherine recognized the little Frenchman—Victor something or other. Had himself a mining claim just upriver a bit.

"Miss-suss . . . Miss-suss Elfers," he gasped when her face finally appeared in that six-inch space she opened up between door and jamb.

"Victor?" And she peered behind him at the other three who waited down in the yard, for some reason not wanting to look up at the door.

"Yes, Miss-suss Elfers—"

"What is it?"

Running his dirt-crusted hand beneath his nose, Victor gushed, "We found 'em dead, Miss-suss Elfers—"

"Found who dead?"

When he told her that Henry and her sister's boy and the hired man were all dead in the upper pasture, Catherine didn't believe him. Not that she went numb with the news. Just that it had to be someone's idea of a sad, sick dream.

But she did start to slowly go numb as Victor and the three strangers were describing what they'd found in the pasture, when suddenly three men sprinted from the tree line at the side of the house, making for the porch.

"Catherine!"

"Norman?"

"Dear Almighty," Gould said as he bounded up the creaky steps onto the narrow porch. "It's Henry and the others—"

"No, no," she uttered almost too quietly, the cold fuzziness beginning to seep in. "This man—a Frenchman, aren't you? He said the same thing . . . b-but it can't be true."

"Come, sit, Catherine," Gould said as he took her by the elbow and got her through the doorway.

It was a long time after he had put her into the chair and left one of the Frenchman's companions to keep an eye on the two little ones that Norman Gould returned to her side. She knew this would all be cleared up when Henry came home near sundown as he always did after a long day in the hay field. Then they'd all learn that it must have been someone else—

"Catherine."

She found Gould kneeling before her, his hand resting lightly on the back of hers. Gazing over his shoulder, Catherine realized a lot of time had passed while she had been sitting there, what with the way the shadows were different now than they had been when she had returned from the milk house.

"Norman," she said softly. "You know Henry will be home soon and he'll tell you—"

"Catherine, I brung Henry down from the pasture," Gould told her, gripping her hand hard, like it was a hoe handle. "Your sister's boy, too. And your mister's hired man."

She stood without saying a word, looked at Norman, then finally whispered, "I suppose you want me to come with you?"

"They're in the wagon. All three," Gould explained. "We brung 'em down to show you."

In a moment she found herself out on the porch, the two little ones holding onto her skirt like a pair of bookends as Catherine stared down at the wagon box. The three of them were laid out, side by side by side, three sets of dusty boots poking out from the edge of a small sheet of oiled canvas.

"Henry?"

"Yes, it's him, Catherine," Gould replied, then turned away. "One of you, go get the baby in the house."

George Greer clambered away from the wagon, stopping midway up the steps to the porch. "Norman—we gotta go now," he said with great apprehension. "Gotta get her and the children outta here."

"Yes, yes," Gould agreed with a little irritation. "If them reds are letting the wolf out to howl, then chances are they'll be coming back soon, Catherine."

Greer turned to Whitfield, who was sitting on the wagon seat, reins laced through his fingers. "Get that wagon into the barn and hurry—we gotta get."

"We ain't taking the wagon?" Whitfield asked.

"No," Gould said. "Going on foot. Can't take the chance of staying to the road."

"W-where?" Whitfield stammered. "Where we gonna go to be safe now?"

Gould started down the steps with Catherine in tow, then stopped and took the basket with the fussy baby inside from Greer as he shuffled back onto the porch. Holding the woman's elbow, Gould dropped step by step to the yard and started past the death wagon on foot. "We're lighting out for the Cones' place on Slate Creek."

Chapter 10

Season of *Hillal*
1877

BY TELEGRAPH

WASHINGTON.

**Overhauling the Indian Department
Generally.**

WASHINGTON, June 7.—Secretary Schurz, today, by order, created a board . . . to examine into
the methods now in force in the finance and
accounting division of the Indian bureau,
especially as to an analysis of the money and
property accounts of Indian agents, and whether
the accounts of agents are rendered in accordance
with the law and regulations; whether any
expenditures are made without proper authority
and whether the present system is such as to show
at all times the condition of the money and
property affairs at each agency . . . particular
examination will be made as to the number and
compensation of employees at each agency, and
whether they are given or allowed to purchase
subsistence or clothing in violation of the law . . .

To avoid the Shadows' village that stood near the mouth of Slate Creek, Shore Crossing decided the three of them would drive their stolen horses into the hills, where they could follow the upper trail along its rugged contours on their way north; heading back to *Tepahlewam*. It proved difficult for them to keep that small herd together. Here and there along the steep slopes a horse would wander off the narrow path, then another.

Shore Crossing finally gave up and let them go. It did not matter, because the three of them still had several good horses as well as the rifles to shake in the faces of those who had dared call him a coward.

Once they had put two tall crests between them and the white man's settlement, the three warriors turned off the upper trail to begin their descent. No sooner had they returned to the Salmon River Road than Shore Crossing spotted a rider approaching.

"He is coming from the north," he told his two companions who rode out on the flanks of their stolen herd.

Swan Necklace visibly stiffened as he and Red Moccasin Tops watched the white man draw closer.

"It is the one called Cone,"* Shore Crossing announced as soon as he recognized the Shadow who waved to them some distance away. "We will stop and give him some good advice."

Now that they had slowed, the weary ponies milled off the road, tearing at the tall grass growing in scattered patches between the trail and the river.

"Cone!" he sang out in a good imitation of the white man's tongue.

The Shadow grinned, clearly relieved that Shore Crossing recognized him. But the white man's eyes flicked nervously to his two companions, then to the stolen horses and back to the two warriors again, before coming to rest on Shore Crossing. Cone cleared his throat and began to talk haltingly in the *Nee-Me-Poo* tongue.

"Good horses, strong horses. Where you going?"

"*Tepahlewam*," Shore Crossing answered. "Where you going?"

"Slate Creek," Cone replied in English. "Home."

---

*Charles P. Cone

Nonetheless, Shore Crossing understood the sound of those Boston Man words. "You have never been bad to my people."

Cone's eyes narrowed as he suspiciously regarded the young warrior. "No, I have always been good to the *Nee-Me-Poo.*"

"You know these horses, don't you, Cone?"

"Y-yes, I do," the white man answered nervously. "John Day ranch horses. You buy them from Elfers?"

"No, we kill men. Take horses and guns."

"K-killed the men?" Cone's face went tight, drained of color and pasty.

"You have never been bad to my people, so I will give you some good advice, Cone."

"Yes, good advice," he echoed nervously, the tip of his tongue licking at his lower lip.

"My people are on the warpath," Shore Crossing explained, pausing a moment while the Shadow looked again at the other two warriors.

The white man repeated, "Warpath."

"You are alone, Cone?"

"Y-yes."

"We will not harm you," Shore Crossing sought to relieve the Shadow's fear. "But it is dangerous now for a man to be out here alone. You go home, stay there."

"That is good advice," Cone said, lightly tapping his heels into his horse's ribs. "I will go tell the others about the warpath."

"Some white men will already know." And he was sure Cone understood what he meant.

"Thank you. I will go now to tell this news."

"Do not get in any fights against us, Cone," Shore Crossing said as the white man passed him by, knee brushing knee. "You are a good man and should not get yourself killed!"

With those last few words he flung at the fleeing Shadow's back, Shore Crossing saw Cone tear the hat from his head and wave it as if in answer while he galloped out of sight.

The three young men hadn't gone much farther down the trail before they saw another rider approaching from the north.

"Red Moccasin Tops!" Shore Crossing shouted to his cousin gleefully.

"I see, brother! It is my shooter!"

"Shooter?" Swan Necklace asked.

"Two summers ago, that Boston Man* shot me in the back of my head at his store," Red Moccasin Tops grumbled, his eyes narrowing cruelly. "Now I'm going to finish him."

"Only after he knows who will kill him!" Shore Crossing advised as the Shadow neared them, drawing back on his reins.

. Chances were the white man didn't recognize Red Moccasin Tops, he figured, but from the look on his face the white man clearly realized that he had plopped down in a bad situation with both feet.

"Hep-hep-hah!" the Shadow yelled at his horse before it had even come to a complete halt, sawing the reins hard to the right.

"Shoot him, brother!" Shore Crossing ordered as he brought his rifle to his shoulder and sighted in on the fleeing man's back.

He fired, seeing the Shadow's hat fly off his head. An instant later his cousin fired his new rifle. The white man spun off his horse into a clump of tall grass and brush.

Red Moccasin Tops whooped, brandishing his rifle aloft as he screamed in utter glee.

"Come on!" Shore Crossing commanded. "We'll make sure he's finished!"

They loped their horses up to the spot where the Shadow had fallen beside the trail. Both of them peered at the white man's legs sticking out from the thick underbrush, watching the britches and boots for some time.

"I think he's dead," Red Moccasin Tops ventured.

"I knocked his hat off."

"But *I* knocked him off his horse!" Red Moccasin Tops boasted.

Shore Crossing grinned at his cousin. "As it should be. This Shadow cheated our people in every trade we made with him. And he shot at you. So now you have killed him. It is very good."

Yelping again in joy, Red Moccasin Tops said, "But he didn't have a gun for me to take from him."

"No, he did not."

---

*Samuel Benedict

"Then I will keep his horse."

Shore Crossing nodded in agreement. "The horse is yours, brother," he said. "It is your coup."

Whoop-whooping, the younger man wheeled his pony about and reined it up beside the white man's horse. He leaned over to snag the drooping reins, then rejoined the small herd of stolen animals.

"Let's take our prizes back to *Tepahlewam* now," Shore Crossing said.

An easy grin finally spread across Swan Necklace's face. He answered Red Moccasin Tops's wolf howl with one of his own. Shore Crossing joined them as they put the horses back into motion.

They were warriors now. Let no man ever doubt that. He and Red Moccasin Tops had drawn Shadow blood.

Which meant they had started a war.

Samuel Benedict barely breathed.

His head was foggy, but with his ear against the ground Benedict could easily hear the horses approaching. How he wanted to open his eyes, but he didn't know for sure just where he was lying—or if the red sonsabitches would see his eyelids part into slits.

The hooves came to a halt nearby, and he heard the bastards talking. Two voices. But he had seen three of them. Where was the third? Damn, he wanted to open his eyes . . . to leap up and run—but Sam realized that he wouldn't stand a chance, not with the way his leg burned.

He'd be Injun bait before he got very far.

The two of them kept talking. . . . Benedict was pretty sure one of the three was in that bunch that had tried to break into his store late one August night back in '75. He had yelled out at the pricks that his store was closed, but they kept shouting and shoving against the door, so he fetched the scattergun he kept under the counter, always loaded with buckshot and handy for driving off any of the sparky bastards.

He hadn't worried about giving them a warning shot, goddammit. Flinging back the door, Sam let them have the first barrel. Benedict heard the pricks scream in pain and alarm with that sudden roar and bright muzzle flash. Isabella was sobbing behind him, wailing and yelling, too as the little bastards lunged off into the summer darkness.

Benedict had decided he'd show them once and for all, so he stepped out onto the porch in front of his store and spotted the shadows scattering for their ponies left at the tree line. Dropping from the low porch onto the dust and grass, he had taken a half-dozen more steps, deciding just who would get the second goddamned barrel as the red pricks scattered for their lives. The shotgun roared into the black of that night.

Just shy of their ponies, one of them fell, crying out to his friends. Two turned back and struggled to get that screaming one off the ground. Benedict hoped he was gut-shot, for it would be a long and painful way to die. Served the little prick right.

Turning to his left, Benedict snapped open the action and ejected the spent shells. He pulled two fresh loads from his front pants pocket and shoved them home. Snapping the breech closed, the storekeeper braced the stock of the scattergun against his hipbone and cocked both hammers. Wheeling the muzzle at the dim, starlit forms, he yanked back with his finger, immediately realizing that he had made a mistake, and pulled both triggers that instant after he had found a likely target and clenched his eyes shut against the muzzle flash.

Benedict had opened both eyes just as he heard a grunt. The son of a bitch was flying through the air, landing on his belly.

Realizing he stood right out in the open without a loaded weapon, Benedict had turned on his heel and sprinted back to the store, yelling at Isabella to get down behind the counter. By the time he had pulled the empties out of the two-eyed stage-rider scattergun and stuffed in two new loads, Sam had reached the porch—snapping the barrels closed against the breech. Benedict found the troublemakers had scooped up their wounded and hightailed it into the dark.

Good riddance to the little pricks.

As he lay there now listening to the two voices, praying he could keep his breathing shallow, Samuel Benedict remembered how good it had felt to drive the little bastards off like that. Figuring it would teach them not to come strutting around his place no more.

But then he recalled that he had to teach the red bastards one more lesson. That was last spring, little more than a year ago, when Isabella called to him from the store. He was working outside when one of them bucks came flushing out the door with Isabella squawking behind him.

"He's got some liquor!" she was squealing. "He's got some of our liquor!"

The brazen bastard saw Benedict and leaped into a sprint. But Samuel was quick enough with that pistol he kept tucked into his belt whenever any red niggers were about. There in the midst of a half-dozen other warriors standing around in the yard, Benedict pulled his revolver and popped the son of a bitch in the back.

Damn if when he turned the dead man's body over with his boot toe Samuel didn't find the bullet had blown out the front of the prick's belly, busting that stolen whiskey bottle in the process. Waste of not only a bullet, but a shameful goddamned waste of some good whiskey, too!

Pricks—

He wanted to be sure they had gone now—to open his eyes and be sure when he heard the hoofbeats fade. How his side hurt and he wanted to take a deep breath, his lungs crying out so. Wondering if he shouldn't just stay right here.

Someone would come looking for him. After all, Isabella knew he was out looking for stray cows. Someone would come soon enough. But what if they didn't?

How he wanted to get to his feet and run. But he waited, that ear pressed against the ground hearing the hoofbeats quickly fade away.

Letting his breath out as quietly as he could, Benedict felt the blades of grass brush against his nose, his hairy upper lip, too. And lay there a while longer just to be sure before he cracked one eye into a slit. Then opened the other slowly, looking about without moving his head.

The red bastards were gone. Sure enough. They'd left him for dead, by God.

Now all he had to do was figure out how bad off he was and get himself on down to Slate Creek to tell the others the little pricks had let the wolf out to howl.

Son of a bitch, but now was the time to finish off all them red niggers, once and for all. With war finally come, white folks and the army could rub out every last one of 'em: bucks, squaws, and nits, too.

Ever' last one of 'em hardly worth the bullet it'd take to blow 'em to kingdom come.

*   *   *

Here beside Round Willow Creek at the western edge of the *Tepahlewam,* Shore Crossing raised his arm and the three of them stopped their small herd of stolen horses.

He waved his nephew over. "You look very fine on your new horse."

Swan Necklace patted the roan's withers. "And I have a fine gun now, too. Never had a gun before."

"Plenty of shells?" Red Moccasin Tops asked.

"Got me some, yes."

Then Shore Crossing said, "The camp is just beyond those trees ahead. I want you to go in to announce that we are coming with our horses."

"You want me to tell the village?" Swan Necklace asked in sudden excitement.

"Yes. Show them your horse, and the rifle we took from the Boston Man. Tell the camp that Red Moccasin Tops and I have killed five of the Shadows who have done our people badly. Tell them that news so they will be ready when we ride in."

"You're coming soon?"

"Yes, Nephew," Shore Crossing assured him. "We will give you a few minutes to tell everyone so that it will make for a grand parade when we run our horses through the camp."

Swan Necklace *kee-yi-yied* like a coyote as he reined the big roan about in a tight circle, kicking it hard with his moccasin heels and leaping away. Shore Crossing and his cousin sat grinning at each other.

"This is a good day," Red Moccasin Tops said.

He nodded, finally realizing that from the moment he had left the rendezvous camp at *Tepahlewam* he—Shore Crossing—had held the destiny of more than seven hundred of his people in his hand. No more could they sneer at him and call him a coward. He alone had been brave enough to start this war that would free his people from the tyranny of the Shadows.

"Yes. This is a very good day!" Shore Crossing exclaimed with joyous certainty. "And for you and me—the two men who saved our people from the reservation—all of our days will be good from now on!"

Chapter 11

Season of *Hillal*
1877

Sun Necklace got to his feet as the youngster raced into camp on a strange horse. Big Morning, his older brother, stepped up beside him. Sun Necklace sensed those first claws of fear wrap themselves around his belly.

Young Swan Necklace started yelling as he came in sight of the first lodges, but it took a moment for Sun Necklace to understand what the exuberant youth was shouting as he brandished a carbine high over his head, his big roan frightened and sidestepping as women and children began to crowd in around him.

"What does this mean?" asked *Hemackkis Kaiwon*, the man called Big Morning or Big Dawn.

"The boy will tell us what has become of Red Moccasin Tops," Sun Necklace replied with steely resolve, fearing desperately for his son's life.

He hadn't slept at all last night, his belly tight with apprehension from the moment the three young men rode off on their two old horses. When he found them leaving, Sun Necklace had leaped atop his own war pony and easily caught up with the trio not far from camp.

"Come back home, Red Moccasin Tops," he had ordered.

But his son had stiffened his backbone and quickly replied, "I am not a boy anymore, Father. You cannot order me about

as you once did. For many winters now I have been old
enough to become a warrior."

Sun Necklace had glanced at Shore Crossing. "Nephew,
you are the cause of this trouble for my son. Because you did
not go after the Shadow who murdered your father when you
should have, because your pride has been pricked now . . .
you will take my son from me so that some Boston Man can
kill him far from his family."

"I will bring him back a hero, Uncle," Shore Crossing had
vowed. "Or he will die with me, become a true warrior of the
Nee-Me-Poo."

"Good-bye, Father," Red Moccasin Tops said as he turned
his horse away.

Shore Crossing put his old pony into motion, Swan Necklace riding double behind him.

"Son!" he had cried in desperation, his voice no longer
drenched with paternal bluster.

But the young men said nothing more as their backs grew
smaller and smaller, then disappeared through the trees. Sun
Necklace had sat there for a long time on his war pony, wondering how he should feel now that his son wanted to prove
that he was a man, old enough to rise or fall by his own hand.

But all night Sun Necklace had lain awake in such gut-
wrenching fear: wondering if this was what his own father had
felt. Still, this was something different: the two cousins had
been drinking, if not that morning before they left, then
surely the night before when they had caused a disturbance
at the dance.

And he brooded that what the cousins had set out to do
would in all probability ignite a war, would with all surety
change the lives of the *Nee-Me-Poo* forever.

At first he had grown sad, his heart cold with despair at
the fate awaiting his people. Then, gradually, his heart
warmed with anger, boiled with fury. Perhaps the time had
come for their people to rise up in glory once more and throw
off the yoke of the white man!

"Swan Necklace!" he hollered apprehensively now as he
lunged forward, grabbing hold of the leather rein and stopping the youth's horse. "Where is my son?"

The youngster was grinning, his whole face radiant with the
glow of unbridled victory. "See my rifle? I took it from a
Shadow. We killed him! We killed him for his rifle!"

On the other side of the roan Big Morning reached up and snatched the carbine from Swan Necklace. He inspected it with admiration. "This is a good rifle!"

But Sun Necklace did not care about the rifle. He repeated his question: "Where is Red Moccasin Tops?"

"They are coming!" Swan Necklace declared, twisting about on the back of the big Boston Man horse. "Right behind me! They wanted me to come first and tell everyone to be ready when they brought in their guns and horses!"

"G-guns and horses?" Sun Necklace echoed, sudden joy shoving his apprehension aside. "Both of them, they are alive?"

"Yes—alive!" Swan Necklace roared. "There! Look! They come!"

Of a sudden the huge crowd became animated all over again: shouting, crying out, the women *u-u-uing* with their tongues in exultation. Beyond the fringes of the gathering Sun Necklace could see the bobbing heads of several horses—perhaps as many as he had fingers—then he saw the heads of the two young warriors as they herded their captured ponies in among the lodges. Everyone was cheering, some men shouting their war songs in deep voices, women crying out in falsetto celebration.

"My son! My son!"

"Father! Look what we have brought!" Red Moccasin Tops cried as he approached.

"Get down, Swan Necklace!" Big Morning ordered, tugging on the youngster's arm.

"This is my horse!" the youth whimpered as his uncle began to pull him down.

"I will bring it back to you," Big Morning promised as he leaped onto the roan's bare back once Swan Necklace hit the ground. He settled himself and raised the youngster's rifle aloft, tapping the big horse in the ribs so that it started walking slowly through the tightly packed crowd.

Now it was Big Morning who was leading the two warriors through the joyous throng.

"Come, Swan Necklace!" Sun Necklace shouted above the tumult and put his arm around the youngster's shoulders. They fell behind his brother on that big roan horse. "Swan Necklace—walk with me and my son, the brave warrior known as Red Moccasin Tops!"

"I am truly a warrior now, Father!" the young man hollered down at them as he brought his stolen horse up beside Sun Necklace.

His eyes were filled with glistening tears of joy as he gazed up at his son in deep admiration and pride. "Yes," he said, his voice cracking. "Today . . . you are a warrior. And you, my son . . . you have reminded all of us of something we have forgotten."

"What, Father?" the young man cried over the rising excitement and noise from hundreds of throats. "What have I reminded you of?"

"You make us all remember what it means to be a warrior for our people!"

Lepeet Hessemdooks was his name. Two Moons.

An older warrior of more than forty winters, he had lived about as long as Big Morning and Sun Necklace. His father had been a noted Salish warrior who had come to live with the Wallowa after he married a Nez Perce woman. Two Moons was their firstborn. And now he had grandchildren, a man who had enough winters behind him that he had watched the slow, painful dissolution of the old existence once lived by the *Nee-Me-Poo*. Enough winters behind him to know this war would bring about their final ruin.

Joining several of the headmen and chiefs in White Bird's lodge late that morning, Two Moons and the rest debated their misgivings about surrendering to a life on the reservation. Although they had guaranteed Cut-Off Arm they would bring their bands to Lapwai, many of these leaders still harbored grave doubts that they were doing the right thing.

So again this morning they had talked and talked—some arguing that they should stay on their old lands and fight the soldiers if they came. Others declared that what they should do was wait until later in the summer when their best warriors would return from the buffalo country, and then all the bands would be at full strength and could decide to go to war.

But a few claimed there was no way to defeat the white man, who was as numerous as the stars. Back and forth the deliberations rumbled until they suddenly heard the growing tumult outside the council lodge.

An old man came to the lodge door and yelled at the chiefs, "Now you will have to go to war!"

Closer and closer the shouting men and keening women came, along with a call heard constantly above the din: "Prepare for war! Prepare for war!"

"What can this mean?" White Bird asked, his voice shattering the stunned silence in that council lodge.

Suddenly the door flap was hurled aside and one of White Bird's young nephews poked his head inside, announcing, "You old men are talking of peace and war for nothing! Three boys have already started the war. They have killed some white men on the Salmon and brought their horses and guns to this camp. War has already come!"

The headmen stared at one another in disbelief. There was little left to debate now. Nothing else to do . . . but prepare for war.

In moments Two Moons stood on the outskirts of the noisy throng being pushed this way and shoved in that direction as the crowd followed Big Morning on through the heart of the village. People from Toohoolhoolzote's small band were the next to come running to learn of all the excitement. White Bird's and Looking Glass's people clamored to hear the stories, too. Suddenly all the manifold emotions pent up within these people for season after season came flooding forth, their long-held fears of the soldiers suddenly overridden by this surprisingly sweet taste of victory over a few Shadows.

Two Moon realized these people were like a pack of hungry mountain lions now, the scent of blood become strong in their nostrils.

To all of those clamoring noisily around the horsemen, those most hungry for talk of war, for the joy of any victory, Big Morning repeated over and over, "This is the horse and this is the gun the young men have brought back!"

As he shook the rifle in the air, the throng erupted anew. Then he shouted, "You must all remember that we have to fight now!"

There at the center of the swelling crowd stood the fomenters, those who thought only of their selfish pride, men like Toohoolhoolzote and the other *tewats,* the shamans of the Non-Treaty bands' Dreamer faith. These medicine men were awash in glory now.

On all sides long-suppressed anger and resentment were boiling to the surface. Feelings of unbridled excitement at the prospect of war animated some in that growing crowd, while alarm and dismay cloaked the dark emotions of others. Only those who were overjoyed at the certainty of war could exult at this sudden turn of events in their lives. The rest knew not what to do. Where to turn. Who to follow.

Two Moons moved along the fringe of the gathering as it continued to swell. It had taken very little time for the entire village to stream into the open—women returning from their root digging, men coming in from their work among the horses—everyone converging on the vanguard of the procession where Big Morning harangued the warriors, where many hot-blooded young men began to clamor for someone to lead them on a second revenge raid.

Suddenly, Big Morning halted his horse in the jostling crowd and twisted around, pointing now at his younger brother. "He is the one to lead us! Sun Necklace will take us to kill those who have wronged us! Sun Necklace!"

Immediately the warriors in the throng set up the chant: "Sun Necklace! Sun Necklace!"

It was plain to Two Moons that it did not take much to convince Sun Necklace that he should lead the second raid. He looked over those who clamored around Sun Necklace to go along—many of them untried, untested youngsters. It was one thing to do what the three had done when the whites were not expecting trouble. It would be something altogether different now that the Shadows had raised the alarm and would be prepared for warriors to sweep down on them.

So besides his son and Shore Crossing, Sun Necklace asked Toohoolhoolzote to ride along, then carefully selected seventeen of those whom he could count on to protect his own life in battle. Counting his brother, Big Morning, that would make for twenty-one who sprinted back to their lodges to snatch up paint and weapons, shields and bullets.

If any man should lead this second raid, Two Moons ruminated sadly, then Sun Necklace was that man. No one had ever questioned either his courage or his judgment in battle. In fact, his reputation had been made some summers before when, along with Looking Glass and his warriors, Sun Necklace had sculpted his standing by counting many coups during a battle far away in buffalo country that pitted their friends, the Crow, against their inveterate enemies, the Lakota.

Two Moons saw the young man headed his way at a sprint

now, eager anticipation written on his smooth, unlined face. He put out his hand to stop the youngster.

"Stick-in-the-Mud, you have been asked to go on Sun Necklace's raid?"

The man nodded, his eyes wide, bright with exhilaration. "We will strike back now, after all these winters. We will give back blow for blow!"

He let Stick-in-the-Mud go.

As he turned and watched with misgiving, Two Moons noticed that none of the young men of the Wallowa band were clamoring to join Sun Necklace's war party.

It is good, Two Moons brooded. *They must realize how terrible it would be to make themselves a part of this blood-letting after their chief has worked so tirelessly to hold war at bay.*

"Where is Joseph?"

Two Moons turned to find the old woman, *Tissaikpee,* the midwife to Joseph's woman, stopping at his elbow when she asked her question.

He said, "He is across the Salmon."

Tissaikpee wagged her head. "He is not part of making this war, is he?"

"No." Two Moons explained, "He and Ollokot went back to butcher some cattle so they would have plenty of meat for their families before we go on the reservation in two days—"

Then he stopped talking suddenly, realizing what he had just said. And he recognized the dismay clouding the old woman's face.

"But now . . . ," and his voice trailed off for a moment, "now we won't be going to the reservation."

She said nothing more to him but turned slowly away, raising her arms to the sky and beginning to wail as she started back to the birthing shelter.

For many, many seasons now, these bands had been suffering outrages at the hands of the whites. Two Moons realized that this call for war was not a sudden and unexpected event come with the return of the three brash young instigators. No, because of all the wrongs that had been done them, these *Nee-Me-Poo* people had been made ready for a long, long time. And now that they were enjoying their last few days of freedom, talking of the old life, celebrating as they would never celebrate again—these *Nee-Me-Poo* had grown angrier and angrier.

They were a people who were hardened for war by years of abuse and deceit. But Two Moons knew they were also a people in no way prepared for what this war would do to them.

"Joseph," he whispered sadly under his breath as he turned from that tumultuous gathering of the warriors who were beginning to return from their lodges, young men eagerly streaming toward Sun Necklace with their ponies and their weapons. "Joseph, where are you now that your people need your steady hand?"

Without him here, Two Moons knew, the war fever would run amok. Without Joseph here to talk for those who could not defend themselves, the brash, strutting, bellicose war-talkers had no one to cool their ardor.

Two Moons felt his eyes sting as he watched Sun Necklace and the strident Toohoolhoolzote lead the war party out of camp, headed south from *Tepahlewam* for White Bird Creek and the Salmon River settlements.

He felt his heart grow heavy as he trudged away from the throngs, watching a woman here, and a woman there, hoist herself up on the back of an old, steady travois pony to yank the lacing pins from the front of her lodge. One by one, the women yanked those long, peeled shafts from their holes, slowly unfurling the heavy buffalo hides . . . preparing to flee this place at first light.

A short while after the bold war chief and the brazen *tewat* led the raiders out of camp, White Bird and Looking Glass called for another council. Some who were already infected with the war fever protested that the question had been settled. There was nothing left for the chiefs to debate. War was at hand. All that was left to do was prepare for the soldiers.

Yet steady hands like Old Rainbow cautioned reason and restraint. By the time a gibbous moon had risen and the council dispersed, most of the leaders had decided it best to wait and see what the white men would do now. There might yet be a chance for peace.

And if all hope for peace was ruined, the least they could do was pray that their best warriors would return from the buffalo country soon.

But, no matter what, they had to abandon *Tepahlewam*

now. Evil had visited this place. Some expressed that they would return to their homes in the valleys far from this once-sacred ground, and others said they would climb higher into the mountains now, making it harder for the soldiers to find them. Come morning, they would finish striking their lodges and go.

No telling how Sun Necklace's war party would tear through the white settlements now, making all the more trouble for the *Nee-Me-Poo*.

Two Moons needed to find Joseph, to bring the chief back before the clans scattered to the winds. Dispersed in those small bands, the soldiers would easily slaughter them, Two Moons realized. With so many of the chiefs pulling in so many different directions, thinking only of war and fighting—they needed Joseph here now to think about the good of the women and children.

But by the time the council broke up it was too dark for him to start for the Salmon. In the gray before morning came, the old man decided, he would ride for the river. This might well be the only chance the *Nee-Me-Poo* had to make some kind of peace with the Shadows.

Joseph was a patient talker, an accomplished diplomat. If any man could fashion something out of this tragedy, Joseph would.

Chapter 12

Season of *Hillal*
1877

Joseph found it hard to sleep that last night of their trip to the Salmon. He tossed beneath his blankets, mostly lay staring up at the starry sky dusted with clouds—thinking of *Ta-ma-al-we-non-my* back at *Tepahlewam*.

Any day now she was due to deliver their child.

Her name meant Driven Before a Cold Storm, and he grew so anxious to get back to her that he finally decided that it was futile to try sleeping any longer. Arousing the others in the cold darkness, Joseph spurred the two women into packing up their blankets and the small hunting lodge, while he helped his brother and the four other men load the butchered beef onto a trio of travois and the backs of several pack-horses.

Joseph's party had been here beside the river for the better part of six days, having returned to the east bank of the Salmon from the rendezvous meadow by the lake to slaughter some of the cattle the Wallowa band had left behind to graze in the tall grass after they crossed the river in their journey to *Tepahlewam,* and eventually to the reservation. When they abandoned this wandering life Joseph and Ollokot wanted to have plenty of meat for their families. There was no way of telling what they would face when they crossed the Lapwai boundary tomorrow. . . . There it was again.

That word—*tomorrow.*

Up from the Salmon he led the party, climbing the steep slopes that carried them ever higher toward the Camas Prairie, where the *Nee-Me-Poo* women were harvesting this season's crop of *kouse* and camas roots they came to dig from the ground early every summer near the Split Rocks. Reaching the entrance to the Rocky Canyon, Joseph turned and gazed back at the others strung out along the wide trail the Wallowa had used for countless generations. But this was to be their last journey here.

Good that his child should be born free, in these final days before their freedom would be no more.

Catching his breath, he watched Ollokot's wife, *Wetatonmi,* and Joseph's own nearly grown daughter, *Hophop Onmi,* whom he had named Sound of Running Feet because of how the tiny one had loved to run about with wild abandon as soon as she had learned to remain stable on two feet. With those two women and their three travois ponies walked *Welweyas,* the half-man, half-woman of the Wallowa who for nearly all his life had preferred to wear the traditional dress of a woman.

Farther back down the trail came the men with the nine other horses laden with beef: Joseph's old friend, Half Moon, and his young nephew, Three Eagles; also the warrior whom missionaries had once given the Christian name of John Wilson before he abandoned the white man's faith for good, returning to the reservation and the Dreamer religion. Behind them all rode Ollokot, bringing up the rear protectively.

Joseph smiled in the gray light of day-coming. He did not have to see Ollokot's face to know for sure who it was at the end of the procession. It would be his brother. They made an able pair, these two, he realized again. He himself always stepped to the fore, to be the first into whatever his people confronted. And Ollokot—his loyal, steadfast brother—always saw to it that the rear was protected, that no stragglers were left behind in the march, that . . . that no one could attack those at the end of the column without suffering his wrath.

They really were two of a kind, he decided as he put his pony into motion, starting into the canyon of the Split Rock. Both of them knew that should they be required to offer their lives up for their people, each of these brothers would willingly give that ultimate, and most sacred, sacrifice for the Wallowa band.

When they reached the camp, Joseph decided he would let the others continue on to Ollokot's lodge with the travois and those quarters of butchered beef. But he himself would peel off and hurry for the squat separation lodge a *Nee-Me-Poo* woman would erect away from the rest of the village when she was nearing her time to deliver.

Closer and closer he felt himself drawing to her now at this hour when she might need him most. Close enough that the faint smell of woodsmoke tickled his nostrils. Some of the bands must already be up and rekindling breakfast fires.

But when he studied the eastern sky ahead Joseph realized it was far too early for the camp to be rising for the day. There was no reason to make an early march; there was nowhere for them to go for this one last day of freedom. Strange that he should smell woodsmoke this early. But perhaps it was only the remnants of last night's lingering fires rising from the lodges, fanned to a fury while the people sang and danced, courted and coupled, before the *Nee-Me-Poo* fell upon their robes for that next-to-last night of freedom.

Each time Joseph thought about it—and he could really think of little else except the child's coming—Joseph sensed an immense pain in his heart. So he did his best to push aside the utter sadness of these last steps toward the reservation, these last steps away from all that their life had been . . . thinking of the child that was coming to them. Be it a boy or be it a girl, this infant would not live the freedom its parents knew, but it would certainly know love—

"Thunder Traveling!"

Suddenly he was aware of the horseman riding out of the brush ahead, bursting into view on the trail taking them to *Tepahlewam.* It had to be one of his people, to call him by his given name rather than the *Shahapto,* or white, Christian name first given to his father. Like most of the Wallowa, Joseph had renounced the white man's religion when it failed to protect his people from the greed of those pale-skinned Shadows who first brought the *Book of Heaven* to the *Nee-Me-Poo,* along with plows to cut up the ground and their shovels to scratch for gold.

"Two Moons!" Joseph cried with no little joy. It was good to see this long-time friend, an older warrior and respected counselor. "You are up and about early! Going off to hunt here as the sun has barely begun its journey across the—"

"I came looking for you," Two Moons interrupted stonily.

"M-me?" he stammered a moment, instantly afraid. "It isn't . . . trouble for Cold Storm?"

"No," the older warrior said. "Your wife is in no trouble—"

"Has she delivered our child?"

"No, not that I know of."

Nonetheless, something in his belly gave him warning. "Then why do you come looking for me here before the rising sun has even entered the canyon?"

"To bring you back from the river," Two Moons declared. "Our people need you."

"For what purpose?"

"The camp is breaking up this morning, going back to their homes—"

"Going back?" Shaking his head in confusion, Joseph said, "We don't have to leave *Tepahlewam* until tomorrow—"

"They are fleeing. Last night they began to take down their lodges and bring in their horses—"

"Fleeing?"

"Some are going back to their homes," Two Moons explained. "But others say they are planning to go higher and higher still into the mountains where the soldiers won't find them."

He heard the women coming up behind him with those three laden travois, the poles scraping the canyon trail as his belly twisted with alarm. "*Sua-pies*? What of the soldiers?"

Two Moons let the tragic tale pour out, from the beginning of the taunts suffered by Shore Crossing to the return of the three killers with the horses and rifles of those white men they had murdered. "As soon as they reached our camp yesterday afternoon, nearly everyone cheered what the three young men had done to cover themselves in blood to start this war."

"How many Shadows did these foolish ones kill?"

"Five, I think."

"It—it doesn't have to be war," Joseph ruminated, his mind racing on what to do as Ollokot and the others came up to them.

Two Moons protested, "It's too late—"

"No, surely it's not too late. We can go to Monteith, have him send a runner to bring Cut-Off Arm here before the soldiers come looking to punish any of us."

"When the murderers returned, a few in the camp began to grieve because of what we knew would happen," Two Moons explained. "But most of the people went into celebration. Toohoolhoolzote and Sun Necklace organized a war party that rode off to seek out more of the white men who have wronged our people—"

"How many went with them?"

"Two-times-ten, no more than that."

His heart sank. Quietly he asked, "And what of old White Bird, and Looking Glass? Did they call for revenge and the blood of white men too?"

Shaking his head, the older warrior replied, "No. They did their best to stop things—but sadly most of the young men came from White Bird's band, the rest from Toohoolhoolzote's."

Overwhelmed with despair, Joseph reached out and grabbed a handful of Two Moons's shirt. "Did . . . did any of our people join this war party?"

"Only one, Geese Three Times Lighting on the Water."

Releasing his friend's shirt, Joseph only realized how angry he had become when that anger started to subside, the fire slowly being replaced by an undeniably hollow ache for what he now sensed was irrevocable, by a despair for what was now utterly inevitable.

"Perhaps as you say, we can still make some sort of peace," Two Moons advised gravely, the look on his face betraying his words of hope.

"We must pray it will be so." Joseph wanted to join in that hope with all his heart, but of all the Shadows he had known, there wasn't one he could turn to now. Not one he felt he could trust.

So Joseph rested his hand on the shorter man's shoulder and told Two Moons, "But even if we talk to Cut-Off Arm and make some sort of peace with him, because of what these three fools have done—because of what Sun Necklace's war party is on their way to do now—the white men will certainly take away everything we were going to have on the reservation. Now the soldiers will greedily strip us of what little would have been left us for our new life among the Treaty bands, just as the soldiers always do to those they defeat."

When he heard Ollokot sigh deeply, Joseph turned to gaze sadly at his brother.

"This time, Joseph . . . it is for our people to fight," Ollokot said. "Fight . . . or die."

"Mamma, I see Papa coming down the road."

The instant her four-year-old daughter, Emmy, raised the call, Isabella Benedict stepped out from behind the wet clothing she was hanging across the yard on a line strung between the house and the store and gazed down the path that led in from the White Bird Road.

"Looks like he didn't find none of them cows," she replied grumpily and pulled another wet shirt from the basket.

A fiery redhead of Irish ancestry, Isabella had married Canadian-born Samuel Benedict back in '63 when she was no more than fifteen. Four children later, she hadn't seen her thirtieth birthday. But she hadn't lost a drop of her spit and vinegar.

By gum, if he won't expect me to go looking for them cows now me own self, she thought as she lapped the damp shirt over the line and dug in her apron pocket for a clothespin. Then she stopped and stared again at her husband as he approached. Something was wrong, terribly wrong, with the way he was sitting that horse. Not riding it high and handsome, but clutching the horse like he was about to fall off. Now she saw that wasn't his horse.

"Isa—"

When Sam's voice choked off the way it did, she knew something was terrible wrong. And started walking, reminding herself to walk.

"Isa—Isabella!"

Then she was running, her long dress whipped between her lean legs like a damask table runner, her old ankle boots scuffing across the grassy yard to meet him.

"Mamma?"

"Stay with the little'un!" Isabella snapped at her daughter without stopping or turning, and kept running for Sam.

She was at his side the moment the strange horse came to a halt beneath the big tree that shaded the yard stretching between their wayside inn and the short path down to the mouth of White Bird Creek at the Salmon. He smiled weakly at her as he held out an arm. That's when she saw: nearly the entire back of his left leg was soaked with blood.

"Oh, Sam—what the hell you gone and done to yourself?" she asked as she dove in under his arm, throwing one of her own around his waist to pull him off the horse.

"Injuns," he growled as he dragged his right leg down and struck the ground on his left, grunting in pain.

"Injuns?"

"Sh-shot me," he groaned as the hottest pain seemed to pass. "Get me to the tree . . . there."

She did as he ordered. "Who, Sam?" And she knelt with him, letting him lean all his weight on her as they came down quickly onto the grass.

Benedict lay back against the tree trunk, gasping, his eyes half-closed. "Three of them little pricks."

Then she noticed his other leg, just as bloody if not worse. "Goddamn, they shot you more'n once!" she shrieked.

"I don't 'member no more'n one bullet," he gasped and opened his eyes. "Don't know how they got me in both legs, for they didn't get the horse."

"That ain't our horse, Sam."

He wheezed, "I know. Think it's Elfers's. The bastards took mine. Later on, this'un come up to me all by itself."

"Who? Who shot you, Sam?"

"One of 'em was in that bunch I run off two summers back," he said, squeezing her hand till it turned white. "I know he was."

"I'm gonna get some bandages; then we're gonna take you into the house where they can work on you—"

"No," he interrupted. "Get over here, Emmy."

The girl trotted over, her baby sister propped on her slim hip. "Papa—you're hurt."

"You gotta go for help, Emmy."

"Me, Papa?"

"Want you to take my horse and go fetch Hurdy Gurdy."

"Mr. Brown? You want me get him to help you?"

Isabella stood and took the baby girl from her daughter's arms. "Go do what your father tells you now. Get Mr. Brown and tell him come quick."

At that very moment some ninety miles north as the buzzard would fly, General Oliver Otis Howard was stepping onto the dock at Lewiston, accompanied by U.S. Indian Inspector Erwin C. Watkins. This was still a woolly frontier town, no matter how kind the description: a Snake River settlement growing hand-over-fist by the week, already sporting a grist- and a sawmill, a local newspaper, and quite a number of enterprising merchants making hay off the gold miners.

Two weeks earlier they had departed military headquarters in Portland for a tour of army posts and reservations in Howard's Department of the Columbia. Over the past year the general had grown increasingly irritated that he had to deal with as many as fourteen Indian agents in his region, each one of them wanting a little something different, perhaps a little something more from Howard's soldiers than the general was able to provide them.

"It is not scriptural to obey so many masters," he was fond of grousing about those carping and conniving civil servants who plagued his department.

But now the general had the large-boned Watkins along, and Watkins clearly outranked those mealy-mouthed, frustrating agents. Besides that, Howard simply liked Watkins as a man. A Civil War veteran like himself, the inspector was a hale-fellow filled with Christian wholesomeness as well as unbounded courage.

So with tomorrow, the fifteenth of June, being the deadline he had given the Nez Perce to be on the reservation, Howard had decided it would be prudent of him to return to this area in the event there was the slightest trouble with the Non-Treaty bands not living up to what they had agreed to do.

To greet Howard and Watkins as they stepped down the steamboat's gangplank was a small crowd of townsfolk, mostly curious people who showed up every time one of the steamers puffed its way upriver to Lewiston. On the dock stood the man in charge at Fort Lapwai, Captain David Perry.

Saluting the post commander, Howard next held out his hand and addressed Perry by his brevet, or honorary, rank. "How are things with Joseph, Colonel?"

"All right, by last accounts, General," Perry replied, then shook hands with Watkins before turning back to Howard. "The Indians are, I think, coming on the reservation without trouble."

That was the sweetest piece of news Howard had heard in years. He grinned within his neatly trimmed beard. "Praises be, gentlemen. We've circumvented a war by holding firm—steadfastly firm, I might add. I venture to say the Indian problem is all but put to rest now."

Charles Monteith, the agent's younger brother, who was serving as reservation clerk, finished introducing himself to Inspector Watkins, then told Howard, "The Indians appear to be acting in good faith, so we suppose they will make no trouble in coming in."

All around this group a small crowd of curious and interested Lewiston residents cheered those hopeful sentiments and gave the general three hearty huzzahs for dousing the fears of an Indian war. It had been a long, long time since Howard had experienced this kind of praise and adulation.

These people have been scared, he remembered. *They've been afraid for the better part of a year that war could break out at any moment, with the slightest provocation. But you've done it, Otis. By Providence! You've gone and saved them from a war!*

"Mr. Watkins has some matters to attend to here in Lewiston for the next two or three days," Howard announced as the small group turned and started toward the ambulance Perry had brought up from Lapwai.

"I'm seeing to the civilian contracts for the Umatilla and Nez Perce reservations," Watkins explained.

"Then I'll be taking you to the fort alone, General?" Perry asked.

"No, Colonel—I believe I can keep myself busy here in town," Howard told the officer. "Now that it appears affairs with the Nez Perce are quietly falling into place, I think I'm going to enjoy a few days of peace in Lewiston myself."

Chapter 13

Season of *Hillal*
1877

"You mustn't run away!" Joseph cried at a small group pushing past him on their way out of camp by the time he and Ollokot reached the village at *Tepahlewam*. "No reason to be afraid—you have done nothing wrong!"

"The soldiers will come looking for us!" White Bird wailed as he stepped up between the lodges. "All must join now. There is blood. We will be punished if we delay our escape!"

Joseph dismounted. "We look guilty when we run away," he explained.

White Bird shrugged, turning slightly to gesture at the frantic activities of those breaking camp. "I am afraid it is too late for talk now—the war has started. Look at these people—they are running for their lives before the soldiers come searching for the killers and find us instead."

"We must wait for the soldiers to come," Joseph protested. "Then we can make us some kind of peace with Cut-Off Arm. It would be better than running and fighting, because too many women and children will die—"

"Too late, too late," White Bird groaned, wagging his head.

"Why do you say it is too late?"

"I told Sun Necklace not to go; I argued with Toohool-hoolzote," White Bird explained, "said they mustn't take all my young men with them. That would leave my people with no protection when the soldiers come."

"But there doesn't have to be a fight when the soldiers come," Joseph consoled him.

"There will be a lot of fighting," White Bird whimpered in protest. "So we must join in the war now."

Joseph reached out and put his hand on the older man's shoulder. The venerable war chief turned and looked into Joseph's face. "Where will you go, White Bird?"

"*Sah-pah-tsas,*"* he answered with regret. "The Drive-In near the Red Rocks."

"Yes, on the Cottonwood." Joseph reached down and seized White Bird's wrist affectionately. "We will see you soon."

The old man gripped Joseph's wrist tightly, refusing to let go, and asked, "You are coming to join us there?"

"I don't know," and Joseph shook his head. "My wife— she is about to give birth."

"Her time is soon?"

"Perhaps today. Tomorrow at the latest."

Finally releasing the taller man's arm, White Bird scrutinized Joseph's eyes carefully, as if to read what lay behind them. "Will you turn your back on the rest of us and take the Wallowa into the reservation now?"

Sensing such heavy responsibility weighing upon his shoulders, Joseph said, "Some of my people will surely want to surrender now that there is trouble, now that the smell of blood is on the wind. But the Wallowa will gain nothing by giving up to the soldiers. No matter what has happened, who committed the murders . . . I know the white men will look at all the chiefs the same. In their eyes now, you and I and Looking Glass are equally as guilty as Toohoolhoolzote or Sun Necklace."

"Then we must run away to the hills and prepare to fight, Joseph."

He wagged his head sadly. "For now, I know we can't run away. We must have time to think, to figure out how to put out these first flames of war."

White Bird stared into the taller man's face, saying, "Those first flames are no longer small enough for you or me to put

---

*Also rendered in the historical literature as *Sapachesap,* a cave close to the traditional home of Looking Glass's people on the South Fork of the Clearwater River out, Joseph. Sun Necklace and his warriors are fanning the fire hotter. Already the flames are out of control."

"I cannot stand by and do nothing. I must do what I can," Joseph vowed.

"May the Creator guide your steps," White Bird said. "No matter what path you choose for your feet."

Without another word, White Bird turned away to rejoin his people already streaming away from *Tepahlewam.*

"Ollokot."

"Yes, Joseph."

"See that our people do not tear down their lodges and run away before I can talk to them."

Ollokot caught Joseph's arm and asked, "Where are you going?"

"To see my wife," he said, his eyes turning sad, "to learn if I have become a father again."

"What the hell you fellas doing back here so damn quick?" asked John J. Manuel as he stepped off the porch. The two horsemen brought their lathered mounts to an ungainly halt in the yard of the house Arthur Chapman had built at the mouth of Chapman Creek, here beside the White Bird.

"Never did get anywhere near Mount Idaho," explained forty-year-old Patrick Brice, an Irish immigrant who had come to Amerikay in the stinking hold of a ship filled with those who were fleeing the third potato famine to devastate the old sod.

Despite his seventy-four-year-old bones, James Baker swung out of the saddle like a young cavalryman and landed right in front of Manuel. "We see'd a war party up on the divide, John. Better clear out and pronto."

"Coming this way?" asked George Popham, Manuel's father-in-law, his eyes narrowing with concern as he stepped onto the porch.

"We damn well didn't stay long enough to ask 'em," Baker snorted, grabbing hold of Manuel's vest with one hand. "Now you gonna believe me and get your family out of here, son?"

"Where the hell us to 'spect us to go?" Manuel demanded defensively. This was the home he had bought from Chapman a few years back; this was his business—where his family was sinking its roots. He glanced quickly at his wife, then at his six-year-old daughter, Maggie. "They catch any of us out on the road to Grangeville, there ain't no getting back. Better we stay here—"

"My place," Baker huffed. "It's better'n yours here case they put us to siege. I cleared the trees clear round the place, and I got a good field of fire from ever' side of the house. And if they try to burn us out, I allays got that stone cellar they can't burn. You ain't got much time to get your family away from here, John."

A few hours earlier old man Baker had been down near the Salmon River Road when the Benedict girl came riding up the White Bird Trail, scampering for the Brown homestead bawling the news that her father had been shot through both legs by the Injuns and had just reached home, bleeding something terrible. So just before noon Baker gathered up his most trusted hired man, Conrad Fruth, and together they rode off for the Manuel place, a little more than a mile on up White Bird Creek, intent on spreading the alarm among the local folk.

At first he was planning to ride on over the White Bird Divide with Fruth, alerting the settlers near the Camas Prairie like Paul Revere himself, but at his first stop John Manuel talked him out of that notion.

"We don't know for sure what's going on," Manuel argued. "You know Sam Benedict's played hell with them Nez Perce, and they may just be squaring things with him. I doubt it's a war, Jim. Why don't you and Fruth go on back to your place? You both'll be one helluva lot safer there than you will be up on the divide, should any young bucks catch you two out with their blood all worked up over shooting Sam."

Baker had relented and taken Fruth back to his place down White Bird Creek. But the old man was back about an hour later, this time with Patrick Brice along. The Irish prospector wasn't about to sit around Baker's place and wait for a war party to come pay their respects. Together the three had decided that safety lay in numbers and ridden for the Manuel ranch. After John, his father-in-law, Baker, and Brice argued it all over again . . . Baker and Brice decided they would head off to Mount Idaho to let folks know something evil was afoot.

But here they were, back again, turned around by a band of horsemen they had spotted heading up the White Bird Divide.

"Them Injuns might've followed you boys back here. Damn it all," Manuel drawled, maintaining a strong vestige of his thick Virginia accent. He set his jaw, having come to a decision. "George, s'pose you get Jennet and the chirrun saddled up—"

"I ain't going, John," George Popham interrupted sternly. "I figure to stay here and fight 'em off when they come. That way, I'll give the rest of you a little more time to get clear of the place."

Manuel felt a sudden swell of sentiment burn in his breast as he gave his father-in-law a quick, fierce embrace. Amid the swirl of her long, honey-blond hair, Jennet Manuel pressed against her father the moment her husband, John, knelt to sweep up their eleven-month-old son from the porch.

Manuel held out his hand for his daughter. "C'mon, Maggie."

After Jennet had climbed into the saddle, John handed the boy up to his mother.

Patrick Brice stopped beside the horse and waited while John Manuel mounted, then hoisted six-year-old Maggie up behind her father. Brice stepped back from the horse. "I've decided to stay with George."

For a moment Manuel measured the immigrant with no small admiration. He cleared his throat and said, "Lock the doors ahint you, Patrick. There's extra shells in the chest by the door, and a rifle in the corner, too."

"Better you get now," Popham growled, slapping the rump on his daughter's horse.

"I love you, Father!" Jennet cried as they kicked their horses away from the house.

Baker spurred his animal to the front of the line, leading them downstream along the narrow trail. They were bound for the sanctuary of the old man's stone cellar. Just the place John Manuel figured he could keep his family safe from all harm.

Little Maggie had never seen her mother so frightened before. Jennet Manuel's tanned cheeks were almost pale as the bleached muslin of her apron by the time they got on horseback and started out of the yard.

The old man, clearly older than Maggie's own gran'pa, kicked his horse vigorously so he could ride in front of them all. Maggie clung to her papa like a deer tick, pressing her cheek against the damp warmth of his back.

"Christ Jesus in heaven!"

The moment that gray-bearded old man swore, Maggie poked her head around her papa's side to give a look, discovering some two dozen warriors suddenly appearing on the road that was taking them toward the Salmon—as if they had sprouted right out of the ground!

What devils they looked to be, their faces mean as they started shouting.

As close as the horsemen were to old man Baker, it was no wonder they hit him so many times with their arrows. Maggie could hear the bowstrings *pung, pung, pung* as the shafts were rapidly released. And she could hear the old man grunt as each one struck him, even though her papa was already wrenching their horse around, yelling at Mamma to get moving.

"They got me, Jack!" Baker cried as he flopped to the ground. "Good-bye!"

Maggie twisted herself around as far as she could while still clinging to her papa, finding Baker lying in the middle of the road, his chest, back, and arms bristling with the shafts. Then Maggie realized she and her father were in just as much danger as the warriors screeched and yowled, galloping their way. But the Indians weren't all using bows.

Maggie heard the *pop, pop* of the guns behind them . . . just before her father groaned and suddenly he wasn't there for her to hold onto anymore. She was just righting herself behind the cantle on the broad, bare rump of the horse when the first arrow pierced her upper arm.

Squealing in pain, she twisted to look at the shaft quivering halfway through her tiny arm, the pointed end glistening with her own blood. Before she could take another breath, the day got bright as a meteor show and she found herself on the ground.

With her head pounding like a drum, wondering why she was so dizzy and sick to her stomach, Maggie put her hand to the back of her head—feeling how the arrow had hit her skull, slashed along under the scalp, and was now hanging there beneath a flap of skin and her long blond hair, the same honey color as her mama's.

"C'mon, Maggie!"

"Mamma!"

Maggie was trying to stand, wobbly and stumbling about, when an Indian dismounted nearby, walked over to where her father lay groaning and clutching at the bloody wound in his hip. The warrior shot Papa in the back of the neck with an arrow. Maggie's father quit moving, stopped moaning.

"For the love of God, Maggie—run!"

Wheeling about at the sound of her mamma's warning, Maggie found her mother lunging to the ground and diving into the brush beside the road, the young boy straddling her hip. Following her mother into the timber, the girl cried out each time a twig or limb reached out to snag the arrow stuck through her bloody scalp, tearing at the lacerated skin like cruel fingers ripping off her hair, making a sound each time like someone ripping a strip of coarse muslin.

But she blindly followed her mamma's waist-length blond hair . . . running faster and faster—picking herself up after every fall to run ever faster because Maggie could hear the Indians closing in behind them, hooves pounding, voices bellowing and screeching.

Her mamma shrieked as she zigged this way and zagged that through the branches and undergrowth. Maggie wondered why her mamma had forsaken the trail and headed into the woods when it would have been easier and faster to escape if they stuck to the trail.

Then just as their house came in view through the tall trees, she heard the horsemen come alongside her on their heaving ponies, two of them lunging past her, their horses wet with lather as they raced up along either side of her mother. One of them reached out with his arm, swinging a short club at Mamma's back.

With that blow across her shoulders, Jennet Manuel stumbled, her eleven-month-old boy spilling from her arms as she spun to the ground with a shrill yelp of pain when her knee struck a large, exposed rock. She had barely rolled over onto her back, clutching her injured leg in both hands and sobbing, when the warrior with the club reined back, wheeled his pony, and dismounted near Maggie's mamma.

From the woman's throat burst an unearthly shriek as the warrior stepped between the sprawl of her legs and dropped to his knees.

Jennet Manuel flung herself onto her side, attempting to

crawl away, clawing for the little boy who sat sobbing just yards from her, swiping dirt and leaves from his face.

Maggie could see that her mother's cheeks were scratched, that her knee was badly cut and oozing, soaking through the dress the warrior flung aside as he shoved at his breechclout and dropped between her mamma's legs.

Two other Indians gathered to watch and pin her arms down as the white woman screamed and screamed beneath the first warrior. Maggie stood there, stunned—one of her tiny, bloody hands gripping the arrow shaft that pierced the other arm—mesmerized by how the warrior bounced up and down on her mother until Mamma quit screaming and began to sob, her mouth opening and closing, opening and closing, over and over again with no more sound than a pitiful squeak coming out as the Indian kept on bouncing atop her.

It wasn't until the warrior climbed back to his feet to stand there over Mamma that Maggie became aware of the loud voices coming from the direction of the house. Running to the edge of the trees where one of the two watchers seized her arm and spun her around, she looked up at the warrior and found his face painted, grinning down at her.

"Maggie!"

It was Gran'pa's voice. She called out to him at the house.

Then it seemed the edge of the timber came alive with more of the painted warriors. A whole line of them stepped out of the shadows there among the trees when two of them started yelling at the house in their Indian talk. Gran'pa talked Indian with them. Arguing, angry words. It must have pained him deeply to watch the Indian hurt his own daughter.

Maggie was wondering when Gran'pa was going to shoot the Indians and kill them all for what they had done to old man Baker, and her papa, and how they'd hurt Mamma too— when Gran'pa and the Irishman stepped from the doorway and stood stock-still on the porch for a moment. Then the two of them laid down their weapons, a rifle and a shotgun, at the edge of the steps, before turning to disappear into the house again.

Three of the warriors—a real old and wrinkled one, along with a young one and a man about as old as her own father— mounted up and rode their ponies to the house, where two of them leaned over and scooped up the firearms left at the edge of the porch.

With a whoop the pair raised the firearms in the air to show them to the others back at the line of trees as the three riders wheeled their horses and loped toward the timber. The warrior who had hurt her mamma let out a joyous yelp and leaped atop his pony to join the rest as they all rode off through the trees toward the Salmon with a clatter of hooves.

Maggie eventually turned at the sobs growing louder, finding Mamma dragging herself along the ground on one knee to reach Maggie's little brother still sitting there in the dirt, shrieking piteously, leaves stuck to his teary face and snotty, red nose.

"Oh God, oh God," Jennet Manuel kept repeating as she scooped up the boy and cradled him across her arm, wiping dirt from the child's mouth.

Maggie tried to reach up to swipe some tears from her cheek with that wounded left arm, and for the first time since she and her father had fallen from the horse, young Maggie sensed something wrong with that left hand that wouldn't do as she commanded.

Slowly lowering the arm, she studied her wrist curiously, realizing how bent it was, how the sharp bones poked against the inside of her skin.

Finally beginning to cry quietly, Maggie thought about the old man, thinking on how the Indians had killed Papa, too, on how they had hurt Mamma by wrestling with her on the ground.

But Gran'pa had given the Indians the weapons . . . and that had made the scary warriors go away.

Maggie sat cradling her misshapen arm across her lap, crying not so much for the pain in her broken wrist but because she knew nothing would be the same for any of them ever again.

Chapter 14

June 15, 1877

"You mean you ain't gonna do a damn thing about this?" Samuel Benedict shrieked in disbelief.

Wagging his head, H. C. "Hurdy Gurdy" Brown looked down at the seriously wounded Benedict lying there in the shade of an overhanging tree. "Sam," he began matter-of-factly, just the way a person always did when he was about to deliver unsettling news, "I figger them Injuns is only squaring accounts with you."

"S-squaring accounts!" Benedict yelped, his dismay hurting more for the moment than the wounds in both legs.

Brown was kneeling beside him, where he now patted Benedict's arm. "You know damn well how you been so hard on them Nez Perce, Sam. Shot up a bunch of them bucks, even killed one, too."

"The little pricks had it coming!" Sam growled as Brown stood beside him on creaky knees. "Shit, Brown—me getting shot don't mean all the rest of you ain't in big, big trouble, too!"

"I don't see no one else riding in here hollering that we got a war on, Sam," Brown said benignly, staring down at Benedict.

Sam couldn't believe Brown was taking all of this so calmly. "So you're just gonna ride on back home, easy as · you please?"

Brown glanced at Isabella Benedict, then said, "Looks to

be them bullets went right on through his legs, Mrs. Brown. I suggest you just wash them holes up real good with cold water and let 'em bleed till they start to knit on their own.''

"N-nothing else?" Isabella asked.

"Less'n you got some sulphur to pour in them holes, ain't much else a body can do with bullets what gone on through."

"Damn you, Brown," Benedict grumbled as he watched his neighbor turn away and shuffle toward his horse.

"You brought this on yourself, Sam," Brown said without turning around. He stopped as he reached his horse and flipped the reins over the animal's big head. "Better you thank your lucky stars them Injuns didn't get down off their ponies to finish the job they started on you, 'stead of riding off and leaving you for dead."

"When they come for you—," Samuel hollered as Brown swung up into the saddle and started from the yard, "don't 'spect me to come help you or yours!"

Benedict closed his eyes, his anger and disappointment still hurting more than his wounds . . . but those wounds were beginning to nag at him something fierce once more.

"You want I should get some cold water, Sam?" Isabella asked, kneeling at his elbow, pushing a sprig of red hair off the bridge of her nose.

"Yeah," he answered, opening his eyes and finding his wife's face near his.

"All right—we'll do what Brown said and wash them bullet holes."

"Damn his eyes anyway," Sam groused as he watched Isabella and the children start for the house.

By the time his wife was finished cutting slits in his canvas britches and dabbing water on the painful wounds, Sam heard the sound of approaching voices and footsteps.

"Isabella, get the children in the house!" he ordered, shoving her away. "Get 'em inside and bring me a gun now!"

The woman and children were just reaching the door when five unarmed men burst into the yard on foot. And they weren't dressed like Indians.

The moment one of the group called out to Isabella, Sam recognized the man: August Bacon, a Frenchman working a mining claim over on the west side of the Salmon.

"Bacon!"

Benedict watched the five wheel around to gaze at the tree

line, where they eventually spotted him lying in the shadows, then started his way.

After listening to Sam's story, the French miners decided they'd best return to their camp so they could retrieve their rifles and some ammunition.

"But I will stay," Bacon said. "Your woman will need someone to help you."

"Thank you," Sam whispered, glancing up as Isabella stepped over with a rifle in one hand while the four miners turned away for the Salmon in a hurry. He said to Bacon, "While them others is gone for your guns, maybe you can help my wife get me into the house."

"What is this one?" Bacon asked as Mrs. Benedict handed the Frenchman her husband's rifle. He turned it over and over in admiration.

"That there's the finest breechloader I own, Bacon," Sam declared as he painfully dragged his feet under him, ready to pull himself up against the tree trunk. "It'll knock down a horse anywhere from here clear to the river, and make a hole big enough you can shove your fist through one of the red pricks."

"Good."

"Believe me," Benedict vowed with a grunt as the Frenchman knelt, shoving his shoulder beneath Sam's armpit and rising with him, "you'll want that rifle when those sons of bitches come for us."

Harry Mason wasn't the sort to get scared at the first frantic alarm given by any of his skittish neighbors, but then . . . he wasn't the sort not to be ready for trouble either. He was smart enough to know that men like him and Sam Benedict shared the worst reputations among the Nez Perce, neither of them missing an opportunity to skin any of the Injuns on a trade, cheat them here and there when they could, and generally be hard on the red-bellies.

So any news of Indian trouble just naturally got Harry Mason's attention.

Along about two o'clock when William Osborn rushed into Mason's store to sound off about the Indians killing a couple of Frenchmen over on John Day Creek, Harry was napping on a cot in the corner of his store beside the White Bird. Two days before, while driving some cattle down the road into some new pasture, he had injured his right eye when he snapped himself with the frayed end of the bullwhip he was using to herd the cows. Bright light brought a fierce pain to the eye, gave it a sandy, gritty feel, just the way it had back in Massachusetts when he went snow-blind as a youngster.

Turns out, Harry hurt himself with the same whip he had used earlier that very spring to drive off a pair of young Nez Perce warriors, lashing them from his store and right on out of the yard.

So for the better part of two days now he had been lying here, while his sister, Helen, and her husband, Edward Walsh, ran the place for him till that eye no longer troubled him. Just now, Harry was beginning to think he might make do with some sort of eye patch, maybe even a dark bandanna tied around his head so that it lay across that right eye and he could keep the left one open, when his brother-in-law came flying in with the news.

Mason and William Osborn had ended up marrying sisters back in '67, a few years after both men came west in search of Idaho gold. There never had been an abundance of women out here. But a couple years ago Harry's Anna took sick and died after a grueling struggle that quickly sucked everything out of her. That left him alone to work the store and the rest of it until he finally convinced his sister, Helen, that she and her husband needed to come west, where Edward Walsh could make a living for himself. Without that arm Ed lost to the war against the Confederacy, Walsh wasn't doing well. Harry Mason always had been the sort to take in family, put a roof over their heads, and give his kin some gainful work to do.

When Osborn left to warn his wife about the Indians killing those Frenchmen, Mason sat on the edge of his cot and with that one good eye studied those three employees of his who had gathered around the small checker table in his store to smoke their pipes and tell their outlandish stories as they whiled away the afternoon, seeing as how Harry didn't have anything better for them to do until the cows needed to be brought in from the upper pasture that evening. Those three hands—William George, Frank "Frenchie" Chodoze, and old man Shoemaker—just sat there dumbly looking at one another, then at Harry, as if they were waiting for Mason to decide for them what they should do about the Indian scare.

"Get me that needle gun down from behind the counter, Frenchie," he instructed François Chodoze. "And grab that cleaning rod, them rags, too, under the counter for me."

One by one the men got up and started to move about the store, retrieving their own and Mason's weapons.

"William," Harry called to the youngest of his employees, "want you to go spread the word on down the creek from here."

"The word?"

"See you get to all the places between here and the Salmon. Tell 'em what we heard: the redskins killed two Frenchmen upriver on John Day."

George rode off and the other two men took to working over the weapons with Harry—unloading, cleaning and oiling, then reloading every one of the rifles and revolvers just in case the killing of those two Frenchmen was no isolated, random attack.

William George hadn't been gone for more than a few minutes when he came scurrying back, bringing an aged miner with him. "Bumped into Koon on the trail, Harry. G'won—tell Harry what you know."

Clearing his throat, the tobacco-toothed Koon said, "They did their damnedest to kill Sam Benedict this morning."

Harry shook his head, "Sam's a hard-ass on them Indians. Likely this is all over something Sam started with his shooting at 'em a while back."

Koon licked his lips and protested, "Sounds to me like them Injuns is out killing folks."

"Them Frenchmen, and now they shoot up Sam Benedict," Harry pondered dolefully, rubbing the gritty eye. "William, I want you and Koon to head up to the Baker place. Tell that old fella to hurry on in here. I figure our buildings are easier to defend, sitting here in the middle of the wide open the way we are."

William George nodded. "I'll take that fast horse of your'n."

Then Harry concluded, "Tell everyone else you run across on the way there and back to bring their families here, too. Tell 'em we got the strongest place right here to hide their women and children, up on the mountain right behind our place. Now, go."

* * *

"Jennie! Looks like we got company for the night!" hollered Benjamin B. Norton as he heaved himself out of the wicker chair on his front porch and stood, watching the two freight wagons approach, each pulled by a six-horse hitch as they rumbled heavily into the yard of his wayside road-ranch and stage-stop raised here at the foot of Craig's Mountain to serve travelers plying the road that pierced the pitch and heave of the Camas Prairie between Lewiston and Grangeville.

Jennie Norton stepped out the open front door, grinding the flour on her hands into the apron tied around her waist. Behind her came their nine-year-old son, Hill, and Jennie's sixteen-year-old sister, Lynn Bowers.

"It's Lew and Pete all right," Norton called as he descended the four steps into the spacious yard of Cottonwood House, a combination hotel, saloon, general store, and horse-breeding ranch Norton ran some eighteen miles northwest of Grangeville, Idaho, near the headwaters of Shebang Creek.

Luther P. Wilmot waved to those on the porch as he pulled back on the reins, then leaned against the brake squealing in protest. He turned on the high spring seat to watch his partner, Pete Ready, bring his bright-green, high-walled Pittsburgh freighter to a halt directly behind his.

"Bound for Mount Idaho, are you, Lew?" Norton asked as he shook hands with Wilmot the moment the teamster dropped to the ground.

Jabbing a thumb at his wagon, Wilmot said, "Yep. Supplies for the Vollmer and Scott store." He turned to Mrs. Norton and nodded politely. "Howdy, Jennie."

She smiled. "Lew, you and Pete care to stay for supper?"

"Don't believe we will this evening," Wilmot refused as he peered at the sky. "Still a lot of light left, so we'll get on down the trail a ways till we're forced to camp for the night."

"Hill's gonna be disappointed," Norton warned, gesturing to his son. "Way out here, why . . . the boy hankers for a new face and new stories. Sure we can't get you fellas to stay?"

"Nawww," Wilmot repeated. "We'll take a cool drink from your spring, though."

The three men started toward the corner of the house. Looking over his shoulder to find that his son had not followed them, Benjamin Norton asked in a whisper, "What you hear of Injun troubles?"

Ready and Wilmot stopped in their tracks. "Injun troubles?" Wilmot echoed. "Don't know nothing 'bout no Injun troubles."

"You haven't seen any of the bucks out?"

Ready shook his head. "Ain't seen an Injun since we got past Lapwai, Ben."

"Why you asking?" Wilmot inquired suspiciously.

Norton glanced again at the porch guardedly, then said, "There's been talk the past couple days, 'bout them Non-Treaty bands gathered down at the lake near the Split Rocks. Time for 'em to go on in like the army ordered 'em to."

"What sort of talk?" Ready asked.

Norton wagged his head. "Just that . . . folks around here feel there's something afoot."

This time it was Wilmot who asked, "Been any trouble?"

Ben shrugged. "Dunno for sure, fellas. Hell, with us being stuck way out here so far a piece from Mount Idaho and Grangeville too, why . . . I was hoping the two of you might tell me what's up with the Injuns."

"Ever'thing I've heard says the Nez Perce are being peaceable," Wilmot explained. "Last I knowed before we rode up to Lewiston, they had their women and children with 'em over on Camas Prairie, which means they ain't fixing up no war parties. If they was planning on making some raids, them bucks would first see to getting their families away somewhere safe, put the women and kids where the soldiers couldn't get to 'em. I wouldn't pay no mind to any rumors you hear from some of them scared ones, Ben."

Norton pursed his lips thoughtfully a moment, then admitted, "S'pose you better call me a nervous Nellie, Lew."

At the sound of footsteps the three men turned to find Jennie Norton appearing around the corner of the house.

She grinned apologetically and asked, "What you men up to here?"

"We come over here so the children couldn't hear us, dear," Ben explained. "Lew and Pete haven't heard a thing of trouble."

She told the freight men, "I think you ought to stay."

Wilmot glanced at Ready and said, "Figger to push on, Jennie."

Mrs. Norton faced the teamsters. "You may say nothing's going to happen, but too many folks been talking over at Mount Idaho, and Grangeville too."

"That's only talk," Ready tried to reassure the woman.

"There's enough omens, fellas," she argued. "But even if you're right, sure would make me feel a lot safer if the two of you could stay for the night."

Wilmot flicked a glance at his freighting partner, then told her, "I'm sorry, Jennie. We gotta make good time. Need to be in to Mount Idaho afore noon tomorrow with these supplies or we get docked by Vollmer for getting in late. Listen, if them bucks was out doing their devilmost, we'd seen something of 'em, wouldn't we?"

"So you won't stay?" she repeated.

"No, we can't," Wilmot apologized. "Sorry that you're feeling less'n safe. But I'd sure like to get home to my own family."

She drew her lips into a straight, grim line, then said, "You two fellas have a safe trip."

The three of them watched Jennie turn and head for the house, disappointment in her walk.

"Didn't mean to upset your missus, Ben," Wilmot said.

"We're all a little jumpy past few days," Norton expressed as all three heard the sound of hoofbeats and turned toward the spur that connected the road-ranch with the nearby Mount Idaho–Lewiston Road.

As the lone rider slowed out front, the trio stepped around the corner of the house and into the yard to greet the horseman.

"By damn, thought it looked like you, Lew!" Wilmot cried out.

Swinging down from the saddle, Lewis Day held out his hand. "Luther P. Wilmot! You going or coming with your wagons?"

"Bound for Mount Idaho," Wilmot said.

Day shook hands with Ready and Norton, then said, "On my way to the commander at Fort Lapwai with a message from L. P. Brown."

It was almost as if a drop of January ice water suddenly spilled down Norton's backbone. "Message?"

Day nodded. "Too many of them Injuns acting too unfriendly last few days. Loyal figgers their war chiefs is working 'em up for one last hurrah now that they gotta be on the reservation tomorrow."

"How you know that?" Wilmot demanded.

"Couple fellas seen 'em practicing war manuevers out there at the Rocky Canyon lake," Day explained. "So all the folks for miles around are streaming into Mount Idaho for protection."

"Can you stay the night?" Norton asked, glancing over his shoulder at the house. "I know it'd make Jennie feel safer."

Day turned to Wilmot and Ready, then to Norton. "I really can't—gotta push on soon as I can borrow a fresh horse off Ben here—but these two fellas might stay."

"They're pushing on too," Ben said in resignation.

"We've got ground to cover afore bedding down for the night," Ready explained to Lew Day.

"C'mon then," Norton said as he started them toward the barn where he kept many of his prized horses. " 'Cept for my stallion, you can have your pick of the three best runners, Lew."

Chapter 15

June 14, 1877

She was hunched over in her garden, pulling up spring on-
ions and a small head of big-leafed lettuce to add to the
supper she had heating over the fire in the house, when Isabella Benedict noticed that it had grown cooler.

Straightening, with the basket suspended from one forearm, she looked to find the sun just then slipping out of sight
beyond the hills across the Salmon just down White Bird
Creek. Amazing, she thought, just how quickly it became cool
once the sun had abandoned the sky in this country, even of
an early summer night.

Taking only two steps toward the house, Isabella stopped,
brushed a long sprig of red hair out of her eyes, then suddenly
spotted them on the hillside above the house. The heathens
were just sitting there, watching her. Sure enough planning
what they would do to her if they got their hands on a white
woman.

But rather than running, rather than showing them she
even knew they were there, Isabella turned slowly and continued to the house. Once inside, she flung her basket down
beside the fireplace where she had started supper and went
to the tiny room just off the parlor where Samuel lay on a
small, low bed.

"They've come, Husband," she announced as the girl carried her little brother across her hip into the room.

Benedict was raising himself up on an elbow when the

Frenchman stopped at the doorway to the small room. Samuel looked at the miner. "You got shells in your pocket?"

August Bacon patted both pockets. "They won't get in your house."

"Go to the door and keep watch for 'em while I send my family away."

"Away?" Isabella repeated two octaves higher with shrill despair.

"Take the children and get into the woods," Sam ordered.

"And you?"

"I'll hide here, Isabella," he snapped. "Now go."

She bent to kiss him on the mouth, then ran her fingers down his cheek, saying only, "Sam. Sam."

Then she turned, sweeping the children before her, herding them toward the back door and into the side yard, where she headed straight for the gate that would lead them to a path winding back into the hills.

But Isabella had no more than reached the gate and swung it open when she spotted the three horsemen approaching from that last stand of trees up the path. She and the children didn't stand a chance getting to the timber.

"Get back!" she hissed at her four-year-old daughter, reaching out to snatch the baby from Emmy's hip.

Together they wheeled and sprinted back to the house, diving in through the back door as she heard the horses, even heard the savages' voices behind her as the Indians reached the gate. She heard it clatter open when one of them swung the gate so hard it struck the garden fence with a violent, noisy crack.

Sprinting through the parlor, Isabella reached the small room. "Sam!" Frightened to find her husband gone from his bed.

At the loud, booming roar of a nearby gunshot, she wheeled in a swirl of her skirt, knocking down the small toddler. "Get behind me!" she shouted at the children.

Then came a smattering of rifle fire from the Indians, their bullets smacking against the house, one of them shattering something made of pottery on a shelf in the pantry, another bullet clanging against a cast-iron kettle or skillet. She was turning back into the parlor just as she heard the wind slammed out of the Frenchman's lungs in one loud gust, watching Bacon being driven backward in the air, landing on the floor right at her feet.

Isabella saw the smear of shiny crimson where the miner had slid across the floorboards before he came to a stop. Bacon looked up at her, gurgling, his lips moving as his fingers patted the dark, damp petals of the blood blooming on his chest. The fingers stopped moving as she watched, his lips, too. Then his eyes no longer blinked and she could smell how he had soiled himself at the moment he died.

Emmy screamed, lunging against her mother, as Isabella watched the warriors break through the front door. Clutching both her children against her when the Indians stepped close, she steeled herself—ready for them to kill her, even to dishonor her, which men like her husband had always called "a fate worse than death itself."

But at least she would live, able to go in search of Samuel. As the ugly warrior with the twisted grin stepped up before her, Isabella swore she would never tell Sam how they had shamed her. And she would make the children promise never to tell their father what they had watched.

"You go nah," the warrior said in nearly understandable English.

"Wh-what?" she stuttered in utter surprise, not comprehending that this painted, blood-splattered warrior could speak her tongue.

"Go," he repeated and turned slightly, pointing at the door. "You go nah."

Gulping, Isabella nodded dumbly. "We'll g-go."

She started toward the door, stepping over the blood smeared on the floor, smelling the dead Frenchman's bowel stench, the hem of her long skirt slurring through the long, gleaming patch of crimson.

"Go Man-well huss," the warrior said, his strange words catching her at the door.

"Man-well?" she asked as she turned back to the Indian. "Oh, Manuel. Yes."

"Man-well huss."

"Huss?" she repeated that word, too. "H-house?"

"Yesss, huss. Uh-ther woe-man at Man-well huss."

Must be he was referring to Jennet, she thought. Another woman was already there. So, was he saying that woman was safe there?

"Thank you—I'll go now," she said quietly, sensing deep-felt gratitude for this savage who was freeing her. Isabella Benedict folded her children against the billows of her bloody dress and pushed a path for them through the two dozen warriors, saying, "I'll take my children to the Manuel house."

"General, sir?"

Howard turned, finding his former aide-de-camp, the post's officer of the day, saluting at the open doorway. "Major."

Then the officer turned to Captain Perry and clicked his heels together, saluting again. "Colonel?"

"Something urgent, Major Boyle?" Perry asked as he returned the officer's salute and used the man's brevet rank.

"A message addressed to you from Mount Idaho, sir. Brought in by a civilian courier." Captain William H. Boyle held out the twice-folded paper between them.

"Thank you for your prompt attention to this, Captain," Perry replied, beginning to open the message.

"Do you wish me to wait while you read it, Colonel?"

"By all means," and Perry's voice trailed off as his eyes danced over the scrawl.

Howard watched the first deep furrow crease Perry's brow but waited until the post commander finished reading what plainly was important enough that it was carried here by courier across some sixty-two miles of all-but-uninhabited frontier.

With the growing warmth of that late afternoon, Howard slowly removed his heavy coat, folded it neatly, and laid it over the back of the chair here in Perry's office at Fort Lapwai that fourteenth day of June. That morning the post commander had managed to prevail upon Howard not to remain in Lewiston while Watkins went about his business of securing supplies for the next six months. With the captain's insistence, Howard finally agreed that he would be more comfortable out at the fort while they awaited the arrival of the Non-Treaty bands. The two of them had no more than made that twelve-mile ride from Lewiston to reach Perry's office when the Fort Lapwai quartermaster and officer of the day showed up with the message.

"The citizens of Mount Idaho are in an uproar," Perry began his explanation. "This comes from their spokesman, L. P. Brown. He owns an inn and a store there as I recall."

"An uproar?" Howard repeated, settling in the chair against his folded coat.

"Brown writes that many of the settlers in the area are very concerned with the large gathering of the Non-Treaty bands near Rocky Canyon."

"What have these citizens got to be concerned about?" Howard felt himself bristling. "Isn't the Nez Perce gathering on the Camas Prairie less than a day from the reservation? This message from Brown only confirms that the Non-Treaty bands are but a matter of miles from surrendering tomorrow, right on schedule."

"Brown says it's been reported to him that the bands camped at the lake have become insolent and their actions indicate trouble from them."

"Trouble?"

"The warriors have been parading around full of bluster, and they're boasting that they will fight any soldiers sent to put them onto the reservation. They've come into town to buy ammunition and powder too."

"So it sounds as if this Brown fellow is duly alarmed?"

Perry shook his head. "That's the strangest thing, General. He says he isn't alarmed—just thought it well to inform me of what was going on among the bands. He says they are on the lookout for the soldiers coming. So, he nonetheless ended his letter by requesting that I send troops. Hmmm, here it is—'as soon as you can, a sufficient force to handle them without gloves, should they be disposed to resist.' "

The general waited a moment for Perry to continue reading, but when the captain did not, Howard asked, "So what are you disposed to do in this situation, Colonel?"

Perry's face relaxed. "I trust Brown's assessment of things, General. Come morning, I think I'll send a couple of men with an interpreter down to Mount Idaho to see for ourselves what the state of things is."

"If nothing else," Howard agreed, "I figure you'll placate the settlers that you're doing *some*thing about their complaints, Colonel."

"Then you agree with my response to this message, sir?"

"By all means, Colonel," the general answered. "Send out your party in the morning and we'll find out for ourselves just what in God's name has got those civilians so stirred up down there."

*   *   *

Lew Wilmot and Pete Ready got their cool drink from the spring while Lew Day walked off with Ben Norton to have his pick of the horse breeder's finest for the final leg of that ride of his to Fort Lapwai.

In a matter of minutes, Day was re-saddled and heading north, disappearing around a bend in the trail, as the teamsters were climbing back onto their wagon seats, intending to cover a few more miles before darkness forced them to stop for the night. Just about the time they were ready to slap leather down on the backs of those twelve freight horses, a small wagon rumbled into sight, rattling off the road and into the Norton yard, a high wheel spinning until it clattered back onto the ground.

John Chamberlin sat perched on the springless seat; behind him his pregnant wife and their two young children huddled in the wagon bed. Hungry for any news after two days of rumors had compelled them to make for Cottonwood House, Chamberlin hung on every word as Norton, Wilmot, and Ready related the latest rumors of Indian trouble brewing over at the Rocky Canyon lake. With the way his missus was latched onto her husband's arm, it was no small wonder that Chamberlin begged Wilmot and Ready to stay the night.

"I already asked 'em to, John," Ben Norton grumped.

Chamberlin looked squarely at Wilmot. "You're the best shot in these parts, Lew. Case there's trouble, my family would be much obliged to have you and your rifle with us."

"Everything's gonna be fine," Wilmot soothed. He heaved the brake forward and slapped the reins down again. "Hep! Hep!"

As the two freighters rolled out of the yard, Norton stepped back and rested an elbow on one of Chamberlin's iron tires, watching the teamsters disappear down the road for Mount Idaho. "You figure on staying here for the night?"

"Was hoping we could," John Chamberlin admitted.

"I think Jennie would feel a whole lot better if I packed her and the others up and we headed for Grangeville," Norton explained.

"Head out in the morning?"

"No. She's wanting to go right now," Norton admitted.

After glancing at his pregnant wife a moment, Chamberlin

nodded. "I think that'd be for the best, Ben. If you don't mind, we can unload these sacks of flour and make room for you folks in the back here. That way you don't need to take the time to hitch up another wagon."

Nodding in agreement, Norton pushed away from the wagon, heading for the porch. "I'll get Jennie to make up a bag of what she needs for a few days and we'll get started—"

At the sound of approaching hooves, Chamberlin suddenly twisted sideways on the wagon seat and Norton turned on his heels, starting for the back of the wagon. Out of the trees burst Lew Day on that racehorse of Norton's, its magnificent head held low, those four white socks flashing in the last of the afternoon's light with every eight-yard lunge the legs took. Instead of gripping the reins, Day had his white knuckles locked around the saddle horn.

Ben Norton found his heart hammering as loudly as those oncoming hooves, his mouth instantly gone dry: Day couldn't have been gone more than fifteen minutes, twenty at the most.

Ben's hired man, F. Joseph Moore—who had originally sold Cottonwood House to the Nortons, then promptly went to work for the new owners—stepped out of the barn as the lathered horse sprinted into the yard with Day dragging back on the reins, grunting with painful gusts each time the high-bred racer sidestepped, hoof-chattering, to a halt.

Norton bounded up. "Lew! What the devil you doing b—"

"Injuns!" Day cried in interruption, his eyes wild with fear.

"Damn, but you're shot!" Joe Moore exclaimed as he trotted up from behind.

"Bastards got me," Day gritted out the words as he peered back over his right shoulder at the damp stain.

Moore and Norton held up their hands, helping the horseman out of the saddle.

"What in blazes happened?" Chamberlin asked as the other two men sat Day down right there in the middle of the yard.

"I spotted three or four of 'em on up the road some," Day began. "Near the Old Board House, up against Craig's Mountain."

"I'm going to get Jennie and some bandages," Mrs. Chamberlin promised as she clutched her swollen belly and climbed down with a rustle of her skirts brushing over the wagon seat.

"They jump you outta ambush?" Norton asked.

"Nawww," and Day winced as Chamberlin gently probed around the entry wound at the back of his right shoulder. "They did their best to act friendly, and the bastards even rode with me a while—but I had a bad feeling, so I figgered I'd stir the pot and see if the soup come to a boil. Told 'em I was getting cold with the sun going down and wanted to ride faster, so when I got that racer of yours pulled ahead of 'em . . . the red niggers fired on me."

"Shot you in the goddamned back!" Chamberlin growled.

"When they did, I kicked that horse for the thick timber a mile on down the road," Day confessed. "That's where I fell outta the saddle and pulled the horse into the brush with me."

"The sonsabitches follow you?" Norton asked.

"That they did, Ben. But back in the timber the way I was, I held 'em off till they decided to give up shooting and ride off."

"Must've thought your scalp wasn't worth the trouble, eh?" Chamberlin asked wryly.

Day watched Jennie Norton coming down the steps, her hands filled, the two Chamberlin youngsters right behind their mother. "Soon as I figured they was gone, I pulled myself into the saddle, held on tight all the way here."

"God's grace got you here," Jennie Norton said as she handed Joe Moore the cotton strips, then slipped two of her fingers inside the hole poked in the back of Day's shirt. With one smooth movement she ripped the fabric so she could peer closely at the wound in the fading light. She made a clucking sound; then the woman declared, "Glory be, if it wasn't by God's grace alone got you here, Lew Day!"

Chapter 16

Season of *Hillal*
1877

Bewildered, Shore Crossing watched Sun Necklace talk briefly with the white woman; then—like the woman at the last place they raided—he let this one go free with her children too.

Sun Necklace had grown very, very angry when he discovered Red Elk had raped the first woman, so angry the fighting chief struck Red Elk across the cheek with the back of his hand, the way a man would strike an errant woman. To shame him.

Then the chief had ordered his own son, Red Moccasin Tops, and Shore Crossing as well to accompany him out of the trees to the white man's building where the two Shadows had appeared and willingly laid down their firearms. Shore Crossing picked up the shotgun, and Red Moccasin Tops retrieved the rifle before Sun Necklace ordered the war party to abandon the place.

Leave?

Shouldn't they have killed those two Shadows? Shore Crossing brooded. But he had bitten his tongue and ridden away from that house with the others. Red Elk brought up the rear, sullenly licking his pride.

But now as the woman shuffled her children into the growing darkness, Shore Crossing could keep quiet no more.

"Fighting chief," he said, turning and stepping up before

Sun Necklace, "I do not understand why you are letting the woman go. Just as you freed the last woman—"

"We do not make war on women," Sun Necklace snapped. "The white man's soldiers do . . . but we do not make war on women."

"But, Uncle—that one was the bad whiskey man's woman. She had a hand in shooting at your son, and a hand in killing the lame one called *Dakoopin*."

Instead of throwing his anger back at Shore Crossing, Sun Necklace turned and flicked an angry glance at his son. "Red Moccasin Tops knows that a *Nee-Me-Poo* warrior does not harm the helpless. There is no honor in that, Shore Crossing. Didn't my son kill the whiskey man who shot him?"

Red Moccasin Tops answered for himself, "Yes, Father. Early this morning."

"Then to kill women and children would be beneath a warrior's standing," Sun Necklace said, turning to glare at Shore Crossing.

The war chief stepped outside the door to address the rest of the warriors impatiently clamoring at the front of the house after the woman fled. "This is the place that sells guns and bullets to the other Shadows. Look for those guns and bullets, now. And, remember, this is the whiskey man's home—look carefully so you can find his whiskey. I am very thirsty for it!"

Samuel Benedict lay belly-down in a clump of brush some thirty yards from the northwest corner of his house.

The pain in his legs came and went in slowly rising waves so severe that when he finally admitted he could not take any more Sam bit down on a short twig his fingers discovered in the grass after he crawled here in his escape.

When the Frenchman and Isabella got him inside and onto the small bed near the parlor that connected the house with the store, Benedict tried to sleep. He had been awakened by Isabella's sudden cry of alarm, opening his eyes to find that the sun had fallen and twilight was imminent. He ordered her to flee with the children, and as soon as they were on their way he grabbed for his pistol on the bedside table, finding it wasn't loaded.

Just as he was going to shout at Bacon to bring him some cartridges, Benedict heard the Frenchman yelling that the Indians had reached the front yard. Stuffing the pistol under the mattress, Sam twisted painfully off the bed and onto the floor, crabbing to the nearby window, where he pushed up the sash, then hoisted himself over the sill and dropped to the damp ground. From there he started to crawl, somehow got to his feet—

—just as he heard the big breechloader boom. His heart exulted for the Frenchman . . . when Sam heard the crack of those lighter carbines. It sounded like a dozen or more shots. Then he waited for Bacon to answer back with the breech-loader a second time.

But he never heard the big gun fire again.

By the time he reached the brush thirty or more yards from the house on his way down to the river, Benedict owned up that the brave Frenchman was likely dead.

As he lay there in the grass, Sam wondered what the little pricks were doing in the house. Every now and then he could hear something breaking, but he could not be sure what the devil was going on because he was hiding way back here, far from the front of the place. Probably for the best.

Yet, as the minutes crawled past, Samuel Benedict came to realize that those red niggers weren't going to wait for darkness to continue their rampage. Some of them came around the corner of the house, inspecting the ground. They pointed off in his general direction, then disappeared again. He figured the sons of bitches were bound to come looking for him soon.

But if he could reach the footbridge across White Bird Creek . . . he might be a lot safer on the other side. Cover himself with leaves and hide till morning.

Though it hurt him to pull himself to his feet against a sturdy birch sapling, Benedict started forward, the twig still clenched between his teeth. If he could make it across the creek . . .

Step by agonizing step he teetered toward the footbridge through the fading light of that afternoon—inching along so slowly that he had time to select his steps so that he wouldn't make a lot of noise busting through the brush. Then no more than fifteen yards of open ground was all that lay between him and the creek bank. He'd make a fine target of himself as he stumbled for the end of the bridge—

Almost there, Sam heard them coming. Thinking if he

could just lie flat on the bridge they might not see him.

But from the way the red bastards suddenly began to yelp he knew they had spotted him.

There at the edge of the water he reached out and grabbed for the two rope spanners, dragging himself forward with that first clumsy lunge onto the bridge. Benedict looked over his shoulder, his attention drawn to the crowd of warriors. One of them stepped away from the others, slowly bringing a rifle to his shoulder.

It was the little red prick who had shot him that morning!

The muzzle spat a long tongue of flame before he could duck. An unseen fist slammed him in the chest and hurtled him into the air, tumbling, spinning. A moment later Samuel Benedict sensed the sudden, surprising cold of White Bird Creek swallow him whole.

"Look there, Brother!" Shore Crossing cried to his cousin as he burst out of the brush not far behind the wounded Shadow.

The light was fading, but he was certain it was the same white man they had confronted on the trail early that morning.

"I see! It's the whiskey man!" Red Moccasin Tops roared as he stepped from the edge of the group.

The rest who had joined Shore Crossing in following the blood spots and tracks halted immediately and let Sun Necklace's son continue alone.

"I thought you killed him this morning, Nephew!" Big Morning chided.

Red Moccasin Tops whirled, fury on his face, the new rifle before him. "I shot him, yes. Both of us saw him. He was dead, Uncle."

"Then who is that?" Bare Feet demanded as the Shadow stumbled onto the rope-and-plank footbridge crossing White Bird Creek.

Growling, Red Moccasin Tops whirled back to face the whiskey trader. He started marching toward the Shadow. "This one? Why—he is a dead man!"

The bullet from his carbine struck the Shadow so hard it spilled the whiskey peddler backward over the thick rope that served as one of the bridge's handrails. After somersaulting twice, the Shadow hit the noisy, snow-swollen water and started floating downstream, past the warriors, who hurried to the creek bank to see what became of him for themselves.

Face-down, arms and legs spread, the body cartwheeled slowly around in the current as it was washed into the middle of the stream. For a moment the dead man's foot caught an overhanging branch, but the body soon tilted and was freed to float on out of sight for the Salmon.

"Now he will stay dead!" Red Moccasin Tops bellowed in triumph. "Back to the whiskey trader's house! I have grown as thirsty as my father!"

Once allowed to flee the house with her daughters, Isabella Benedict reached the thick timber and tall brush sheltering the bank along White Bird Creek. Here within earshot of the gurgling, rushing stream, she settled down within the bushes with her two children to watch the warriors moving about in her house as the afternoon light continued to ripen.

A handful or more warriors suddenly streamed out of the house, knelt in the yard, and one of them pointed at the ground—before immediately taking off for the creek.

They swept right on by her, entering the trees not far from where Isabella cowered with her babies. The heathens were off on some deadly errand.

She was still choking on something sour, something hard to swallow, thinking it must be her thundering heart that had risen into the back of her throat. Still not quite able to believe they had let her go, telling her to hightail it for the Manuel place. Telling her they had allowed another woman her freedom . . . wondering again if it was Jennet. Could it be that these savages weren't really killing every white man, woman, and child in sight—not really raping every female old enough to give the smelly bucks their horrid pleasures?

It had to be a trick, a terrible trick, she convinced herself as she huddled there, clutching her children close, feeling her oldest girl sobbing silently, no sound, only the unsteady quaking as Emmy shook against her mother's rib cage beneath the shelter of that arm.

A single gunshot startled her. That wasn't a weapon fired from the house, but from the bunch that had rushed past her hiding place not too long ago. She waited and waited for more gunfire, then figured the warriors must be getting spooked themselves, shooting at ghosts.

Agonizing minutes later, the same bunch emerged from the trees and returned to the house.

She waited them out. A long time. Listening as they ransacked the place, breaking and clattering, busting and shattering. Roaring with laughter and shrieking their war whoops. *Damn it all—they must have found the cache of whiskey,* she thought.

It was getting cool here in twilight's shadows by the time she saw them mounting up in front of the store and streaming off. But instead of heading upstream along White Bird Creek where she had figured they would return to the Camas Prairie, the bastards were riding down for the Salmon.

Bound for H. C. Brown's homestead.

The summer breeze coming off the nearby Salmon rustled the week-old *Lewiston Teller,* the newspaper H. C. Brown sat reading on his front porch late that Thursday afternoon, the fourteenth of June.

"Brown! Brown!"

Lowering the paper past his eyes, H.C. peered about, looking for the source of the faint voice that had called out his name.

"The Indians, they are coming! Indians are on their way!"

He spotted them—four men on the opposite bank of the river, waving to him and jumping about as they hollered across the Salmon, pointing downstream.

"Indians are coming!" they repeated.

Flinging his newspaper aside, Brown didn't need any more prompting. Not after what had happened to Sam Benedict that morning. Dammit if Benedict wasn't right after all!

"Albert!" he bellowed for his brother-in-law as he shot to his feet. "Get my sister down to the boat! Injuns coming to butcher us all!"

Albert Benson and his wife brushed past Brown as he dove inside the house. He could hear his sister shrieking in terror as her husband dragged her toward the riverbank, where they kept a large rowboat tied to a narrow floating dock. H.C. went to the corner of the front room and took up the old needle gun. Opening the action, he saw there was a copper cartridge seated in the action. He snapped the breech closed and took the hunting pouch from the peg near the door. Raising the flap, he found the pouch filled with more than two dozen cartridges.

Enough to get them out of danger, across the Salmon, maybe downriver in the rowboat they often used rather than going horseback to one of the stores for supplies.

Dashing out of the house, Brown took a few steps toward the dock, where Benson was just then helping his wife totter into the boat.

"Wait there for me, Albert!" H.C. hollered, then wheeled toward the rocky outcrop that jutted from the side of the hill behind the house.

Reaching the top of the jagged granite a few minutes later, Brown huffed to a halt. From here he could peer up and down a good piece of the Salmon River Road, as well as look across much of that ground lying off toward White Bird Creek too, over where the Benedict place lay. That's where he saw them—at least a handful at first, then a lot more made their appearance through the trees on the wooded trail leading to Sam's store.

Leaping off the rock, Brown skidded, bounding down the slope two or three yards at a time, nearly falling twice, but somehow keeping himself upright as he skidded onto the bottom behind the house, where he immediately started sprinting for the riverbank.

"Goddamn rope!" Albert Benson was grumbling in frustration as he struggled with the knot mooring their rowboat to a fence post embedded in the bank.

"Cut it!" Brown yelled as he sprinted up.

Benson raised his head, his eyes imploring—like a trapped animal's. "I ain't got a knife!"

Bending, H.C. pulled his folding knife from a pocket, snapped open the blade, and slashed the rope. "They're right over yonder by them trees! We gotta get!"

Scrambling into the boat, Benson made it rock so much that his wife screamed in fear that he would swamp them. The moment Albert got seated, Brown passed his brother-in-law the rifle, then heaved against the floating dock to cast off the boat. Once it was easing into the current, H.C. leaped in and went to his knees at the bow.

"Row, goddammit!" he ordered, taking up one of the oars himself.

Together the two men used the oars like canoe paddles,

digging deep in the Salmon as they heard the cries of the warriors.

His sister shrieked in horror. Brown looked over his shoulder, finding more than a handful of the red bastards emerging from the trees on their ponies, halting right at the floating dock. Some of them brandished firearms.

"Row for it!" Brown screamed. "They got guns!"

The first bullet whined harmlessly past Brown's head as he ducked, feeling lucky. Then more of a ragged volley erupted from that shoreline behind them.

"Dig with that paddle, Albert!"

"Can't—"

"I said *row*, goddammit!"

Then H.C. suddenly spotted the blood oozing between Benson's fingers where he gripped his upper arm. "Paddle for him, Sister!"

Just as she rocked forward to take the oar from her husband, H.C. felt his own shoulder burn.

Brown looked down, finding the bloody furrow a bullet had carved across the top of his upper arm. Flexing his fingers in that hand, he figured he could still grip the oar.

"Dig, Sister—dig with all your might!"

As they pulled at the snow-swollen Salmon, the boat slowly turned sideways in the current and was swiftly carried away downstream. Brown listened as the gunfire slowly faded behind them. Eventually no more angry bullets hissed past their heads the way wasps did when he knocked down their muddy nests from under the eaves of the porch.

Eventually he and his sister managed to get the boat over to the west bank, where he jumped into the shallows, seizing the bow with his good arm so he could lunge toward the grassy shore. Only then did H. C. Brown realize his sister was quietly sobbing, her eyes clenched shut as she continued to stab her oar into the water, blindly rowing, still fighting the river as if it were the embodiment of those savages who had come to murder them all.

"We're safe," Benson cooed at his wife the moment the rowboat lurched against the riverbank.

"That's right, Sister," Brown said, his own voice cracking as he reached out and took hold of her wrist, stilling her frantic oar sweeps, each one biting more at the air than she bit into the river. "We're safe for now."

Chapter 17

June 14, 1877

"Sounds to me like all the rest of 'em figger Baker's place is closer," William Osborn declared after listening to what messenger William George had to say when he returned from spreading the alarm to the neighbors.

Harry Mason nodded, turning all of it over in his mind. He dragged the big turnip watch out of the pocket in his canvas britches, snapped open the case with his dear, departed Anna's photo inside to protect it from fading, and found it to be just past six o'clock that Thursday evening. "So everyone you saw said they were heading up to the old man's place?"

George bobbed his head. "Afore I turned back for here."

"All right," Mason relented. "Let's get those two horses saddled and hurry up there ourselves then. The more guns we got at Baker's, the less chance the Indians gonna try something slick on us."

In less than a quarter-hour, Mason had those who would ride the horses among the rest starting on foot for the Baker homestead. At the front of the group rode his sister, Helen Walsh, who was holding her young daughter, Masi, on her lap. On the other horse sat the two eldest Osborn children and little Edward Walsh. Walking behind the two animals were William Osborn and his wife, Elizabeth, along with two more of their four children. William George and Harry Mason brought up the rear on foot. They didn't have far to travel before they passed the Benedict place, which stood on the other side of White Bird Creek, then quickly crossed the narrow footbridge and started upstream for the Baker homestead.

The group was no more than twenty yards from the darkened, too-quiet house when Harry heard the hoofbeats, then some scattered whoops, even before he saw the warriors appear out of the growing gloom. Mason sprinted to the front of the group with George. The war party halted some distance away in the shadows, their ponies restless, standing there as if they were thinking over the situation.

"Ain't it the damnedest luck?" William Osborn grumbled as he came up to stand at Harry's elbow.

"Come talk!" an Indian voice called from the twilight.

"We chance talking to 'em?" William George whispered at Harry's right elbow.

"Hell no!" Mason snapped.

He knew how much these red-bellies hated him for all the cheating and skimming and back-stabbing he had done against them. *Talk?* Harry Mason knew what awaited him if those goddamned red-bellies got anywhere close enough to him to talk.

The voice called out again, "Come talk! Come talk!"

"No!" Mason hollered back now as his one good eye flicked left and right, quickly landing on Baker's orchard and garden. "Just you stay there so no one gets hurt—"

Out of the deepening indigo of evening he saw the bright yellow flare spew from the muzzle of a distant rifle. Heard that first round slap through the branches and leaves right over their heads. Instantly every one of the women and children set up a caterwauling that Harry would never have thought possible.

"Get into the orchard!" he ordered, waving his rifle toward the fence line at the same time he was whirling to grab hold of the horse Helen and little Masi were riding.

Like a clot of worker ants, the whole group turned as one and clambered toward Baker's orchard and garden, around which the old man had constructed a fence to protect his fruits and vegetables from his own marauding cows. Within the corral stood grass already grown some three feet tall this early in the season.

"Get down in the grass!" Mason ordered the first of the children diving between the fence rails. "Get down!"

A few bullets sang overhead as the warriors made the final turn from the road and started into the yard. Harry vaulted over the fence and tumbled into the grass just as a bullet kicked splinters from a nearby post. Both of Mason's horses immediately clattered off toward the timber.

"There goes our only chance for escape," muttered William George.

"Ain't any of us gonna get out of here on those horses anyway, Billy," Harry reminded him. "Just stay down. And you kids hush up! They can't see us to shoot us, but they can damn sure hear where you are if you keep bawling like you are!"

Behind him the mothers shushed their children, perhaps even clamping hands over the mouths of those who hadn't been made believers by Harry Mason.

A bullet buzzed through the grass. William Osborn yelped in surprise.

"They get you?" Harry asked in a harsh whisper, trying to spot his friend through the tall grass and deepening shadows.

"Just my hand," Osborn grumbled.

"How bad?"

"Shot off the end of my little finger."

"Wrap it up. Should stop bleeding."

"We gonna shoot back?" Osborn asked, grumpy with the pain.

Mason vowed, "They come any closer, I sure as hell am."

Minutes later when some of the warriors dismounted and started to advance, Harry fired a warning shot in their direction. The Nez Perce stopped and ducked for cover.

"We talk!"

"No!" Mason shouted back. "You go, or I kill you!"

"*We* kill!"

That might be, Harry thought, but he said, "Lots of you will die, you come any closer!"

The last slivers of light were rapidly draining from the sky as the warriors appeared to be arguing over the likelihood of flushing the whites out of the garden. As long as they were arguing about it among themselves, the Indians weren't going to rush the fence line surrounding the tall grass where Harry had them hidden. Still, every now and then one of the warriors fired a shot toward the garden, more and more unsure of where the settlers were hiding as the shadows blackened.

And for every Nez Perce bullet, Mason or Osborn or George answered back, firing a round at the warriors.

"Let's keep 'em edgy," Harry kept reminding the others. "That way they'll be thinking on just how many men and guns are in here when they figure to get brave and want to rush us."

But he still wasn't about to sit there and wait for the Nez Perce to work up the courage for an assault.

When slap-dark had crept on down off the mountainsides and swallowed the valley of White Bird Creek, Harry whispered to the other two men, directing them to gather up the rest of their charges and follow him out of the back of the orchard, beyond the fence line, where they could take up new hiding places across the stream.

At the creek bank, Harry and the other men were the first to wade across in order to find themselves a good ford, then returned for the first three of the children. Helen Walsh hiked up her dress and waded right into the cold, rushing torrent with them to reach the far side. On the second trip across with the children, Elizabeth Osborn dropped off the bank into the stream, immediately lost her footing, and came up with a sputter to stumble on across, shivering and mumbling a blue streak.

Wet and cold, they were nonetheless that much farther from the savages, Harry thought as the women settled the children within a thicket that completely hid them while the first stars winked into view. Now came an even scarier time. With darkness those bastards could slip up out of the black and be on you before you realized it.

"Listen!" William George announced in a sharp whisper.

The hair on the back of Mason's neck was standing. He listened, figuring George must have heard one of the warriors creeping up on them.

"Horses!" William Osborn whispered as the sound faded.

"You figger they're leaving, Harry?" George asked.

"Could be laying a trap," Mason advised suspiciously. "We can afford to wait some and see what we hear from over at Baker's place before we leave this brush."

Sanctuary, some would call it. A hidey-hole is what it was. The sort he and his brothers had always sought out when they were children back in Massachusetts. Always hoped to find just the right spot where no one else knew your hidey-hole when they came looking for you in a game of hide-and-go-seek. For now, *sanctuary* would do nicely.

He couldn't read his watch in the dark, but Harry was sure more than an hour had passed since they had crossed the creek. He heard some slow, deep breathing, so he was sure a number of the children were sleeping, their heads resting in their mothers' laps.

"We can't stay here, fellas," Mason finally whispered.

"Where you figger to go?" William George asked.

"Back to my place. Safer'n staying here till it's daylight, when they can catch us out in the open," Harry explained.

"All right," William Osborn relented.

Mason got the rest awakened and standing in the thicket, preparing to recross the stream, when George stepped up to Mason's elbow. The young man had never been a particularly brave sort, so it sure as hell surprised Harry when George grabbed Mason's arm.

"Mr. Mason, I ain't going back to your place with you."

He studied the intensity on the hired man's face. "You can't stay here, Billy."

"I ain't," and George shook his head. "I figger them folks up on Camas Prairie oughtta know of the troubles."

"You're gonna walk up there by yourself?"

George nodded. "I think I can find my way."

Mason shook the young man's hand, squeezing it hard. "Good luck to you."

Harry watched his employee turn into the darkness and start upstream, following the White Bird as it climbed its narrow, confining valley.

It was slow going in the dark for the rest of them as they struggled alongside the road that led them downstream toward the Salmon River, slow helping the children along, carrying those youngsters so frightened they didn't want to move, their mothers clucking like hens with their broods, the two men staying well ahead of the women and children to be sure they didn't stumble into another war party. It proved to be such slow going that William George caught back up with them as Mason's group approached the Salmon River Road.

Harry was surprised when he heard the hired man coming out of the night. "What happened? You see some Injuns?"

Osborn shook his head and shrugged, admitting, "Got turned around somewhere in the dark."

"That's all right, Billy," Mason said. "You tried a brave thing. You think you could find your way over to Mount Idaho?"

George shook his head. "Not sure. Only know by going the road."

"All right—I'm gonna tell you how."

As soon as William George believed he had enough of Mason's directions to get himself cross-country in the dark, the young man bid the others farewell a second time, promising to get through with word of the attacks and depredations if it took all the rest of that night.

For those who had remained with Harry, it took three, maybe four, times as long to plod back to the Mason place by keeping to the timber as it would have traveling on the road without the children. But by the time the sun was coming up, Harry had convinced himself he was smelling woodsmoke. Maybe nothing more than his lifelong association of sunup with cooking breakfast over a fire.

"I'll be go to hell," William Osborn marveled just about the time Harry spotted French Frank and old man Shoemaker stepping out onto the porch of the Mason store.

"Got something cooking?" Mason asked as his bunch came out of the woods and approached the porch.

"Just what we could find after them Injuns made a mess of ever'thing else, Harry," Shoemaker admitted.

Hurrying up the steps and to the door, he peered into the store. Mason's heart sank.

Osborn said, "They was looking for guns and bullets."

"And whiskey," Shoemaker grumbled.

Mason turned to the old man. "Where'd you two go off to hide?"

French Frank grinned and tossed his thumb over his shoulder. "We get out. Go to trees. Stay down."

"They never come looking for us," Shoemaker continued. "Likely didn't know we was anywhere about the place. The two of us didn't come on in here till it started to get light. My meat bag was hollerin' for fodder by then. Damn, if I wasn't hungry! Had to fix me some breakfast."

"You boys can stay if you want," Mason offered, "but soon as the children eat, I'm taking everybody across the Salmon."

"Across the river?" Shoemaker echoed. "What the hell for?"

"Lay out the day," Mason said. "While the little ones eat, Bill and I are going to stuff as much food as we can in a couple of burlap bags and take 'em with us. Stay over across the river where them Indians aren't likely to go, and wait till dark."

"Then what, Harry?" Osborn asked.

"Then we'll recross the Salmon and follow Billy George ourselves," Mason replied. "After sleeping out the day, we can head out on our own. Way I see it, we should reach Mount Idaho by sunup."

After Jennie Norton bound up Lew Day's wound the best she could with some clean cotton bandages that stanched the flow of blood, Ben Norton, John Chamberlin, and Joe Moore emptied the Chamberlin wagon of its load of flour, hauling the hundredweight sacks inside the Norton house. With the weight of the women and children in the back of the dead-axle wagon, not to mention the wounded Lew Day as well, Chamberlin's four horses would have enough of a load to pull now. It made a lot of sense to lighten the load as much as they could before setting out for Grangeville once twilight was done deepening the hues of the timber around them.

When Norton and hired man Joe Moore returned from the barn with the two saddle horses they would ride, Ben found Chamberlin helping Lew Day hoist himself back into the saddle atop that racer. "What the hell are you doing, John?"

"He said if I didn't help him, he'd get up there his own self," Chamberlin apologized as Day straightened atop the horse.

"You strong enough to ride, Lew?" Norton asked as he stopped beside Day's knee.

"I got here, didn't I?"

"I figgered you for the wagon, Lew. In there where you don't have to worry 'bout hanging on—"

"I'm up here now, Ben," Day sighed stoically. "Let's get going."

Without another word, Moore and Norton rose into the saddle as Chamberlin clambered onto the seat alone. Behind him in the wagon box were his pregnant wife and their two small children, along with Jennie Norton, her son, Hill, and Jennie's sister, Lynn Bowers. It was just past 9:00 P.M. as they pulled out of the yard and started down the south side of the divide for Grangeville. Overhead, the stars shined brightly in a moonless sky, but visibility was good.

After no more than a half-dozen miles, Ben Norton spotted the flickering light of a campfire up ahead at one of the wide spots in the road where travelers preferred to camp on their way across the Camas Prairie. As they drew closer, he spotted the two high-walled freighters with their tongues down, a dozen horses grazing in the meadow just beyond.

A figure rose beside the flames, rifle in hand, and quickly stepped back to the edge of the firelight.

"Ho there, fellas!" Norton called.

"That you, Ben?"

As a second figure emerged from behind one of the wagons, Norton answered, "It's all of us, boys. Chamberlins, and Lew Day too."

Pete Ready came into the firelight with his carbine in his hands. "Lew Day?"

"Goddamned right," Day grumped as he brought his horse to a halt in the light.

Luther Wilmot was beside him in a heartbeat. "You run into trouble?"

"One of the red bastards shot me in the back."

"Damn," Wilmot sighed, then whistled low as he stepped around to peer at the bloodstained back of Day's shirt, blinking in disbelief. "You better get down here and sit by the fire, Lew. Get warm and I'll rustle you up some coffee to drink, too—"

"We ain't staying, Lew," Norton interrupted. "Figure to make Grangeville afore first light."

Wilmot swallowed, looking first at Chamberlin on the wagon seat, then at Joe Moore in the saddle, and finally at his wounded friend again. "Least you can leave Lew here with us. He ain't in no shape to be busting ass down this road to Grangeville in the dark with you, Ben."

"I figger he can make his choice," Norton admitted.

Wilmot gazed up at his friend. "You figure to push on with the rest of these folks, Lew?"

"Yep. I need someone to look at this hole the niggers put in me," Day groaned, leaning forward on the saddle horn. "I ain't getting no better."

"Maybe both of you should come with us, too," Norton suggested hopefully. "Better we're all together—"

"We already put the teams out to graze, and I'm 'bout ready for the bedroll myself," Wilmot explained. "We'll get us some shut-eye and rest our stock, then be on the way afore first light."

"Can't talk you into coming with—"

"Nawww," Wilmot said forcefully this time. "You got plenty of guns. Them four Injuns who shot Lew Day won't jump all of you, not now."

Norton swallowed hard. "Ain't just us. I'm afraid for the two of you staying here by yourselves."

"We'll be fine, Ben," Wilmot repeated.

"All right," Norton relented. He waved Chamberlin on, watching the wagon rattle away with the women and children. Joe Moore fell in right beside Lew Day, who rode no more than a few yards behind the tailgate.

Then Norton leaned over and shook hands with Lew Wilmot and Pete Ready.

"So long, fellas," he said as he straightened back in the saddle. "This is likely the last time we'll see you boys alive."

Chapter 18

Season of *Hillal*
1877

The only lodges standing that night after Joseph had returned to *Tepahlewam* belonged to his Wallowa band. Those loyal few were the only ones who stayed.

At the news of attacks made on the white settlers, visitors from the Treaty bands immediately flushed like coveys of frightened quail and streamed north across the reservation boundary. Looking Glass led his people north across Camas Prairie to camp on Cottonwood Creek, where they would wait to see what developed with the soldiers. White Bird's people and Toohoolhoolzote's band, most of whom could be counted among the war faction, had started southwest for the Salmon River and the scene of the murders—but not without first leaving some spies behind. That handful of scouts had orders to keep an eye on Joseph and Ollokot, so afraid were the war supporters that they believed the brothers would turn traitors and take off for Fort Lapwai.

That night in his darkened lodge, Joseph lay awake, anxious for the birth of this child. By tradition, his wife would keep herself apart from the rest of the village. So he waited for the midwife to come tell him when the child had come.

But the night remained quiet. No one stirred. What few women had been sobbing earlier that evening had evidently fallen asleep. Joseph knew the despair they were feeling. All of them, no matter what family they were a part of, no matter what band they belonged to, they were all *Nee-Me-Poo*.

And that meant the Shadows would make war on the innocent as well as those guilty of the killings.

So quiet was it in his village that black night. He wondered if he should pray . . . asking of *Tamalait* a special blessing for his woman and the child to come. Pray especially for those who were being drawn into this war that would destroy the very last of what the *Nee-Me-Poo* possessed.

Pray too for the white settlers who were in the middle of the conflict, even for Cut-Off Arm, who would soon lead his soldiers against the warriors.

And as Joseph sat up, deciding he would find his pipe and tobacco pouch in the dark of his lodge, he figured he should pray for White Bird's young warriors who had started it all, pray, too, for Sun Necklace's war party, who were shedding more blood at that very moment—

—when a bullet smashed through Joseph's lodge. Right over his head. Splintering the lodgepole just behind his bed before it sang out the back of the lodgeskins.

An angry voice called out from the hillside. Joseph couldn't be positive, but it sounded like white man words. Someone speaking a language Joseph had never learned.

He lay on his side, listening as the warning shouts faded, his heart hammering, his prayer pipe clutched in his hand.

Someone wanted to scare him, perhaps to frighten his Wallowa band very, very badly. A lone white man come here to do what he could to drive the Wallowa onto the reservation. Or perhaps one of those warriors who wanted a fight very, very badly—enough to attempt fooling the Wallowa into believing it was a white man out for blood. To goad the Wallowa into joining the war.

Joseph clutched the prayer pipe against his breast and began to cry hot tears. He cried for them all.

Most especially for those yet to die before the war could end.

Lord, how he was coming to hate the old man's grousing!

Patrick Brice turned to George Popham and whispered, "You stay put right here. I'm going to have me 'nother look at the back of the house."

"You ain't gonna get yourself killed, is you?" Popham begged with an anxious pinch in his voice.

"I'll be right over here a little ways," Brice explained. "You stay put."

The Irish prospector crawled off far enough that he didn't think he would have to hear more of the old man's noisy laments. As if he hadn't already seen enough to make a blithering idjit of himself—but then he was forced to listen to Popham sobbing miserably one moment about watching the rape of his married daughter ... when the next moment the old man whipped himself into a crimson fury at the Indians—vacillating back and forth all night, ever since they had abandoned the house to Jennet Manuel and her two children.

It had shocked Brice the moment the warriors took his Henry repeater and the old man's shotgun, then calmly as you please rode off without killing the two of them there and then on the front porch after they had surrendered their weapons. Popham had hugged his sobbing daughter and grandchildren as Brice watched the warriors ride away; then the immigrant suggested to the old man that they all skee-daddle away from the place as fast as possible.

"We ain't gonna have us 'nother chance like this," he had whispered to the old man while Popham wiped tears from Jennet's cheeks. "They could be changing their minds and come back to finish us, George."

Popham had gazed down into Jennet's face before he turned to Brice, saying, "We'll wait here for the night. Go fetch John's body in the morning and bring him back for a decent burial."

Angry, and scared clear to the worn soles of his old boots, Brice had said, "Awright, so we stay till morning—"

"And watch out for Jennet and her babies," Popham interrupted.

"So if we stay till morning, the least we can do is get away from the house and hide out there in the woods where we ain't so easy to find."

After considering that for a moment, Popham had turned to Jennet, saying, "We won't be far away, honey. You need me, you just come outside and gimme a call. Two of us just gonna lay low till morning. Maybe you should bring the children out with us, too—"

"No, Pa," Jennet protested with a hollow sound. "I want 'em to sleep in their beds, inside their house tonight. They lost their pa today—so I don't want Maggie and her little brother to feel like they gotta lose any more of what little they still got."

As twilight approached and the first stars blinked into view overhead, Brice noticed three warriors appear on the hillside above the house. They dismounted and sat on the slope, doing nothing more than staring down on the place. Keeping watch perhaps. But he had never pointed them out to the old man. As long as those bastards just sat there on the hillside, then there was no reason to raise an alarm.

Maybeso they were just keeping watch on the house, come back to keep an eye on that white woman and children, too, just like him and George were doing.

After dark Brice and Popham watched a lone candle move from window to window, then come to rest as it grew colder out at the edge of the timber where he and the old man kept up their vigil. In that growing silence, the father, this old grandfather, began to quietly curse the red savages for what they'd done to his daughter's family.... Minutes later Popham would cry a little before more angry curses tumbled from his lips.

After taking about all he could of that for hours, Brice settled back against the trunk of a tree, wondering what the hell he and the old man would do if the bastards returned for the woman and her children, came back to murder two defenseless white men—because that's just what they were. Neither of them had any more of a weapon than a belt knife, maybe a folding knife down in their pockets. They'd given away their firearms to the enemy to save their hides.

From time to time the horrid image of the rape kept coming back and Patrick would have to struggle to push it out of his mind. How the little boy flew out of his mother's arms as she stumbled; how the warrior knelt between her legs as Jennet began to shriek, pulling his breechclout aside and flipping up her dress to expose the bare tops of her legs above her stockings so he could ...

And then Brice would remember how Popham had listened to his daughter's screams, fighting with himself on whether or not to rush out there to kill the son of a bitch and likely get himself killed in the bargain—swearing to Brice that if they murdered Jennet after raping her, then he would go out there and kill as many as he could before they got him.

But one of their leaders had come up to stop any more of

the warriors from raping Jennet, then turned to the house to offer them a chance for escape. All they had to do was—

And that made Brice ashamed. Angry with himself that he had surrendered his weapon rather than die with it in his hands.

So the Irishman was relieved that he had crawled over here away from the old man where he found he could doze a little, jerking awake suddenly at times to look at the house, then gaze up at the hillside in the starshine for those three warriors . . . but he couldn't see them any longer after it grew so dark. So he closed his eyes again, deciding that morning would come soon enough, when he and Popham could be slipping away for Mount Idaho at first light.

It was so dark and cold in Brice's dream that it seemed damn real when he came to sometime later, groggy and gritty-eyed. Brice found it still dark, yet the stars above the hill back of the house were in new positions. Some time had crawled past—

There, he heard that sobbing again . . . but this time it wasn't what he figured for his dream. And it sure as the devil wasn't old man Popham's voice.

Curious, Brice leaned forward, rocked onto his knees, and started crawling toward the whimpering. Closer and closer he drew to the sound, hanging back at the edge of the brush where he could approach the side of the house, the better to hear it more plainly. Perhaps one of the children had awakened with nightmares and Jennet was trying to console the child.

Then he realized it had to be little Maggie. What was she? Six or seven?

Of a sudden Brice saw her out of the dark, his ears locating her at the same moment—finding the child huddled, her knees drawn up fetally beneath her chin there beside some brush at the tree line. She jerked when she saw him, skidding back clumsily the instant she realized he was crawling toward her—emitting a pitiful squeak of terror that so reminded him of a wounded animal with its tiny leg caught in a trap, so weakened by its efforts to free itself that the animal could no longer fight back, couldn't even cry out very loudly.

"Maggie," he whispered the moment he stopped, spreading his arms out to her. "It's Patrick. Patrick Brice."

"Mr. Brice," she said, clambering to her feet and rushing

toward him, sobbing even as she took her first step, cradling her skinny left arm tightly against her tummy.

He was managing to get to his feet as she flung herself against him. With her face buried in his belly, her cries were muffled. He stroked her hair.

"What you doing out here now, Maggie dear?" he soothed softly in the dark. "Should be in there with your mamma and your wee brother, sleeping the night away till—"

"They killed 'em, Mr. Brice," the girl interrupted with a steely cold that belied her tiny voice.

He knelt before her, staring directly into her eyes. "Killed who, Maggie? You sure you wasn't having yourself a bad dream from all what's happened to you, and only come outside sleepwalking so—"

"No!" she said fervently. "They killed my mamma and brother."

"The Injuns?"

"Yes," Maggie declared, taking a step back and pointing to the house. "Hit 'em both with a big stick and dragged 'em away."

"How come they didn't get you?"

"I was in 'nother room, looking for the pee pot to use, when the Injuns come in the house," she whispered, pressing herself against Brice again. "I sneaked up to see when I heard their funny talking. Saw what they did to my mother and little brother. And I saw when they come looking for me, but I hid out back against the pantry so they never found me in the dark."

"Your mother?" He could not believe it. "She's killed?"

"When them Indians was gone, I went looking for Mamma—but I didn't find either of 'em. I s'pose the Indians dragged 'em off to cut 'em up, maybe chop off their arms and legs—"

He gently peeled the child away from him and held her out at arm's length there on his knees so he could stare directly in her eyes. "Don't go talking like that, Maggie dear."

"It's true—"

That's when he noticed how she winced as he gripped the tops of her arms. "What is it, girl?"

"My arm," she whimpered, gazing down at the left arm. "I'm feared something's broke it hurts so bad."

Gently brushing his fingers down past the crusty arrow

wound, on down to the lower arm, Brice felt the tight swelling, the hard knot that was surely the splintered end of a bone. He looked into her face for a long moment, trying to decide if she could take what was to come . . . Then he realized she had already endured far worse, seeing her family butchered.

"Maggie, I'm gonna have to set your arm," he explained quietly at the same time he pulled his folding knife from the patch pocket on his coat.

She glanced down at the knife, but her eyes did not flinch. "It's gonna hurt, ain't it?"

"But the arm's gonna feel much better after we do it," he confided. " 'Sides, I don't think I can take you off anywhere till you're ready to travel."

"We gonna go get away from those Injuns?"

"Yes, Maggie," he promised.

He had her sit on the ground right where she was and wait for him while he crawled off into the timber a short distance, searching for some willow saplings he could hack through with the knife. With three pieces, each cut a little more than a foot long, Brice returned to her side, where he used his knife to trim two long strips from the bottom of her muddy dress. Maggie was able to help him hold one of the splints against her arm as he gripped the other two and tied them in place just above the elbow.

Then he started singing low, working hard at remembering the words of that ages-worn Irish lullaby his mother had sung to him so long ago. All the better to keep her mind on anything else while he seized the crook of her elbow in his left hand, snatched her tiny hand in his right.

Then he asked, "Maggie, what was that I heard?"

"What?" And she stiffened, starting to turn.

"Over there—"

And the moment she turned her head to see for herself, Patrick hauled back on the arm. The child released a shrill cry the instant the muscles went into spasm. When he slowly allowed the muscles to contract again, Brice felt how the bone ends slipped back into place against each other. No longer overriding crookedly.

She sobbed as he quickly bound up the wrist end of his splints with that second piece of her grimy dress. She could no longer bend the arm at the elbow, which minimized the movement of the broken ends of the bone and therefore lessened the pain. He'd only done this sort of thing once before, on a Chinaman who was crushed in a rock slide near his mining claim.

"There now, it will get better and better from here on out," he promised, settling onto his rump and dragging her into his lap. He laid her head against the crook of his shoulder and wiped his fingertips down her wet cheeks. "It's bound to be better for us from here on out, Maggie dear."

She was quiet for a long time there, tight against him in the cold darkness. "I ain't got no one now, Mr. Brice. The Injuns killed everybody else I had."

"We'll find them, Maggie," he vowed. "Come morning, we'll find the bodies and give 'em a decent Christian burying. Your grandpa will see to that, wee one."

"Grandpa. I forgot my grandpa," she said in a quiet voice. " 'Cept for him and me . . . all the rest are dead now."

Chapter 19

June 15, 1877

L ew Wilmot could sense the dampness stab him deep in his thirty-eight-year-old bones when he dragged himself out of his bedroll just past three o'clock that Friday morning, the fifteenth day of June.

"Pete," he said quietly, awakening his freighting partner, "be light enough for us to move out soon."

Pete Ready sat up, rubbing his gritty eyes, watching Wilmot lay some more wood on the coals of last night's fire.

After setting what remained of last night's coffee on the flames to reheat, Wilmot led the twenty-eight-year-old Ready out to the good grass where they brought in the horses they had hobbled at sundown. As an additional precaution, the wary Wilmot had side-lined the twelve animals for the night. What with all that talk of the Nez Perce bucks getting frisky, it simply didn't make any sense for the two of them to make it easy for any youngsters who wanted to steal some white men's horses.

"Don't think I got any decent sleep last night," Wilmot admitted as they started leading the first of the teams back to the wagons.

"You neither?" Ready asked. "I must've kept one eye open all night, Lew."

"I could swear that was gunfire I heard 'bout the time we was stretching out in our bedrolls," Wilmot reflected.

Ready was quiet a moment more as they started backing

the first pair of horses into their traces on Wilmot's wagon. "You figger Ben and them other folks run into some trouble on down the road after they left us?"

He sighed deeply, thinking back on the faint rattle of gunfire they had heard about an hour after the Nortons and Chamberlins passed on by their camp. "Hope not." Then he tried to shake off the cold gloom by proclaiming, "Hell, I can't even swear what we heard was guns at all."

By the time they had hitched up the animals, drunk some coffee, and smothered their fire, the sky was starting to lighten just enough that a man could read the trail ahead of him. The teamsters rolled into the coming of that day.

About the time the first of the sun's rays were streaming on the Camas Prairie, they had put some three miles behind them—when the first shriek reverberated from the rolling hills that descended off Cottonwood Butte. Suddenly the air was filled with the yips and cries of festooned warriors erupting from the timber lining a dip in the trail ahead.

Vaulting off their high seats onto the muddy, misty ground, Wilmot and Ready sprinted for the head of their teams, fumbling to unhitch those twelve horses. Dragging the trace lines back out of the iron rings, the teamsters bellowed at the animals, slapping and goading the horses into motion, driving them away from the wagons before the men leaped onto the bare backs of their faithful, steady lead horses.

When Wilmot and Ready got started back down the trail for Cottonwood House, Lew glanced over his shoulder, finding the warriors less than a quarter-mile behind and closing fast atop their buffalo ponies. As he lay low over the neck of the tall, muscular animal, Wilmot began thinking of Louisa—how his heart burned with his deep love for her. Images of their four young children darted through his mind. A moment later as he chanced a look back at their pursuers, Lew Wilmot tried to conjure up an image of that child due any day now. Would it be a boy or a girl? Would this one look more like Louisa or like him?

Wilmot had come here from Illinois when he was but a lad himself—his father moving the family to Oregon on that great Emigrant Road. Having grown up all those years in this country, he had never done a goddamned thing against these Cayuse or Palouse or the Nez Perce . . . so why the hell were they screaming for his blood?

Wilmot had no idea how far they had been running after abandoning their wagons. A mile now, maybe a little more, on past the place where the two of them had camped last night. That would make it. . . . More than four miles they had run these sure-footed wagon horses as if they were long-limbed racing stallions.

When Lew looked back now he found no more than two warriors still following them.

A damned good thing too, because the animal beneath him wasn't cut out for this sort of buffalo chase. It was built for slow-paced hauling power. He could feel the faint shudder in its lights as the critter heaved for air, every one of its massive muscles straining to carry the huge, big-boned body up and down the pitch and heave of the trail faster than those lean, grass-fed Indian ponies.

"Lew!" Ready called from right behind his left knee.

Wilmot turned, afraid the warriors were on them.

But the moment Lew twisted around, Ready shouted, "I can't see 'em no more!"

Sure enough—as they continued that gentle climb up the Cottonwood Divide to the Norton place, the trail disappearing back through the trees was bare of horsemen.

Starting to slow his exhausted animal, Wilmot prayed, "Maybe we outrun 'em, Pete."

Ready swallowed hard. "A good thing, Lew," he admitted sheepishly. "I forgot to grab for my pistol when I come down off my wagon back there."

"Y-you don't have a gun?"

The younger partner shook his head.

"S'all right," Wilmot reassured him as they slowed the horses to a walk, both men constantly twisting around on those bare, damp backs to peer behind them as if they didn't really believe they were getting this reprieve from certain death. "Better we get off this road now and go across country."

"Where to, you figger?"

"Grangeville. It's still the closest."

Ready glanced at the lone pistol Wilmot had stuck like the hoof of a goat in his belt, then said, "Them Injuns gone back for the wagons, ain't they, Lew?"

Wilmot nodded.

"We lost all them supplies Vollmer paid us for—"

"But you got your hair, Pete," Lew grumbled as he started

his horse off the trail, reining into the timber to begin their climb up the slope that would lead them over Cottonwood Divide and down to Threemile Creek. "Just remember that. You still got your goddamn hair."

Jennie Norton sat clutching her nine-year-old son, Hill, against her, the other hand gripping the sidewall of the Chamberlin wagon. She was sure that she was digging her fingernails into the wood so fiercely that they must be bleeding. The wagon bounced and weaved down the rutted, rainsodden road, racing to stay ahead of that pack of shrieking heathens who had suddenly appeared out of the black of night not very long after they passed by the teamsters' camp.

Beside Jennie sat her eighteen-year-old sister, Lynn Bowers, who wrapped an arm around the three-year-old Chamberlin girl. The pregnant Mrs. Chamberlin was pressed against the opposite sidewall, one arm holding her little toddler, another daughter. Behind the wagon galloped Jennie's husband, Ben, their hired man, Joe Moore, and the wounded courier from Mount Idaho, Lew Day, the three of them atop straining, wide-eyed horses that dutifully followed the springless wagon as it shuddered and slid its way through every twist and turn in the dark ribbon that was taking them toward the Cottonwood Divide.

For some time now—she didn't have any idea how many miles—John Chamberlin had somehow managed to keep the light wagon ahead of the yelping savages. But gradually, the heathens drew near enough that they began to fire random shots at Ben and the other two horsemen.

"Don't you ladies fret none yet!" Chamberlin hurled his voice over his shoulder in the cold air. "Those Injuns aren't near enough that you should worry! We keep ahead of 'em like we are . . . we'll make it! We'll make—"

"Chamberlin, stop!"

It was Ben who called out from the rear.

Jennie watched her husband and Moore reining up. The saddle on that third horse was empty.

"Stop, John! Stop!" Jennie hollered frantically, afraid they were going to leave the three men behind.

Chamberlin jolted the wagon to a halt, then vaulted off the seat to run back toward Norton and Moore, who already had Lew Day suspended between them, his head sagging from his shoulders.

"They hit him again!" Ben shouted as they reached the back of the wagon.

Together with Chamberlin's help, the two of them heaved Day over the back gate, where Jennie went to her knees. With some help from Hill, she managed to drag Lew toward the front of the bed while John Chamberlin clambered back atop the seat and slapped reins down on the backs of his two horses as he threw off the brake. Behind them, Norton and Moore lunged back into their saddles and were kicking furiously as the warriors appeared at that last bend in the road.

Closer than ever before.

"Stopping for him may have just cost us our lives!" Mrs. Chamberlin scolded her husband and Jennie, pinning her daughter against her belly, swollen with another child.

"You could run off and leave a man—a friend—to those devils?" Jennie demanded as she peered down at Lew Day with those eyes everyone said were soft and large, like an antelope's.

Jennie found Day's eyes staring up at her, gratitude welling deep within them—at least when he didn't clench his eyes shut with every rise and fall of pain as the wagon rumbled into a gallop. Then she noticed a fresh smear of blood about the size of her small hand. It glistened high on his belly.

A gut wound, she thought. Painful as hell, and it would take an unmercifully long time for him to die.

"Lookit 'em!" the Chamberlin woman shrieked. "They're almost on top of us!"

By then her two young girls were screaming, goaded to a frenzy by their mother as John Chamberlin repeatedly shouted for his daughters to be quiet. No matter that the woman was right, Jennie thought—they had indeed put their lives in danger to stop for Lew Day when he was knocked from his horse. Every jolt made the wounded man grunt where he lay groaning in her lap.

"Jennie!"

It was Ben shouting. She looked up to find her husband barely staying atop the saddle, clutching the back of his left thigh, weaving now.

"John!" she yelled at the driver, twisting away from Lew Day for the tailgate. "Benjamin's hit!"

As Chamberlin began to pull back on the reins, another bullet smacked into the side of Norton's horse. When his animal pitched to the right, Ben started to dismount onto his injured leg. She watched that leg give way under him as Norton spilled into the middle of the road. Joe Moore had his horse beside the crumpled man in a heartbeat, leaning off to grab that hand Norton held up as he got to his knees. Snatching Moore's wrist in one hand, clutching the stirrup with the other, Ben managed to lurch toward the wagon as the screeching got louder than it had ever been.

Jennie peeled her legs from under the wounded man so that she could scramble to the back of the wagon to help pull her husband in.

"Damn," Lew Day growled as he sat up and propped himself against the sidewall, "now they got Ben, too."

Reaching the rear gate, Norton was barely able to start over the gate before Chamberlin slapped the horses into motion again. Jennie managed to reach out and snag her husband's hand, heaving backward with all she had to yank him over the gate and into the wagon box before he fell off.

Suddenly Chamberlin's horses were screeching with that shrill, eerie, humanlike cry that made the hair on her arms prickle. The wagon lurched to the side, tilting slightly on two wheels as one of those horses stumbled forward onto its front knees and promptly went down in a heap.

Thrashing in terror, the other horse attempted to hurtle around the fallen animal, lunging against the singletree and nearly tipping the wagon filled with screaming women and children as they collided with one another. Clattering back onto all four wheels, the wagon slammed to a halt against the dead horse.

Painfully rolling himself over the sidewall, Lew Day flopped to the ground with a grunt and crabbed behind the horse carcass just as Joe Moore's animal was hit, screamed, and flung its rider into the middle of the road. Another shot split the darkness. Disbelieving, Moore stared down at his left hand, finding that a bullet had clipped off two of his fingers— then he, too, dove for cover behind his own fallen horse. He and Day quickly began to return the warriors' fire, holding the Nez Perce off as Chamberlin helped the wounded Norton get the three women and all the children over the sidewall and under the wagon box as a bullet brought down the second of Chamberlin's noisy horses.

Jenny clutched young Hill against her as Lynn sobbed with a wheeze each time she dragged in a breath.

In a matter of seconds the Nez Perce had dropped every one of the animals. Three of the four men were badly wounded.

And these horrible, bloodthirsty savages likely had them surrounded already.

Chapter 20

June 15, 1877

Hill Norton gazed into his mother's pretty face, not believing the fear he found reflected there, refusing to believe what she was demanding of him.

"I ain't going without you!" he protested.

She seized her son's arm, yanked him close, and embraced Hill. Then Jennie Norton held him away from her and gazed squarely into the youth's eyes while she said, "You and Lynn, I want you both to run for it while you still can."

Lynn Bowers started to argue, "Jennie, I can't—"

"You've got to do this for me, Sister," Mrs. Norton pleaded in a husky whisper. "Get my son out of here before the end comes to us all."

Hill could feel the tears welling up in his eyes, and he angrily swiped them away with the backs of both hands. He didn't know if they were tears of terror or sadness or if they were tears of fury that he felt for the Indians, for his family's plight, maybe even for his mother ordering him away into the black of night and the unknown.

How could she ask him to leave her and his father, both wounded the way they were? How could she expect that of him after what had happened to the Chamberlins when they had tried to slip away?

From that moment when he had crawled under the wagon with his parents and the others once the horses were dropped, Hill had listened to the steady crackle of the enemy weapons, hearing every bullet slam into the wagon box or ricochet off an iron wagon tire or moistly slap into one of the dead horses. He could tell the warriors were moving about, inching closer and closer out there in the dark—just from the telltale cracks of those carbines.

It wasn't long before the messenger from Mount Idaho was hit again—then hit a fourth and fifth time too. After they had been forted up here for better than two hours, Lew Day started begging for some water. Hill's father whispered to his son, explaining that was what happened to a man who was bleeding out: he got real thirsty. So it came as no surprise later when Lew Day began whimpering, pleading for someone to bring him anything to drink from the wagon, anything at all, because he couldn't move for all his wounds.

"I can't stand him moaning over there no more," grumbled Ben Norton as he started to scoot backward from beneath the wagon box. "He keeps on crying like that, he's gonna draw more of their fire."

"Don't leave us, Ben!" Jennie Norton begged.

Nonetheless, Hill's wounded father crouched at the side-wall for a moment, then stood suddenly, hurriedly peering into the wagon box for one of their canteens.

The boy heard the two sharp cracks of the Indian carbines, saw the muzzles spit fire in the black of that night. The first bullet clanged against a piece of the iron furniture somewhere on the wagon. But the second smacked into his father's good leg.

Ben Norton collapsed, spinning to the ground in a heap as the canteen flew from his grasp and he gripped his right thigh with both hands. Hill stared transfixed at the gleaming patch of blood appearing on his father's leg as Mr. Chamberlin dragged Norton beneath the wagon box once more. Not hard to see that black ooze seeping up between his father's fingers, even in the dark.

"They got you bad," Chamberlin whispered.

"May—maybe you oughtta take Jennie and the rest and get the hell outta here while you can, John," Norton advised grittily.

Even in the shadows beneath the wagon box, Hill could still see how white his father's face had become. More than anything else, the boy was afraid he was going to have to lie here and watch his father die.

"I'll go and ask them to let us go, Ben," Jennie Norton offered.

"Don't be stupid," Norton snapped at his wife.

"I can't let you bleed to death here," she argued. "We gotta get you to some help."

"No!" Ben Norton growled, clenching his eyes and gritting his teeth for the pain. "You go out there, you're good as dead, Jennie . . . that, or worse—when they grab you and drag you off. I ain't watching that happen to you—"

"All right, Ben," she relented softly. "I thought it would be worth a try. Maybe they won't hurt women and children."

For a moment Norton looked at Chamberlin, then into his son's face. And finally he said, "Awright, Jennie. S'pose you give it a try. Ask 'em to let you go, but don't go out there far enough for 'em to grab you. If they do anything funny, I want you close so you can get back in here quick."

Hill wanted to cry out at that moment, to scream that they hadn't asked for his arguments against sending his mother out there in the open to beg for their lives. As he watched his mother crab her way around the side of the wagon in a crouch, the boy figured they could have stayed right there for the rest of the night, holding the warriors off just the way they had been—

—when the bullet struck his mother, slicing through both her calves. As she collapsed in a ball, screeching in pain, Jennie Norton slammed the side of her leg against a wagon wheel, dislocating her ankle.

It wasn't very long after John Chamberlin dragged her back under the wagon that the neighbor told the others he was leaving, going to make a run for it with his family. Scooping up both of the sobbing children, the parents shushed their daughters, then slipped away into the brush at a crouch.

For some time after that Hill did what he could to help his father and mother with their wounds. When his father's hands began to cramp more than the man could bear, Hill interlaced his own fingers over the wound that continued to ooze no matter how much pressure any of them applied to it.

Then off in the distance, the boy heard some screaming, at least two different voices shrieking out there in all that black—followed by several gunshots . . . when everything went quiet in that direction and for a long time the night fell

silent. Except for a final crack from one of the guns that surrounded them.

As the following minutes snailed past, Hill came to understand just how critical their situation was if no one could slip
away to bring help back. None of the five adults uttered a
thing for the longest time, but the boy figured that was because they were all brooding over the screams and the gunshots, too. *Like me, the grown-ups must figure the Injuns got
the Chamberlins,* he thought.

It grew so unearthly quiet, with nothing else to do but
think.

Just about the time Hill was beginning to figure Lew Day
must have finally bled to death, thinking that his own father
must have lost so much blood that he was no longer conscious, Benjamin Norton's eyes fluttered open and he spoke
to his son.

"Hill . . . you gotta try to get away."

"I won't let him go!" Jennie Norton disagreed, trembling
like a dried cottonwood leaf in an autumn gale while she
clutched Hill to her as if he were still a babe.

"Woman," Norton whispered, "the boy's gonna be killed
here with the rest of us if he stays. Let him and your sister
go. Least they'll have some chance of living."

For several minutes Hill's mother didn't speak, staring at
the ground, making no sound but her labored breathing. Then
she relented, tears glistening on her cheeks as she turned to
her sister and told her to take off her heavy wool skirt,
shimmy right down to her petticoat and bloomers so she
could run faster and maneuver through the brush and timber.

That's the moment it finally struck Hill that they were going to make him leave them behind. His protests did no good.
And when they made him see that someone had to go for
help or they'd all perish right there . . . then Hill took a deep
breath and squeezed his eyes to shut off the tears.

More scared than he had ever been, Hill leaned over and
hugged his father before he wrapped his arms around his
mother and pressed his head against her breast for what he
knew was going to be the last time he would ever hold his
parents.

Reluctantly he pulled away from her, quickly turning to slip
his hand inside his aunt's trembling fingers, and together they
stole into the night.

*   *   *

When her boy and sister left, the night seemed to close in all the tighter around Jennie Norton.

Her husband was the first to lapse into a deep and merciful sleep. Only once did she think about how much blood Ben had lost from that second terrible leg wound, only once did she wonder if he would ever awaken again . . . and then she thought no more about it.

It was much later when she realized that Lew Day wasn't begging for water anymore.

When Jennie worked up nerve enough to call out to the hired man, she asked, "Is . . . is Lew still alive, Joe?"

There was nothing but silence for a moment, long enough that Jennie began to worry that Moore had himself been killed during one of the intermittent exchanges of gunfire. Then just as she was about to give up and figure she was alone—

"I heard him breathing, Mrs. Norton," Moore replied with a hush that nonetheless seemed to split the stillness of the night.

"The Indians . . . ," she wondered out loud, "you suppose they're still out there?"

"I reckon they are—"

When their question was answered as more than a dozen shots rang out, bullets hissing past, clanging against iron fittings on the wagon, or splintering the box timbers.

"You got any bullets left you over there, ma'am?" Moore asked her a while later when the Nez Perce stopped shooting again.

Jennie dragged herself over to her husband's body and collected what cartridges she could scrounge from his pockets. Then she pulled herself back around the other side of Ben Norton's legs. "I got some, Mr. Moore. But I don't think I can get 'em to you—"

More gunfire shattered the rest of her explanation.

"I'll come for 'em, Mrs. Norton," Moore offered when the noise died away. "You're hurt worse'n me. Stay put where you are."

Before Moore returned to his shelter between the two big carcasses of the Chamberlin team, he scrounged through every pocket for cartridges, even dared to take a peek in the wagon box for another weapon. That's where he found an old hunting pouch filled with a horn of powder and some wadding. And in the dark, the nimble fingers on his good hand touched the trigger guard and stock of a weapon.

"It's a shotgun, by damn!" he said in a joyous whisper.

"Ben's," she explained. "He brung it along in the wagon."

Digging through the pouch, Moore stopped to look into Jennie's pretty face and said, "But your mister didn't bring no shells. Just powder and wads."

Her short-lived hope was all but dashed. Looking away, she admitted, "It doesn't matter, Mr. Moore. Those Injuns gonna figure out soon that there's only one of us still shooting back."

The hired man affectionately cupped her chin in the hand missing those two fingers and said, "Ma'am, long as there's a few bullets for my carbine and some powder for Ben's ol' shotgun . . . Joe Moore's gonna keep the sonsabitches off the rest of us. You trust to that, Mrs. Norton."

The Indians must have heard him crawling off, because they fired a few more shots their way. But Jenny stretched out flat on her belly, draping her arm over Benjamin as if the two of them were at home in the bed they had shared for some thirteen years. She clenched her eyes shut and listened as the hired man fired his rifle.

Then she heard the boom of that shotgun and looked up in surprise.

A few minutes later Joe Moore fired his carbine again. She was watching now, her chin resting on the ground, her arm laid across Ben's chest, when the shotgun went off again: its long, bright tongue of yellow-orange flame sharply defined against the paling of the sky far, far away to the east at the edge of the Camas Prairie.

She started to weep, almost wanting to laugh for joy— maybe out of sheer madness—because Joe Moore was shooting nothing more than powder and wads at the night. Laugh crazily because those goddamned Indians wouldn't know any better, but the warriors did understand the big noise of that deep-throated shotgun, and they damn well must respect the way the weapon spit out flames every time the hired man fired it in a different direction.

Keep the red sonsabitches honest, she thought.

Then she suddenly felt self-conscious, sorry that she had cursed even in her thoughts. Jennie glanced at her husband's pale, ghostly face and was relieved that he could not hear what was in her mind, could not hear it cursing the savages.

Looking out from where she hid under that wagon, Jennie noticed something different about the distant horizon as she lay there with her chin on the damp ground, a cheek resting against her Ben's chest. The sky was changing, the stars no longer bright and sharp. Then she realized that she must be looking east. That the sun would be rising soon.

Jennie Norton began to cry silently again, lying there listening to her husband's feeble heartbeat. Trying her best to remember how to pray—for her son.

Pleading that the red sonsabitches wouldn't get him and Lynn on their way to fetch up some help.

Praying God would save some of them.

Chapter 21

June 15, 1877

Hill Norton was certain the toes of his boots were all but rubbed clear through. Sore as his feet were, and blistered for all the chafing they had endured through the countless soakings in every little stream and creek he and his aunt were forced to cross, unable to dry his wool stockings before they scurried on through what was left of that terrible night. Somehow they managed to cross the far edge of the Camas Prairie in the dark.

His Aunt Lynn didn't say much except to encourage him when his will to go on seemed to flag. Hill was glad she never sounded gruff. He was doing the best he could, and any scolding from her sure didn't help get him up and down these rolling hills on his weary legs any faster, his lungs burning for want of air, his cheeks whipped by the clumps of spindly brush, his knees scraped and bruised for all the times he had stumbled in the dark as they trudged overland, making for the tiny community of Grangeville. Always staying well clear of the road where the Indians might be lying in wait for them.

Only once during their harrowing journey did Lynn Bowers tell her nephew, "You must do your best to keep up, Hill. We've gotta reach Grangeville before sunup."

"If we don't?" he had asked as he wiggled his toes in his soggy socks, feeling the sole on one wet boot working itself loose of the stitching.

"We'll have to hide back in the trees till dark again," she

explained dourly. "Can't take the chance the savages will find us in broad daylight."

That explained it. How Hill Norton and Lynn Bowers crossed that rugged piece of open, rolling prairie overrun with wild-eyed warriors just the way red ants would boil out of their hill he had poked a stick into. All those miles in the dark, stopping only twice to catch their breath before struggling on.

Make it to Grangeville before first light . . . or sit out another day. And that would mean that they wouldn't get any help back to his mother and father until the following morning. Unaccepting of that possibility, Hill Norton thrust himself against the unmovable granite wall that was the last of his endurance, and somehow, he kept on.

Only once did he tell his aunt, "What about the Chamberlins? They run off, Lynn. Ain't it likely they got some help coming already?"

"We can't slow down," she had chided him that one time he felt his spirit sagging beyond redemption. "We can't count on nobody but us, Hill. Your mother . . . and specially your father, too, they're counting on us."

He could not deny that. After all, just about the only thing that stuck in his mind throughout the entirety of that long and dangerous journey for the nine-year-old boy was his remembrance of those two faces. How his father's had grown so white in pain, so pale with the inexorable loss of blood. And his mother's: how those soft, doelike eyes still pleaded with him even as he stumbled on.

With nearly every step, his fears swelled along with his aching feet—afraid not of the Indians, not of failing to reach Grangeville by dawn. More so it was his fear that his mother and father had sent him away to save him. He convinced himself that they knew help would not arrive in time to save them . . . so he figured they must have ordered him away simply to spare him the horrible death they might already have suffered.

Then after all those hours and miles, somehow in the black of that night, he and his aunt got separated. How he had wanted to holler, to scream for her. But instead he had stopped and strained his ears . . . and heard nothing. For the longest time he stood absolutely motionless, thinking he might well be dozing with his eyes open: standing on his feet, dead asleep.

Eventually he set out again, alone this time, determined to make it across this rolling prairie by himself, guided by nothing more than the bright dusting of stars far overhead. Those stars might just as well be on the outskirts of Grangeville, the place seemed so far away. On into the night . . . hour after hour, mile after grueling mile—

He blinked and blinked again, then realized it must be some hot tears in his eyes. Hill realized he smelled that smoke he'd suddenly spotted rising in columns just beyond the fringe of trees. Down the slope below him lay the muddy ruts. And around the next bend in that wide wagon road lay the few scattered buildings of Grangeville. He'd recognize that final curve in his sleep.

Everything was gray and moist and misty, too, with the coming of the sun's first light while he lunged down the side of the gentle slope now, taking huge leaps. Hill could feel his lungs filling to bursting, so much that he wanted to yell out his joy, his relief, finally to bawl with all that he had kept bottled up all night long—when he struck the rain-soaked road and suddenly heard the sound of approaching horses.

Hill Norton froze, turning back to his right—staring, waiting for the approaching danger from out there on the prairie. He could feel the blood drain out of his head. Hoofbeats from the direction of Cottonwood House meant only one thing: Indians coming after him, maybe even Indians come to attack this tiny settlement of Grangeville.

But then he realized the echo of the hoofbeats had fooled him. Hill turned left, saw the bobbing movement of riders— a half-dozen horsemen headed his way, the six of them emerging around that last bend before he could find sanctuary in Grangeville.

And just as young Hill Norton started to shriek and dart back into the brush at the bottom of the slope, one of those horsemen called out to him.

"Ho there!"

He jerked to a halt, spinning on his heel. That wasn't no Injun!

The boy stood there quaking with pent-up fear as the riders came up and one man dismounted.

"Hill? That you, Hill Norton?"

He tried to speak but couldn't. So he only nodded.

All of them were studying his torn, muddy clothing, his bloodied hands, the scratches marring his face. "What you doing out here all by yourself?"

Then he was gushing, like someone had pulled a cork out of a tavern-keeper's beer keg, telling the story of the teamsters and Lew Day, the wagon race from the Indians, and how the warriors had killed them one by one.

The man slowly sank down on one knee in front of Hill and opened his arms, enfolding the boy into a fierce hug that made Hill Norton want to bawl right there. "You 'member me, don't you, young man? I'm Mr. Fenn. Frank Fenn."

"M-Mister Fenn, yes. I do 'member you."

The man held Hill out at the end of his arms. "My bunch, we're from Mount Idaho. We come to spread the word there might be trouble brewing." Fenn stood, dusting off the knee he had stuck in the damp soil between the wagon ruts. "But from what you just tolt me . . . it's plain that trouble's already boiled outta the pot and spilled into the fire."

"My . . . folks. I-I promised 'em—"

"First thing the six of us gonna do, young man—is get you back to town and put some food in your belly," Fenn explained. "And while you're doing that, we're gonna go . . . go find your people, Hill. I promise you that. We'll find your people."

Another day was coming, hinted at behind the hills to the east, when Sun Necklace shouted that they were giving up their chase after the pair of wagon men the war party had bumped into not all that long after they broke off their siege of the white people the warriors had surrounded for most of the night, abandoning that one wagon and all those dead horses by the side of the road.

It was too dangerous, Sun Necklace explained to the grumbling warriors. To approach close enough to the wagon in the dark was far too risky for what rewards they might find. Not with that loud gun spitting fire into the night. After all, the war chief rationalized, there couldn't be much in that little wagon that had been more filled with women and children as it tottered down the road attempting to flee Shore Crossing and the others.

Earlier, in the dark, some of the Shadows had stumbled

right into a few of Sun Necklace's warriors as they attempted to flee the wagon.

Later on, Stick-in-the-Mud reported that he and some others had killed the white man with bullets from their guns, stabbed both of the children, then held the woman down as they took their pleasure and vengeance on her, one after the other until they were tired. Only then did they decide not to leave the woman alive, Stick-in-the-Mud boasted. So he shot an arrow into the woman's breast and they left her for dead near the bodies of her man and the two children.

"Sun Necklace is right," Shore Crossing agreed now as some of the other warriors griped about giving up the chase. "Leave these two wagon men be and let's go in search of something worth our while. If we are to waste bullets killing these Shadows, then we should at least get some plunder for our trouble."

Sure enough, that's what the war party found in the two wagons the wagon men had abandoned on the trail that led back toward the crossing of the Cottonwood. Because those two Shadows were too frightened to put up a fight, they had ridden away on two of their horses, leaving behind the rest of their teams and a pair of wagons.

So Shore Crossing was more than jubilant when Sun Necklace finally broke off the chase, admitting that those two wagons filled with plunder were worth far more than the lives of two frightened Boston Men.

Morning was on its way by the time they returned to the high-walled white man freight wagons. Warriors leaped from their ponies and swarmed over the green and red sidewalls, slashing the ropes tying down the canvas covers stretched across the beds.

Shore Crossing was the first to vault up the tall wheel and fling back one of the tarps to peer at what treasures waited inside. He had had enough experience at the white man's stores to know good plunder from so-so squaw goods. And he knew enough to recognize the potent liquid in those colored bottles he spotted now. With the fiery liquid's own sort of *wyakin* power, Sun Necklace's war party would be re-fortified to go in search of more victims who had wronged the *Nee-Me-Poo*!

Reaching down into a wooden case as several others were clambering up and over the side of the wagon like a swarm of hornets on a puddle of sugar-water, Shore Crossing grabbed a bottleneck in each hand and brandished them aloft with a roar.

Rejoicing, he announced that they had captured a case filled with twelve bottles of thick, sweet-smelling, syrupy brandy, along with another dozen baskets filled with bottles of fizzy champagne.

Red Moccasin Tops pulled out one of those dark glass bottles, studied the paper glued on it a moment, then whacked the end of its long neck over the sidewall. White foam and liquid spewed like a geyser from the broken glass. Handing one of his unopened bottles to Red Elk, Shore Crossing snatched the broken one from Red Moccasin Tops and held it a few inches from his lips as he tilted his head back.

The rush of foam and bubbles poured into his mouth, over his nose and chin in a happy, fizzing torrent.

Blinking his eyes, Shore Crossing pulled the bottle away from his face and sputtered, coughed, and almost gagged with the way the bubbly liquid tickled his nose and throat.

"Here," he said, handing it back to his young cousin and holding up the unopened bottle. "I will drink this instead."

Everyone roared when Red Moccasin Tops sputtered and spit out his first drink of the foamy liquid, just as Shore Crossing had done. But he tried again and started guzzling, then kept on drinking until he had emptied the bottle in one long, gasping series of deep swallows. Inside and around both wagons the two-times-ten were yelling and laughing together again. Shore Crossing realized they hadn't been this happy since the war party left the dead man's store where they had discovered that first keg of whiskey.

Slowly he pulled the mouth of another bottle from his lips, slathered up the thick, sweet brandy with his tongue, and kicked at the corner of the canvas still draped over a portion of the white man's plunder. Shore Crossing knew a whiskey keg when he saw one. Forget this sweet, thick syrup that he had been drinking. And forget those bottles of bubbly foam that tickled his nose.

He had just discovered more of the potent, hard-smelling, mind-numbing, courage-endowing whiskey!

By the time the sky became gray enough to recognize the tops of the waving prairie grass from the sky behind it, Jennie Norton realized the war party must have left.

She hadn't heard anything from them for some minutes . . . or was it hours? She had no way of knowing, numbed the way her mind was with the terror, not to mention the pain in her wounds.

Jennie had torn a wide strip from the hem of her long dress and made two crude bandages with it, knotting them tightly around both calves. Later on she saw no fresh, moist blood on the bandages, so Jennie figured the bleeding had stopped. Still, she could think of nothing to do for that ankle of hers, lying swollen and twisted at the end of one leg, the tender, puffy skin already growing purple as indigo dye.

She began reckoning how she might drag herself into the brush and start for Grangeville on her belly once she got rid of the confining skirt that would only get tangled and caught on the clinging branches. No more than two miles this side of the settlement lay the John W. Crooks place. . . . If she could just reach it before tomorrow morning . . . maybe she might find she'd have enough strength to crawl that far—

Jennie heard voices. Rolling onto her shoulder as she tugged the bloodstained skirt down off her bloomers, she realized it was Moore's voice. He must be talking with Lew Day.

Amazing that the courier was still alive. Last night in the dark when Day fell silent, Jennie was sure the man had died. Just the way her Benjamin had gone quiet, slipping further and further from her as the night crawled on. Lew Day was wounded more times than her Ben . . . so why should he live with all those holes in him and Benjamin slide into death?

"Mrs. Norton?"

The hired man's voice.

"It's Joe Moore, Mrs. Norton," he called to her again. "You got any water over there for Mr. Day?"

"N-no," she said, finding her voice cracking from disuse.

After Joe asked if there might be anything in the wagon bed, she told him she couldn't stand up to find out because of her leg wounds, because of that broken ankle. Then Jennie asked him why he just didn't come on over to check in the wagon himself.

"Them Injuns might've left some scouts to keep watch on us, ma'am," Moore warned. "They're likely watching us, so if I stand up—"

"You're right, Mr. Moore," she confessed with a bitter

sigh. "Your guns are the only thing kept the savages off us last night. If you move out of hiding, if they shoot you ... then they'll come in here for the rest of us."

"Truth is, Mrs. Norton," Moore admitted, "I can't get over there myself. One of 'em made a lucky shot in on me and put a bullet in my hip. Cain't move my leg—"

"Please just get me some water!" Lew Day begged her, interrupting the hired man.

She spotted the satchel the Chamberlins had left behind, its flap open and the contents half-spilled across the ground at the edge of the road where the family had taken off into the dark. Among the waxed bundles of foodstuffs and sulphur-headed lucifers lay a tin cup.

"I got a cup, Mr. Day," she declared. "Maybe I can find a puddle of rainwater what ain't dried up. Or just scrape some of last night's dew off the leaves if I have to."

"Any—anything, Mrs. Norton," he pleaded in a splintered voice. "P-please."

Dragging herself over to retrieve the cup, Jennie pulled herself into the brush by planting one elbow and inching forward, then planting her other elbow before dragging herself a little farther—foot by foot, no more than that at a time.

She found some broad-leafed prairie cabbage that had collected a lot of droplets through the chilly night. Lying among the thick clumps, Jennie licked one leaf after another until her mouth was no longer so dry. Then she began holding a single leaf over the cup and scraping its glistening surface against the rolled, soldered edge of the tin. Leaf by leaf, she slowly drew each one back, collecting the moisture drop by drop as it spilled down the inside of the cup for Lew Day—

Hoofbeats!

Oh, God! Now they've come back to finish us!

She twisted with a jerk of terror, pain shooting clear into her groin. Gasping, she stared down at her legs, afraid she would wet herself in fear—finding her bloomers muddy, grimy, bloodied from her two wounds.

The hoofbeats were coming closer. Several horses, many horses!

Jennie Norton knocked over the cup as she pressed her head down into the grass and covered it with her forearms. Hoping they would not see her, not hear her breathing, not spot her trembling here in the brush.

A horse . . . just one, was at the wagon. Footsteps—one of the sonsabitches stomping around the wagon, likely finding her Benjamin dead . . . Oh, no . . . the heathen was coming toward her now—

Jennie heard the click of a hammer, not knowing if it was a pistol or a rifle. Knowing only that the godless red savage was about to shoot her. Better that than to defile her. Better to die with a bullet in her brain than to live with that nightmarish vision of them rutting between her legs for all the rest of her days—

"No! Don't shoot!" Joe Moore screamed. "For Chrissakes—it's us! Can't you see it's us!"

She heard the footsteps shuffle even closer in the grass as the hired man pleaded some more.

"That's Mrs. Norton!" Moore shouted. "For the love of God—that's Jennie Norton!"

More horses came pounding up suddenly, lots of hooves now. Voices calling out. Angry shouting.

Gradually she opened her eyes and dared peek through the crook of her elbow at the man standing over her.

"M-my God, ma'am. You . . . why—all covered in mud and bloodied up the way you are—I took you for an Injun in the brush."

He knelt beside her as she slowly inched her arm down from her face. And she realized he must see that she was crying.

"It's all right now, Mrs. Norton. My name's Frank Fenn. We come to get you. Come to tell that your boy got through, ma'am. By the grace of the Lord . . . your boy Hill got through to Grangeville."

Chapter 22

June 15, 1877

Captain David Perry pulled his hat down snugly on his head and stepped out into the grayish first light of this fifteenth day of June. He stopped at the edge of the porch and returned the salutes of those two soldiers who next stepped around their mounts and climbed into the saddle, joining a civilian already on horseback.

Then Perry asked, "Corporal Lytte, do you fully understand your orders?"

Joseph Lytte of Perry's F Company, First U.S. Cavalry, nodded as he settled in the saddle between Private John Schoor, also of the same company, and half-breed Joe Rabusco, one of the agency interpreters. "Yes sir, Colonel. We're dispatched to Mount Idaho to look up a man named Loyal P. Brown who sent you a message about the Injuns stirring up some trouble."

"And when you find Mr. Brown?"

"You want us to see for ourselves if the Injuns are causing trouble for the settlers in that area, Colonel."

"And besides doing that snooping around for me, what else have I asked you to do, Corporal?"

The thirty-three-year-old, Ohio-born Lytte grinned a little sheepishly before he admitted, "You want us to make Brown and the rest of 'em feel like the army is staying right on top of things."

"Yes, Corporal. Make those civilians feel like they're getting their money's worth out of their army. Mr. Rabusco, you are under this soldier's command, understood?"

"Yeah, Colonel," the half-breed replied tersely.

"Very well." Perry snapped another salute to his soldiers and took a step back from the edge of the porch as the breeze picked up, scented with rain. "I'll expect you men back before the week is out."

The captain watched the three turn their horses away, heading east for the road that would lead them south along Lapwai Creek before it climbed over Craig's Mountain to the Cottonwood, on across the Camas Prairie where the Non-Treaty bands had been gathered for more than a week now, on to the community of Mount Idaho to find Loyal P. Brown.

When they were gone from sight, he stepped back into his office, closed the door, and sighed, weary of all the paperwork a real soldier had to do anymore, now that there were no more Confederates to fight or Modocs to round up and hang, now that it appeared everything had been put to rest over in Sioux country.

Now his First Cavalry had become nothing more than constables with no Indian wars flaring. Perry sank into his wooden chair with a squeak, realizing that in the span of less than five short years he had become nothing more than a bureaucrat.

Harry Mason had them running the best they could—what with the women slowed down by their ankle-length dresses and the little children being dragged along in spite of their short strides. Harry figured their one chance to get through to Mount Idaho was to make it to the boat landing near the Osborn cabin a half-mile or so up the Salmon. Maybe they could row upstream part of the way, then go in overland once they couldn't row any farther. Maybe a good place to put in and start cross-country would be that French claim, where some of Chodoze's parley-voo friends worked their placer outfit.

Bill Osborn, French Frank, and Harry all carried small burlap bags now, each of them filled with what food the warriors had neglected to leave behind in the ransacked house and store. Back behind a loose board in the pantry Helen Walsh had located a small cache of food. In one stone crock was some bread and a little butter cake, and in another crock they found some cold beef. Hungry as everyone was after what they had endured last night, Harry had nonetheless allowed no one any more than a bite or two; then the rest was stuffed away in those three sacks for their journey over the White Bird Divide to safety.

Only old man Shoemaker had elected to stay behind at the store. "I got to let them calves out to graze," he declared. " 'Sides, them Injuns don't think an ol' coot like me is worth a bullet. Now you go on by yourself, Mr. Mason—and get the rest of them outta here."

So they had darted from the store as Shoemaker calmly headed for the barn. Mason wondered if the old man would live out the day.

Less than ten minutes later when they were approaching the boat landing, a party of warriors came into view up the road. Spotting the white people, the horseman began to whoop and bellow.

"Back to the house!" Harry roared, pushing, shoving the children and women before him as he pitched his burlap sack aside.

Sweeping up young Edward Walsh in his arms, Mason was the last to reach the store with his nephew, just as the war party burst into the yard. Osborn already had French Frank and the two women dragging crates and furniture up to the doors, barricading themselves the best they could, while Harry went to the back wall and used his pocketknife to chip through a wide spot in the chinking between the logs. Through that tiny hole he poked the barrel of his Winchester and prepared to knock one of the bastards off his pony as they began to dismount at the side of the house.

"Don't, Harry!" William Osborn warned.

"Why the hell not?" he demanded, angry at the interruption.

"Maybe we got a chance to talk our way outta this," Osborn reasoned. "But you go shooting one of 'em, there won't be no talk. I know a little Nez Perce, so maybe I can palaver our way out of this."

"Bill's right," Elizabeth Osborn begged. "We gotta give it a try, Harry."

Mason wanted to shoot one of the sons of bitches anyway, to go down fighting. But seeing how the group beseeched him, he relented. As he slowly dragged the barrel of his carbine from that hole in the chinking, Harry was suddenly struck with the overwhelming sense that he was as good as dead right where he stood.

Osborn turned away and stepped over to the side of the only window in that front wall, where he hollered, "*Clatawa!*"

"What's that mean?" Mason demanded.

"I told them to leave."

"They aren't gonna leave," Harry snorted with despair. "And we're never getting out of here alive either."

"I'll try getting them to talk," Osborn suggested as he slipped between Mason and the Frenchman, inching up to that lone window and putting himself in full view.

An immediate volley rattled the timbers surrounding the window and splintered through the door nearby. Bullets came crashing through the panes.

"Give 'em billy-be-hell!" Mason shouted as he leaped to his feet and whipped around, pointing the Winchester out the window.

French Frank stepped into the open with the other two at the same moment, preparing to fire back at the warriors, when the Nez Perce released a second volley.

"You g-goddamned devils!" Osborn groaned as a bullet toppled him. He spilled backward, tripping over the Frenchman who already lay twitching on the floor, a bullet hole in his forehead.

Mason staggered to the side, propping himself against the windowsill, doing his best to hold onto the rifle, to pull the trigger again—but finding he couldn't, not with the way blood was streaming from both arms. The weapon clumsily tumbled from his grasp as he settled backward onto his haunches, listening to the shrill cries of the warriors out front, the haunted wailing of the women and children behind him echoing in his ears.

As he peered down at himself, Harry could feel the painful heaviness of his left arm. But his right forearm was shattered. The bullet that had gone through the left had splintered the Winchester's forestock before it drove shards of lead and wood into what was now a useless right arm.

A third noisy volley made him flinch as pieces of timber and chinking went spinning overhead. Rubbing grit from his eyes, Mason spotted the two thin tick mattresses supported on their rope-and-pine frames.

"Helen! Get everyone under them beds!"

As the two women shuffled the children toward the beds at the back of the room, Mason tried one last time to hoist up his repeater. Perhaps if he could only rest it across one knee, he might just get one, maybe two of them, when the bastards came busting through the door.

But he couldn't even pick it up with the weakened left arm, much less the shattered right arm. Instead, he sprawled onto the floor and began pumping his legs, shoving himself across the floor toward the others when Helen started shrieking in horror. Twisting about was agony, but Mason looked back over his shoulder, finding a bare bronze arm at the broken window, one of the bastards swinging a burning bundle of smoky rags onto the cabin's puncheon floor, where it smoked and raised a horrible stench.

Harry crawled all the faster as the children set up a deafening caterwaul, what with the stifling smoke filling the room. Just as he reached the mattress where his sister Helen was waving him in, Mason turned back to look at the door where the sons of bitches were slamming themselves against the weight of those crates and sacks. At the window he spotted a warrior standing boldly in relief as he hurled a second bundle of coal-oil-soaked rags into the cabin.

Dragging himself across the last yard of bare floor, Mason slid beneath the bed where Helen held a corner of the tick up for him. Elizabeth Osborn had the last of her children scampering beneath the other bed as more of the warriors joined in to heave their shoulders against the door, gradually shoving the massive wooden crates and hundredweight sacks of beans back so they could leap inside after their quarry.

With no more gunfire coming from the house, Mason brooded, *the bastards know we're good as soup. They won't have to burn us out now—*

"Kill 'em, Harry!" Helen Walsh growled as she shoved her revolver into his bloody left hand. "Kill as many as you can!"

But he didn't have the strength.

Staring down at his lap where she'd laid the pistol, he couldn't get the hand to grip that weapon, much less raise it and fire at the warriors who were storming in around the barricade of boxes and bags, all of them shrieking in victory.

He felt so helpless: "If . . . I could only shoot—"

Suddenly the thin tick was yanked back and there stood

three warriors staring down at him. Sick grins crossed the red bastards' faces as they shouted and pointed to the other bed. Then, as Mason watched, two warriors leaped onto the other mattress and began to jump up and down, laughing and screeching in evil joy until they flushed the children and Elizabeth out of hiding.

From out of nowhere one of the warriors kicked him. Harry cried out and tried to raise his left arm to protect himself as the son of a bitch kicked him again. Then another warrior seized Mason's right wrist, yanking on the shattered arm.

A hot, blinding pain shot straight up his arm, through his shoulder, and right into the back of his head as the warrior dragged Mason from behind the tick and into the middle of the floor while the white man screamed nonstop in utter agony.

Foot by foot, the Nez Perce warrior repeatedly lunged with Mason again and again across the floor. The others kicked at him, stomped on his head, and spit at him drunkenly.

It became more than he could stand, reckoning how they were going to drag out this torture for as long as they could . . . make it last for their own goddamned enjoyment.

The drunken bastards. Red niggers never could handle their goddamned whiskey.

Harry struggled to twist his whole body about even though he felt his right arm was about to tear itself loose at the elbow. Gasping with the blinding pain, he gazed through squinted eyes at his sister, at Elizabeth Osborn too—watching as both women were dragged up by the hair, one of the dirt-crusted hands suddenly ripping Helen's dress down to her bodice.

Mason groaned, clenching his eyes, not daring to witness any more, not wanting to live any longer.

His eyes snapped wide open, clear and steady of a sudden as he stared up at the red son of a bitch who was twisting his arm off. Harry growled, "Oh, go ahead and shoot me!"

Still clutching the wounded man's bloody right arm suspended between them, the warrior yanked a pistol from his belt, placed the muzzle between Harry Mason's open, angry eyes . . . and laughed as he blew the white man into oblivion.

*   *   *

Frank Fenn's companions helped him pick Jennie Norton up from the ground and carry her to the back of the wagon, where they settled her near the tailgate. Then they brought Lew Day and Joe Moore to join her in the wagon box before the rescue party began struggling to remove the harness from John Chamberlin's dead horses.

That's when the others decided one of their number, James Adkison, should race back to Grangeville and bring out more volunteers to escort the wounded into the settlement.

Eventually the rest muscled the wagon clear of the carcasses and backed a pair of their riding horses on either side of the singletree. Two of the rescuers, brothers John and Doug Adkison, chose to ride atop their horses they had just hitched to the wagon. Electing to bring up the rear, Fenn joined George Hashagen and Charles Rice when they stepped over to untie their horses from the nearby brush.

With the shrieks of immortal banshees riding out of the maw of hell, the peaceful dawn erupted in war cries and gunshots as a war party appeared at the top of a nearby hill.

Suddenly Fenn and the others were bellowing as they clumsily leaped into the saddles atop their frightened mounts. Already the Adkison brothers were kicking and yelling at their horses, bolting the wagon into motion. Doug Adkison cried for the wounded Day and Moore to stay low and hang on as the wagon careened away from the ditch at the side of the road.

"No!" Jennie Norton screamed, flailing helplessly between Moore and Day. "They didn't get Benjamin in the wagon yet!"

Joe Moore lunged out for her. "Mrs. Norton, get down!" He grabbed Jennie at the last moment, preventing her from pitching over the tailgate as the wagon weaved onto the road.

The Adkison brothers steered their team of saddle horses around the two dead animals.

A bullet whistled past their heads. "D-don't leave my Benjamin!" she whimpered, watching their backtrail as the wagon lumbered away from her husband's body lying by the side of the road, stretched out in the tall grass.

"We can't!" groaned Lew Day as Fenn, Rice, and Hashagen twisted about to fire random shots over their shoulders, each of them galloping right behind the wagon, courageously forming a rear guard. "They'll skin us all alive if we take time to fetch up his body."

Joe Moore nodded, his grimy, powder-blackened face grim. "They can't do no more to hurt your mister now, Mrs. Norton."

Jennie cursed herself for not pleading with them to put Benjamin in the wagon bed even before they hoisted her over the tailgate. Now she was abandoning him in death, something she had never once done in life.

Side to side the frightened, untrained saddle horses whipped the wagon along that muddy, rutted road, racing into the new day's light as Jennie watched the war party gaining, slowly gaining, on Fenn, Rice, and Hashagen. She saw how tight their faces were with fear—figuring they realized that within moments they might well be joining Benjamin Norton in death.

"It's . . . it's help comin'!"

At Joe Moore's exuberant cheer, Jennie turned about painfully, peering up the road as the wagon took a wild bounce. Galloping off the spur that led to the Crook place and onto the Mount Idaho Road were at least eight to ten riders.

John Adkison twisted about on his horse's back, his unkempt hair whipped by the wind as he shouted back to those in the wagon, "It's my brother Jimmy, by damn! He got through to fetch more men! Whoooeee!"

"The red-bellies are laying off!" Lew Day announced, then groaned loudly as the springless wagon bounced over a rock in the road, one wheel spinning free in the air until it came back down with a teeth-jarring jolt.

Twisting around again, Jennie peered beyond the three rescuers on horseback, finding that the war party was indeed slowly reining up.

"They spotted them others coming out for us!" Moore shouted lustily. Then the hired man reached out and gripped the back of her blood-crusted hand. "We're saved, Mrs. Norton. Don't you see? We're saved—"

"But not my Benjamin," she sobbed, hiding her face in her hands as her head sank to her lap.

"They cain't hurt him no more, ma'am," Moore cooed. "We'll go back and get him—that's a promise. But, till then, the bastards can't hurt your husband no more."

Chapter 23

June 15, 1877

Helen Walsh shrieked as she had never screamed before the instant her brother's head snapped violently and the back of his skull blew off in a red splatter.

In the next moment, the Indians surrounding her were howling as they clawed at her clothing. Cowering in a corner, the children were screeching even louder as Elizabeth was yanked to her feet by her hair. In a matter of heartbeats the warriors stripped both women naked to their stockings and boots, knocking Helen down and throwing Elizabeth Osborn back onto the mattresses as their young children scampered aside like a brood of chicks a fox had flushed from the hen-house.

Helen bit down on her tongue as a warrior backhanded her little Edward when he tried to reach his mother. But she angrily slapped one of the Nez Perce and attempted to lunge toward her whimpering son as his older sister, Masi, pulled Edward back from the growling warriors. The girl swept her brother into her arms, then turned protectively toward the corner.

Almost as if young Masi instinctively realized what these red heathens were going to do to their mother.

Helen's head was smacked to the side with the brutal blow delivered by the warrior she had just slapped. She staggered, collapsing on her hands and one knee, seeing a warrior already climbing on top of Elizabeth, two more of them holding her arms and legs as she thrashed against the attack.

Then Helen realized she was being stretched out by some hands too, smelling their rancid grease, the firesmoke and dirt as their faces and arms and bodies loomed over her. The others pulled back slightly the moment they got her pinned on the mattress. She looked up through her puffy, swollen eyes in time to watch the Indian pull his breechclout aside just before he flung himself upon her.

She was sure he would rip her apart—*but that'll be all right,* she thought. *At least I'll be dead.*

One after another the warriors took their turns at both women. Eventually, somewhere in the middle of it all, Helen lapsed into sweet, blessed unconsciousness . . .

Suddenly she came to, having no idea how long she had been out. Helen did her best to cover her nakedness with her arms in front of the savages as a half-dozen or more of them backed away from the mattress together, settling their clothing and laughing. That is, all but one of the heathens.

As the children continued to wail, this lone savage stood there between the two naked women and surprised them both by speaking a little English. "You go now."

"You're . . . you're setting us free?" Helen asked, trembling like a leaf with shame and fear. "Letting us go?"

"You go Lewiston. You go Slate Creek. You go where you like. Go now."

Then the warriors were gone, hurrying out the door, onto their ponies. Their hoofbeats faded in the last of that day's sunlight.

Masi came over with a thin blanket for her mother, then handed another to Elizabeth, whose dress still hung from her shoulders although it had been ripped completely down the middle.

"I . . . I wanna change my dress before we go," Mrs. Osborn said with a hollow voice.

Helen wanted to give this friend a last shred of dignity, so turned away slightly when she asked, "Where do you think we should go?"

"Anywhere," Elizabeth said, clutching the blanket around the tattered billows of her clothing.

"I figure to head out for Slate Creek," Helen suggested, summoning up the last vestiges of her courage. "It's getting late, but we might just make it there before it gets too dark to go on."

"Find me a dress," Mrs. Osborn said quietly as she started to hobble away, her legs scratched and bloodied beneath the bottom of the blanket. "A bl-black dress for mourning my William."

Helen realized she didn't have anything of the kind for herself, then thought of Edward. In a couple more days her husband would be getting back to this house from his trip and he'd find the ruin of it all, discover the three bodies, and likely go crazy wondering where she and their children had gone. Wondering if the heathens had stolen his wife and their young'uns.

Yet Helen Walsh knew she couldn't stay here. Not with the bodies of the three men lying right there in pools of blood. Not after . . . what the warriors had done to both women there in front of the children.

When they both had dressed, Helen and Elizabeth picked up those three burlap sacks with the bread, cake, and cold meat still inside and started the youngsters upriver. The sun was going down, and the air was growing cool. Helen brooded on how good a nice, hot bath would feel.

Then she realized that no matter how hard she might scrub, likely she would never feel clean again.

Fort Lapwai
June 15, 1877

Dear Mamma,
Well, our Indian troubles, that we thought all over, have begun again, and this time the officers here seem to think it means business. General Howard is here again, and an Indian inspector from Washington is at the Agency. The thirty days that was given the Indians to come onto the Reservation expires today, and early this morning a party was started from the post to the upper part of the Reservation to see if they were keeping their promises. The party came back an hour ago, riding like mad people, and brought with them two friendly Indians that they met on the mountains and who were bound for the post and the Agency. The Indians had been riding

all night and said other Indians, not friendly, were after them. These Indians bring word that the Indians have murdered four settlers up by the mountains, and that they are holding war dances, and that White Bird is riding round his tent on horseback and making circles on the ground, which is his way of declaring that they have taken up the hatchet, etc.

General Howard sent at once for four companies more to move up here and has sent off for hard bread and all such things that troops on a scout need. Things look exciting.

The story of the Indians is corroborated by a letter sent to the General from some settler up in the region asking for help and stating that the Indians were making trouble already and saying, "For God's sake, send plenty of troops. Don't handle them with gloves on." I have heard officers discussing it, and the general impression is that if the Indians have begun, the troops are in for a summer campaign. General Howard said, "I wish the Doctor was here, but I will dispatch at once for Dr. Alexander, who is at Wallula, and he can join us at once." My first thought was that I was glad John wasn't here, but I know he would feel that his place was with the troops from the post he belongs to. If there is trouble, he will have to go anyway, as soon as he gets back. So I expect that all my delight in getting him back will be spoiled by knowing he will have to leave me again at once. We here will feel perfectly safe. The post will not be left without a good garrison. Two companies of infantry, at least, will be left here. But how anxious we will be about the little party out after the Indians. It is all horrible!

Mrs. Boyle just ran down the back way for a minute to discuss the matter for a little. She says it makes her feel sick. It is dreadful to think what might happen, but I can't think these Indians, those we have seen so often, are going to fight the troops. General Howard, the inspector, the Agent, and Colonel Perry and the aides are all just now counciling together as to the country and best plan of action. I wish John was home, and I wish the Indians were at the bottom of the Red Sea. I don't feel as if any other matter deserved consideration this morning.

. . . I do wish Doctor would come home. I feel as if the bottom was knocked out of everything.

Emily looked down and saw how her pen was trembling so. It was almost as if she were holding her breath and she couldn't take another until he got back to her. How she wished he was there to put his arms around her.

Oliver Otis Howard stirred from his chair at the sudden hubbub out on the parade and stepped from Captain Perry's quarters onto the porch and into the early-afternoon light to watch the five riders hurriedly dismount from their lathered ponies in front of the quartermaster's office at the south end of the post grounds.

They appeared to be those same two soldiers and that half-breed interpreter—the three men Perry had dispatched early that morning to make the long journey to Mount Idaho in hopes of determining why the settlers in that area were so alarmed at the Non-Treaty bands presently on their way in to the Lapwai Reservation.

But with them were two more riders: Indians.

Howard stepped off the porch and started across that end of the parade for those five riders who stopped among a gaggle of soldiers and officers in front of the commissary. He realized he was already distressed that the three had returned after no more than a matter of hours—on lathered, done-in army mounts.

"Get them inside, Colonel!" Howard barked at Perry. "This is not meant for general gossip!"

The curious soldiers and anxious officers turned, finding the general approaching. They self-consciously began to back away from the five new arrivals. Perry quickly ushered Corporal Lytte and Private Schoor, along with Rabusco and those two Nez Perce, into the office and closed the door as soon as Howard shoved his way past the muttering crowd beginning to grow outside.

Otis slammed the door behind him. "What's going on, Colonel?"

Perry wagged his head, saying, "Just what we were trying to find out, General. I've sent for Whitman to help Joe translate." The post commander immediately whirled on Rabusco. "Tell it to me again: what did these two say to you that made you turn around?"

"Them two, Nat Webb and Putonahloo, not silly young men," Rabusco answered gravely. "Them two say they're killing white men."

"Who's killing white men?" Howard demanded, a cold knot tightening in his belly. Just when everything had seemed to be in place for making a success of his Nez Perce policy, enough of a triumph to wash away the stain of that debacle over the Freedmen's Bureau . . . now some of the young bucks in the throes of their Dreamer religion had gone off and pulled the rug out from under him.

"Non-Treaty," Corporal Joseph Lytte explained.

"White Bird's warriors," Rabusco clarified.

"When? And how did this happen?" Howard demanded.

He could clearly see how agitated the two Nez Perce became as they began to repeat their story for the interpreter. Rabusco had to stop them constantly, waving his hands for quiet that would allow him to make some sort of translation here and there throughout their tidal wave of information. The whole lurid tale of it came out in a hodgepodge of warrior names, places, and incidents. Disjointed as it was, the story nonetheless spelled out that at least two, perhaps as many as four, warriors had taken off from the village gathering at the head of Rocky Canyon to exact some sort of revenge against a white man who had killed the father of one of those avenging warriors.

By the time that Perrin Whitman and agent John Monteith arrived in a sweat from their sprint across the parade to confirm Rabusco's terrifying translation, Howard was working hard at convincing himself this would prove to be only an isolated incident.

The general sighed and told them, "I have heard nothing that convinces me this is anything more than one young buck getting in a last, bloody lick against this fellow Ott who was absolved of murdering the man's father."

"But, General," Whitman began, "it wasn't Ott the warriors ended up killing. They murdered another man—Devine.

A Salmon River settler who also harbored no kindness for the Nez Perce."

"This isn't good," Perry intoned, wagging his head.

"We'll surely keep an eye on things," Howard observed, intent on not letting the somber mood get out of hand. "The bands are on their way in, just as planned."

"But, General—this doesn't bode well for getting the Non-Treaties onto the reservation," Perry argued. "I suggest that we send some emissaries from the agency right to their camp on Camas Prairie, see if they can settle things down and convince the chiefs to get their people to Lapwai before any more incidents stir up the white settlers to retaliate against the Nez Perce."

"Yes," Howard ruminated, combing fingers through his graying beard. "If the settlers start taking revenge for that murder, then the Non-Treaty bands will take their revenge . . . and we'll soon have a general war on our hands."

Perry turned to Whitman. "Perrin, I want you and Agent Monteith to convince Chief Jonah to go talk to the Non-Treaty chiefs—convince them to get on their way here and do all they can to quiet things down right away."

"I'll send Jonah along with another," Monteith suggested. "A good man for this job would be James Reuben."

"The one who helped translate when Joseph and the chiefs were here?" Howard asked.

Turning to the general, Monteith said, "He's Joseph's nephew. A treaty Indian, like Joseph's father-in-law."

"Very good," Howard replied hopefully. "I'm sure these two emissaries of yours will find that the murders are the handiwork of a few rebellious young bucks who have merely stepped out from the control of their chiefs."

Chapter 24

June 15, 1877

After trudging a few miles up the Salmon from her brother's place while the shadows lengthened, Helen Walsh led the others out of the timber, hurrying them across the open ground and in the back door of the Titman place. The warriors had been here, breaking everything they did not take with them as they scrounged about for weapons and whiskey.

Her gut flamed once more with the nightmarish memory of their repeated assaults, smelling again the stench of their stale, whiskey-sodden breath, feeling them rip her apart inside as each one in turn grunted over her. Just that remembrance made Helen start to retch, but she caught herself and swallowed down what little bile there was left in her stomach.

Watching her wipe her mouth, Elizabeth Osborn and the children stood quietly in the utter silence of the place.

Turning to them all as she dropped the two sacks she was carrying, Helen said, "I want all of you to look around for anything to eat. Anything. Bring it here so you can share it with everyone else. And, Masi—I want you and Annie to go out to the barn and see what you can find out there to eat."

As the children scattered to search under every overturned table and tick, to search in every drawer and on every shelf still nailed to a wall, Helen glanced at Elizabeth and wondered if her friend was feeling the sort of numbing shame she herself was suffering.

Perhaps that was why Elizabeth hadn't spoken to her much after they lit out from the Mason place, hadn't said a thing at all about what the warriors had done to the two of them.

It wasn't long before her daughter Masi and Elizabeth's girl, Annie, were back from the barn. Masi proudly carried a large pail she set at her mother's feet.

"You found that? Wonderful," Helen enthused as she hugged both of the girls. "Milk is just the thing to have with our supper."

After calling the rest of the children over and having them sit in a small circle at the middle of the floor in the ransacked front room, Helen and Elizabeth distributed some of that food the three men had stuffed inside those mill sacks. They located two tin cups, dipping them into what little milk the Titmans had urged from their cows before they up and abandoned the place. But there was enough that the children could wash down their bread, the butter cake, and a little cold meat for each of them.

"Ain'cha gonna eat, Mamma?" Masi asked innocently, licking at the filmy mustache across her upper lip.

"I'm not hungry, children," Helen lied, sensing the pangs stab through her like a twisting butcher knife she wished the savages had used on her instead of their . . . their . . . but she squeezed away that thought. Although she hadn't eaten for more than twenty-four hours, Helen Walsh had no appetite and couldn't bear the thought of trying to swallow any food. She knew it would likely come right back up. Better that the children were fed—

Suddenly a face appeared at the front window, like an odd, out-of-place portrait surrounded by the broken panes of glass the warriors had shattered. Two of the children shrieked. Helen and Elizabeth each grabbed for a child, at the same time searching for some object lying on the floor they could use as a club. Then Helen recognized the face.

"Mr. . . . Mr. Shoemaker," she gasped with no small relief, her heart pounding. "You startled us."

"I been comin' on your backtrail," he admitted as he stepped into the open doorway from the narrow porch, his soppy boots still soggy on the timbers, his clothes damp and clinging to his skin. "After I got them calves out on their pasture, figgered I'd just as well light out to see you got in to Slate Creek awright, ma'am."

Helen watched his weepy eyes dart over the children as if he was weighing what he could say. With his next words, Shoemaker's voice dropped into a husky whisper. "By the time I was coming in from the pasture, I see'd the Injun ponies out front of the house, ma'am. When the shooting started I took off back of the barn. Climbed down into the crick under the brush and stayed up to my neck in the water, hoping like hell them bastards didn't come find me. Stayed there a long time after it got quiet in the house. Later on, I come up to the window and found wasn't nobody left in the place. So I reckoned I'd come after you and the children."

"We're glad you're with us now," Helen admitted, but doubted that the old man could offer them any protection if the warriors decided to return for more of their abuse or to simply kill them all.

"I figger to catch my breath here, Mrs. Walsh," Shoemaker explained as he sat and started to untie one of his soggy broghams. "Dry my stockings a bit, then I'll push on down to Slate Creek."

Thankful for his company, she said, "We'll be ready to go when you are, Mr. Shoemaker."

"Oh, no, ma'am," the old fellow retorted quickly as he dragged the first shoe off, and the stocking with it. "I don't think you and the young'uns should go on with me."

Elizabeth Osborn got to her feet to stand beside Helen. She asked, "You're talking about going alone, yourself?"

"I think it's best I leave you and the children here," he explained as he wrung out that first stocking on the bare floor.

"You wouldn't leave us here alone, Mr. Shoemaker!" cried young Annie Osborn as she leaped to her feet and rushed over to clamp her arms around the old man's neck.

Helen watched as the hardened, resolute look on Shoemaker's face suddenly softened.

He gently wrapped his arms around the child and brought her into his lap, his weary, bloodshot eyes misting. "Y-you wanna go with me, Annie?"

"Take me when you go, please," she begged.

Peering up at Elizabeth, Shoemaker said, "If your mamma says you can come with me."

Elizabeth glanced uncertainly at Helen for a moment, then said to the old man, "Yes. You can go, Annie. But you do what Mr. Shoemaker says. When he tells you to hush, you be quiet as a field mouse."

Annie got to her feet and lunged against her mother. "I know, Mamma. I won't say a thing because the Injuns gonna hear me. I won't make no trouble for Mr. Shoemaker."

He pulled off his second sock and was wringing it as he said, "We'll go through to Slate Creek by way of the timber. Get some help, then c'mon back to fetch the rest of you."

Helen nodded. "We'll find a place to hide till you do."

After knotting his broghams once more, Shoemaker stood and gazed at the two women. "I'll be back for the rest of-you. Don't neither of you ladies worry 'bout that."

Then the old man knelt before the child. "C'mon, Annie girl. You're gonna ride to Slate Creek."

"P-piggyback?"

"A real horsey ride, li'l'un," Shoemaker said as he rose with the girl on his back, her tiny arms locked around his loose throat wattle.

At the door he turned again one last time to the two women. "Annie here's gonna give me a hand bringing you back some help."

Then Helen Walsh and Elizabeth Osborn watched the grizzled old field-worker step through the doorway and into what that night would bring them all.

From that moment on, it was almost as if she were holding her breath. To see if the old man really did make it to Slate Creek to bring back a rescue party . . . or if they were all destined to die at the hands of the heathens.

Less than an hour after seeing treaty chief Jonah Hayes and Joseph's nephew, James Reuben, off for the Nez Perce encampment, David Perry heard hollering out on the parade. He went to the door and stepped onto the porch that ran the width of the duplex residence he and his wife shared with the FitzGeralds just in time to watch those two Nez Perce returning to the post on their very weary ponies, accompanied by two civilians he did not recognize.

As the quartet reined up in front of Perry late that afternoon, dragging with them an instant crowd of the curious and the concerned, the captain had figured the pair for civilians from the settlements. White men. But when he peered under the brims of their hats, Perry could tell the riders were Indians. Likely members of the Treaty bands who were in Mount Idaho on some business when the uproar started. Both of them sat horses clearly done in by their ordeal of crossing the rolling prairie and the Craig's Mountain Divide between Grangeville and this Lapwai post.

"My name's West," one of the men said a bit breathlessly as he reached inside his shirt and fumbled. "Brown—he give me writing for you."

The second added with a thick accent, "Chapman."

"Ad Chapman?" Perry asked.

"Yes, Chapman's this man's friend. *Tucallasasena* is Looking Glass's brother," the first rider replied in his uncertain English as General Howard stepped up to Perry's elbow.

"Looking Glass's brother, is he?" David peered over the parade quickly, seeing how the wives and children of the post were converging on the scene.

He turned and found Emily FitzGerald and Mrs. Boyle too, both of them looking on with the creases of concern graying their long faces. Too much activity, far too much, for any of them to attempt to keep this a secret any longer now.

"Where is this message from Mr. Brown?" Howard asked impatiently, leaning against the porch railing and holding out his hand.

The general took the paper from the rider, unfolding it as he stepped back to stand beside Perry. Together, they both coolly read in silence:

MOUNT IDAHO, 7 A.M., Friday, June 15, '77
COMMANDING OFFICER FORT LAPWAI:

Last night we started a messenger to you, who reached Cottonwood House, where he was wounded and driven back by the Indians. The people of Cottonwood undertook to come here during the night; were interrupted; all wounded or killed. Parties this morning found some of them on the prairie. . . . One thing is certain, we are in the midst of an Indian war. Every family is here, and we will have taken all the precautions we can, but are poorly armed. We want arms and ammunition and help at once. Don't delay a moment. We have a report that some whites were killed yesterday on the Salmon River . . . You cannot imagine people in a worse condition than they are here. . . .

> Yours truly,
> L. P. Brown

So stunned was he by Brown's message that it surprised Perry when the other Nez Perce courier held out his own folded paper.

"A second message, General," Perry commented.

"Tucallasasena," the half-breed began, "he come out of Mount Idaho 'bout a hour after me. Catched up with me on the road near Craig's Mountain."

Howard appeared to give the riders no mind as he took the page and opened it, both he and Perry seeing that Brown had written it an hour after the first message they had just finished reading. The captain's eyes flashed across the words written by an increasingly agitated L. P. Brown:

I have just sent a despatch by Mr. West, a half-breed. Since that was written the wounded have come in . . . Teams were attacked on the road and abandoned. The Indians have possession of the prairie, and threaten Mount Idaho . . . Lose no time in getting up with a force . . . Give us relief, and arms and ammunition . . . I fear that the people on Salmon have all been killed, as a war party was seen going that way last night. We had a report last night that seven whites had been killed on Salmon. Hurry up; hurry! Rely on this Indian's statement; I have known him for a long time; he is with us.

> L. P. Brown

Perry looked up from the page, blinking with worry as he took a step closer to the railing. Deep concern gouged a furrow between his eyes as he glowered at the half-breed and Looking Glass's brother.

Apprehensively Perry took a deep breath, then said, "All right now—you must explain to us exactly what's going on at Mount Idaho."

*   *   *.

Afternoon

Mamma, dear,

I only have time to write a few lines, as the mailman will be here. Oh, Mamma, we have just heard such horrible news. The Indians have begun their devilish work. An Indian and half-breed came in this afternoon with dispatches from Mount Idaho, a little settlement up on the mountains. The Indians have murdered seven more men on the road and also have attacked an emigrant train killing all. They broke one poor woman's legs, and she saw them kill her husband and brother. They say everybody is gathered into this little town. They want help, and arms, and ammunition immediately. They say in the most piteous manner, "Hurry, hurry, hurry. We are almost helpless and bands of Indians are all around us." They fear the settlers in the ranches around them are killed, as nothing is seen of them.

Our post is all in a commotion. The two companies of cavalry will leave in a few hours. They don't dare to wait even for more troops, though dispatches have already been sent everywhere to gather up the scattered troops in this Department. My dear old husband will have to follow Colonel Perry's command, as soon as he gets back here. These poor people from Mount Idaho say, "One thing is certain. An Indian war is upon us." You know these devils always begin on helpless outlying settlements. Mrs. Boyle and I have just been sitting looking at each other in horror. Poor Mrs. Theller is busy getting up a mess kit for her husband. Major Boyle remains in command of the post. The talk among the officers is that there will be a great deal of trouble.

I will write more before I turn out the lamp for the night.

Chapter 25

June 15, 1877

"Shush!" Helen Walsh hissed at the children.

Elizabeth Osborn instantly looped her arms around two of the littlest youngsters and clamped her hands over their mouths lest they cry out.

"Stay down!" Helen warned them all.

"T-they come back?" Mrs. Osborn's voice cracked with undisguised fear.

Helen felt that very same terror. Only difference, she figured, was that she could swallow hers down and Elizabeth could not. If this was going to be the end, Helen thought it better to see it coming, to know death was on its way, to prepare herself and the others.

So if those horsemen just now reaching the tree line in the distance were another war party who had tracked them here—or even the first bunch of heathens who were returning for more of their depraved assaults—then she damn well hoped the bastards would out-and-out kill her right off rather than subject her to their unspeakable tortures. Kill her two children too, she prayed. Better that than ever witnessing again what they had been forced to watch done to their mother—

Those weren't headdresses. And those horsemen didn't ride like bareback warriors sat atop ponies.

They were . . . white men!

"Eliz—Elizabeth," she stammered, finding her mouth gone

dry from those moments of panic and dread that suddenly drained from her the way a leeching poultice could draw poison from a boil. "We're safe now."

Mrs. Osborn scooted slightly on her rump, still holding the little ones tightly against her, and poked her head over the windowsill, staring toward the side of the Titmans' yard. Then Elizabeth began to cry, silently—only her mouth ratcheting up and down slowly, tears streaming from her eyes. Not making a sound.

"Old Shoemaker must've gotten through," Helen declared, reaching out to grip one of Elizabeth's grimy hands. Squeezing the hand, she whispered, "We must swear to each other, for all time, that we won't ever tell what happened to us."

Elizabeth Osborn gazed into Helen's eyes with a blank expression.

"Swear it," Helen prodded. "Swear you won't ever tell what those savages did—how they ruined us."

Mrs. Osborn turned slightly to peer at the riders slowly coming to a halt just beyond the line of trees.

"Swear it, Lizzy! Swear not a word of what they done to us will ever cross your lips," Helen demanded.

Turning back to look at Mrs. Walsh, Elizabeth finally nodded. In a barely audible whisper, she vowed, "Never will I say a word of what they done to me—"

"Ho, the house!" one of the riders called as he threw up an arm and stopped the dozen or so men with him.

It was clear the horsemen had halted where they could wheel into the timber should they find themselves under attack by the savages, Helen thought as she stood, knees beginning to tremble. Fatigue, lack of food, all the hours and miles—but mostly the nightmarish terror they had somehow endured. She slowly pulled back the broken, ill-hung door with a loud scrape and stepped into the twilight shadowing that front porch.

"Ma'am?" the rider croaked with no little surprise as he nudged his horse forward.

With no more than that one word, she could hear the faintest rolling resonance of a Southern accent. "I'm Helen Walsh."

He took his hat off politely, his eyes clearly jarred by her disheveled appearance. "William Watson, Mrs. Walsh. Your husband in there with you?"

She dragged a hand under her nose, jutted out her chin, and said, "No, Mr. Watson. My husband has been killed."

"The Injuns?" he asked, replacing his hat snugly.

"Yes," she replied as she heard the sound of feet shuffling out the door and coming to a stop behind her skirts.

All those horsemen sat frog-eyed as they peered over the two women and those pitiful children.

"Just you ladies and the young'uns?" Watson asked.

"Yes," and Helen felt like she needed to sit. Slowly lowering herself to the front of the porch, Helen settled as the dozen riders dismounted with a squeak of their saddles.

Watson gave orders for two of his horsemen to enter the house and assure themselves that no one else was inside, then look for any weapons and ammunition they might find. He posted four others around the house to keep watch for a war party that might try to slip up on them.

The group's leader stepped over to Helen and removed his hat again. "You been through hell, ain'cha, ma'am?"

"W-we just wanna go where we'll be safe," she begged, still rooted on the porch.

He peered up at the woman. "That's what we come for, Mrs. Walsh. Last night an Injun woman named Tolo* come in from the Nez Perce camp over on Camas Prairie. She walked twenty-six miles to Florence, up in the hills yonder—where all of us are working our claims. Damnedest thing: that Injun woman coming to warn us." Watson sighed. "She brought word that some of their bucks was whiskeyed up and killing white folks over on the Salmon. I asked for volunteers, and these fellas got under way with me last night. We been taking folks over to Slate Creek, so that's where I'm fixing to take all of you when we light out from here."

Her damp, red-rimmed eyes studied some of the mud-crusted, shaggy, poorly dressed miners; then she asked, "Any of you men have families over here along the Salmon, Mr. Watson?"

"No, ma'am. Ain't none of us from these parts," he confessed as he ground a boot heel into the damp earth, glancing around at the six miners who had remained with the horses when he dismounted and dispatched the others to search the

---

*Tulekats Chickchamit, sometimes rendered in the Nez Perce language as Tula

house. "A time like this, howsomever, a man does what needs doing. Time like this, Mrs. Walsh . . . we're all like family now."

Late in the evening of the fourteenth, after the warriors had finished off all the whiskey in their store and torn off into the night, Isabella Benedict returned to the house, where she stretched a quilt over Bacon's body, the most decent thing she could do for the Frenchman now that she knew they had to leave. While her daughters waited, Isabella quickly gathered a few things and a little money she figured they would need for food and a bed in Mount Idaho, placing everything she was taking in a large muslin sewing bag.

Only then did she plunge into the darkness of White Bird Canyon, heading upstream now that the night gave her and the girls some measure of safety. Almost immediately they ran across the contorted, bloody, arrow-ridden body of old man Baker. She hurried the girls on by, doing her best to clamp her hands over their eyes.

Not far beyond Baker, she had to steer the children clear of John Manuel's body lying by the side of the trail, just outside the fence line. It proved to be such slow going for them to reach the Manuel place in the dark, picking their way through the timber along White Bird Creek and listening for warriors.

Even though the Indian had told her she could leave with the children, told her she could flee with them here to the Manuel ranch, Isabella wasn't about to trust any Indian now.

Reaching the house, Isabella had shared a joyless reunion with Jennet Manuel and her two children. Evidently brought in by the commotion of her arrival, Patrick Brice and George Popham had sneaked in from the brush outside where they had been hiding ever since the warriors looted them of their only firearms.

"You should try to come with me," Isabella had begged Jennet more than once.

"I won't leave long as I know John's out there," Mrs. Manuel whimpered like a wounded animal. "Don't know if he's dead or alive—so I'm not going off till I can see to his body."

Isabella stood staring at the three adults in wonder, then gradually realized the men didn't have the nerve to venture far from the house and the brush to see if John Manuel truly was dead or if he somehow still clung to life.

Gazing at her own two daughters, Mrs. Benedict decided she didn't want to chance making that long walk over the divide to Mount Idaho by herself. After Brice and Popham once again ducked out of the house to stay hidden in the brush, Isabella and the girls stayed the night in the Manuel house.

All the children had fallen to sleep like logs, curling up right where they were on the plank floor, while Jennet and Isabella kept watch at the parlor window. Sometime shortly before midnight Isabella spotted a handful of riders moving slowly out of the inky darkness. She had tapped Jennet on the forearm, then pressed her finger against her lips before pointing at the starlit yard. Mrs. Manuel nodded that she had seen the horsemen.

But those six riders moved on past the house without venturing any closer. A half a dozen warriors, feathered up and each one carrying a rifle of some sort in his hands. They scared Isabella to her marrow. The next bunch of the bastards to happen along might not treat her and the young'uns near so kindly, might not let them go free as you please.

So as soon as the riders had passed, Isabella gently shook her two girls. "We've got to sleep in the woods tonight, little ones."

Without a word of complaint, they both got to their feet, sleepily kneading some knuckles into their eyes as they followed Isabella out the back door and into the dark timber. When she found a likely spot where she could keep an eye on both the house and the wagon road going by, Mrs. Benedict settled back against a tree trunk and let her daughters drift off with their heads resting in her lap.

She herself slipped in and out that night, awakening at every little noise floating out of the blackness of the brushy hillside beyond the Manuel house. At times she felt like crying out—hoping it was a rescue party—but bit her lip instead to keep from alerting any of the roving war parties.

Once, she heard a voice calling out from beyond the yard, "Mrs. Benedict. Mrs. Benedict."

But Isabella knew it had to be an Indian trick. A few of them knew enough English to sound white as that. And she realized the warriors knew exactly who she was: wife of the "store man" who had shot at several of them when they tried to steal from the store goods. She wasn't about to let the bastards know where she was hiding.

As soon as the sun came up the morning of the fifteenth, she heard a few faint sounds from the brush around them, thinking Popham and Brice must be moving around, checking for John Manuel. Maybe he wasn't dead, she considered. Isabella kept herself and the girls completely silent, not daring to make a sound if those noises weren't the white men.

Through that day Isabella huddled in the brush with her girls, watching as horsemen crossed and recrossed the hillside, descending to the road where Manuel had lain bleeding after the attack, leaking his life into the dirt of this land he had tried to put roots into, like her own Sam.

As the sun went down that Friday, she had no earthly idea where Sam could be. If he were still alive at all.

But Isabella did know one thing with rock-hard certainty: she had to get away from here, not spend one more night or another day. No matter the cost, she had to get the girls to Mount Idaho.

As soon as it was dark enough, here before the moon rose in the east and without worrying to tell another soul, Mrs. Benedict ushered the two little ones out of the brush and started up the steep, all-but-barren hillsides that would lead them over the White Bird Divide to Camas Prairie.

If she made it there with her daughters by the time the sun appeared . . . they just might have a chance to reach Grangeville or even Mount Idaho. No matter what the odds were against reaching the top without being captured or killed . . . she and her babies might just have a chance.

Chapter 26

June 15, 1877

John G. Rowton had nearly all forty of his men spread out in a long line, searching the tall grass and brushy thickets as the sun eased down that Friday afternoon ... because there was still one more person to find somewhere near the carcasses of those wagon horses abandoned beside the Camas Prairie road. Perhaps one more body to bring in.

Rowton's day had begun just before dawn as he and the others were preparing to set out to warn families southwest in the direction of Henry C. Johnson's ranch that the warriors were more than just rambunctious and making trouble. The red sons of bitches were killing and looting something terrible—what with the way they'd done their devilment with the Nortons. His riders were barely settling onto their saddles when young James Adkison galloped into Grangeville with word that Frank Fenn's rescue party needed rescuing itself. They were just starting down the lane from old man Crooks's place when Adkison came larruping up on his lathered horse.

Sure and be damned, if that wasn't a sight when Rowton's men reached the Mount Idaho–Lapwai Road to see that wagon barely staying ahead of a pack of the red devils! No sooner did those forty-some horsemen fan out across the road than those cowardly Nez Perce decided to turn around and hightail it out of there, but quick.

Never could count on those spineless buggers to put up any sort of a fight when the odds were anywhere close to even!

The other two Adkison boys, who were perched aloft the
horses hauling the wagon, pulled to a halt among Rowton's
men, gratitude plain on their pasty faces as Frank Fenn and
the other two riders reined to a halt behind the wagon.

"You gotta go get my husband!" demanded a scratched-
up, disheveled woman the moment she sat up in the wagon
bed.

What for all the blood and grime smeared on her face, not
to mention all the mud caked in her hair, John didn't recognize the woman as he eased his horse along the sidewall.
"Ma'am?"

"Mr. Rowton—please: you gotta go get my husband!" she
implored, clasping her hands together prayerfully. "These
men, they left him behind when more Injuns come along—"

"You know me?"

She tried to scoot closer to him across the wagon bed, but
it was plain to see she was in agony as she shifted her bloody
legs. "Can't you see? I'm Jennie Norton, Mr. Rowton."

"Glory," he whispered under his breath, startled at her appearance: blood crusted every bare patch of skin and stained
her clothing; blackened grime was scrimshandered into every
wrinkle, mud smeared on near everything else that wasn't
bloody. "Mrs. Norton, you say Benjamin's back there?"

Joe Moore inched himself a little higher along the sidewall
and spoke up to defend the others. "He's dead, John. We'd
a brung him, but them bastards jumped us afore we could get
him in the wagon."

Rowton touched the brim at the front of his hat. "Mrs.
Norton, we'll go get your Benjamin now."

"There's others," Moore declared before Rowton could
start away.

That brought him up short. "How many?"

"A family. Chamberlins," Moore said with a wag of his
head. "Man, wife, and two young'uns. Li'l girls they are."

Rowton felt his face blanch, his mouth drawn into a straight
line. He struggled to keep his composure as his eyes were
drawn back to Jennie Norton. "We'll get your husband,
ma'am. We'll find 'em all."

Because the wagon had reached the outskirts of Grangeville at that point, Frank Fenn, Charles Rice, and George
Hashagen all turned their horses around and joined Rowton's
search party, backtracking the road toward Cottonwood

Butte. It surprised John when they actually found the body of Benjamin Norton lying right where Fenn's party had abandoned it alongside the road—still undisturbed, not mutilated, hair intact.

Dismounting, Rowton split up his men, leaving a few to stay with Norton's body and the horses, sending the rest into the tall grass and man-sized thickets of brush to see if they could find some trace of what direction the Chamberlins might have taken in their flight. Wasn't long before one of the men off to John's right called out that he'd found a body. It was Cash Day hollering for them all to come join him, waving them over.

By the time Rowton and the others crowded into the small copse of trees around John Chamberlin's bullet-ridden body at the bottom of a swale, they all fell silent at the heart-wrenching sight of the settler clutching his dead three-year-old daughter, Hattie, in his cold arms.

"Jesus," someone whispered almost prayerfully in the stony silence.

Something under the dead man's legs caught John's attention as he stepped closer to the body. Rowton knelt, gently turning over the corpse, starting to tug at a long piece of bloody cloth that immediatcly came alive, shrieking with an inhuman sound.

"It's a young'un!" one of the men yelled as Rowton stumbled back, totally surprised.

It was a moment before he recognized the figure as a little toddler, small enough that she had been hiding beneath her dead father for . . . for what must have been a horrid eternity.

Settling back on his knees, Rowton gathered the child in his arms and had begun to soothe her when he noticed the strange way the tot was whimpering through her bloodied lips. Studying her closely, John could see how the tip of the youngster's tongue had nearly been severed. The blackening tip lolled around the front of her mouth, held only by a thin strand of flesh. His first guess was that the baby had so annoyed the warriors with her crying that the savages had tried to hack off her tongue, but the more he looked at the ragged cut, the more John was convinced that it couldn't be the work of a knife.

Rowton figured the toddler must have fallen in making their escape in the dark, perhaps when the father had stum-

bled carrying the child in his arms. And that must have surely
been when this little one nearly bit her own tongue off with
her tiny, sharp teeth. But in looking over the youngster now,
he saw there was simply too much blood smeared across the
girl's chin and down her neck to account for that nearly severed tongue. Gently pulling the collar away from the crusted
skin where blood had dried, Rowton discovered a deep, oozy
wound low on the toddler's neck.

"Gimme your kerchief," he asked Frank Fenn. "Wrap it
round her neck."

"Looks to be the godless devils tried killing this li'l'un,
too," Fenn grumbled as he gently wrapped his greasy bandanna around the tot's neck, bandaging the jagged wound as
the child winced, howling in pain.

"She's lucky they didn't make sure of it after they stabbed
her in the goddamned neck," Rowton cursed, feeling his face
burn with anger at warriors who made war on women and
little children. The youngster resumed wailing, thrashing her
arms and legs not only at the pain being caused her neck with
the bandanna but also for terror of these strangers.

"Here, give her to me, John," Fenn offered, holding out
his arms.

When he had handed the child over and Fenn began cooing
at the tot, Rowton stood and said to the others, "That's the
three of 'em, fellas. Which means there's only one person left
to find. Mrs. Chamberlin."

"I'll lay odds they took her with 'em," one of the men
observed.

"Nawww, not likely," another countered. "Kill't her for
sure."

"Why you say that?" someone asked.

"She was . . . with child," the man declared, somewhat self-
conscious about speaking of a pregnant woman.

"That's right," George Hashagen agreed. "Red niggers
wouldn't want nothing to do with a woman carrying a child
in her belly."

Off to his side, another man growled, "Then she's a dead
woman, for sure."

Rowton himself shook his head sadly. "Don't think they'd
drag her off with 'em, fellas. Leastways, I never heard of the
Nez Perce ever taking women prisoners to make 'em their
wives like other tribes over the mountains." He sighed. "I

figger we'll find her body out there, somewhere."

"Dragged her off for sure," a man muttered as the forty spread out again and started combing through the brush and timber once more.

More of the men were grumbling among themselves now too. Rowton couldn't blame them, nor hold them at fault for all their bravado and brave talk about what they would do when they got their hands on the red bastards who could do such a thing as kill one child with a rock to her head, stab another in her neck—a tot no more'n a babe.

"Rowton!"

He started toward that cry at a sprint. The closer he got, the more noisy the commotion became—men shouting, their voices cursing as they tumbled through the brush and shoulder-high grass, other voices pleading.

"Stop, ma'am! It's us! It's us!"

Then Rowton heard the woman's cries, more like the wails of a wounded, frightened animal, as a half-dozen men surrounded her and got Mrs. Chamberlin stopped there at an opening in the tall brush. She was hunched over in a crouch, her clothes torn, muddied, her dress barely clinging to one shoulder, the other crusted with blood darkening her pale skin. The way the woman thrashed this way, then that, John Rowton thought he spotted an ugly, oozy wound above her right breast. Not a neat, round hole—no, more a jagged wound. Just the sort of ragged laceration that led him to believe she had yanked out an iron arrow-tip herself, ripping the flesh of her own breast when she did.

More dried crimson streaked her cheek where she had been struck repeatedly beneath one eye so puffy it was all but completely shut. She continued to growl like a cornered animal as John inched up with the others, closing the ring on her. She held her hands out in front of her, fingers like claws, slashing them at Rowton when he dared to step near her.

"We found your husband, ma'am," he explained an instant before she collapsed to her knees as if giving herself over to her fate.

Her swollen lips moved. "They . . . they—"

Rowton knelt before her, not sure if he should reach out to touch the woman just yet. "I know what happened here, Mrs. Chamberlin. They killed John. Hattie too. But your little one, she's gonna live."

He watched how those words changed the light in her eyes—not near so dark and deep as a bottomless pool where she had been sinking only a moment before he gave her something to cling onto.

"M-my baby?" she asked with a pitifully small voice.

"She's gonna be fine."

Wagging her head, Mrs. Chamberlin groaned, staring down at herself. "I thought they was all dead. Killed by them . . . by the ones who held me down. Ones who done that shame to me."

His heart burned in anger at the warriors who had committed such crimes against this family; his heart bled for how this woman had been so savagely violated.

Reaching out, Rowton took one of her crusted hands in both of his. "We wanna take you to Grangeville now, ma'am. You with your baby, too. Gonna take you both where those devils can't never touch you again."

As soon as William Watson got Helen Walsh, Elizabeth Osborn, and their children back to the Cone brothers' little community at the mouth of Slate Creek, he rolled up his sleeves and went right back to directing the construction of their fortifications.

Because of his war experience with the Second Missouri Light Artillery, Watson was elected to supervise the digging of narrow trenches where the men stood twelve-foot timbers on end to form a palisade anchored three feet in the ground. This log stockade extended around Harry and Charles Cone's store and way station they had lawfully purchased back in 1861 from a Nez Perce named Captain John. Right from the start, the Cone brothers had established a reputation for treating the Indians well, unlike the downright belligerent and dishonest reputation of other "store men" the likes of Samuel Benedict and Harry Mason.

Watson had explained to the menfolk who were coming in from up and down the Salmon that they should fell logs from the edge of the nearby timber not only for use as their pickets but by cutting down the trees at the fringe of the settlement they would give themselves a far better field of fire in the event of attack. So while men like Hiram Titman, E. R. Sherwin, and Mr. Van Sickle joined Watson's miners, the women followed along behind the trenching crews, filling in the cracks between the upright timbers with smaller logs and saplings so that no stray bullet could find its way into the compound.

Helen Walsh and Elizabeth Osborn, along with their children, all lent their help as soon as Watson and the miners from Florence brought them into that sanctuary of Slate Creek. The Missouri emigrant took no small pride in getting the women and their young'uns safely back to this rendezvous for area settlers. Shame was—he was struck now as he looked around at the bustle of the construction—nearly every woman here was a widow, most every child already an orphan.

Oh, the children, he brooded that cloudy evening of June 15. How brave they had been so far, staying so quiet without so much as a whimper or a sob . . . as long as no one mentioned Indians or Nez Perce or their fathers. The slightest slip of the tongue like that and the little ones began to scream in unholy terror—reliving what they had been forced to witness over the past day or so.

Despite what those three warriors told Charles F. Cone less than two days back—saying they wouldn't harm him and suggesting that he should go tell others that they were going on a rampage—most of the men flocking here to Slate Creek weren't anywhere near as optimistic as Charley. Chances were damned good the war parties would get liquored up, work their blood into a boil, and then it wouldn't matter what white man they ran across.

"Goddamn the red bastards," Watson grumbled as he turned aside with the small keg of powder he was lugging down into the stone cellar of Charley Cone's house. *War's a madness meant only for men,* he brooded as he descended into the lamp-lit darkness. *God knows it should never be visited upon women and children.*

He set the keg down at the center of the bare room, there beneath the cellar's only furniture—a small, simple wood table—then made his way outside to retrieve the third of the five kegs of black powder. When he was finished hauling the last of them into the damp cellar this experienced artillery veteran planned to join all five with a running fuse that could be lit with one match at the cellar entrance, then drape a bedsheet over the table to hide his hidden cache of death. If the Indians attacked their fortifications, Watson and the other thirty men would do their damnedest to defend the forty women and children they would send down into this stone cellar below the fortified house.

Should all appear lost at the palisades, with the red bastards breaching the stockade and flooding into the compound, Watson had chosen a half-dozen miners who each swore they would light the fuse before their dying breath. So with seven of them vowing to make that final retreat to these stone steps, William was sure one of their number would still be alive to reach the cellar door in those last moments of their unsuccessful defense.

Stopping to wipe his forehead with a greasy bandanna, he watched Helen Walsh as she shoveled dirt back into the trench beside Mrs. Catherine Elfers at the wall. Then Watson noticed a similar gravely lined face worn by Elizabeth Osborn. Neither of the women had said anything of the cruelty they had suffered at the hands of the drunken warriors. They didn't have to. What depravity they had endured was plainly written in their eyes.

Once again this war veteran realized why it would be better to blow up the stone house, killing every woman and child huddled inside, than allow any of them to ever again fall into the hands of the Nez Perce sonsabitches.

He went through these preparations with his cache of gunpowder because William Watson realized the men might not be capable of holding back an all-out assault, especially because of that nearby bluff overlooking the Cone house on the east. It continued to nag at him so much that Watson finally ordered a handful of the men up that slope to solve this tactical problem by digging a rifle pit at the crown of the bluff where he would post a round-the-clock rotation of two-man watches.

"From here," Watson explained to the thirty miners, settlers, and store men whom he had gathered with him at the just-completed hollow scraped out of the rocky ground, "our pickets can watch over a good piece of the country here 'bouts: up and down the river, and the hills back of us too. They'll signal the rest of us early if they spot any war parties coming our way."

"That's right," agreed E. R. Sherwin. "Look down there. No matter if them Injuns come along the road hugging the side of the Salmon or they stick to the high trail up along the canyon wall—we'll still see 'em coming afore they're on us."

"What about that bridge down there?" asked Hiram Titman as he pointed down at the span crossing Slate Creek to the north.

"Awful close," Charley Cone added. "Come night, the Injuns could slip across the bridge and get right up to the walls afore we'll see 'em."

"Maybeso we'll make it hard as we can for the bastards to get across," Watson said. "At sundown every night, I'll send out a detail to pry up the cross-planks on that bridge and bring 'em into our stockade for the night."

"Damn fine idea," Harry Cone complimented Watson, slapping him on the back of the shoulders. "High as Slate Creek's running now, them Injuns won't be swimming cross it to get to us."

"That's right," Watson said as he surveyed east, south, then west. "I figger they'll rush us from another direction."

When he started down with the rest of them as it was growing dark, William Watson realized that all his people had to do now was wait.

Watch . . . and wait.

Chapter 27

June 15, 1877

"How soon can you be ready to depart, Colonel?"
When General Howard asked David Perry that question late of the afternoon, the captain gazed squarely at his superior and, without the slightest hesitation, responded, "We will leave at first light, sir. Everything is in place, except for some additional transportation I'll call down from Lewiston."

With those civilian messengers and their Nez Perce counterparts all racing in here to Fort Lapwai with their discouraging reports, it was clear that the army needed to move and be about its business without the slightest delay. For too long, so it seemed, they had dawdled in their dealings with the Non-Treaty bands, and now Oliver Otis Howard could see just what his liberality and evenhandedness had gotten him. Dead citizens and a territory just now being ravaged by the first flames of an Indian war.

That afternoon Howard had penned a message to be carried back to Loyal P. Brown in Mount Idaho, hoping to reassure those panic-stricken civilians that the army had received the two dispatches and that help was indeed on its way:

> *... [I am sending] two companies of cavalry to your relief... Other help will be en route as soon as it can be brought up. I am glad you are so cool and ready.*

Cheer the people. Help shall be prompt and complete. Lewiston has been notified.

Yours truly,
O. O. Howard

Next he dispatched his aide-de-camp, First Lieutenant Melville C. Wilkinson, off to the nearest telegraph at Fort Walla Walla to wire his orders for additional troops he wanted brought in from around his department, as well as his request to engage twenty-five Indian scouts. First Lieutenant Peter Bomus would take Wilkinson in a buggy to Lewiston, where the quartermaster had Howard's order to hire, for fifty dollars in coin from a local stage company, a buckboard and team that Wilkinson would drive on to Walla Walla.

Because Captain Perry had only two companies of cavalry at Lapwai—no more than a hundred men at most—the general summoned two more cavalry companies under Captain Stephen G. Whipple to hurry over from that reconnaissance he had sent them on in the Wallowa Valley, in addition to calling up a large complement of foot soldiers stationed at Walla Walla, southwest of Lewiston, to come as quickly as possible by steamer, along with three months' supplies and rations.

Finally, the last item of business before taking his supper was to have Perry's quartermaster, Lieutenant Bomus, contract for the services of a string of pack mules and their handlers from the Lewiston freighting company of Grostein & Binnard for the coming campaign.

After bolting down his supper with a few of the unmarried officers, since his wife was already on her way to visit family in The Dalles, David Perry huddled with Howard to plan their strategies for the next few days. Both believed that it should take no more than a week to bring the murderers, outlaws, and renegades to bay and force the rest onto the reservation. With the guilty warriors tried and quickly hung, life would return to normal at Lapwai and Howard could start back to Portland.

The captain expressed how relieved he was that his wife wasn't there that day when all hell was breaking loose. She was a high-strung woman as it was, Perry explained to the general, and easily given to theatrics. Had she been there to watch him preparing his troops to take off in pursuit of the murderers who already had innocent blood on their hands, he told Howard, she would have been inconsolable at best, maddeningly hysterical at worst.

"Despite my optimism on just how quickly we can wrap up this action against the Non-Treaty bands," Howard turned the subject away from such raw, personal issues, "it might take longer than my assessment."

"I choose to share your optimism, General."

"I'm still not comfortable in sending you out with so few men, Colonel."

"Permission to speak freely, sir?"

"By all means."

Perry tugged at his tight collar as if chafing at the symbolic restrictions of their officer corps. "As you stated the case: We could wait, sir. Yes. Until the other troops arrive, then march after the warrior bands as quickly as possible. With reinforcements, I could be assured of a decisive victory, once I get the bands to stop, hold, and engage my large force. Or . . ."

"Or what?" Howard asked when Perry turned aside and grew thoughtful.

"Or I can take what cavalry we have here now and go in pursuit of those warriors who surely can't number many more fighting men than I will have along under my command."

"I'm not so positive of your assessment of their numbers, Colonel. I think with the news we've been getting from the civilians that it's certain none of the Non-Treaty groups are coming onto the reservation as they promised," Howard reasoned.

After all, this was the very day those bands were to have reported to the Lapwai agent.

The general continued, "Which means that we must prudently take into account Monteith's estimate that the chiefs have as many as two hundred fighting men available to throw against what troops you'll lead against them."

"You're having second thoughts on me getting under way as soon as possible, sir?"

Howard scratched his chin whiskers, deliberating. "No," he finally declared. "Brown over in Mount Idaho is clearly in dire straits."

"My mission, General?"

"Yes—well, I don't want you concerned with treating with the chiefs and their warriors, Colonel," Howard advised. "No reason to waste your time convincing the chiefs to turn over the murderers to us for trial."

"They wouldn't give the guilty parties over to a white man's justice anyway, would they, sir?"

"Certainly not. Despite the protests of those leaders of the Treaty bands like Jonah Hayes and James Reuben, who tried to convince me this afternoon that the murderers are few in number and beyond their chiefs' control. And they most certainly won't turn over the murderers, since they have no faith in the white man's justice system after seeing our justice system fail them so many times in the past."

"So my objective, General?"

"Put an immediate halt to the depredations, Colonel Perry. If you can do that and that alone until reinforcements arrive and I can lead them to rendezvous with you ... the rest of this campaign will be nothing more than mopping things up."

Perry's chest swelled with the pride he felt at leading this spearhead against the enemy. "I concur completely, General: we must crush this rebellion quickly, with all force necessary. Even if my two companies encounter all two hundred warriors you and the agent fear might be arrayed against us, each of my men is the equal of at least ten of those Nez Perce. Besides, I can't imagine those warriors standing and giving us their best, sir. I don't see it in their nature."

"It is true the Nez Perce have never raised arms against the white men or our government." Howard measured the officer before him a moment, then asked, "You're very optimistic that you'll have this war over and done with before I get the reinforcements in here, aren't you, Colonel?"

Perry nodded and smiled. "I believe we'll have the Non-Treaty bands on the run the moment they sight my cavalry, and from there on it will be no more than a chase where we have to follow their fleeing backsides, General."

After his conference with General Howard, Perry watched the sun fall and the stars wink into view across the deepening indigo sky, growing more anxious as the hours passed. Then at dusk the post bugler stepped out to the center of the parade and blew "retreat." Pacing the long porch that extended across the front of the duplex he and his wife shared with surgeon FitzGerald's family, the captain grew all the more convinced that he could wait no longer for Lieutenant Bomus to bring that string of pack mules over from Lewiston.

David Perry had come to a decision.

"General," he said breathlessly as he stepped inside the parlor of his residence, where Howard was engrossed in his reports at a small table by lamplight.

"Colonel Perry—"

"Sir, I request permission to depart tonight."

Howard straightened. "Tonight?"

"As soon as I can put my companies into light marching order, sir."

Howard stared at the floor, scratching his beard thoughtfully. "Tonight."

"Time is critical in a situation such as this," Perry argued. "The murderers have already had two full days to plunder and rape and kill, General. Putting some cavalry in the field as quickly as possible—tonight, in fact—no matter that it would be only these two companies, is better than making no show of force at all."

Howard looked up and seemed to study the captain's face a long, anxious moment. "You won't wait for the mules to get here?"

"I'll take the five mules we have here, sir. We'll pack what rations and ammunition we'll need until you rush the mule train to catch up to our rear."

Howard finally nodded. "Very well, Colonel. Get your column under way."

He had turned on his heel and was back out the open door before he realized he was on the long front porch, searching the parade in the last dim light of dusk. There—he spotted the man.

"Major Trimble!" Perry suddenly called out to the commander of H Company, First Cavalry, using the officer's brevet rank as the captain was crossing the corner of the parade, making for the cavalry barracks.

Of late H Company had been reassigned from Fort Walla Walla. Their march here to Lapwai, in addition to some six weeks of field duty in recent months, made Trimble's men more fit for the campaign trail than was Perry's own F Company.

Joel Graham Trimble came to a stop at the bottom of the steps, placed one foot up, and greeted the post commander by his brevet rank. "Colonel?"

"How soon can you have H Troop ready to ride?"

Instantly yanking his foot off the step, the forty-four-year-old straightened, the slight off-cast in the one eye that had suffered a serious wound at Gettysburg twitching noticeably. "Within the hour. Do you plan to embark without our supply train?"

Perry's voice was confident as he gazed into that one eye Trimble had pinned on him, "Each company will take along two pack mules that will have to do until the train catch up. I'll leave word for them to come on with all possible speed once the train arrives here. I trust that it won't take them long to join us if they follow along with dispatch. Meanwhile, we can leave this evening in light marching order with those two pack mules for each company."

"Very good, Colonel. You'll be leading F Company?"

"Yes. Be sure the men carry three days' cooked rations. An additional five days' rations uncooked with each company's supplies. Report to the quartermaster's depot and draw forty rounds for each carbine, twenty-four loads for their side arms. An additional hundred rounds per man on the pack animals. Light marching order. Ready within the hour, Major Trimble?"

"Yes, sir."

Perry watched this older officer turn and start away for the barracks before he hollered into the twilight, "Mr. Theller!"

"Yes, Colonel?" This junior officer, a first lieutenant with the Twenty-first Infantry assigned to Fort Lapwai, was already approaching the porch, having grown aware of the hubbub of sudden activity at Perry's residence.

Of the men he was taking with him, Theller had the least experience in battle. "You heard, Lieutenant?"

"Yessir."

"I need a junior officer to ride in command of F Company." He looked steadily at the infantry officer.

"Cavalry, sir?"

"Exactly. Are you the man to command my men, Lieutenant?"

"By all means, Colonel!"

Perry nodded with gratification at the junior officer. "See that Sergeant Baird alerts our troop and they are prepared to march inside of an hour. You understood my ration and ammunition orders to Captain Trimble?"

"Yes, sir."

"Very good, Mr. Theller," Perry replied. "Draw your rations and distribute the ammunition. We're going to stamp out this brushfire and stamp it out quick."

Like many of the officers in the frontier army, David Perry had learned to soldier during the War of Rebellion against the secessionist states of the South. Early in '62 he had earned a commission as a second lieutenant in the First Cavalry, and by that July he had earned his promotion to first lieutenant for action in battle. By November of '64 Perry had advanced to his captaincy, the rank he now held as commanding officer at Fort Lapwai. As the Civil War was gasping its last in the spring of 1865, Perry won his first brevet for gallant service in the Battle of Five Forks on 1 April. The next day Jefferson Davis evacuated Richmond and the fighting was all but over.

Later, when the First Cavalry was transferred to the Northwest following the Civil War, the captain struck a decisive blow against a large party of Snake and Bannock warriors on the Owyhee River in Idaho the day after Christmas in 1866. For his leadership in that victory Perry received his second brevet to the rank of lieutenant colonel. Then, during the campaign in the Lava Beds against Captain Jack's Modocs a few years later, his F Company saw more action. Perry himself suffered a wound during fighting at Tule Lake in 1873.*

So this was not a man untried in battle, nor a leader hesitant in a fight. No less an Indian fighter than General George Crook himself had publicly expressed his admiration for Perry's own abilities as an Indian fighter.

Of the men at Fort Lapwai that night of 15 June, eighteen and seventy-seven, Captain David Perry was *the* man to lead those two companies of cavalry against the Nez Perce uprising. He knew firsthand what Indian fighting was all about. And the captain recognized when bold action must be taken.

Now was not the time to delay.

Howard's former aide-de-camp, Captain William H. Boyle of G Company, Twenty-first Infantry, would remain in command of Fort Lapwai until the reinforcements arrived and he would depart with Howard and the pack train.

With Lieutenant Parnell's and Captain Trimble's wives visiting over at Fort Walla Walla and his own off on holiday at

---

Devil's Backbone—vol. 5, The Plainsmen Series

The Dalles, only one officer's wife was still in residence at the fort: Mrs. Delia Theller. She moved up to stand beside General Howard after kissing her husband farewell, and the lieutenant turned aside to join his men as the sergeants began to bawl their stirring command of, "*Mount!*"

Perry nudged his horse to the edge of the porch directly in front of Howard. He could tell by the look on the department commander's face that Howard fully agreed to his not waiting until morning to go in search of the Nez Perce. "Good-bye, General."

"Good-bye, Colonel. You must not get whipped."

"There is no danger of that, sir."

Howard saluted. "Colonel—I know you will make short work of this."

The captain saluted and without another word reined left. To his three officers he gave the order. "Right—by fours—MARCH!"

Ninety-nine enlisted men set off on their march—no more than sixty-five miles to reach Mount Idaho. Joe Rabusco and a dozen unarmed Treaty Nez Perce who would serve as scouts streamed along either side of the formation, quickly loping to the front of the column.

It was just past eight o'clock when the captain led his detail into the dark, moving south down the Mount Idaho Road.

Almost from the time they left Fort Lapwai, Perry's command entered a mountainous country sparsely dotted with heavy timber and scarred with deep ravines, which slowed their march through the black of that cloudy, moonless night, not to mention the rain that began minutes after they were on their way, a rain that made the trail muddy and extremely slippery—dangerous footing for the horses by day, a treacherous situation by night.

So dark was it that Perry grew increasingly suspicious of an ambush by scouting parties that might be keeping an eye on the post for sign of a soldier column. By one o'clock he ordered Second Lieutenant William Russell Parnell, junior officer of Trimble's H Company, to take the advance with a platoon of skirmishers.

David Perry understood that there was not a better officer to have along on this campaign than Parnell, a forty-year-old Dublin-born Irishman who had served with distinction in the British Hussars, a unit of foot. After transferring to the Lanc-

ers, Parnell had participated in the capture of Sebastopol during the Crimean War and was, in fact, one of a handful of
survivors from that fabled "Charge of the Light Brigade" at
Balaclava who had ridden on, on into the mouth of death
with the six hundred.

After immigrating to America in 1860, this large-boned
man who taxed the strength of his mounts volunteered for
the Union Army in the Civil War. Following his capture by
Confederate troops at Upperville in 1863, Parnell managed
to escape and return to his lines, seeing service in the Shen-
andoah Campaign despite the fact that he still carried a minié
ball in the bone of his left hip. In addition, the lieutenant
bore the scars of several deep saber wounds, one of which
had severed his nose.

As a prisoner of war he had received no medical attention
for that deep, suppurating wound that caused the bone to
corrode and fall away, leaving a gaping hole in the roof of
his mouth, an affliction that made it difficult for him to speak
clearly. After the war, Parnell had a metal plate constructed
to cover the hole, which permitted him to articulate so others
could understand him.

By the end of the war he had reached the rank of lieutenant
colonel and had been awarded two brevets for gallantry in
action. With things quieted back east, Parnell moved west
with the army. During a fierce skirmish against hostiles on
Pit River under the field command of General George Crook,
Parnell garnered another brevet, earning himself the honor
of being called lieutenant colonel in the regular army. Like
many of the officers in the Northwest, he too had participated
in the Modoc War.

Moving into the vanguard this dark, rainy night, Lieutenant
Parnell deployed his skirmishers 200 yards in front of the column and posted outriders 150 yards from both flanks to prevent
any surprise ambushes. The march was taking longer than Perry
had hoped, what with those small-footed mules so notoriously
balky where the footing was uncertain. So during that night
Perry was compelled to order brief halts not only to allow the
five heavy-laden pack mules to catch up with the rear of the
march but also to give Parnell's skirmishers time to maneuver
through the thick brush on either side of the wagon road and
to cross the deep ravines ahead of the column. A soaking night
seeped into the coming of a drizzly dawn.

At midmorning, 16 June, Captain Perry ordered a halt in the yard at Cottonwood House after a march of forty-plus miles. It was plain as sun the battalion's horses were not in the least conditioned to the demands of the campaign trail. Directing the column to dismount in a field behind the house where the men removed their saddles and turned their horses out for a roll and to graze within a fenced pasture, Perry next deployed Parnell's pickets to warn of any approaching horsemen.

"The men can fall out and cook their breakfast," he declared to his officers, gazing down at the face of his pocket watch. "Two hours. We march away at noon."

In the distance, Perry spotted three huge columns of smoke. Perhaps burning haystacks. Maybe the homes of settlers. The captain turned to this experienced Irish soldier, Lieutenant Parnell. "Search the buildings," he ordered as he turned slowly, looking over the tranquil scene here at Cottonwood House. Hard to believe a raiding party had been here at all.

Upon close examination, Perry's men found some wagons beneath a shed near the house that had had their contents disturbed as the warriors rifled through the supplies. And inside the Norton house itself, it was plain the raiders had intended to burn the place to the ground. They had thrown a burning firebrand into a trunk that contained clothing and papers, but the lid had fallen and snuffed out the flames before much damage was caused.

There was some brief excitement when two of the pickets brought in a lone Nez Perce dressed in civilian clothing. At first Perry suspected he might be a spy from the Non-Treaty camp they were pursuing, but Joe Rabusco came over to explain that the rider was a Treaty man from Lapwai who had followed the column alone in hopes of joining the other twelve who had enlisted as scouts for the captain.

"Abraham Watsinma," Rabusco introduced the horseman.

"Very well. He's under your command now," Perry said as he sent them to rejoin the other scouts.

As the search of the Norton road ranch continued, company cooks started fires and prepared breakfast while most of the men curled up in the grass right among their grazing horses to catch a little sleep while they could. These ninety-nine weary cavalrymen had now been awake for something more than twenty-four hours.

Chapter 28

June 16, 1877

Mamma,

We have just watched the little party of two companies start off at dusk. General Howard remains here. If John had been here, he would have been out tonight marching with them. I can't help but feel glad that he is not, but I know he will feel he ought to have been here, and General Howard was so much concerned tonight about the command starting off without a medical officer.

It is ten o'clock and I am going to bed. We all feel so anxious. I will write soon again. I have only told you the news we have had that we know is true. Rumors of all sorts have been coming into the post all day. Everything centers here, and you can imagine how we all feel. I hope and pray it won't be another Modoc War. Love to all,

Your loving daughter,
Emily F.

Henawit, the one called Going Fast, did not know which of the white settlers owned this deserted house standing a few miles southwest of the place the Shadows called Grangeville. It did not matter anyway. The frightened Boston

Man and his family had abandoned the place, leaving everything for Going Fast and his friends to plunder.

Disappointed that they did not find any firearms or ammunition, they nonetheless did discover some food already prepared and left behind on a table: cold meat and biscuits, along with most of a fruit pie. Going Fast sat down in the middle of the floor and joined his two companions in a regal breakfast truly fit for warriors. After promptly filling their bellies, the trio located a small keg of whiskey on a box in the corner—enough inside to get all three of them good and drunk.

Accompanied by his young friend *Pahka Alyanakt*, who was called Five Winters, and the older warrior named Jyeloo—who was lame in one leg—Going Fast had left the camp at *Lahmotta* on White Bird Creek early that morning and headed north onto the Camas Prairie in search of booty and horses among those ranches the Shadows were fleeing now that the war scare was spreading like a late-summer wildfire.

Stuffed with food, their heads reeling from the potent whiskey, the warriors took to traipsing around in the clothing they found—men's pants and a woman's dresses too—dancing, singing, drinking, and carousing until all three collapsed into a deep sleep right there in the middle of the rough-planked floor.

Bleary-eyed following a near-sleepless night after returning to Grangeville with John Chamberlin's body, the man's widow, and their two daughters, John G. Rowton had volunteered to join George Shearer's posse going in search of any more survivors now that the sky was turning gray with dawn's first light this Saturday, the sixteenth of June.

Three miles southwest of town as they neared Abner Smith's homestead nestled against the hills, Shearer ordered his twenty volunteers to spread out and keep their eyes peeled for redskins. The moment Rowton halted his horse near the edge of the tree line, alone, he spotted the three Indian ponies grazing in the yard at the corner of the house.

For a moment he sat there, reckoning on his chances of taking the three bastards on his own—recalling the pitiful sight of that Chamberlin woman as she scrambled away from her rescuers like a terrified animal, remembering the wounded, inhuman cries that had escaped her throat as Rowton's party finally surrounded her and escape became impossible. But as much as he hungered to kill the three of them by himself, Rowton decided it prudent that he turn back to fetch Shearer and the others. Just in case there were any more of the murdering bastards in the area.

Where there were three of the niggers, there'd always be many times more.

"Shearer!" he shouted as he came in sight of the volunteers who were reaching the road that would take them through the timber to the Smith place.

"What's got you lathered?" George Shearer asked in a distinctively southern drawl as he perched the butt of his double-barreled Parker shotgun on the top of his thigh and watched Rowton rein up beside him.

"Three ponies," John said breathlessly. "Injun ones . . . just easy as you please . . . out front of the Smith house."

Shearer grinned, patting the shotgun while he looked over the volunteers. "You fellers remember what that boy, Hill Norton, told us these red neegras done to his family out on the road?"

Rowton looked at the anger clouding the faces of those twenty volunteers as all grunted their assent.

Then Shearer looked squarely at Rowton. "Ain't none of us ever gonna forget the sight of that poor Mrs. Chamberlin, fellers—knowing full well what they done to her, a fate that's nigh wuss'n death."

The whole bunch yipped like coyotes with the scent of prey strong in their nostrils. John couldn't help but feel ready to string a few of the red bastards up himself, maybeso just to make their dying long and hard to serve as a lesson to all the—

"So let's go see 'bout catching us some red bucks and chopping off their balls afore we kill 'em real slow!" Shearer goaded his band of twenty.

As one they shot away, still bellowing for blood, their horses wild-eyed and wide-nosed as the twenty-one tore across that last half-mile to Ab Smith's homestead, where Rowton believed they could finally start giving hurt back for hurt.

His head was pounding as if someone were swinging a *kopluts* against the back of his skull. . . . Going Fast came suddenly awake, sensing the rough wood board against his cheek.

He blinked his eyes, slowly remembering that he had fallen asleep from the powerful whiskey right where he had collapsed half-in, and half-out, the door to the Shadow house. As he dragged up his heavy head from the planks, Going Fast realized he could actually hear the pounding—growing louder and louder.

In an instant his instincts told him it was the hooves of many horses. No one at the *Lahmotta* camp knew they had come here. Chances were it was not another war party out to plunder the scattered homesteads on this part of the Camas Prairie.

Rocking up to his hands and knees, Going Fast crawled back inside the open doorway, hollering to his sleeping friends, "Hurry! Hurry! Riders coming to catch us!"

Together the three of them struggled to maintain their balance as they lurched off the porch, landing in the yard about the time they spotted the riders approaching down the road at a gallop. Their three skittish ponies shied when the trio stumbled among them. Going Fast heard the pop of the first gun, recognized the hiss of a bullet as it sped overhead.

His head aching, he vaulted atop the bare back of his horse and brought it around, finding Five Winters already mounted and kicking his heels into his pony's ribs.

"Come on! Come on!" Going Fast shouted at the older warrior, who was struggling to control his frightened horse long enough for him to mount.

Poor Jyeloo was so lame, lacking any strength in one leg, that he could not easily mount this pony dancing about in a circle. That, and the man was older, slower from a long-ago war wound in his back. Still somewhat drunk too.

Going Fast bumped his pony right against Jyeloo's to hold it still, reaching across with one arm to do what he could to help pull the lame man atop the frightened sidestepping pony.

"Help me!" Jyeloo screamed. "I can't—"

Two bullets burrowed into the ground near the hooves of Going Fast's pony, scaring the animal. A heartbeat later another bullet whined past his ear and slapped against the house. His horse started prancing away from Jyeloo's pony.

"Here!" Going Fast hollered. He leaned to the side, holding his soldier rifle out between them. "Take it and defend yourself!"

His own pony whipped itself around as if stung by wasps and reared with a whinny. The last thing Going Fast saw as he struggled to hold onto his animal was Jyeloo frantically gripping his horse's mane with one hand, the other gripping that soldier rifle, valiantly struggling to kick that lame leg up and over the animal's back, desperate to drag himself off the ground.

Then Going Fast's horse bolted away. And he realized he had failed to leave his cartridge belt with Jyeloo. The soldier rifle had only one bullet in it. The lame one didn't have a chance against so many.

Admitting to himself that he had never been so scared for his life, Going Fast galloped in the wake of Five Winters, the two of them clattering past a stand of trees and racing across a narrow strip of pasture for the slope they would ascend in escaping south for the encampment at White Bird Canyon.

Escaping from the murderous Shadows still firing bullets over their heads.

John Rowton was exuberant to see how quickly they were closing in on that last warrior struggling to mount up and rein his pony away from the Smith homestead. An instant later the red bastard pulled himself atop the horse and flailed his legs to get his horse moving.

At Rowton's knee rode George Shearer, whooping and sometimes growling like that big black-haired mastiff one of the shopkeepers kept chained up outside his trading tent in the mining camp of Florence. Shearer sounded just like a snarling dog ready to lunge and latch onto your leg, take a hunk of meat right out of your arm . . . maybe even clamp its jaws on your throat.

Those first two warriors jumped their ponies over the fence that cut diagonally across the back of Smith's pasture there at the base of the hill. Once the bastards were around that knoll, they would have a straight shot up and over the divide to the headwaters of White Bird Creek. And from there the twenty would lose them. That's likely where the whole village of redskins was fleeing.

Rowton kept expecting that third Indian to jump his pony over the rail fence only high enough that it blocked Smith's cows from his garden crops . . . when the warrior's horse suddenly shied and dug in its hooves, skidding stiff-legged to a halt this side of the fence. The Nez Perce yanked brutally on the rein and started to come around for another try at the jump when he spotted Rowton and Shearer, along with all the rest clattering up behind them.

The Indian surprised Rowton by leaping off his pony, spilling in the grass. But the warrior rolled onto his feet and lumbered away, hobbling unsteadily along the fence line in a futile race.

Rowton leveled his pistol at the Indian's back and pulled the trigger. He knew the bullet struck the bastard from the way the Indian jerked, paused in his ungainly flight, then lurched away again in a painful hobble. Maybe, John figured, he'd hit him in the leg or hip.

By now Rowton was slowing his horse, so quickly was he closing the gap on his prey. Shearer was off to his right, and some of the others were sprinting up to fill in the gap between them. More guns popped now—pistols and carbines both.

Arms and legs flailing crazily, the warrior flew through the air a good five yards, just as if there had been a small charge of powder exploded underfoot. He went sprawling in the knee-high grass. While Rowton hauled back on his reins, Shearer's horse slid to a halt directly beside the warrior who dragged himself up on his hands and one knee, his back clearly bleeding in at least three places already. The Nez Perce had lumbered forward no more than a yard, clawing with one hand at his back, when Shearer pointed his shotgun off the side of his horse, holding the muzzles directly over the Indian's back, then pulled the first trigger.

The impact of that arm's-length shot hurled the warrior against the ground, where his hands clawed at the grass, a pitiable high-pitched squeal escaping his throat. Shearer's horse pranced around to the other side of the prostrate Indian, where the civilian leaned to the side, positioning the shotgun's muzzles inches from the back of the warrior's neck, and pulled the second trigger.

With a violent spasm, the body convulsed once, then lay still. Blood darkened the Indian's back, beginning to pool in the grass beneath him. The warrior's shirt smoldered a few moments until the dead man's blood extinguished the powder burns.

"Goddamn, if that didn't feel good!" Shearer roared triumphantly, shaking the double-barreled shotgun overhead as a half-dozen of the volunteers leaped their horses on over the fence, sprinting after the two escaping warriors. "Get em!" Shearer goaded. "Get those sonsabitches too!"

Rowton was staring now, transfixed on the body, when the rest came to halt in a tight circle around Shearer and the Indian. It caught him by surprise when Shearer kicked himself out of the saddle and landed beside the bloody corpse.

"Can you believe it, fellers?" Shearer drawled. "This bastard's still alive!" He pointed at the warrior's hand flexing slowly in the grass as if the Indian was struggling to drag himself away from his killer.

"Bet this son of a bitch was one of them what got to Chamberlin's woman!" someone in the bunch hollered.

"This'un prob'ly killed that li'l girl too," another voice chimed in.

A third man growled, "Likely this bastard chopped off the other girl's tongue!"

"Well now, boys," Shearer declared as he stepped across the warrior, placing a boot on either side of the body so that his feet were planted just below the Indian's armpits. "I s'pose we ought'n show all them other red niggers what we'll do to 'em if'n they go raping our women and killing our young'uns!"

Whirling his shotgun in both hands, Shearer seized the muzzle of the weapon, raising it high overhead for an instant, then hurled it downward into the top of the warrior's head with a dull, moist crack.

"Sakes alive, George—you got the first'un for sure!" one of the volunteers shouted at their leader.

He grinned at those around him. "This neegra's just the first!"

Then the bloodied shotgun was back in the air as Shearer held it poised over his head before bringing it down a second time, now with all the force of both shoulders, driving it into the warrior's head with an even more sickening, mushy sound. Blood oozed from the one exposed ear, gushed from the lips that no longer quivered.

As he pulled the splintered shotgun up and inspected it, Shearer started laughing crazily. "Lookee here, boys! I've gone and busted the goddamned stock on this here red neegra!"

Rowton wagged his head, mesmerized at the blood and

gore splattered over the shotgun's glistening stock and break-away action. He spotted the half-dozen riders returning from the base of the hill, loping back across the pasture to rejoin Shearer's posse. Some of those around Rowton were climbing out of their saddles, shoving through the ring of horses to take their turn kicking the lifeless body again and again.

Rowton swallowed hard, his insides awash with a jumble of feelings. He sensed unmitigated fury at the Nez Perce for what they'd done to the women and children out on the Camas Road, sensed a bloodlust for those less-than-human warriors who could commit such savage acts against the innocent. Killing these sonsabitches in a stand-up, man-to-man fight was one thing . . .

John watched the others finish kicking the body, then roll the corpse over to claw the warrior's breechclout aside, two of the volunteers standing ready with their belt knives drawn.

Without a doubt, Rowton wanted more of the warriors to fall, more of them to pay for what they'd done to the innocents.

But with all the fury boiling around him, John knew this sort of cruel blood sport only made him and the rest of these men no better than the drunken warriors who burned and raped and murdered their way up and down the Camas Road, suddenly realizing that—just like those red bastards—he and the others mutilating this body had become no better than a pack of animals themselves.

Chapter 29

Season of *Hillal*
1877

The moment Going Fast and Five Winters raced into White Bird's camp at *Lahmotta,* broadcasting the Boston Men's attack on Jyeloo, young warriors came running from all directions. In less time than it took for a man to eat his breakfast, three-times-ten were mounting up with weapons in their hands or hanging from their backs, following Going Fast and Five Winters back to the north for that homestead where the two had abandoned old Jyeloo to his fate.

But the Shadows were gone by the time the war party came tearing around the brow of the hill and sprinted across the pasture toward the rail fence. Just on the other side they found the lame warrior, his manhood crudely hacked from his body. Blood soaked the tops of his leggings where the Shadows had committed this outrage. Crimson blossoms dotted Jyeloo's shirt where eleven bullets had struck his body. And blood darkened the trampled grass all around the old warrior's head where flies blackened the crushed skull that oozed the dead man's pulpy brain into the dirt already shiny with gore. Near the old man's left hand lay his belt knife.

"I gave him my soldier rifle," Going Fast explained as he turned away from the body, feeling weak at the sight of such brutality.

"The gun is no longer here," said *He-mene Moxmox,* the one named Yellow Wolf, a young warrior of twenty-one summers from Joseph's band of Wallowa. "The Shadows took it with them."

"And Jyeloo's pony too," Five Winters added, gazing around the pasture.

"He died fighting those Boston Men," growled *Pahkatos Watyekit,* the warrior called Five Times Looking Up.

"For this bravery he will always be remembered by our people," vowed *Kosooyeen,* the one named Going Alone.

"He was lame; and long suffered that old battle wound in his back," Going Fast explained as he looked into the angry, stony faces of the others. "But he went down fighting as a *Nee-Me-Poo* warrior."

"Perhaps we should see what we can find at the house?" asked Five Times Looking Up.

"I will take Jyeloo back to camp," volunteered *Pahkatos Owyeen,* the older warrior named Five Wounds.

Going Fast turned aside from the group now and saw the long look on young Five Winters's face. He figured his friend's heart must feel very cold and small, perhaps even racked with guilt that he had been the first to flee, leaving Jyeloo behind without a way to defend himself against the onrushing Shadows. As a means to honor the lame warrior, almost half of the war party elected to accompany the body back to their village near the mouth of White Bird Creek.

The rest followed Going Fast on to the abandoned homestead. They were inside the house looking for clothing, any food, and even more whiskey if they could find it, when Yellow Wolf stepped into the open doorway and shouted.

"A Shadow is coming down the trail!"

"Only one?" asked Five Times Looking Up.

"He is alone," Yellow Wolf declared.

"But we cannot be sure," Going Alone snarled. "Maybe it is a trap."

"Yes," Going Fast agreed. "Maybe he is one of those Boston Men who butchered Jyeloo. Hide! Hide!"

Closer and closer the white man* came, walking down the road toward the house alone and on foot, completely unaware of the danger.

But as the Shadow neared the house, something must have aroused his suspicion. The man stopped suddenly, slowly

---

*Charles Horton

turned around in all directions, and appeared to be listening carefully as he studied the house and the other small buildings from afar. Then he turned on his heel and started away as if he had heard something suspicious or spotted their war ponies secreted at the back of the house.

With a yelp, Going Alone and Five Times Looking Up were the first to break from hiding, followed by the others streaming out the door. Some went sprinting after the white man while the rest raced around the corner of the house to grab their horses.

Sneaking a look over his shoulder, the Shadow saw the warriors racing after him on foot, probably heard those who had mounted and came clattering around the house, hooves pounding, war cries leaping from their throats as the Boston Man scampered for the bottom of a steep hill at the base of which lay a deep, brush-choked ravine.

On horseback, Five Times Looking Up easily pulled beside the Shadow while he nocked an arrow against his bowstring. He positioned the weapon over his victim, drawing back the string at the very same moment the white man turned and reached out in desperation, seizing the arrow and stumbling at the same time.

As the Shadow tumbled into the grass, he yanked on the shaft, nearly toppling the warrior from his pony. Instinctively tightening his knees at the horse's ribs made his pony lunge to the side, away from the white man who vaulted back onto his feet and bounded away in a different direction.

But Going Alone shot into that gap atop his pony, bringing his repeater down, pointing at the Shadow's back as his horse brought him closer. With the first shot from his carbine the Boston Man tumbled forward onto the ground, rolling across the grass. But again he scrambled back to his feet, stumbled away clutching his side, lumbering into his valiant dash for freedom once more.

Working the lever of his repeater before another warrior could claim this kill, Going Alone leveled his rifle squarely at the Shadow's back and pulled the trigger a second time.

With this shot the white man spilled headlong into the tall grass, his legs thrashing a moment before he lay still.

As the warriors dismounted around the Shadow, they discovered that the man was not young to run so far so fast, nor was he old.

"Look!" Five Times Looking Up shouted as he toed the body onto its back. "The Shadow has a pistol that is now yours, Going Alone!"

Bending down, Going Alone freed the gun belt and holster, gazing at the dead man's face, bewildered. "I wonder why he didn't shoot at me with his pistol."

Now his newborn daughter would be a wanderer.

Although Joseph and his people were still in country long roamed by the Nez Perce, he realized his Wallowa would never be allowed to return to their ancestral lands. Though his father's bones slept there in the valley of the Winding Waters—a land he loved as he did his mother—Joseph realized it would never again be his home. He had abandoned it hoping to avoid war.

But even that was beyond his power now.

The morning after the bullets were fired into his lodge, Joseph gathered up his wife and infant daughter, leading his Wallowa northeast from the rendezvous place at *Tepahlewam* to Cottonwood Creek in hopes of joining more of their people just inside the southern boundary of the reservation. No matter that yesterday's was a short journey—the miles taxed the strength of his wife, who had lost a lot of blood delivering their child in the birthing shelter.

As the sun fell that day, four young scouts rode away from camp to watch the Shadows' wagon road, stationing themselves where the trail left Camas Prairie and started over Craig's Mountain, descending to Fort Lapwai, where the Treaty bands lived in subjugation. These four were to keep an eye out for any messengers headed north to the soldier post or the mining community of Lewiston beyond.

And now, this morning, with the alarm raised that bands of white men were roaming the countryside, his *Nee-Me-Poo* hurriedly dragged the buffalo-hide covers from their lodgepoles, preparing to leave *Sapachesap,* this place they called the "Drive-In," a cave situated at the bottom of Cottonwood Canyon where they often cached saddles and other camp equipage as they moved back and forth across the Camas Prairie.* But Looking Glass's people would not be leaving with

---

*This cave was reportedly situated just west of the present-day community of Stites, Idaho.

them. Instead, the *Alpowai* chose to hide and endure on the Clearwater. The women had their gardens planted there, the older chief had explained. His people wanted nothing of Too-hoolhoolzote's war . . . so they would simply go home where they belonged.

"My hands are clean of the white man's blood," Looking Glass angrily told White Bird and Toohoolhoolzote, "and I want you to know they will so remain. You have acted like fools in murdering white men. I will have no part in these things, and have nothing to do with such men. If you are determined to go and fight, go and fight yourselves and do not attempt to embroil me or my people. Go back with your warriors; I do not want any of your band in my camp. I wish to live in peace."

So as a peace chief, a thoughtful diplomat, Joseph no longer had it within his power to prevent the coming war. By tradition, it was not his duty to raise his hands for the coming fight. Instead, he would remain as a civil chief: seeing to the needs of the women, children, and old ones, besides caring for the immense herds of horses.

At the same time, his brother Ollokot would join with the war chiefs. It was they who would make plans for battle. There was no doubt now; the soldiers would be coming. A big fight loomed on the horizon. Joseph would take care of the camp and its people. His younger brother would see to the fighting men.

Taking the reins to his pony in hand now, Joseph stepped up beside the travois that carried his wife and daughter. Not yet able to sit astride a horse, Driven Before a Cold Storm instead lay awaiting the start of the day's journey, clutching the sleeping baby against her.

"I pray we can find rest soon," Joseph said as he knelt beside the travois.

She smiled wanly, reaching out to brush his cheek with her fingertips. "I so wanted this child to be born in freedom. But now we fear the soldiers will chase us down like the wolf runs down the hare. I am scared I won't have the strength to run when Cut-Off Arm comes."

"Rest," he hushed her, leaning forward to press his lips against her forehead. "Save your strength for our child."

Ollokot rode up as Joseph got to his feet beside the travois. "We are ready, Brother."

Joseph squeezed his wife's hand, then turned to Ollokot. "Now we go to *Lahmotta,* the canyon where White Bird Creek flows."

White Bird's people and Toohoolhoolzote's band already had streamed across the southern edge of the Camas Prairie for that favorite campsite at the bottom of the canyon, a place the *Nee-Me-Poo* sometimes called *Lockyah,* meaning "Wood Built across a Stream to Hold Back the Fish," a dam of sorts where his people traditionally fished the waters of the Salmon River every summer near the mouth of White Bird Creek.

As the first of the band got under way, Ollokot sent out warriors to protect the flanks of their march. For the past two days scouts had come and gone from the encampment, carrying word of what they could learn from the movements of the wagon men along the road between Mount Idaho and the agency. Any wagons were sure to have the whiskey barrels on board. It caused Joseph's heart to ache all the more, knowing how bad whiskey was for young men whose spirits already burned with war.

When Joseph loped to the head of the Wallowa band, Ollokot reined in beside his brother. They rode together in an uneasy silence for some time, perhaps each of them remembering how they had argued that terrible night at *Tepahlewam.* Joseph understood that it was natural enough that his brother's heart would follow the way of the eager young warriors.

"Now that war has come," Ollokot had argued, "a warrior cannot turn his face from it!"

But in time Joseph's powers of persuasion had convinced Ollokot that there had to be a better course than to confront the soldiers who were sure to come. When they rejoined the other bands on the White Bird, he planned to call for a council of the chiefs so he could propose that they immediately flee east to the *illahie,* the buffalo country.

"There," he had convinced Ollokot, "we can wait while the wounds of these killings have healed and this current trouble is forgotten."

"And then?" Ollokot had asked in resignation.

"We will see what sort of peace Cut-Off Arm will offer us, so we can return to this country."

"I think the Shadows have a long memory," Ollokot had

grumped. "We might be fools to believe those Boston Men will give us a good peace."

For a long time Joseph had weighed their options. In the end he reluctantly vowed, "If Cut-Off Arm does not deal with us honorably while we are in the buffalo country, then I will lead our people north into the Old Woman's Country, where we will find Sitting Bull's Lakota."

No matter how cheerful he tried to make that option sound, all the paths that lay before them appeared equally grim. So Joseph's heart lay heavy in his breast, not so much because other chiefs and warriors had openly called him a coward for wanting to wait at *Tepahlewam* so they could see what sort of peace the bands could forge with the soldiers when the army came, not even heavy because many had accused him of being a traitor and suspected he would be a turncoat for the Shadows . . . but heavy because he felt he could peer into the days and the seasons ahead, glimpsing what fate now held in store for his people.

Somber and weary, Joseph led his people away from *Sapachesap* for the mouth of the White Bird, knowing that even though only one of his warriors had followed Sun Necklace and taken part in the murderous raids up and down the Salmon, he himself would be blamed for the trouble because of his prominent role in the failure of the recent negotiations, especially because of his past defiance against the agent and Cut-Off Arm. As the other bands had packed up and abandoned *Tepahlewam*, Joseph had despaired that he no longer held any power to determine the future of the Wallowa. Now that was held in the hands of the soldier chief.

If he were given the chance to sue for peace, Joseph vowed to do what he could on behalf of all the *Nee-Me-Poo*. Somehow he would have to convince Cut-Off Arm and Agent Monteith that even though ten, perhaps fifteen, white lives had been taken already, those lives had been sacrificed only after the young men had soaked their hearts with Shadow whiskey. Besides, Joseph would argue, that slaughter of a few whites along the Salmon and up on the Camas Prairie had to be weighed against twenty-four long winters as the Boston Men raped *Nee-Me-Poo* women, stole *Nee-Me-Poo* horses, cattle, and land . . . twenty-four long winters as the miners, cattlemen, and settlers wantonly murdered Joseph's people.

Here on the hillside where he could look down on *Lah-*

motta, into that bottomground along White Bird Creek, Joseph recognized how this traditional campsite had been chosen for defense generations ago. Backed by the Salmon River to the west, they were flanked on both sides by high ridges and deep ravines. Atop nearby buttes the chiefs could post sentries to watch for the approach of any soldier column. The scarcity of level terrain at this traditional camping ground would serve the bands well should the white men choose to attack. Here a few warriors could hold off more than twice as many as their number.

Turning his pony about, Joseph hurried back along the column to reach his wife's travois. There he leaned over and held down his hand, smiling. But when she raised her hand to touch his, she seized it, squeezing fiercely.

"Stay close, Joseph. I am so afraid for your daughter."

Tears stung his eyes. "Do not fear, woman. Our daughter has been born in freedom."

He stayed with the travois on their way down the long slope toward the great encampment where the other bands had already erected a forest of lodgepole cones, spreading their smoke-blackened buffalo-hide covers over them. Somewhere near the creek he would help his eldest daughter erect their lodge.

Then he would wait.

Joseph knew he could do little else but wait and brood that Cut-Off Arm held the power now. The *Nee-Me-Poo* could only wait.

Would the soldier chief come to punish his people with a harsh and unjust peace?

Or would he send his soldiers?

Chapter 30

June 16, 1877

He was a mishmash of contradictions, this Arthur Chapman.

At thirty-six, he stood tall, spare, and every bit as lean as a buggy whip. He still had plenty of his hair: black as the bottom of a tar spring did it spill across his shoulders. Born in Iowa, Chapman was no more than seven years old when his family moved to Oregon during that monumental western migration upon the Emigrant Road. His father soon became one of the founders of Portland.

This inland Northwest was a country rife with possibilities for a likely lad. Seeking his own brand of adventure at the ripe old age of nine, young Arthur carried dispatches for the army between The Dalles and Fort Walla Walla during the Rogue River Indian War. By the time he turned fifteen, Chapman had settled on a piece of ground beside White Bird Creek, near the mouth of a stream that would soon bear his name. It was there he began raising cattle and breeding horses, as well as operating a ferry across the Salmon River at the mouth of the White Bird. Because of his daring bravado and his uncanny ability to navigate his ferry across the swollen, raging river, even during the most tumultuous spring flooding, folks in the area began calling him Admiral, or simply "Ad" for short.

Ad Chapman it was, and always would be.

In '74 he sold his ranch to John J. Manuel and moved north

to a new homestead he built on Cottonwood Creek some eight miles from Mount Idaho out on the Camas Prairie, where he continued to breed horses. Around the time the Nez Perce started kicking up a fuss, Chapman boasted owning some four hundred head of prime stock that grazed in his pastures in the shadow of Cottonwood Butte.

Oh, not that there wasn't a ticklish rumor about Ad and his horse-trading practices that cropped up every now and then: a story that claimed he had sold a horse to a warrior named White Eagle, then later taken the horse back by force. But that wasn't really anything more than talk. Not that Chapman hadn't tried to get the horse back, mind you—when Ad found out how the red bastard had cheated him by trading him three old horses, all soon to come down with the colic. Truth was, Ad was plagued by a short-fused temper, and when he went off looking to even the score with White Eagle, Chapman only got himself whipped pretty good by some of that Indian's friends.

Such affairs as that didn't do much good to endear the Nez Perce to Ad Chapman, even though he had married an Umatilla squaw a few years back, even though he spoke real good Nez Perce too. The couple had a young boy, and now his wife was expecting another child come early fall.

Hard as he tried, Ad couldn't seem to win with either side—not with most of the Nez Perce, who distrusted him to one degree or another, and not with some of the whites who considered him a traitor because he had married an Indian woman and fathered a half-breed child. Truth was, Chapman didn't endear himself to some folks simply because he called it as he saw it. If an Indian acted bad, he was due a thrubbing, Ad believed. And if a man stole a horse, he was due a hanging.

That's how Chapman came to be the leader of the bunch who caught a warrior named Wolf Head who was accused of stealing a settler's horse and some cows. Once the white posse got their hands on the Nez Perce warrior, they hanged him from the closest tree and left the body twisting in the wind for the better part of a week simply to scare hell out of the other bucks who might feel frisky enough to purloin some white man's horses or some beef on the hoof.

On top of all that, there was a story going the rounds that the Non-Treaty bands didn't trust him any farther than they could throw him because they claimed he had stolen some of their cows and sold them off to Chinese miners up at Florence and Elk City in the mountains. Hell, if those Indians didn't take better care of their stock than to leave their cattle run through Chapman's upper pasture, they deserved to be missing a few cows!

Such was the delicate line he walked between the white world and red in these parts. For good or bad, there honestly wasn't a man who possessed more experience dealing with the Non-Treaty bands than Arthur Chapman. In fact, over the years, he had forged quite a bond with chief Looking Glass and a few of his headmen. Ad figured when you got right down to it, that steadfast friendship had to go a long way to proving he wasn't so bad a fella to the Nez Perce.

But that friendship with Looking Glass and his bunch might have been reason enough some of the citizens who had flocked into Mount Idaho and Grangeville at the first whisper of trouble resented it when Chapman was elected to captain the volunteer company formed to defend the communities against the uprising. It made no never mind to Ad Chapman—there were more important things to concern him now than a few ruffled feathers of those shopkeepers and gentleman farmers. This was war.

He recognized this situation for what it was, right off. Back on Thursday afternoon, two of his Nez Perce friends—Looking Glass and Yellow Bear—rode over from the big gathering they were having at the head of Rocky Canyon on Camas Prairie to let Chapman know that some of the young bucks had gone on the warpath and had already killed seven white men by that time. A damn honorable thing of those two old friends to come warn him at a time like that, even going so far as to suggest that he clear out till things quieted down. No sooner had he gotten his wife and son started away, his two hired men coming along with Ad's three prized breeding stallions, than they spotted a war party headed for his ranch.

Chapman figured he might well owe Looking Glass his life for that warning, because it had been a horse race all the way to the outskirts of Mount Idaho.

Sprinting into the tiny settlement barely ahead of those warriors screaming for his blood, Ad dropped out of the saddle in front of Loyal P. Brown's hotel and began spreading the alarm, shocking one and all with the news of the Salmon

River murders. By nightfall the folks flooding into town had formed their own militia company and elected Chapman as its captain. As soon as he had mounted pickets to watch all the approaches to town, Chapman asked for volunteers to carry word to Fort Lapwai.

That's when Lew Day had stepped up. Within minutes, the courier was on his way to Cottonwood House.

In the predawn darkness of the following morning, June 15, Chapman had slipped out of town and back to his ranch to keep a planned rendezvous with Looking Glass and Yellow Bear. Just before five o'clock, as the sky was graying, he rode up to his friends, a bit surprised to find them accompanied by two other warriors. The four grimly related the names of the settlers who had been killed up to that point in time, including some white folks on the Camas Prairie. It shook Chapman to his boots when Lew Day was reported as being among the dead.

That's when Ad knew he couldn't stand back and ask for any more Mount Idaho volunteers to make that deadly journey. So then and there he asked Looking Glass's brother if he would ride from Mount Idaho to Fort Lapwai. Without hesitation the warrior agreed to carry word to the soldier post.

A half-breed named West took off about seven that Friday morning, carrying a letter from saloon-keeper Brown. About an hour later, *Tucallasasena,* the chief's brother, set off with a second note from Brown to the post commander at Lapwai. Ad figured one of them would get through and bring the soldiers running.

Once those couriers departed, the men of Chapman's militia went out to gather up their dead, along with what survivors they managed to find. One small band of volunteers ran across Hill Norton, scared out of his wits, near the edge of town. And a little while later some other men managed to coax a hysterical Lynn Bowers to accompany them to Brown's hotel, where Loyal P. and his wife, Sarah, were nursing the wounded and feeding everyone for free out of their stores. By afternoon more than 250 souls had converged on the mountainside village.

Chapman figured if there were any others who hadn't made it into town by sundown that Friday . . . they weren't coming. Likely dead by now.

Knowing the pitiful story of Mrs. Chamberlin and her daughters, the rest of the women murmured softly among themselves on what fate awaited them and their children if the warriors attacked the town in strength. Chapman, Brown, Rowton, and a few others kept every able-bodied man at the barricades they had thrown up at both ends of the street and tallied their firearms. There weren't enough rifles to go around so when a new watch arrived to assume their rotation on the picket line, those going off-duty handed over their weapons to the fresh guards. Ad never told another soul just how pessimistic he felt about having enough firepower to hold back all those warriors Looking Glass had warned him were busting loose from the encampment at Rocky Canyon.

But there were some peaceful, idyllic moments nonetheless as twilight came down that Friday night, the fifteenth. Most of the mothers were having a dickens of a time getting their frightened children to lie down and drift off to sleep, so the town's finest voices agreed to sing some lullabies for the wee ones. James Adkison sang "Nearer, My God, to Thee" and "Onward Christian Soldiers"; then John Rowton climbed a tall pine tree standing inside their makeshift stockade and with his melodious baritone sang a heart-wrenching rendition of "I'll Remember You, Love, in My Prayers."

As it grew dark that evening, Chapman listened all the more intently to every sound drifting in from the night, brooding on those women and children gathered in this tiny settlement, each of them so scared they could hardly close their eyes and sleep. For now it didn't make any difference that a few folks here in Mount Idaho had done their level best to cheat or steal from the Nez Perce. No matter that most of the citizens were guiltless in every way.

In a dirty little war like this, Chapman realized, travail and gnashing of teeth always visited itself upon the guilty and the innocent alike.

Having been awake most of the night, Ad was aware when the overcast sky turned gray. Plain that the sun would refuse to shine this Saturday morning, the sixteenth. The blackening horizon promised a day of rain. All they could do now was wait, and wonder if the couriers got through to Lapwai.

Then wait some more.

By midafternoon, Ad Chapman grew tired of waiting. He asked for volunteers to join him on a scout up the road to

Cottonwood House. Eighteen men mounted up, heavily armed, and followed him out of Mount Idaho for Grangeville. They found that settlement battened down and prepared for the siege those townsfolk expected at any moment; then Chapman's militia pushed north onto the Camas Prairie.

Just past four o'clock Ad figured they had to be getting close to Norton's place, what with Cottonwood Butte looming on the left. Up ahead at the bottom of a swale lay the spot where Wilmot and Ready had abandoned their wagons with all that liquor aboard—

Suddenly, no more than a mile away up the road, he spotted horsemen, a damn lot of horsemen, coming on at a good clip, a double handful of Indians out front.

But just as the other civilians were about ready to piss in their britches, Chapman saw those telltale guidons snapping in the cold breeze.

"Hold on, there—that's cavalry, fellas!" Chapman announced, hearing the audible sigh shudder through the eighteen men around him. "If I know anything, it's horse soldiers."

The others were starting to whoop and holler as Ad Chapman put heels to his horse. He didn't know who had gotten through to Lapwai—the half-breed or Looking Glass's brother—and it really didn't matter much right then.

All that was important now was that the army had come and they were about to give back hurt for hurt and put down this short-lived uprising. If nothing else, it was time to teach them murdering bucks a lesson, but good.

"Any of you in command here?" Captain David Perry asked the twenty-some civilians who had halted in the middle of the rain-soaked road, squarely in front of his cavalry, no more than a handful of miles north of Grangeville.

After that three-hour stop to eat breakfast and recoup their horses, Perry had gotten them under way again by noon. They hadn't come all that far from Norton's place when the soldiers started running across dead horses on the road, an abandoned wagon here and there, and the tall, wispy columns of smoke in the distance that signaled another ranch had been put to the torch.

By midafternoon they ran onto the two wagons positioned across the road, hundreds of cigars littering the ground, other trade goods strewn everywhere. Near the wheel of one wagon lay an empty whiskey keg. Perry's column had just left the scene of that rampage behind when the skirmishers up front announced the approach of horsemen. The strangers turned out to be a band of white men.

"The men elected me their captain," replied a lanky sort who urged his horse away from the group and stopped by Perry.

The officer studied the age beginning to show on the younger man's weathered face: those chiseled features, that huge, unkempt walrus mustache, but mostly those dark eyes rimmed with fatigue where a strange light nonetheless glimmered. Something in those eyes instantly made him wary as he shook hands with the rawboned civilian.

"Ad Chapman's the name."

Perry introduced his officers, then asked, "What's the situation at Grangeville and Mount Idaho?"

He was relieved when Chapman declared neither of the communities had been attacked. As more of the civilians moseyed up to get in on that conversation held at the middle of the road, it became apparent there were roaming bands of bandits, looters, and murderers who dared not attempt the strength of the towns where the settlers had gathered as the alarm spread.

"The Injuns crossed the Camas about noon today, Captain," Chapman explained.

"What direction?"

"Toward the Salmon River." Chapman pointed to the White Bird Divide, then crossed his wrists atop his saddle horn.

Perry wagged his head, feeling the deep fatigue in his bones. Sixty miles, in just shy of a twenty-four-hour march. "My men have been on the march since last night."

"It's for damn sure them Nepercy know all about your bunch of soldiers," Frank Fenn spoke up.

"Yep," George Shearer said with a hint of a Southern drawl as he shifted a carbine across the crook of his left arm. "That's why they're skeedaddling to the Salmon now, Cap'n."

Chapman said, "They get across that river with all them horses and cattle they stole—"

"All their goddamned plunder too," Shearer growled.

Ad Chapman nodded and went on. "Them Nepercy manage to get all that across the Salmon, why . . . I don't think you or nobody's cavalry gonna ever catch 'em in the mountains."

Alarmed for the first time that his quarry might well slip from his grasp if he did not act, Perry asked, "How soon do you suppose till they make their crossing?"

The leader of the volunteers peered at the sky. Then Chapman ventured, "Sun be going down soon. I'll lay they won't cross till sunup tomorrow, so they'll have 'nough time to get all the women and animals across in daylight."

"Tomorrow morning," Perry repeated, deep in thought.

"Once they're on the other side of the Salmon," Shearer warned, "they're in their mountains . . . and you'll never catch 'em."

"Even with a month of Sundays, your cavalry won't never catch Nepercy once they get into those mountains across the river," Chapman repeated ominously.

For a long moment, Perry studied the faces of his officers for some clue as to their mood; then he quickly glanced over his two companies and their limited supplies. He sighed, turning back to the civilians.

"Gentlemen, do you have any guess how many warriors we would confront?"

With a shrug, Chapman's big horseshoe of a mustache twitched as he spoke, "Don't matter how many warriors they got along, Captain. I've lived with and around these Injuns since I was a tad. If anybody knows the Nepercy, it's me. I speak their talk good as any Nepercy buck. Ain't that right, fellas?"

The other civilians either nodded or grunted their agreement.

Then Chapman continued, "So you mark my words when I tell you that these bastards are yellow-backboned scoundrels. Cowards of the first stripe, Captain. It don't matter how many men they got against your soldiers, 'cause they ain't gonna put up much of a fight once you tear into 'em."

"These red niggers showed how they're better at ganging up on two or three white men at a time," George Shearer snarled. "They ain't fighters. The sonsabitches is nothing more'n thieves, rapers, and back-shooting murderers."

"They won't stand and fight you, Captain," Chapman assured.

Perry was brooding as the militia leader went on with his explanation, for he was worrying. Should he allow the warrior bands to escape across the Salmon with all their plunder, without making any effort on his part to prevent it, then he knew he would be open to censure . . .

"Why, Colonel . . . if I had the hunnert men you got with you here and now, don't you know I could whip them Nepercy myself. If'n I only had your rifles—"

"You'll have that chance if you want it, Mr. Chapman," Perry offered by way of interruption, measuring the civilian.

"Meaning you want us to come along with your soldiers?" asked Chapman.

"Subject to military orders, of course."

His brown teeth gleaming beneath that bristly black mustache, Chapman grinned wolfishly at Perry, saying, "Captain, I wouldn't miss this fight for all the gold in Elk City."

Oliver Otis Howard came awake with a start.

Not long after sunset he had gone to bed in the Perry residence. As dark as it was outside now, it had to be close to midnight . . . or later.

Stepping into his britches and pulling a tunic over his sleeping gown, the general shuffled past the table bearing those reports he was writing and immediately flung open the door. A commotion was growing outside on the darkened parade. Loud voices, and the most shrill, urgent one among them all was a woman's. A knot of people and horses was moving his way.

"What's all this, Captain?" the general demanded as he stopped at the edge of the porch.

William H. Boyle, presently in command of the post, stepped over, dragging a large Nez Perce woman by the arm. In turn, she was yanking on the reins to a jaded pony. Boyle saluted and said, "General, this here's the wife of Jonah Hayes."

He studied her face in the dark a moment. A robust, fleshy woman. "Yes, I thought I recognized her. He's the acting chief of the Treaty bands."

For the first time Howard noticed another Indian woman, younger, who had inched her pony up behind Hayes's squaw. She hadn't dismounted in the starshine.

Then the big woman was talking loud again, nonstop. Yet it was her manner that most alarmed the general. A tiny warning bell clanged in the back of his mind. "What's the problem?"

"I have an interpreter on his way, sir," Boyle apologized. "Can't understand a thing she's saying." Then he turned at the sound of footsteps. "Here he comes."

Even before Alpowa Jim came to a halt among them, Howard was wringing his hands with anxiety and instructing him, "Find out what she's got to say."

The two of them spoke for a few moments—she in her loud, passionate voice and he in hushed tones. Then the half-breed blinked like Gatling gunfire when he turned to Howard.

"General, this Hayes woman, wife of the—"

"I know who she is," Howard interrupted, made short-tempered by the woman's agitation. "Just say why she's here and what she's so all-fired excited to tell us!"

With a gulp, the interpreter explained, "Hayes woman says the Nez Perce—them Non-Treaty bands—they fixed up a trap for your soldiers gone from here last night. Them soldiers you sent away run right into their trap. And . . . and—"

"And *what*, my good man?"

Alpowa Jim's eyes were blinking like volley fire again. "And . . . they all been . . . been wiped out!"

Chapter 31

June 16–17, 1877

Not long after he finished listening to all the stories, fears, and charges of those citizens huddling in Grangeville, Captain David Perry assembled that trio of his commissioned officers. Back on the road he had made sure the three were in on all that Chapman and the other civilians had to say about the strength and lack of fighting resolve in the Nez Perce warriors. Trimble, Theller, and Parnell deserved to have some voice in the steps he was about to take.

"If we allow the Non-Treaties to escape across the Salmon without making a wholesale effort to catch and punish them," Perry summed up his feelings for the others, "then I'm assured the citizens of this territory will hold the four of us, if not the army in general, in great contempt, gentlemen."

"These folks have been through hell," Edward Russell Theller observed, his eyes glancing at an open patch of ground where some women and children were gathered. "They deserve our protection, Colonel."

Perry nodded. "Many of their complaints have to do with the Nez Perce stealing stock from the local ranches—so these people are anxious to get back what belongs to them and see the thieves get punished to the fullest extent of the law."

"We ain't constables, Colonel," Parnell grumbled, his brogue still thick with the peat of his birthland. "All due respect, sir . . . we're soldiers, so we do a soldier's job. Not no sheriff's duty to chase after horse thieves."

"Lieutenant, I was given General Howard's orders to come down here to determine how best to put this outbreak to rest and capture the guilty parties," Perry explained, looking into the faces of the three. "But lately, I've been considering more and more about how and why the general didn't box me in with orders that were unnecessarily restrictive."

"Please explain, Colonel?" Trimble asked.

"It's my belief that General Howard gave me enough freedom to handle the situation as I see fit, since I would be on the ground. Back at Fort Lapwai, none of us had enough information for him to give us restrictive orders when he dispatched us on this mission."

"So you're saying we're going after the Injuns?" Parnell asked, a measure of cheer returning to his voice.

"Gentlemen, I do not believe I am overstepping my authority in the slightest if we give chase to that village we know is hiding the murderers and giving comfort to the guilty parties."

"But our men have been in the saddle for the better part of the last twenty-four hours, sir," Theller argued. "Which means they haven't had any decent sleep in more than thirty-six hours."

"And the horses are weary too," Perry agreed. "Nonetheless, I am prepared to march this command after the Non-Treaty village so we can prevent its escape across the Salmon. We must put ourselves into attack position around their camp before first light and engage the warriors at dawn."

After waiting a moment while he studied their faces for any more misgivings, Perry continued. "I brought you here to ask for your opinions. I know it is unusual for a commanding officer to do so—but I feel as if we are confronted by unusual circumstances and I would like to proceed only if we're all riding forward together."

Parnell glanced at Captain Trimble quickly, then spoke up. "Sir, I'm all in favor of attacking that village before it can escape."

"The same goes for me, Colonel," Trimble agreed.

Then the three of them turned to gaze at the last man, Edward Russell Theller.

The lieutenant cleared his throat and told Perry, "All right. It's unanimous. So we should get this battalion moving, sir."

Perry felt the surge of that old excitement electrify his very sinew. "Damn right, gentlemen. Inform your commands we are moving out in thirty minutes."

After leaving three men from among both companies to stay behind, posted to guard the battalion's excess equipage, Perry sent his Nez Perce trackers forward, threw out both skirmishers and flankers, then started those one-hundred-some cavalrymen for the canyon of White Bird Creek.

When it came time to march against the enemy, the two dozen or more civilians Ad Chapman boasted would be coming along failed to show up. The citizen militia numbered no more than eleven, including Chapman, when they loped up to join the column setting out to prevent the Indian village from crossing the Salmon.

It was 9:30 P.M., Saturday, the sixteenth of June.

Those ninety-nine weary enlisted men, four officers, and their dozen Nez Perce trackers had climbed out of their saddles upon reaching Grangeville at sunset. They found fewer than forty men, women, and children huddled behind an upright stockade they had erected around Grange Hall.

Minutes later First Sergeant Michael McCarthy watched about half of the fifty-two men from his H Company straggle back from the tall grass where they had picketed their horses as the shadows grew long. The rest had already kindled fires and put beans on to boil.

"Get them white dodgers cooking, boys," he ordered them as he moved among the dozen or so fires the hungry troopers surrounded. "You'll damn well want something in your bellies afore the cap'n comes whistling up his night guard."

"So we gonna bunk in here for the night, Sarge?" asked Corporal Roman D. Lee.

"You better pray we do, Cawpril," McCarthy said, his voice still laden with much of that Newfoundland Irish heritage of his. "We been in the saddle for something shy of twenty-four hours now, so if you boys don't need a rest, then those poor mother-loving horses you rode here sure do."

The beans smelled bloody good. Their fragrance was suddenly reminding his stomach of just how long it had been since last he had swallowed anything of substance.

McCarthy had wandered south from Canada as soon as he was old enough to leave home. After a short time in Vermont he had ended up migrating to Boston—good Irish town that it was. There he had knocked around until he landed something solid as a printer's devil. Seeing how he was only fifteen

when the Civil War broke out, the most an eager young lad
like himself could do was follow the war with every edition
and extra of the newspaper.

By the time the Southern states had been defeated and
brought back into the fold, McCarthy had tired of the smell
of printer's ink and signed up for a five-year enlistment in the
army. Sent west to Jefferson Barracks near St. Louis, where
the army trained him to be a horseman, McCarthy was
promptly shipped off to a First Cavalry outfit to fight Apaches
down near the Mexican border. Wasn't long before they
moved McCarthy, now wearing corporal's stripes, and some
of his mates north to Oregon country, where they ended up
chasing half a hundred poor Modocs around the Lava Beds
for the better part of a year.

In fact, he had been in on the chase and capture of Captain
Jack himself. A downright sad thing that was, McCarthy often
thought, how the chief's friends and headmen had turned on
him. Sad that most of those traitors went free and Jack hung
at the end of a rope.

McCarthy pushed an unruly lock of his auburn hair out of
his eyes in that glow of the firelight and continued oiling his
Colt's .45-caliber service revolver. He knew that should he
ever pick up four out of every five of this company's carbines,
he would find them rusty, fouled, and unfit for service in an
Indian fight. Joseph and Mary, he'd tried! At least he'd keep
his own weapons ready, waiting for those beans to boil, when
the trumpet suddenly blared—

"Joseph and Mary!" he grumbled, completely caught by
surprise when Trumpeter Frank A. Marshall blew the stirring
notes to "Boots and Saddles" as the last shreds of twilight
faded and night was dripping down around them. It was nudg-
ing nine o'clock.

Lumbering to his feet, McCarthy poked the oiling rag into
the back pocket of his light-blue wool britches, then stuffed
the cuffs with their wide yellow outer stripe into the tops of
his dusty, scuffed black boots. A few of the closest horses
whinnied, as if the beasts had already learned some of the
goddamned bugle calls themselves.

Of a sudden, the bivouac came alive. Sergeant Isador
Schneider came trotting up. The man skidded to a halt,
slapped heels together, and saluted, "First Sergeant! Compliments of the major—prepare to march!"

Goddammit, he liked this German, he did. No matter that it was hard for McCarthy to understand him at times, Schneider always managed to say enough, always spoke most of it clear enough that McCarthy understood the transfer of orders from that fleshy Irishman Lieutenant Parnell, or this command come directly from Captain Trimble.

"Cawprils!" McCarthy bawled like a wounded calf. "You heard our orders!"

"But, Sarge!" whined Farrier John Drugan with a hint of Boston Irish in his voice. "We ain't got our supper boiled!"

"Eat them god-blessed beans if you want," McCarthy growled, waving off the complaint. "Or dump 'em when you put out your fires. Just make sure you're in the saddle when that trumpet blows. This army's going on the march!"

The corporals had half the grumbling men moving away into the dark, carrying the throat latches they would use to bring in the horses by rotation as the men began to throw the still-damp saddle blankets across the broad backs and cinch down those god-awful, ass-numbing McClellan saddles. In a matter of minutes their camp was alive with the bustle of soldiers given very little time to move out. Some of H Company chose to drag their kettles off the flames, where they started scooping the half-cooked white beans into their mouths, while others were content to soak their hard bread in the hot bean water or in their coffee before chewing it down. But the first sergeant got every man jack of them off his arse and moving when his horse was brought into bivouac.

If Michael McCarthy had anything to say about it, H Company was not going to be bringing up the rear on tonight's march because his men were the last who were ready to ride. No, sir—when Colonel Perry gave the order to "march," H Company, First U.S. Cav, was gonna be there right at the front of the column, leading the way. If they were going to be fighting Injuns by sunup, then First Sergeant McCarthy was damn well gonna see that his men wouldn't have to eat any other company's dust on their ride into that battle.

Joseph and Mary, but these weeds were no get-up-and-move-out bunch of soldiers! A matter of months ago many of McCarthy's men had been signed up during recruiting sweeps through cities back east. Since shipping out from Jefferson Barracks, these "Custer's Avengers" hadn't drilled enough to make them marksmen with their carbines or confident in the saddle. But Sergeant McCarthy's headaches weren't limited to his green-broke shavetails. Even those soldiers who had been on duty for some time out here in Nez Perce country ended up spending most of their days acting as clerks, blacksmiths, carpenters, and tinkers. A few served their officers as dog-robbers.

Even if the troops had been given ample time for target practice, a penny-pinching army never provided enough expendable ammunition. And if the troops were kept too busy with other mundane duties, it meant their horses suffered a lack of training, most tending to shy at the unexpected and loud noises that would come with battle.

"Get up, god-blame-it!" McCarthy growled as he plodded around the fires, intimidating his men away from those kettles of half-hard beans and barely boiled coffee. "That gun cleaned?"

"Y-yessirsergeant!"

"Where's your blanket?" he shouted to another, then kept on stomping through the bivouac, goading each reluctant, weary soldier into action.

"Got your extra cawtridges?" McCarthy demanded of another who clumsily kicked over a kettle of half-cooked supper when he stood to salute too suddenly. "You'll be begging for want of bullets 'stead of beans by morning, soldier!"

McCarthy brushed the droopy ends of his shaggy reddish-brown mustache away from the corners of his lips while he kept probing through H Company's bivouac—prodding, cajoling, wheedling, jabbing men into motion as Perry's battalion prepared to march away into who the hell knew what.

Even a few bloody rumors were flying faster than any of these men were moving, goddammit. Word from those civilians cozied up with Colonel Perry said that the soldiers could creep right up on that Injun village while it was still dark . . . and wait for first light to sink their teeth into the camp.

Joseph and Mary! If that tale be true . . . then these poor mothers' sons would be crying for a shitload of bullets by morning, and all the beans in Idaho be damned!

By gor, if these men of his Company H weren't about as frayed as an old rope!

Lieutenant William Russell Parnell couldn't blame any of them for drifting off to sleep, even though they'd been or-

dered to stay awake now that Colonel Perry had called a halt
for the battalion, here at 1:00 A.M. among the skimpy timber
at the head of the canyon, after marching some ten miles from
Mount Idaho in the dark. The slopes below them descended
some twenty-six-hundred feet in a precipitous three-mile drop
to White Bird Creek itself. Somewhere between there and
the Salmon River a few miles farther down the valley was
where Perry figured they would find the village.

For the last three hours the column had stumbled through
the dark, groping its way past the lake where the Nez Perce
had been camped until a day or so ago, if for no other reason
than to make sure the village had abandoned the area.

Parnell wasn't totally sure, but as he peered at the face of
his pocket watch in the dim starshine it appeared to be just
before two o'clock in the wee hours. An ungodly time for
man or beast to be up and about—unless that man was with
a beast of a woman!

He chuckled to himself as he strode over to his first sergeant, noticing how many of the bone-weary horses had lain
down on the slope beside their riders to fall asleep.

"McCarthy," Parnell whispered. Perry had given his officers strict orders for the utmost silence.

The sergeant turned, snapping a salute as he came round.

"I need you to keep moving 'mong the men," the lieutenant explained. "Shake 'em, whisper in their ear, kick 'em in
their arse if you have to—but help me keep these shavetails
awake or it will be our hides."

"They ain't had decent shut-eye in—"

"You have my orders, Sergeant," Parnell interrupted.
"They must stay awake so we can move out at an instant."

McCarthy stared east. "Gonna be a while till sunup—"

"You're a damn fine sergeant, McCarthy," Parnell interrupted, gripping hold of the slim, shorter McCarthy's tunic in
his beefy hand. "I've served with many a good fighting man on
the Continent and here in Amerikay, but you're one of the finest
I've ever had ride into a scrap with me. Don't go mucking things
up so I have to put you on report for running away with your
mouth. Now be a good soldier and keep these men awake till
we jump this village the trackers found up ahead."

"Yes, sir," McCarthy replied as Parnell freed him. The sergeant turned and started off down the ragged line where
H Company had dismounted and ground-hobbled their

horses to remain close at hand; then collapsed into the damp, dewy grass right where they were.

There was grumbling when the first sergeant went through the ranks—to be sure, there was some grumbling. And Parnell knew most of it came from the Irishmen among them, more so than from any of those pig-loving Germans. God knows—they had enough Germans in this man's army, and sure as hell too goddamned many of them in Parnell's H Company!

The big, fleshy lieutenant who could tax the resources of all but the sturdiest of cavalry mounts hungered to fire up his own pipe while they waited here in the dark above this cleft of a narrow canyon. But Perry had issued orders forbidding both fires to boil coffee and light their pipes. *Rightly so,* Parnell brooded. This close to the red buggers, sneaking up on their savage bums the way they had—no telling just how close the colonel's scouts had brought them to the village when the halt was ordered.

Those trackers were out now, feeling their way on down the canyon of White Bird Creek to locate the village before they would return to the battalion with their report. Stopped here in the black gut of a starless night, what troopers were still awake gazed down the steep, grassy slopes that dropped some twenty-six-hundred feet to the bottomland below. This ridge where Perry had ordered this halt until dawn stretched a little more than a mile to the west of that low mountain spur rising south of Grangeville. Nearly barren of timber, the ridge curved abruptly to the south, ending only when it reached the Salmon River. In those intervening seven miles, the undulating terrain descended more sharply at first, then gentled out near the creek bottom.

Pulling a sizable pinch of pipe tobacco from the ever-present leather tobacco pouch he kept stuffed inside his tunic, Parnell stuffed the wad inside his cheek and nestled it with the tip of his tongue. He stifled the cough that came with its bitter taste. Old goddamned shit, this army weed was. Likely been around since the bloody war—

The lieutenant hurtled into motion at that first bright flare of a sulphur-headed lucifer one of the men struck in the blackness at the head of the canyon.

"Snuff it out!"

That was McCarthy's growl Parnell heard as he raced up to the soldier who whipped his hand in the cold air to extin-

guish the match he had just positioned over his well-worn
pipe bowl.

"Goddamn you, soldier!" the lieutenant snarled as he
lunged up before the private, finding it to be one of Perry's
F Company, a trumpeter who nervously shoved his trumpet
and cord behind his left elbow.

Parnell felt like throttling him—making the son of a bitch
the first casualty of the coming fight. "What's your name,
bugler?"

"J-Jones, sir."

"No bloody pipes," McCarthy hissed as he stepped in between the bewildered soldier and the fuming lieutenant,
clearly set to jump right into the middle of that trumpeter.

"Remind 'em all again, Sergeant," Parnell whispered angrily instead, an ugly edge to it. Times like these reminded
him why there was two classes of fighting men in the American army: them that led, and them what had to be led. "Keep
telling 'em there'll be no pipes till after we've whipped us a
bunch of red-bellies."

"I don't figger there's gonna be much of a fight for me
today, sir," John M. Jones declared.

Parnell glared at him. "Why's that, bugler?"

"I was in the drunk tank me own self when the general put
that old Toohoolhool chief in the guardhouse with me. And
that ugly ol' turnip give me his word as a fellow prisoner that
I wouldn't get hurt if the soldiers and his warriors ever got
into a scrap."

"He say you wouldn't get killed, that it?"

Jones nodded. "It's just what the ol' reprobate hisself told
me—"

Parnell, Jones, McCarthy, and the others nearby turned
slowly as the coyote called from the timbered hillside just
behind his H Company's position. The lieutenant immediately felt the hair rise on the back of his neck with that
howl—something a bit uncanny about the timing of this wild
bay . . . no coyote gonna call out when it's spotted men . . .
The skittish creature would be off and running away—

Then the howl's last note went strangely off-key, quivering,
lasting much longer than any coyote call Parnell had ever
heard. Something imminently forbidding in it.

McCarthy slowly turned from the slope above to look down
at the lieutenant. In that great, deafening silence that swept

in as that final sinister note faded down the canyon, Parnell could see the deeply carved lines of grim resolution appear on his first sergeant's face.

"It's the Injuns, sir," McCarthy whispered dourly. "The bastards saw the bloody match and they know we've come fer 'em."

Chapter 32

Season of *Hillal*
1877

The Nez Perce called him No Feet, but he was not one of their people. No, this man named *Seeskoomkee* had come to live with the *Nee-Me-Poo* quite by the twists of fortune.

His skin was much darker than was the skin of these Northwest Indians. Some say he was an African who had somehow escaped his masters far to the south in California. Most only knew that he had been sold to a succession of owners as his life took him farther and farther north toward Oregon country.

Then three years ago the slave was purchased by a cruel Yakima chief named Kamiakin, who beat *Seeskoomkee*, gave him very little to eat, and provided him little more than a thin blanket to ward off the wind. To punish him for stealing some morsel of food, Kamiakin threw his slave out of his lodge one horribly cold winter night, hoping to teach him a lesson. As the temperatures continued to drop, the slave's bare feet and hands began to swell with frostbite, pressing painfully against the crude iron shackles welded around his limbs.

By morning the damage was done. To save *Seeskoomkee*'s life a tribal physician hacked off both blackened feet and one of the hands.

The Yakima sold No Feet, useless as a slave now, to another nameless tribe, who eventually sold off their property to White Bird's people for what they could barter for him.

Seeskoomkee had been his name from that very day. No Feet.

With the aid of two sturdy walking staffs, he somehow had learned to grittily lurch around in an ungainly fashion on the stubs of what was left of his ankles. It wasn't long before one of the most superb horsemen among the Non-Treaty bands, a warrior named *Payenapta,* the one called Hand in Hand, took the cripple under his tutelage and taught No Feet to ride. Together they braided a special harness that the eager student could step into and use to pull himself atop a pony with only that one good hand. It was nothing less than magical to watch how this lame man, who could barely hobble about, transformed himself into an omnipotent warrior once he was mounted on his pony.

Second only to Hand in Hand in his prowess on horseback. If No Feet had not been born a Nez Perce . . . he was nothing less than a Nez Perce now.

Late yesterday afternoon his people had reached this camping ground located in the creek bottom as the White Bird made its last bend to the south. Here where they were sheltered from approach on the north by twin buttes, no more than thirty conical buffalo-hide lodges stood against the dusky hues of twilight as the supper fires were lit. The three bands in camp boasted some 135 warriors, including those who came and went on their raids.* For the last few days the members of these three Non-Treaty bands had been in full revel as raiders brought plunder, cattle, and horses, along with a number of firearms, into the migrating camp. Not to mention the whiskey they discovered from time to time in the houses of the Shadows and among the white man's wagons crossing Camas Prairie.

It was near twilight last night when one of the raiding parties returned to the village with a large keg of whiskey strapped to the back of a stolen horse. As the fires leaped into the dark, the celebration began. Dancing, singing, drinking, and coupling—life anew now that the Nez Perce had declared their freedom from the dictates of the white man's army and his Indian agent.

Perhaps it was that No Feet had never acquired a taste for

---

*Nez Perce accounts state that there were fifty-five warriors among Joseph's Wallowa, fifty in White Bird's *Lamtama,* and no more than thirty warriors in Toohoolhoolzote's *Pikunan.*

the whiskey because he had been a slave for so long, but he had no more than a few sips of the burning liquid before he and two others joined Hand in Hand to leave the noisy camp. As the sun went down, the chiefs declared need of sending out camp guards to watch the upper canyon. Not everyone could get drunk and carouse, allowed to sleep until midday before arising with a roaring thunder in their heads.

No Feet felt immense pride course its way through him that he had been chosen to come along, especially when Hand in Hand found out that *Wettiwetti Haulis,* called Vicious Weasel, and *Koklok Ilppilp,* known as Red Raven, the other two guards, had brought along a flask of the Shadow's whiskey for themselves! The pair was drunk before moonset, which left only Hand in Hand and No Feet to keep watch through the long summer night.

Above them, along the rim of the canyon, No Feet saw that day was coming. He could recognize that graying line where last night's dusting of stars was beginning to outline the crest of the surrounding heights. Now the brightest of stars were dimming and the sky becoming gray. Dawn would not be long in coming.

He blinked and held his breath, listening to this momentary stillness as time hung in the balance, these last heartbeats before the warming earth would cause the air to move once more. Then all he heard was the rattling snores of those two drunk guards who had been sleeping most of the night.

And then No Feet was sure his mentor was aware of what had changed on the hillside above them.

"Do you see them?" asked Hand in Hand.

Breathlessly No Feet nodded. "That can only be soldiers."

"Soldiers," Hand in Hand repeated the slur. "Come to slip up on our village."

No Feet turned clumsily on his knees, starting to lumber back toward the brush where they had tied their ponies before taking up their watch here on the undulating slopes. He stopped, turned, and looked over his shoulder again. Yes, only white men—soldiers—rode in winding columns like that. Nez Perce raiders would be coming down toward the camp in single file. These were Shadows creeping up on them out of dawn's inky darkness.

That first loud crack of the rawhide quirt slapping against bare flesh brought No Feet around immediately. Hand in

Hand was grumbling angrily as he stepped away from Red Raven and cocked his arm back for another blow, savagely bringing his quirt down upon the shoulders of Vicious Weasel, the second of the drunken guards.

He was cursing them both, ". . . and your mothers' wombs for ever whelping such worthless men! You might as well return to camp right now and start wailing with the old women . . . for both of you are nothing less than women!"

Again and again he rained blows down upon the two groggy men doing their best to roll away from the fury of his attack, from the painful lashing he delivered with each blow from that quirt. They would be no use, No Feet thought as he continued to lurch forward onto his one good hand, propelled through the grass on his knees.

Reaching his pony, No Feet grabbed hold of the braided loop that hung down on the right side of the animal. Rocking himself forward onto one of his stumps, he lifted the other leg and set the crude, scarred stump into the end of the loop. Then with his one hand he pulled himself against the side of the horse, heaved up, and kicked the other leg over. Sitting up, he straightened himself into that comfortable groove behind the pony's withers, dragged the braided loop up, and tucked it beneath his buttocks where it would be out of the way, then reined the animal about in a tight circle.

No Feet stopped next to Hand in Hand. "Do not waste your time on them," he said. "I am already halfway back to camp with the news."

"Yes! Tell them," Hand in Hand said as he backhanded Red Raven when the groggy warrior attempted to stand after his beating.

Without the whoop and war cry he felt surging within his chest, No Feet flailed the pony's ribs with the stumps of his ankles. The animal bolted away, racing down the canyon toward the nearby village.

As the sky continued to lighten behind him, No Feet struggled to stay atop the heaving animal as it shuddered its way down the barren slope into the deepest part of the canyon where the White Bird began its final descent before it joined the waters of the Salmon River.

There they were!

As soon as he spotted the first lodges, No Feet finally freed the beast that had been crying for release inside his chest.

Never before had he ever yelled so loud, nor so boldly. At that moment it reminded him of the shrill cry of a wounded mountain lion, coupled with the battle roar of a boar grizzly. And, therefore, the fierce wildness of his cry truly scared him.

"Awake! Awake, all you free people!" he shouted.

Now the dogs were barking and those ponies tied among the lodges were snorting, whickering, whinnying loudly in their own surprise and fear.

"Soldiers are coming! Soldiers are near!"

Heads were beginning to poke from the doorways in the gray light of that dawn, many rubbing their bleary, red-rimmed, whiskey-soaked eyes.

"Awake and prepare to fight, *Nee-Me-Poo*!" he cried as he raced through the elongated camp. "This is our day!"

At the end of the camp he saw old man White Bird totter out of his lodge, asking loudly, "The soldiers are on their way?"

"Yi! Yi! This is the day of our victory!" No Feet shrieked with joy as the village came to life around him. "For this is the day the *Nee-Me-Poo* are freed forever!"

The instant she heard the horses coming out of the dark, Isabella Benedict dragged her daughters into the brush at the side of the narrow trail that carved its way up the grassy slope to the top of the canyon.

She wanted to wail, sob, gnash her teeth at the damned bloody luck of things; instead, she bit her lower lip and made the little ones crouch down beside her, where they clung like deer ticks beneath her arms in the gray of dawn's coming.

Oh, God—how she had struggled through the last two nights, alternately hiding, then scrambling a short distance across and around the steep hills that enclosed the canyon of the White Bird. Oftentimes too scared to move, what with every faint and frightening sound slipping out of the spooky night. With the little ones she had waited out the days, anxious for the sun to fall and darkness to finally cloak the land so she could lead them out of the brush by the hand, slowly picking their way into the night, feeling their way along the grassy slopes limned with nothing more than a dim starshine.

They'd had nothing at all to eat during their ordeal. And through it all Isabella had been so racked with fear for her girls that she hadn't dared venture anywhere close to the streams for water. Instead, she had shown her daughters how to lick the dews and damps from the rain-sodden leaves right where they hid.

All she could think about last night as the children quietly whimpered beside her was doing her damnedest to make the top of the canyon by daybreak. Up on top they would cross over to the Camas Prairie, from where it would be no more than ten miles into Mount Idaho. The last ten miles of their escape. She figured they could complete that leg of the journey Sunday night, reaching the settlement by sunup come Monday.

And now the sound of hoofbeats—just when the top of the ridge looked so close. Four miles of canyon behind them, no more than a mile of climbing left. If only they'd gotten on top before the sun came up . . .

The horsemen were coming. A real gaggle of 'em, from all the squeak of leather and thud of hooves.

Swallowing down the bitter gall of her disappointment, Isabella let her fear be the goad that drove her back into the brush, where she would hush and hide the children while the war party passed them by on their way to the savages' camp farther down the canyon. In the black of last night, she and the little ones had heard the faint reverberations of the drums, a shrill note sung now and then, as those frightening echoes drifted up the canyon as they climbed for the top . . . getting closer and closer—

A sudden jangle of bit-chain, then the scrape of an iron horseshoe on rock!

Could these be white men?

"Stay!" she whispered to the two girls harshly, pressing down on their shoulders so they squatted on the ground. "Mamma's gonna have us a look an' I'll be right back."

Quickly kissing both girls on the forehead, Isabella wheeled and crawled through the thick brush on her hands and knees for the edge of the trail.

Out of the graying light she saw the first of them take form—shadowy, ghostly apparitions emerging from the clinging fingers of chilling ground mist. The familiar noises alerted her ears that these were white men on creaking saddles, their metal bridles, cinches, and hardware softly clinking in the cold, moist air. But what she saw take shape instead were Indians! Not that they weren't dressed as white men: breeches

rather than leggings, jackets and coats instead of blankets and
war shirts. And they carried rifles instead of bows and *kopluts,* the beloved war clubs of these Nez Perce heathens.

These bastards likely stole that clothing from their victims
and dressed in their plunder. Stole the rifles and abandoned
their bows and war clubs. And those horses too, along with
their saddles taken from some ranch where the settler and
his family now lay dead in a pool of their own blood.

Holding her breath, Isabella shrank back into the brush as
the first of them came parading by, headed down the canyon,
back to their camp, where they would drink their whiskey
and work themselves into a frenzy for another foray onto
Camas Prairie. A second warrior, then a third, and a couple
more . . . she wasn't certain, but she thought she had counted
a dozen of them when a gap appeared in their line.

Those dark faces surrounded by their shorn hair, shaded
by the wide-brimmed hats, slipped on past, and still she heard
even more riders coming from her left. Isabella was confused
as to why these warriors had chopped their hair off to
shoulder-length when those who had raided her place had
worn their long hair in a very traditional manner.

At first it was the buttons she spotted on those coming out
of the gray gloom of swirling mist, damp shreds of the fog
like macabre fingers clinging to the riders as they drew closer,
closer. The big brass buttons on those soldier coats . . . when
she recognized the wide, pale stripe down the leg of those
next two horsemen coming toward her. The same stripes ran
down the outside of the britches worn by the next pair. Riding
two-by-two-by-two.

The dull sheen of a double row of buttons, the faint me-
tallic sheen of the rifles they clutched, the muted squeak of
those hooded stirrups, the gleam of their brass spurs—

Praise God!

She hurtled back into the brush, scrambling like a mother
fox out to protect her young from a voracious weasel come
to raid their den.

"Children!" she whispered sharply as she parted the
branches and pulled them against her breast. "Come! Come!"

Her daughter whimpered, "Th-the Indians?"

"Soldiers!"

A pair of horsemen were almost on top of the three of
them by the time Isabella crabbed her way back out of the

brush on all fours and suddenly stood in the middle of the narrow trail. Those next men in the column suddenly yanked back on their reins, horses grunting with the clatter of bit-chains, the soldiers throwing up their arms to halt those behind.

"A woman!" one of the riders shouted. "It's a god-blamed *white* woman!"

Chapter 33

June 17, 1877

Captain David Perry could hardly believe it himself when word came back from Theller's skirmishers, thrown out to advance down the canyon behind his Nez Perce trackers, of what they had stumbled across on the trail.

Not so much what, as *who*: a white woman and her children—the tinier one encircled in her arms, the other welded to the woman's side. Survivors of terrible depredations, refugees from the unspeakable destruction the savages had committed up and down the Salmon River somewhere below.

Perry loped forward as the column of twos parted for him, two thin slivers of blue peeling aside as the damp mist took on a whitish glow here while the sky was swelling with pre-dawn light. The long, sleepless night had been cold and damp as the men huddled, garbed in their heavy wool greatcoats. Close to 4:00 A.M., as the first gray streaks peeled off the horizon to the east, the captain had ordered the column to mount up and resume their march, starting their descent into the canyon. They had been following an old wagon road down through the steep and narrow gorge for several miles along the winding gut of a dry creek bed, occasionally forced to knife their way through and around the thick, damp underbrush that eventually soaked their legs.

The captain had been thinking just how good a hot cup of coffee would feel in his belly when one of Theller's men came racing back with news that they had stumbled across the civilian and her children.

Perry stopped before her on the trail, struck with how the woman and her two daughters all had hair so blond it was almost white. "Ma'am?"

"I-I'm Isabella Benedict. Wife of Samuel—"

"A trader at the mouth of White Bird Creek, Colonel," explained Ad Chapman.

"You escaped from the enemy village, ma'am?" Perry asked, his heart tugged as she stepped closer to his mount.

So poorly dressed were they: all three muddied, bloodied, scratched, and worn—days of terror etching their sunken eyes with blackened rings of both fatigue and the horror of what they had been forced to witness.

"Please help me," she pleaded. "We been running from the Indians, hiding in the timber since Thursday."

"Good Lord," whispered Captain Joel Trimble.

"I thank my Lord for our deliverance," Mrs. Benedict said as she raised a grimy hand to Perry, imploring.

It was easy to see how her children were shivering in their damp and inadequate clothing. Their lips blue with cold—it was clear all three had been suffering from the elements over the past three nights.

The captain turned to his bugler. "Trumpeter Jones, bring up a blanket from our company supplies."

The moment Perry turned back to look at her again, the woman begged, "Please take me to Mount Idaho with you, sir."

"Mrs. Benedict, we are on our way to attack the camp of those hostiles who have caused all the trouble for you," the captain started to explain. "I cannot take you back to Mount Ida—"

"Just a few of your men to see us back safely," she interrupted, glancing quickly down the canyon, "for the savages are all over these mountains."

"I truly regret that I can't afford to dispatch any of my men to accompany you," he replied, touched by her plight.

Wagging her head, the woman warned, "None of you should go down there, sir. That's a camp of hellions. My husband knew 'em for what they are: the devil's own whelps. And they're just waiting for you to set your foot down in their trap so they can spill the blood of all your men; then they'll dance over your bodies this very night!"

Perry stared at her a moment, sensing the hush swell

around him as Mrs. Benedict's words struck these soldiers he was leading into battle. With confidence he said, "Ma'am, this is a force of trained cavalry going into action against a ragtag band of warriors who have never fought against the U.S. Army. It's utterly scurrilous for you to tell my men they will be killed in the coming fight—"

"You're all gonna die!" she wailed witchily. "And there'll be no one left to get us to my friends at Mount Idaho!" She took her arm from the shoulder of her child and pointed down the canyon. "A massacre is what waits for you in the jaws of the White Bird, sir. You go in there, ain't none of your soldiers coming out!"

The captain didn't like such talk. Not that Perry was superstitious, but this woman's wild claims could do nothing but undermine the readiness of his men as they advanced for the dawn attack. Take some of the edge off their fighting ardor. He glanced at the skyline over his shoulder. Up there, the grasses on the ridgeline were glowing with the fires of sunrise. The light was coming and he had to get his men into position around the village before he could spring his attack.

Perry looked into the woman's ravaged face, her pale skin all the more milky from her deprivation and struggles on behalf of her children. He must do something—

"Mrs. Benedict, I can instruct one of my trackers to return on our backtrail and see you through to Mount Idaho."

"Trackers?"

"One of the Treaty Nez Perce who came along to guide us to the enemy village," he explained. "A friendly Nez Perce—"

"An Indian?" she shrieked. "That's what you'll give me to get us back across the Camas? An Indian?"

"Yes, ma'am. He'll know the way—"

"No!" she cried, shaking her head violently as she took two steps back from Perry, dragging her young daughter against her hip. "No Indian!"

It was plain to see the very idea of being escorted with one of the trackers repulsed her. No matter that he knew the man was one of Jonah's Treaty band, Mrs. Benedict had likely suffered unspeakable outrages at the hands of the raiders and could not be made to look rationally at her situation for the moment.

"All right," he said in a soothing voice. "It's the best I can offer you, because I will not send any of my soldiers with you."

"I beg you, sir," she said, taking one step closer, her dark-ringed eyes imploring him. "My children haven't had a bite to eat in three days—"

"We've marched from Lapwai on limited rations," he apologized, immediately sensing a twinge of guilt for his sudden shortness with her.

"Th-then we'll stay here . . . me and my children," she said, grim resignation clouding her face as she inched back from his horse. "You ain't got no food for us, we'll just have to wait right here for any of your men who will survive what is going to happen when you reach the valley down there. If . . . if any of you return from what waits for you at the bottom."

"If that is your wish, Mrs. Benedict." Perry straightened in the saddle as Trumpeter John M. Jones came forward to give the woman an extra blanket from H Company's stores, then turned his horse back to rejoin the head of the column.

He did not like the nature of what rugged terrain lay below them. The rounded tops of a few hills poked their heads through the rumpled, ragged quilt of ground mist. He did not like what he saw below at all. Perry called to the dark-eyed civilian, "Mr. Chapman."

"Colonel." Ad Chapman urged his horse over to Perry's.

"Take some of these trackers with you and scout ahead for signs of the camp."

The civilian reined away without another word, signaling to four of the Nez Perce to join him. They disappeared down the canyon. Once the five were out of sight, Perry turned to look over his shoulder and called out, "Mr. Theller?"

The lieutenant nudged his horse out of formation and came to a halt before Perry, saluting. "My compliments, sir."

"Pass the word back to the companies, Lieutenant: this is where I want the men to strip off their overcoats and load their carbines. Then I want you to select eight men from your troop. I'm detailing you to lead a squad to serve as the advance guard from here on out."

"What of those trackers you just sent off with that civilian?" Theller asked.

Perry considered them a moment, become wary because of the closeness of the enemy camp, mindful of possible treachery . . . or, perhaps, grown cautious because of this woman's wild claims that a massacre awaited them in the valley below.

"I prefer you to lead our advance, Mr. Theller," Perry explained. "We don't need the help of civilians or these trackers from here on out. We should find the village on our own in the valley."

"Very good, sir."

It took only a matter of moments for the lieutenant to return to the front of the march with his chosen eight. Perry recognized "Jonesy," his bugler, who rode right behind Theller. As he approached, the private pushed his brass trumpet back behind his shoulder and reached down to unbuckle the straps to his saddlebag. As Jones reached the woman and her daughters, he pulled some of his rations from the saddle pocket and held the bread down for the woman.

"We'll be back for you soon, ma'am," Jones promised. "Just soon's we're done with the dirty work and we got this camp of heathens on the run back for the reservation."

"Bless you, sir," she said, her red-rimmed eyes filling with gratitude as the bugler rode past. "Thank God for your kindness."

Theller's men pushed around the knot formed by the rest of the trackers and civilians left on the trail ahead of the column. Perry turned at the sound of the rustle of the brush and found Mrs. Benedict shuffling her children back into hiding. She disappeared among the shadowy willows.

He shifted around in the saddle and stared at the backs of Theller's men as they descended the slope. Dawn was all but upon them. The moment of attack was almost at hand.

"Mr. Parnell!" he called as Theller's detail disappeared one hundred yards ahead. "Column of fours, Lieutenant! Lead them out at a walk!"

Into the valley rode the one hundred.

His name was *Heinmot Hihhih,* meaning "White Thunder."

But history would remember him as *He-mene Moxmox,* or Yellow Wolf, although that was not his chosen name.

Yellow Wolf's mother and Joseph were first cousins. Yellow Wolf had seen twenty-one winters already, so he was no youngster. For the past few summers he had hunted with his friends in the buffalo country beyond the mountains, and he was already an accomplished horseman.

But this would be something he had never done before. This morning Yellow Wolf would be pitting himself against these *sua-pies,* these Boston Man soldiers. None of these *Nee-Me-Poo* had ever fought against the white men the way the Lakota and Cheyenne had struggled against the soldiers for untold summers.

Now he burst from his lodge, just as he had done that night the gun fired and a bullet ripped through Joseph's lodge at *Tepahlewam.* Over his head he pulled the narrow cord from which dangled his whistle made from the wingbone of a sandhill crane. Blowing on it as he rode into battle would summon his *wyakin,* his own personal helper, a warrior's guardian spirit. With his bow and quiver of arrows in hand, Yellow Wolf was ready to fight at No Feet's first cry of alarm: that caw of the raven—warning of soldiers coming.

"O-o-oh! O-o-o-o-o-oh! Sua-pies!"

All around the lame one, other Wallowa emerged from their lodges and willow-and-blanket bowers to hear the astonishing news. Then Toohoolhoolzote appeared, shouting encouragement. And White Bird too. Summoning their warriors.

Over his shoulder Yellow Wolf heard the familiar voices. Turning, he found Ollokot assembling the Wallowa men for action and leading them toward the center of the main camp. With No Feet's first alarm, the young war chief had rushed to the lodge of the aged Black Foot, who owned a great number of both cattle and horses. Many summers ago the old one had traded for the white man's far-seeing glasses when he discovered how they helped him locate his wandering strays in the pockets and ravines, on the rumpled hillsides that had been the rugged homeland of Joseph's people.

As the fighting men from all the bands gathered, Joseph himself came up to stand beside his young brother, distress creasing his face with deep lines of worry. Quickly the chiefs and subchiefs huddled together at the center of the lodges while all around them groggy, fog-headed men stumbled out of camp to catch up their buffalo horses. Nearing the herds, the warriors found the stallions fighting, the mares squealing. Here in the heart of the breeding season many of the animals were hard to manage as they were dragged back to the noisy camp where the women were shrieking and children beginning to whimper with the first twinges of uncertainty and fear.

"Perhaps we can get across the Salmon before they reach us!" one of the little chiefs suggested.

"Yes," another little chief agreed. "In the maze of hills and ravines on the far side, the soldiers will never find us, never threaten our camp. But here at *Lahmotta* . . . we might lose our women and children—"

"You are old women!" Toohoolhoolzote snarled an angry interruption. "This is war."

"Perhaps it does not have to be," Joseph pleaded.

The other chiefs stared at him incredulously. Yellow Wolf could not understand why his chief could be so wrong: could there be any doubt that with the soldiers coming to attack it meant war?

White Bird spoke next. "Joseph could be right," he asserted in that stunned silence. "Perhaps these soldiers have only come for the murderers."

"We will never turn a single man over to them!" Toohoolhoolzote roared. "Kill all the soldiers!"

"No," White Bird counseled. "If they have come only for those who have murdered or stolen from the whites, then we will know soon enough."

"We must fight no matter what!" Toohoolhoolzote bellowed frantically, recognizing how the other chiefs were being swayed to White Bird's persuasion.

"There doesn't have to be a fight," Joseph said. "We should choose some men to go out to talk with these soldiers who are coming. Go meet them some distance from our camp so our women and children are safe. Let's see what these soldiers want from us. Perhaps we can make a peace with them after all the troubles with the settlers."

White Bird turned to Toohoolhoolzote. "But while our chiefs talk to the soldiers we must prepare to defend our village if the white men came to make war on us."

It was agreed and five peace emissaries were chosen to set forth with *Wettiwetti Houlis,* the one known as Vicious Weasel. While they mounted up and set off, a white cloth fluttering on a long staff before them, the chiefs ordered the rest of the men to bring their war ponies into camp—indeed, to drive in all the horses so they would be at hand when the women needed them, should they have to flee the soldiers on their way into the valley.

But all around him Yellow Wolf could see how few people

there were to hear the chiefs' commands. Too many still slept the too-deep slumber that comes quickly after drinking so much of the white man's whiskey. How they had danced and sang and filled their cups from the keg again and again last night! So now fewer than half the camp were stirring to the alarm!

Those prepared to take up arms were fewer than half of the warriors in the village—much, much less than they would need to defend their families if the Shadows came not to talk, but to attack.

Turning quickly, Yellow Wolf counted on his fingers. Including those emissaries who were departing to talk with the soldiers, there were no more than seven-times-ten ready to ride against the certainty that the white man had sent far more soldiers than that to attack this camp!

Once again the *Nee-Me-Poo* were outnumbered.

All through the village older men scampered about, lashing the young men with their quirts, pummeling them with short, sinew-backed bows, trying to awaken the many still suffering the powerful whiskey sleep. Shouting, slapping, striking—the old men moved among the bodies curled here and there where the younger ones had fallen in their revels. Not one more awoke to join those who would protect the camp behind Ollokot and Two Moons.

This gray, cold dawn as these few fighting men stripped to their breechclouts and quickly painted themselves with the favored red and ocher earth colors, it was not only the certainty that they would be outnumbered that gave them pause. It was also knowing that of these few who would be riding out to confront the *sua-pies,* little more than half carried firearms. Of those weapons, many were ancient muzzleloaders from the old pelt-trading days. The rest carried only bows made of wild sheep horn or their *kopluts* to crack against the white man's bones, to crush his skull.

"Yellow Wolf, come!"

He turned to find the handsome Ollokot hurrying his way, leading his cream-colored war pony by hand, wearing his commander's sash over his shoulder, those white man's far-seeing glasses he had borrowed from Black Foot now suspended around his neck by a thick cord.

"Ollokot!"

"Fetch up your horse, Yellow Wolf! I am taking some warriors out to see how our peace-talkers do with the soldiers."

Stuffing his bow into his wolf-hide quiver, the young warrior draped the wide, furry strap over his shoulder and followed Ollokot and more than six-times-ten out of the village toward the mouth of the canyon where the soldiers would emerge onto the rolling bottomground.

Nearing the first bluffs, Two Moons peeled off to the right, taking a three-hand count of the warriors with him. That left Ollokot with close to five-times-ten when his horsemen took up a position on the west side of the canyon behind a low butte. At their backs lay their village of women and children. Between it and Ollokot's men lay a last low ridge that blocked the camp from the soldiers' view. Near at hand stood a pair of small hills where the *Nee-Me-Poo* had come to bury some of their dead for generations beyond count.

Not only did they have a village to defend, Yellow Wolf brooded as they waited in the growing light of this new day, but they had the bones of their forefathers to protect as well.

Pressing those far-seeing glasses to his eyes, Ollokot silently studied the distance. Then he removed them from his face and turned to address the warriors. "It is good," he explained. "I see Jonah and Reuben leading the soldiers down the trail—"

"How many soldiers?" demanded Shore Crossing.

"No more than the fingers on both my hands," Ollokot explained. "To see Jonah and Reuben coming, with no more soldiers than that—this is a good sign."

"How is it a good sign?" growled *Tipyahlahnah Kaps Kaps,* known as Strong Eagle, whose pony stood beside Shore Crossing's.

"They are two Treaty men with good hearts," Ollokot declared. "With Jonah and Reuben riding in front, our peace-talkers can go out to see for sure that the soldiers themselves are coming with good hearts."

"And if those soldiers are hiding behind Jonah and Reuben to fool us as they're riding down on our village?" Shore Crossing snarled. "What then?"

"From here we can race into position and block the trail between the two hills," Ollokot told his warriors. "If our peace talkers fail to turn the soldiers around . . . then it is here that we can block their charge into our village."

Yellow Wolf felt the surge of heat course through his body

as his *wyakin* prepared him for the coming fight. With Two Moons on one side of the canyon and Ollokot's men on the other, they could flank the soldiers, surround them, and cut them off before the white men knew what had happened.

"If these Treaty men and their soldiers did not come to make a peace with us," Ollokot told the hushed warriors, "this is where the war will begin."

So it would be here too that Yellow Wolf knew they would crush the foolish soldiers and this war would end before it ever really began.

Chapter 34

June 17, 1877

Ad Chapman saw to it his trackers hung to the left as they pushed on down the trail toward the valley, the trail taking them down and up, down and up the gently rolling knolls.

The next time he turned around in the saddle, Chapman saw the small army patrol just disappearing from view where they had dipped behind one of the intervening hills. Then his eyes climbed higher still against the far slopes, finding the rest of the colonel's soldiers emerging like a blue-clad snake slithering out of Poe Saddle on their descent. The three groups were constantly in and out of sight of one another as the country grew more broken once they neared the valley floor.

He signaled to the Treaty Nez Perce, motioning the trackers over close enough to give them the order. Abraham Brooks and Frank Husush kicked their ponies ahead of the rest so they could probe the trail around the ridge that came in from the east—hiding everything that lay beyond it.

It was clear from the travois scars and pony tracks crisscrossing this damp ground that they had to be getting close to the village.

The pair was back in no time, loping to a halt to report to him in their tongue.

"Camp is ahead. Smell smoke. See lots of sign."

Chapman nodded, twisting about in the saddle to spot the advance detail of soldiers disappearing behind another intervening hill.

"Go tell that small band of soldiers," he explained in Nez Perce. "I'll go to see the village for myself until you get back."

He watched Husush and Brooks gallop away, then turned to the last two of his trackers. "Stay here. Wait for the others to come with the soldiers."

Then he spurred his horse into motion and started around the grassy knob. The Salmon wasn't far now. Maybe the bastards had camped at its mouth, he thought.

Unable to see the two Nez Perce where he had left them behind, Chapman rode down the gentle slope where the ground would eventually rise abruptly again to form a long ridge. He was watching it for any sign of lookouts or camp guards when he spotted some movement off to his right.

A handful of them, wrapped in their fancy blankets and with feathers spinning in the morning wind as they appeared around the far end of that long ridge. They were making for him, and one of them started shouting.

The Nez Perce words floated across the intervening distance: "What do you people want?"

As Chapman was dragging the carbine out of the boot beneath his right leg, his skittish horse backed a few steps until Chapman squeezed hard enough with his knees to halt the animal in its tracks. He realized his heart was thundering in his chest. Blood roared in his ears. Knowing that bunch was come gunning for him—knowing that he stood alone to start this fight.

"Who are you people?" the distant voice demanded, more shrill this time. "What do you want here?"

Quickly levering a cartridge into the chamber as he heard their voices reach him, Chapman gave the half-dozen of them no more than a cursory look as he turned quickly in the saddle to spot the small detail of soldiers and Shearer's militia angling down the slope behind him. At this distance, he was certain not one of the soldiers or those civilians could understand the words. Likely those soldiers would figure the loud words to be war cries and battle songs—boasting that they were about to lift the white men's scalps.

Nestling the rifle into the crook of his shoulder, Ad Chapman gazed down the short barrel of the saddle carbine and the front blade found the prettiest of them dressed in his bright red blanket. Closer and closer they were coming, eighty yards now.

"What do you people want?"

Most of them were still yelling at him, raising their arms in the air as they pushed their ponies into a lope—coming on faster. Less'n sixty yards. *Them arms in the air: most likely cursing me, vowing what they are going to do when they catch up to me.*

"Whadda we want?" he murmured against the buttstock, letting his breath halfway out of his lungs. "This here's what the hell we want."

He squeezed off the shot, watching the six horsemen jerk back on their reins as soon as the carbine barked.

Levering another cartridge into the chamber, he held on another warrior: high, allowing for a good amount of drop to the bullet's flight—

But the enemy horsemen were already wheeling around and racing away by the time the shot reached them. They were scattering, just like the cowards he knew them to be. If he was going to get another shot at any of them from here on out, Chapman figured, he'd have to shoot 'em in the ass, seeing how they were skeedaddling so fast.

"C'mon back here, you yellow-livered buggers!"

So be it then. They wanted a chase. He jammed a third cartridge into the action and picked up the reins, jabbing his horse into motion.

Ad Chapman would give these red-bellies a chase.

"Trumpeter!" bawled Edward Russell Theller.

John M. Jones jumped his horse around the others and came alongside the lieutenant.

From the moment Perry had dispatched him and his detail into the advance, Theller had pushed them on down the steep grade of the misty wagon road until they got their first glimpse of the widening valley, dotted with gently rolling swells and a jagged ridge in their front. As he led the men up the gentle incline toward that ridge, the lieutenant heard the crack of a carbine.

"Get up here *now*, Trumpeter!" he shouted angrily, moving his advance detail into a gallop with a wave.

Up ahead at the base of the ridge that suddenly popped

into view as they reached the brow of the hill, Theller and his men spotted the lone civilian firing off the second of those two shots from his rifle. Off to the left were a few of Perry's trackers, their horses milling as they watched the mid-distance where a handful of some Nez Perce horsemen disappeared from view around the end of the ridge to the east.

Disappeared no more than an instant before more horsemen suddenly burst into sight from behind an intervening knoll with a flattop that reminded Theller of a loaf of Delia's bread as it came out of the oven.

At the top of the next rise he threw up his arm and halted his detail, having sighted even more small groups of horsemen boiling their way across the bottomground. To the left and to the right those warriors spread themselves into a broad line that stretched from the base of one knoll to the next, effectively barricading the advance of Perry's battalion through that gap slashed between the hills.

He had skirmished with Apaches down on the Arizona border and fought Captain Jack's Modocs too—so Theller was convinced these warriors would turn and run once they were confronted with stiff resistance.

"We aren't helpless settlers you can murder," he mumbled, watching the enemy horsemen starting to sweep closer and closer upon his left flank, where the smoother ground permitted their ponies to move all the faster.

"Trumpeter—now is the time!" Theller hollered. "Blow 'Assembly' for the rest of the battalion!"

Wheeling his horse about as Jones yanked on the bugle cord over his shoulder, Theller hollered, "Sergeant!"

"Sir?" responded the Scottish-born Alexander M. Baird with a thick burr.

"Dismount the men and deploy as skirmishers to meet the Indian charge. I'm going to return to the column, bringing up the rest of the company on the double!"

"You heard the lieutenant!" Baird bawled in his undisguised brogue, wheeling on the detail.

Theller was just threading his horse back through the rest of the men who were coming out of their saddles when he saw Jones press the bugle to his lips and force out the first four stuttering notes of assembly—

But that was all Jones played.

A bullet smashed into the little trumpeter's chest, propel-

ling him backward over the rear flanks of his horse to sprawl
on the ground. Dead where he lay.

On instinct, and feeling he was suddenly about to thrash
around in water way over his head, Theller—the infantry officer—kicked his horse into a gallop, lunging away, crossing
up the slope.

Bring up the rest of Perry's F Company, he kept repeating
to himself as he left his detail behind while Sergeant Baird
deployed them to meet the onrushing warriors.

Bring up that god-blessed F Company.

Young Yellow Wolf raced his horse out of hiding, joining the
rest of those warriors following Ollokot and the older warriors the moment that lone Shadow fired those first two shots.
A low, broad ridge on their left had been hiding the war party
from view until the moment they charged into the open.

While they waited in position behind the ridge, they had
watched Vicious Weasel's peace-talkers emerge into the open
by riding around the west end of the long ridge, angling east
across the bottomground as they hurried to intercept the
Treaty Indians and those soldiers long before any threat
could near the village. Suddenly they saw the six peace emissaries scattering for cover.

Then the echo of a rifle shot.

His attention had been immediately drawn to that lone
rider who did not appear to be a soldier. He was dressed
more like one of the settlers, or those who scratched at the
ground up in the mountains. The Shadow rode a large white
horse and wore a huge cream-colored big-four hat that made
him stand out on the hillside. Some of the other warriors with
Ollokot said they recognized the rider, at least that hat and
horse. Said he was named Chapman—someone who had
caused trouble for the Non-Treaty bands.

Yellow Wolf could believe it. The offer of those peace delegates had not been respected. That civilian in the big white
hat had fired on their peace party!

"Look there!" one of the others shouted.

Not only did Yellow Wolf spot a small band of soldiers
some distance up the slope behind the solitary white man, but
even more soldiers were showing up beyond them. Now this
was going to be a battle!

"I never thought I would see such a fine day for fighting!" shouted the old man riding beside him.

It was *Otstotpoo,* called Fire Body, an elderly warrior acclaimed as a good marksman, who was grinning at Yellow Wolf.

"I feared we would never again protect our people," Fire Body hollered over the hoofbeats, riding knee-to-knee beside the young warrior. "Never take up the gun to protect our land!"

"Ho! Do you see that?" Yellow Wolf hollered, pointing at the small band of soldiers reaching the crest of a low hill.

"We've got them stopped!" Fire Body responded with a joyous yelp.

It took no more than four heartbeats for the old warrior to pull back on his reins and halt at the side of the cemetery hill where the *Nee-Me-Poo* buried their dead. From here in the bottom of the valley Fire Body aimed his far-shooting rifle, stolen by one of Sun Necklace's warriors from a settler's house in the last few days. Two counts after firing the weapon, Yellow Wolf watched one of the soldiers topple backward from his horse.

Suddenly the rest of those soldiers were leaping off the backs of their horses, dispersing in a crouch. Yellow Wolf could even faintly hear those frightened Shadows hollering to one another, they were so close already.

"I got the first one!" Fire Body cheered lustily. "Now, Yellow Wolf—you shoot one too!"

After sending Lieutenant Theller ahead with his advance guard, Captain David Perry rode at the van of the march as he brought the rest of the column down the undulating slope for the creek bottom. The citizen volunteers rode right on his tail. Forty yards behind them came F Company. Another interval of forty yards found Trimble and his H Company bringing up the rear of the march.

More than two miles down from the summit, after descending something on the order of a mile after leaving Mrs. Benedict behind to fend for herself until they finished with the hostiles, the head of the column emerged from a narrow ravine. Below them lay the widening canyon of White Bird Creek—and that meant they could well bump into some camp guards or the village itself at any time now. Day had broken.

"Halt!" he shouted, throwing up his arm.

As the column clattered to a halt behind him, he circled back around the knot of Shearer's volunteers to deliver his orders to Joel G. Trimble. "Pass the word along, Major," he began, using Trimble's brevet rank. "The noncoms are to see that the men have stripped off their overcoats and have them tied behind their saddles. Company sergeants must confirm that every soldier has his carbine loaded."

Then Perry reined about and returned to the front of the column. He kneaded a sore calf with one hand, finding the muscle cramped from the strain required of his tensed, stiffened legs while they were descending one sharp slope after another since resuming the march at four o'clock that morning.

From this vantage point Perry could see how the well-worn wagon road looped itself down the steep southwest side of White Bird Hill before it reached the valley itself. This was the only road leading up to the Camas Prairie, the route the Salmon River settlers relied upon in traveling to and from those settlements of Grangeville and Mount Idaho, to Lewiston far beyond.

To Perry's right, the west wall of the canyon rose abruptly to great heights. No chance of the hostiles escaping around his men there. And beyond the bottomground lay the Salmon River, still out of sight. To his left, looking east, the winding course of White Bird Creek spilled down grassy slopes sparsely dotted with timber, velvet hillsides scarred with erosion ravines thick with brush.

Gazing into the valley, Perry believed the village must lie right where the creek joined the Salmon. Between here and there, only White Bird Hill itself presented an obstacle to them now. Its mass appeared to rise right across the route he had chosen for their advance on the enemy camp.

A long, irregular shadow crossing its top indicated that the knoll must be split in half by a deep ravine. Just beyond that left half of the ridge lay the tree-lined banks of the creek—

It was an immediate reflex action: jabbing his spurs into the horse's ribs the instant he heard that first shot echo beyond the hill. As he reached the top of the crest on his heaving mount, Perry not only heard a second shot but also recognized that it was the civilian named Chapman who was firing at a half-dozen warriors in the mid-distance.

While the rest of the two companies continued up the long slope behind him, the captain watched the scene unfold below him in that rippled bottomground surrounded by broken ridges and the slopes of a series of low hills high enough to conceal the enemy camp, if not its full complement of warriors.

Ahead and slightly off to the left Perry spotted more than two dozen of the Nez Perce streaming out of hiding for Theller, who had halted his advance guard. Their horses appeared skittish as the nervous men milled around their leader. . . . He was probably in the process of ordering them to dismount to fight those oncoming warriors, holding them back by forming a thin line of skirmishers.

Suddenly one of Theller's riders was knocked off his horse. The rest quickly vaulted out of their saddles as if stung by a swarm of wasps. Almost half of the detail's horses wheeled about and whipped away from the troopers who failed to hang onto the frightened animals when they dropped to the ground.

Behind Theller, who remained mounted, the rest of his men still gripped their reins, not yet splitting out with every fourth trooper attempting to manhandle the mounts to the rear.

He doesn't have enough men to spare, Perry brooded angrily, sawing his mount around and spotting the closest noncom.

"Sergeant!" the captain called. "Prepare the rest of F Company to make a charge!"

"You're leading us yourself, sir?" asked Sergeant Patrick Gunn.

"Damn right," the captain growled. "I'm leading you in there, and Captain Trimble will bring H Company on our rear."

As he reined his horse around in a half-circle to find how Theller's detail was bunching on the east slope of that low hill, from the corner of his left eye Perry noticed the civilians break away from his column with an exuberant whoop. The ten of them were bellowing lustily as they clambered over the low rise and on down the gentle descent into the bottomground, bound for Theller's position even as the lieutenant was turning his horse around and racing back for the head of the column above him.

Perry twisted around in the saddle, finding that Trimble had the men of H Troop arrayed in a compact column of eights in anticipation of their charge to support Theller's detachment—

Just then the noisy clatter of small arms yanked his attention completely to the right. Small carbines, repeaters . . . Indian weapons interspersed with the booming reverberation of old muzzleloaders. The cloaking trees and brushy ravine bottom suddenly belched even more riders tearing their way at a fury, their ponies lunging across the grassy bottomground toward White Bird Hill.

In no more than a matter of seconds, Perry fretted, Theller's men would damn well be swallowed up and overrun!

Chapter 35

June 17, 1877

As the ground below him began to boil with warriors, Ad Chapman reined up and did his best to count the redskins the way a cattleman tallied by fives, curling a finger down for every handful he added up. To his reckoning, a little more than fifty horsemen had come to fight the soldiers this day.

So when he accounted for both those friendly Nez Perce trackers and George Shearer's volunteers being thrown in with Colonel Perry's soldiers, that meant they had these damnable Non-Treaties on the downside of two-to-one odds.

Just beyond those naked horsemen in his front, Chapman could make out some of the pale lodges through the leafy trees, what with the mist beginning to burn off. From the looks of things, Ad figured the crazy bastards had pitched camp no more than a mile south of the place he had sold to John Manuel back in '74.

Glancing back across the slope, Chapman noticed about half of the soldiers heading down to reinforce that small detachment whom the warriors were just then sweeping around to flank. Wheeling left front into line, most of the reinforcements were yanking up their Springfields while a few of the noncoms were shoving their carbines back out of the way on their shoulder slings and drawing their long-barreled service revolvers from the mule-eared holsters angled sharply across their hipbones.

Farther back on the heights, the remaining half of Perry's

men were just then moving out in eights, staying tightly bunched as they started down the slope.

From the edge of a large clump of brush where he remained in the saddle, Chapman spotted the ten volunteers suddenly rein around in their tracks, spurring back for the east end of the long ridge behind George Shearer, all of them coming his way.

"That's the way to pluck the daisy, boys!" he whooped, waving his rifle in the air as the militia came on at a gallop.

A bullet hissed past Chapman's ear, yanking him around with a jerk, surprised to find a pair of warriors who had dismounted nearby. One of them held their two ponies while the other aimed his rifle for a second shot in Chapman's direction. No small carbine, that had to be—some sort of buffalo gun to reach across the distance. That second bullet whined past him, close enough to make his asshole pucker. He kicked his horse in the ribs and sawed the reins hard to the right. Time to bust the hell out of that big gun's range.

The troops with their carbines at ready were coming off that last long slope by the time Chapman steered for the other civilians angling back to the protection of that line of oncoming soldiers. Shearer wore a dour grin on his face when Ad wheeled up on his horse.

"Figgered to have all the fun your own self?" the former Confederate major shouted to Chapman over the pandemonium.

Ad grinned and pointed back at the enemy horsemen spilling across the bottom, coming for them like a swarm of ants. "Look for your own self—I damn well saved some for you fellas!"

Shearer didn't get a chance to reply when the nearby brush lining White Bird Creek erupted in rifle fire on their left. As the bullets sang through them, many of the civilians found it hard to control their frightened horses. The volunteers shouted in anger, confusion, and fear.

"Dismount!" Shearer bellowed at the top of his lungs over the growing gunfire.

Then one of their horses reared on its hind legs, almost spilling its rider. When it came down on all fours, the animal tore off with its head down and tail high behind. Not needing any more of a warning, four of the civilians immediately kicked their heels into their horses and followed that first of their number fleeing that exposed position where the long slope eased itself into the creek bottom.

Now the last quartet of the militiamen joined Ad Chapman, heeding Shearer's order to drop from their saddles, every one of them dragging a rifle or carbine out of a saddle boot as he hit the ground.

Flopping to his belly and laying his cheek along the top of the buttstock, Chapman could spot nothing more than puffs of smoke in the creekside brush. No bodies meant no targets. Worse still, what he could see was that more and more of the horsemen were loping into the creekside brush, where they were dismounting to join the first who had begun to lay down a concentrated fire into the civilians.

"You, Charley Crooks!" a Nez Perce voice called from the nearby timber. "I see you, Charley Crooks! Take your papa's horse and go home!"

Then another warrior cried, "This ain't no place to be, Charley Crooks! Get your brother John home with you!"

And the first shouted a warning: "You gonna die here, Charley! You too John Crooks—take your papa's horses home!"

Ad heard the bullet smack into Theodore Swarts lying right next to him. Stifling a yelp of pain by grinding his teeth together, the older civilian rolled over onto his back beside Chapman, blood seeping between the fingers he knitted across his hip.

"We ain't gonna stand a chance we stay here," Shearer grumbled as he crawled up beside the white-faced wounded man.

"Get chewed up if'n we don't get and get quick!" agreed Frank Fenn, sprawled behind Shearer.

"Listen!" Chapman demanded, the hair at the back of his neck rising.

On both flanks behind them they could make out a steady, growing clatter of rifle fire now. Glancing over his right shoulder, Ad realized that the soldiers who had made their charge into the fray now found themselves in the soup, what with a dozen or so warriors streaming around both ends of their wide front, unslowed. Those Indians were dropping to the sides of their ponies, not popping up to make targets of themselves until they had swept completely behind the soldiers, where they immediately fired at the backs of the white men.

That company of soldiers had come to rescue the small detail . . . but in a matter of heartbeats that noisy bunch of soldiers found themselves surrounded.

And that's just where Shearer's bunch was about to find themselves in a matter of seconds if they didn't start moving now.

"God-damn-me!" bawled Herman Faxon as he spun to the ground, both hands gripping his left thigh where a greasy gobbet of blood bubbled over his white thumbs pressed tightly against his britches.

"Don't know about the rest of you," Chapman cried as he scrambled to his feet, dragging the pasty-faced Swarts erect on one leg to start hobbling for their horses "But this fella don't wanna get cut off and wiped out!"

"You heard him!" Shearer bellowed behind Chapman, lending his empty hand to help boost the badly wounded Swarts into the saddle as the brazen warriors burst out of the brush on three sides of them.

Injuns is always like that, Ad thought as terror constricted his throat. *Once they see they have a man on the run, the bastards will be on you like stink on a boar hog.* He leaned off his saddle and held down his arm when two others shuffled over with the wounded Faxon between them. "Hurry with him, goddammit! Let's get the hell outta here!"

The enemy's wild red faces and their crazed shrieks seemed to loom so close they were about to smother Chapman as he got Faxon pulled up behind him and they started away on their frantic retreat.

"Let's get outta here," he growled at the wounded man clinging to him, flaying his horse's ribs unmercifully with his boot heels, "afore we all get blowed right to hell!"

"F Troop—right oblique!" Captain Perry hollered as he stood in his hooded stirrups. "Forward at a trot!"

It was dead certain that Theller's detail would soon be destroyed, if it wasn't already. By damn, Perry decided, he'd lead the charge with F Company himself and pull their fat out of the fire.

With leather squeaking, wide-eyed horses snorting nervously, and metal clanking when the men freed the carbines from their sling hooks, Perry heard them clattering after him as he led F toward that ridge riven in halves by the deep cleft of a brushy ravine. This slope would carry them to the high ground where he could survey the field before making his charge.

Determine the enemy's strength. Deploy his units. Follow through on the attack. First principle: secure the high ground . . .

Over and over he ran the sequence through his mind. Von Clausewitz and others had long said this could work. Wait just a few moments more—allowing Theller's men to become the anvil. Allow those warriors to sweep in and fully engage Theller, surround his small squad, threaten to destroy them in detail.

Then, by God, the rest of F Company would be the hammer—racing into position to catch the enemy from the flank, surprising the warriors from the rear.

His mount carried him onto the high ground, where he could begin signaling orders to the other units.

Perry immediately turned to his right, where Trumpeter Michael Daly was always to ride. Suddenly finding the private off down to the right along the ragged line gave the captain an odd feeling in the pit of his gut. Perry waved his arms, trying to grab Daly's attention. For the longest time Perry's yelling appeared fruitless—forced to shout above the noise of soldiers' voices and war cries, over the incessant boom and rattle of the mixed gunfire swelling on three sides of them, over the clatter of hooves, the squeal of leather, and the grunts of frightened men teetering on the precipice of battle.

Finally Daly spotted his captain and headed his way. "Trumpeter! Sound the charge!"

Perry watched Daly grab for that bugle cord where his trumpet was to hang over the opposite shoulder from his carbine. But this time, the bewildered Daly pulled on the thick strap of woven hemp and found the cord broken. Panic whitened the private's face as his mount lunged to a halt beside the captain's.

"D-don't have it, s-sir!" the bugler apologized in a pinched voice, holding out the frayed end of the cord while he trotted alongside Perry for the edge of the bluff, both of them bouncing in their saddles as they crossed the uneven ground.

"Damn," muttered the captain, disappointment like a cold fist slamming his belly. Somewhere back on their march into this canyon the man's carbine or sling must have rubbed against that cord until it frayed and the trumpet dropped without Daly noticing.

The moment they had spotted Perry bringing the majority of F Company toward the ridge, most of the enemy horsemen broke off their sweeping attack on Theller's harried patrol and streamed to their left as Perry deployed his men just to the right of the lieutenant's squad, intent upon establishing himself on the easternmost part of White Bird Hill. Still mounted and making a conspicuous target of himself among his few men afoot, Theller continued to hold his small advance guard firmly in hand. Clearly these were frightened men engaged in a fierce, hot skirmish on the slope just below the point where Perry reined up the bulk of F Company now.

"Halt!" the captain cried to the soldiers behind him who hadn't been able to urge anything faster than a trot out of their weary horses.

Across the next few moments most of those men in Theller's advance guard below turned as they clawed at their cartridge belts and reloaded, plainly relieved to discover how the rest of their company bristled atop the ridge right to their rear.

Perry quickly came to the realization that he had his men too tightly bunched, but undeniably in possession of the high ground. Scanning the field, the captain calculated he must easily have the enemy outnumbered. In possession of both the high ground and favorable odds! With those two supports of his battle plan propped under him, all he had to do was assure his company commanders kept their heads and they would win the day!

Good—for the moment, Theller's detail was holding the line against the advancing horsemen. Yet . . . if he were to take these two companies and counterattack this mounted enemy swarming across the bottomground, Perry figured those Nez Perce would only fall back to the brush and trees along the banks of White Bird Creek, where the warriors would be concealed. And for his men to pursue the warriors toward the creek would only serve to draw Perry's advance off the high ground and onto that open creek bottom, totally exposing them to enemy fire from cover.

But by remaining up here on this grassy knoll Perry felt the situation looked far better. Holding the high ground meant that this was terrain where his battalion could easily defend against any daring forays of those first few horsemen just starting to race past his right, their bright red blankets flapping as they screamed at his front line, taunting his men just before every one of the warriors dropped out of sight to hang from the far sides of their ponies.

Just looking at what was taking place on the battlefield below him now convinced Perry beyond a doubt against making a counterattack. To pursue the enemy any farther into the valley would be fruitless at best, suicidal at worst.

No, the battalion would make its stand here instead. Across the top of these slopes his two companies could hold their own until the warriors broke off and fled, once the Nez Perce saw they were not going to whip his soldiers. Then Perry would follow them right into their village, nipping at their cowardly heels—

"Dis-MOUNT!" he bellowed enthusiastically, remaining in the saddle for the fight. "Horse holders to the REAR!"

That order was echoed three more times through F Company as the sergeants got their men swinging out of their saddles and snapping throat-latches beneath the horses' muzzles. Every fourth man was aswirl among his three companions, seizing the long leather straps before turning away with a quartet of fractious cavalry mounts, these horse holders led by Corporal Joseph F. Lytte, who had quickly selected a protected swale for the company's animals.

"Deploy skirmish-SHERS!" Perry bawled the order with an emphasis on that last syllable, watching his four sergeants and three corporals fanning the men left and right across the rumpled, rocky ground describing the front slope of the ridge.

Those seven noncoms were seeing to it that in these anxious moments the Germans had no problem understanding what was expected of them, making sure the untried recruits didn't bunch up just as green-broke shavetails had the tendency to do when they were under attack and burrowing in for the first time.

"Three yards!" the captain reminded them on the left flank, standing in the stirrups. "Three yards and no less!" he turned and bawled at them on the right.

These Germans and Irishmen—along with those American-born youngsters who had joined the army because there simply was no other work for them back east—were all slowly deploying, spreading out as they gradually descended the gentle slope toward Theller's advance guard to effect its rescue. As even more naked horsemen broke around the base of a hill on their right flank, some of Company F slowed up to take advantage of the gentle ripples in the terrain, while others promptly went to their bellies in the grass, and a few even slid in behind what few low rocks interrupted the all-but-barren hillside. For those who had nothing more, Perry brooded as he surveyed the success of their deployment, at least the waist-high grass might afford the men some concealment.

Over on his far left, Theller had his detail scattered down the lower half of the slope. At the bottom where the wagon road laced itself into the valley, the civilians were surely feeling the pressure now, bunched like sheep before a winter wind on the side of a low knoll about a hundred yards from the end of Theller's line. For all practical purposes, Perry realized, those few militiamen were now his far—and very much exposed—left flank.

That hill where those ten civilians huddled could prove to be the most critical position on the battlefield, Perry considered gravely, much of his optimism dashed with cold reality. If the warriors flooded around behind those volunteers, the Nez Perce would just as quickly roll those civilians up like an old rug before slamming against Theller's undermanned detail at the end of F Company. And from there the enemy could boil right on around to the shallow swale where Corporal Lytte's men held the company's horses.

They couldn't stand to lose a one of their mounts. Damn good thing Shearer's volunteers were maintaining a toehold on that flank for them all.

Glancing a moment to find Theller wheel his horse and start back up the slope, lunging toward Perry, the captain surveyed the battlefield and decided he now really had no other choice but to hold this ground and prevent the warriors from flanking them on the right—where the enemy would also be in a position to run off their horses. If that occurred, this defensible high ground he had been thinking could be his career's Olympus . . . would quickly become the scene of his bloody Waterloo.

"Trumpeter!"

Daly lunged up on foot, dragging his frightened mount behind him, fighting it when the animal threatened to rear and bolt away. The soldier's once-white face flushed with excitement. "C-colonel?"

"Without your bugle, I need you to ride to the right. Major Trimble," and he pointed off to the west in the direction of the ravine. "Tell him he must hold that ground on top of the ridge. Hold everything between the right flank of F Company and that ravine. Understand?"

"Yessircolonel!" And the short, whipcord-lean Daly flung himself onto the back of his mount without using the stirrup, laying himself low along the withers as he raced away.

"Colonel!" Theller shouted as he reined up.

Perry gestured quickly across the men who had formed a broad skirmish line just below the two mounted officers. "I am turning over command of F Company to you, Mr. Theller. Take control of this line while I reconnoiter our situation."

The lieutenant saluted smartly, relief easy to read on his face now that he and his advance had been reinforced, their fat pulled out of the fire. "By your order, Colonel!"

Peering all the way down the left flank where the volunteers protected the end of their line, the captain felt assured they would hold while he took a few minutes to follow Trimble's men into position on the right.

H Company had been more than 150 yards behind F Company when Perry started his men toward the hill, so Daly was just now getting back to Trimble with the captain's orders. As Perry started for them at an angle across the crown of the hill, Trimble swung H Company left front into line and came about to the right very smartly, setting off up the slope toward the crest of the knoll overlooking that brushy ravine to be feared so.

By the time Perry reached H Company, Trimble already had his men halted and was deploying them from the edge of that ravine across to the right end of Theller's line as ordered. Despite how thin the captain had his forces spread, not one man would be held in reserve this day.

"Every five yards! Five yards and no more!" shouted Joel Trimble.

"The men are in position, sir!" growled William R. Parnell as he loped to a halt near Trimble. "Order the dismount?"

"No, Lieutenant," Trimble said, vigorously shaking his head. "For the time being, we won't dismount. I want you to see to it yourself our left has attached to Theller's right."

Parnell saluted and jabbed his brass spurs into his horse's flanks, reining sharply down the left side of the line formed by H Company's still-mounted troopers.

A sudden flurry of war cries bursting from red throats and boisterous cursing from his soldiers caused Perry and Trimble to wheel about and study the west side of their front. Fifteen to twenty of the enemy horsemen had broken away from the rest and were racing wide to the soldiers' right without even pretending to draw the white man's fire. Instead, they were plainly intending to sweep around the right end of the line, thereby seizing that far western slope of White Bird Hill that stood directly across the deep ravine from Trimble's exposed flank.

Alarm in his voice, Trimble hollered, "They're coming to stampede our mounts, Colonel!"

"Pay them no mind, Major," Perry advised, pointing at the racing ponies. "For a moment there myself I thought they were warriors enfilading our line. But see? Those horses don't have any riders on them. Just loose animals that pose no threat to us. Besides, the ravine separates those wild horses from your flank."

But just as Perry was getting that said, the last dozen men at the far right end of H Company bolted from their exposed position, scampering left to bunch with other men near the center of their line, even though it was plain to see those riderless horses thundered by no closer than a hundred yards from the frightened cavalrymen.

"These men are untested, Colonel!" Trimble apologized angrily as he saluted and started to rein away, intending to correct the problem. "I'll see they are repositioned!"

But suddenly those loose horses Perry thought did not carry any riders instantly sprouted warriors dragging themselves onto the backs of their onrushing ponies. They had been hanging out of sight! Among the riders a few even wore bright crimson blankets tied at their necks, billowing like cloaks as the horsemen galloped past the soldier guns.

A few of the warriors fired a carbine or a pistol before they came upright, and some launched an arrow or two—their deadly work being done beneath the ponies' necks as they hurtled up the gentle west slope of White Bird Hill, then arched back around to their left, where they would reload or nock another arrow in a bowstring before sprinting across the bottomground where the first of those daring riders were just then curving around to begin their second charge on the end of Trimble's line.

Perry turned when he heard several of Trimble's men were shouting with alarm, two of their number leaping off their horses and running toward a third man in his mid-twenties, a fellow soldier whom they reached up to pull out of the saddle where he sat clutching his groin, the pale blue of his cavalry breeches blackening with blood.* "By God's teeth! So this is how they're going to fight us!" Perry shouted at no one in particular now that Trimble had loped away to steady his frightened soldiers.

"S-s-sir? What'd you say?" asked a white-faced private right at the captain's left elbow.

"Damn the bastards!" Perry roared. "These savages won't stand and fight us like men!"

---

*Corporal Roman D. Lee, H Company, First U.S. Cavalry

Chapter 36

Season of *Hillal*
1877

Looking back over his left shoulder as he pulled himself upright atop his lunging pony, Shore Crossing felt certain the bullet from his carbine had struck that mounted soldier. Already the white man was weaving in his saddle while two other Shadows rushed to his side, dragging the soldier off his horse.

Shore Crossing coyote-yelped joyfully at the accuracy of his aim.

"That soldier is only the first of many who will fall!" Red Moccasin Tops screamed as he raced up beside Shore Crossing's pony.

As they reached the top of the knoll split by a deep ravine and passed the soldiers, the trio of warriors popped up on the backs of their ponies, one at a time, suddenly sitting in plain sight now—each one of them wearing his bright red blanket pinned around his neck as he slowed his pony and started down the gentle slope in a graceful arc that would take them back around into the creek bottom, where they could once again kick their animals into a gallop, slipping off the far sides of their heaving horses as they closed on the soldier guns.

"Many more will die before the sun is high!" Shore Crossing vowed in a bellow as he levered another cartridge into the carbine's breech.

His head no longer thundered with pain the way it had when No Feet came tearing into camp, announcing the army's approach. For days now Shore Crossing and many of the other young warriors had remained extremely buoyant with a constant supply of the white man's whiskey. Unlike the many others who were sleeping off the head-thumping effects of the liquor until midday, Shore Crossing had heeded the chiefs' warning call for warriors to ride out to challenge the oncoming soldiers.

He and his most trusted friends, Red Moccasin Tops and Strong Eagle, had been among only half of all fighting men who responded. The rest simply failed to awaken when they were whipped by the chiefs. Perhaps they could *not* move, their minds still too foolish and their limbs far too numb from the punishing whiskey. But now that Shore Crossing and his companions were starting their second bravery run past the end of the soldier line where the deep, brushy ravine prevented the warriors from riding any closer to the Shadows, Shore Crossing felt completely revived, his spirit renewed by the fighting, emboldened by drawing soldier blood and causing the white men to shrink back with fear as his fellow horsemen tore past.

Out of the creek bottom he started up the slope, shoving aside the tail of his flapping red blanket, looping his right wrist into that noose he had braided in the pony's mane, then sliding off the animal's backbone to lie along its heaving ribs.

He and his two friends had decided to wear these red blankets before they rode away from camp behind Ollokot that morning. Bright red targets they would make of themselves— a show of contempt for these foolish soldiers so boldly come to attack their village.

Oh, how the Shadows were scattering, like sage hens, as the three "Red Coats" shot past on their bravery runs, spitting bullets and lobbing arrows among the soldiers.

Another white man collapsed as Shore Crossing was aiming his bobbing carbine under the pony's heaving neck. *Up and down and squeeze,* he reminded himself. Up and down with the rhythm of the animal as it pounded up the slope toward the enemies. Find a target and slowly squeeze as the sights bobbed up and down.

Feeling the carbine buck against his shoulder, Shore Crossing pulled himself up using his right heel hooked along

the end of the horse's spine, dragging himself back atop the
pony's backbone with the death grip he held in that loop of
braided mane.

If that second bullet hadn't hit another soldier, then surely
it struck the Shadow's horse.

As he peered over his shoulder beyond the warriors who
followed him, Shore Crossing watched the frightened soldiers
bunching closer and closer together, many of them dropping
from their horses as they continued to back even farther away
from the edge of the ravine.

He and the others wouldn't have to keep at this too much
longer, Shore Crossing figured; not too many more bravery
runs like these and they would have the soldiers rolling back
over themselves in confusion and fear.

And with that done . . . they could rush in and finish off
every last one of these Shadows.

First Sergeant Michael McCarthy watched a pair of his steadiest hands pull Corporal Lee down from his horse, the badly
wounded soldier groaning as he hit the ground, steadied on
his feet between the two smaller men. McCarthy gasped when
he saw how the front of Lee's wool britches was awash in
blood.

"Joseph and Mary," he murmured a prayer. "A good man
gonna die slow and hard."

"McCarthy!" Captain Trimble cried. "On the double!"

The Newfoundland-born immigrant reined his nervous
horse to a stop before his company commander and saluted.
"What you have for me to do this fine morning, sir?"

"Pick a squad, McCarthy," Trimble said in a clipped manner, in no humor for his sergeant's attempt at raising spirits.
"The best we have. Five or six ought to do it."

"Do what, sir?"

Pointing up the steep slope at the far edge of the ravine
more than thirty yards away, the lieutenant explained,
"Those rocks up there should make an acceptable barricade.
Your squad will see to it that you keep the pressure off the
end of our line."

"Understood, Cap'm," McCarthy said, just loud enough to
be heard above the pounding of his heart. "With us hanging
our arses out in the air the way we'll be up there . . . you givin'
me permission to grab ourselves some extra cawtridges?"

Trimble pursed his lips, then shook his head. "Afraid there isn't anything I'd call extra today, Sergeant. Just see to it your men make every shot count."

Slapping his muddy hand to his brow, McCarthy stoically saluted. "As ordered, Cap'm. Keep the heat off the end of your line!"

Then he was whirling his horse around in a tight half-circle and racing past Trimble, calling out a name here and there: hand-picking the poor weeds who would join him in only-Christ-knows-what-kind-of-limbo, where they had a damn good chance of knocking some of the red h'athens off their ponies . . . or a bloody good chance of never rejoining their mates again; not in this lifetime they wouldn't. Not till they all reached Fiddler's Green together.

The last thing McCarthy saw when he had his six steady hands gathered and climbing for the rocky outcrop was Corporal Lee standing alone.

Riding in the midst of his half-dozen, the sergeant became mesmerized at the sight of the mortally wounded man, watching as Lee wobbled away on foot among the bewildering pandemonium, setting off alone on a slow, lumbering descent of the grassy slope . . . heading for the enemy. Walking like a man possessed through the ranks of his fellow soldiers, plodding down, down toward the naked horsemen as if Lee didn't realize the Nez Perce were swarming over the hillside just below him.

"Joseph and Mary," McCarthy prayed again, suddenly remembering the look of peace on the face of that statue of the Virgin back in St. John's, Newfoundland. "Scoop that poor soul into the palm of Your hand now, Almighty God. And for his sake, do it quick."

"Get your men to those rocks, McCarthy!"

Spinning in the saddle, the thirty-two-year-old first sergeant put his back to Lee once more, spurring his mount anew, goaded by Trimble's frantic cry, leading his hand-picked half-dozen for that low horseshoe of red and black stone.

He was the first to slide his mount to a halt at the back of the quarter-circle opening in the rocks, dismounting and dragging his horse against the side of the outcrop where the rocks stood their tallest, where they might stand a chance protecting these horses from Indian bullets. After all, these animals might well be their only way out. . . .

He was the first to land on his knees at the front of the
natural breastworks where he and the others would be protected as they faced the oncoming horsemen streaming up the
hillside for a fifth run at the right flank as the Nez Perce
continued to enfilade Trimble's entire line.

"Don't wait for me, you weeds!" McCarthy bellowed while
he jammed the Springfield carbine into the crook of his shoulder and thumbed back the hammer with a grimy hand, hearing the others who were dropping here and there around him
in that cozy horseshoe of rocks. "Fire when you got something to kill . . . but don't let me catch none of you shooting
less'n you drop a horse or spill one of them bastards in the
grass."

"Ever' living bullet's gotta count—eh, Sarge?" asked Corporal Michael Curran, crouching on McCarthy's left.

"That's why I picked you six god-blaméd sorry weeds,"
McCarthy groused with a smile the moment after his Springfield bucked and a pony went spilling. "If'n I'd wanted some
boyos to have themselves a wee bit of target practice, I'd
a'brung some of them other sad-sack ladies we left back down
there, you bloody arsehole!"

"Always glad to please me first sergeant!" cried Blacksmith
Albert Myers, grinning every bit as big as McCarthy was in
his unkempt, fire-colored mustache that completely hid his
mouth. "You heard 'im, boys! Let's make us some meat outta
these red-bellies!"

Ad Chapman and the rest of the volunteers had covered no
more than twenty-some yards in their frantic retreat before
the left of Theller's line began to roll up and turn back on
itself too, slowly withdrawing up the slope right in front of
the civilians racing headlong for their protection. F Company
had had themselves enough of the unremitting pressure from
the warriors well concealed in the brush along the creek bank.

With the precipitous withdrawal of Shearer's volunteers,
along with Theller's soldiers turning away and no longer
keeping any pressure to hold the enemy back, the Nez Perce
burst from the trees and willows to brazenly start dogging the
retreat.

Like a nest of hornets Chapman would disturb beneath the
eaves of his house, more than a half-dozen warriors sprinted
right into the midst of Shearer's civilians as they mounted up

and scrambled off in panic. They had no more than started away when Theodore Swarts was hit and, a heartbeat later, his horse was struck—a smack as loud as a bare hand on wet window putty.

Chapman looked back over his shoulder to see the horse lunge sideways, almost going down before it got its legs back under it. Ad didn't know how, but somehow Theodore Swarts hung on, his arms locked around the animal's neck as the handful of screaming warriors closed in. One of the Indians suddenly lunged up right in front of the civilian as Swarts continued to close on him. The Nez Perce had no more than raised his rifle when the frightened white man jabbed his boots into this horse and it leaped at the warrior.

Ducking aside and dropping to his knees, the Indian lost hold of his rifle as Swarts's horse sailed over the warrior. In an instant, the wounded volunteer was in the clear, racing right past Chapman and Faxon riding double on that last horse out of certain disaster.

"Damn," Chapman whispered when he reached the end of Theller's F Company with the wounded civilian barely clinging to him. "If we wasn't just 'bout boiled in the soup there."

He was helpless without a trumpet.

David Perry angrily slammed a fist into the other palm, struggling for an answer as he brooded: a cavalry command without a trumpet on a battlefield was like a ship without a helm!

With all the gunsmoke hanging in the damp air, his company commanders would never be able to see him if he attempted to signal them with his arms. And with all the incessant noise of gunfire and the cries of men in battle, no one but the man next to him would ever hear his orders. Cavalry needed to maneuver. Infantry could entrench and hold out. But horse soldiers were meant to be mobile, even as dismounted skirmishers.

So the question begged itself of an answer—how to move cavalry without a trumpet?

Forced to start left for Theller's F, where he could deliver his orders in person, Perry suddenly noticed how Shearer's civilians had turned out of the fight and were retreating pell-mell against Theller's far left flank, with the warriors slipping out of the creekside brush to make things hot right behind them. In fact, by the time Perry now turned his attention to that side of his line, the Nez Perce had already gained the knoll the volunteers had recently abandoned. From there the enemy was just beginning to lay down a troublesome fire that was falling among the far end of F Company.

"Lieutenant Theller!" Perry hollered above the din as he reined up beside the mounted officer. "Start passing the word, man-to-man if you have to! They're to make a slow, strategic retreat to the right and the rear."

"Right and rear—yes, sir!"

"That's right!" the captain yelled, twisting slightly in the saddle to point at the shallow swale behind them where the horse-holders were already occupied in firing at another bunch of warriors inching closer and closer to them through a shallow ravine that angled up from the creekside brush. "Get your men pushing back toward Trimble's H! Get them to the back side of the knoll where your horses are being held before those animals are driven off."

Theller had an unrestrained, wild look in his eye. "Can't stand to lose our horses, Colonel!"

"Your men don't stand a chance of fighting their way out of this without those horses," Perry reminded him. "Protect those mounts as you pull your men back and rejoin Trimble's company!"

The lieutenant saluted and whirled away, jabbing his horse into motion as he raced to the far left end of the line where the civilians and Theller's soldiers were jamming up in retreat.

Maybe Trimble's H Company has their trumpet, Perry thought. A horn, a horn—my kingdom for a horn!

By the time Perry got his horse turned around and was starting back along the curving crest of the battle ridge, he realized how Trimble's men were in just as poor an order as Theller's troops. Most of H Company was still mounted, but those horses unaccustomed to gunfire were rearing and bucking with every volley of the company's Springfields. The rest of Trimble's men had dismounted, all the better to take aim. Yet . . . those on foot were huddling at the center of the line, not daring to advance any closer to the right flank, where a solitary handful of soldiers held the Indian horsemen off from a high point of rocks above the deep ravine, nor did those men on foot dare to get any closer to the left flank, where an irregular stream of Theller's F Company were bunching up for protection.

If control wasn't seized—and now—disarray was sure to sweep over his battalion.

"Major Trimble!" Perry shouted, finding the officer starting his way from those stalwarts barricaded behind some breastworks near the ravine. "I need your trumpet!"

He saluted. "My apologies, sir. My man's lost it somewhere on the trail coming down in the dark."

"By God's eyes . . . that's two of them lost last night!" Perry roared in frustration.

Gazing over Trimble's shoulder, Perry watched how word of the retreat was leaping from man to man among Theller's F Company on their left. As soon as a soldier got the word to start moving to the right and rear there was no stopping him. Now even more of Theller's right was bunching in with Trimble's left.

"Colonel, look!" Trimble cried, suddenly grabbing his post commander by the elbow to twist Perry around.

Just down the slope from them the entire left side of F Company was completely disintegrating. It was clear that those pressured, harried, frightened men had watched how the left flank of their own company started to pull back, hurrying away and thereby leaving a gap between those who were already retreating with hopes of joining up with Trimble's H Company and those being left behind.

But wholesale panic didn't break out until the wounded hell-bent-for-leather volunteers blended in with the terrified recruits scrambling to get turned around and retreat for their lives—with the warriors breaking from the brushy confines of those trees dotting the creek bank, screaming and shooting right in among the civilians at the tail end of the disintegrating line. A few warriors were even popping up right behind the held horses!

Dashing to the rear, the remnants of F Company were racing headlong for the swale where the frantic horse holders had their hands full with the mounts that were rearing, snorting, twisting, and bucking while bullets landed in among them. As Theller's men clambered to their feet, abandoning their line . . . a soldier dropped. Then a second, clawing at the air with both arms as he spilled into the knee-high grass.

Every five or ten yards in their retreat, another soldier spun to the ground, some of them scratching at their backs, clawing at their death wounds. Six men down in less than a minute.

No longer was there any order on the left. And what little remained on the right existed only in pockets of a few soldiers here and there where those steady veterans bravely resisted the impulse to retreat with the rest.

Just how did this happen? Perry's mind cried out as despair seized him by the throat. How in the hell had his men outnumbered these warriors two-to-one only to have this fight turn into a full-scale retreat within the first five minutes?

As Perry twisted his horse around, doing his best to spot anyone with stripes on their sleeves—corporals or sergeants, any noncom who could hear him above the clatter of guns and the screams of the enemy—all he needed was a few good men who could help him regain control of this disintegrating command.

If he didn't . . . Captain David Perry understood . . . then this retreat would become a rout.

Chapter 37

June 17, 1877

I n their mindless panic a few of Theller's F Company were throwing aside their weapons and madly dashing for their horses.

Captain Joel G. Trimble couldn't blame any of those untried, untested recruits for breaking and running—what with that relentless fire coming from the brush all around them: front, flanks, and now even the swale at their rear. At the very least, those frightened soldiers were only following the cowardly example of the citizen volunteers who were already whipping their horses in a mad retreat back up the canyon.

Rats abandoning the ship, he silently mouthed the words. Cowardly rats, every last one of the militiamen boasting what they were going to do when they finally cornered the Nez Perce, the sort who had been grumbling that they wanted to be at the head of the march so they would be the first to get in their licks. And look at them now! Scampering back over the hills like scared jackrabbits!

"Major Trimble!"

Yanked back to the moment, he turned in the saddle to find Perry threading his mount through the men of H Company who were on foot and those who had remained on horseback.

"Colonel!" Trimble hollered. "I could use your help to hold these men—"

"Major, this must be an orderly retreat," Perry gushed his interruption.

"R-retreat, Colonel?" Trimble bristled. "I respectfully request that I take H Company and make a charge against the enemy."

"Charge?" Perry echoed, his brow knitting in disbelief.

"Yes, sir: straight through the enemy to the Salmon River—"

"That would result in our utter annihilation, Major," Perry snapped in that way a commanding officer silenced all debate from his subordinates. "Nothing less than the death of us all. No, Major. To save what men are still alive for the moment, we must seize the upper hand and begin our retreat *now*."

"But . . . Colonel." Trimble felt exasperation well up inside him like a poisonous, festering boil about to erupt. They still had more soldiers than Nez Perce on this battlefield. He held no doubt they could still wrench victory from what was swiftly becoming a disastrous rout . . . but David Perry wasn't the officer to snatch victory from this naked rabble—

"Listen to me!" Perry snarled impatiently. "We must act quickly or suffer a resounding defeat. Our withdrawal must be *orderly,* Major. Two men at a time. No more than two. The rest will cover those who are falling back. An orderly retreat back to the top of the canyon where we can find a defensible position—or this ground becomes our Little Bighorn."

"Yes, sir!" Trimble replied and saluted, feeling stirred not to lose a single man between here and safety on the Camas Prairie, despite the cowardice or ineptitude of the battalion commander. "I'll pass along the order."

Thank the Lord he had a few veterans in H Company. Even though those old files could see how the rest of the line was falling apart, even though they could see how F Company had already been flushed like a panic-stricken band of barnyard chicks, even though everyone else around those old veterans was acting without reason . . . those few steady hands had refused to budge until they were ordered to.

"Sergeant Reilly!" he cried as he halted behind the closest noncom. "Start this side of the line back to the canyon! No more than two at a time while the rest cover them."

"Aye, Captain," said Patrick Reilly.

"Make it orderly, Sergeant," Trimble hollered over the growing tumult around them. "Keep a firm hand!"

From there he quickly located John Conroy at the left of

the ragged line H Company was still somehow holding against the daring horsemen who raced past, hanging from the far sides of their ponies, stalwartly refusing to bolt and run with Theller's escape. Farther down the slope Trimble spotted both of his steady Germans, Sergeants Isidor Schneider and Henry Arend. Likely those two were holding the men around them because their soldiers were more afraid of that pair of cast-iron-tough sergeants than they were of the screaming warriors swarming out of the creek bottom.

By the time the first of his men got turned around and started for the rear, Trimble could no longer see any of the volunteers. Disappeared up the canyon, well on their way back to Mount Idaho.

Slowly, slowly, he had his troops pulling back in some semblance of order, while F Company was no longer a company of soldiers. Theller's men had become like a band of wrens or sparrows, flitting wildly away from the fighting as if an owl or a hawk were swooping down on their tails—

Trimble instantly recognized the lieutenant far off to the right in front of him, well ahead in the retreat. Theller was hatless, trudging along wearily, the muzzle of his carbine clamped in his right hand, dragging the butt across the grassy slope. Not even making an attempt at running, no. Moving much more slowly than any of the rest of the men he no longer commanded. Weaving a bit from side to side as if . . . he was in shock. Not in control of himself. Perhaps even wounded.

Trimble kicked his horse into a lope. "Mr. Theller!"

The lieutenant stopped immediately when Trimble called, then turned slowly as Trimble brought his horse beside him. Theller stared up at him, blinking, as if not recognizing the captain.

"Are you . . . are you wounded, Lieutenant?" Trimble asked.

"No. No, I'm not, sir," he replied vacantly.

The captain twisted in the saddle, spotting one of his steadiest veterans. "Lieutenant Parnell! Bring that horse over here!"

Parnell and two of Sergeant Arend's men came up and quickly boosted Theller into the saddle. No sooner was he atop the horse than he dropped his carbine and grabbed the reins with both hands, frantically kicking his spurs into the panic-stricken mount.

"That's a goddamn thanks for you," one of Arend's soldiers grumbled as they stood there a moment, watching Theller tear off, racing for the gentler east side of the slope that would carry him to the top of the canyon.

Staring at the fleeing lieutenant a moment longer, Trimble became aware of the rifle fire coming from that distant outcrop of rocks where Sergeant McCarthy and his half-dozen were still working their trapdoors with studied effectiveness. Everywhere else on the battlefield the enemy was swarming, noisy, belligerent, and cocky. But nowhere near that squad of riflemen hunkered down behind the pitiful breastwork of rocks were the horsemen pulling their deadly shenanigans.

"That's some brave men back there, Major," Parnell observed, admiration thick in his voice.

The captain had spotted McCarthy's squad too. But now Trimble realized those seven men were so separated from the rest of the retreating company, for the most part with their backs to the rest of the battalion, that they hadn't heard the order to retreat . . . that they hadn't seen the full-scale retreat already in process across the rest of the battlefield.

By the time Trimble got his horse turned and started yelling at his other sergeants, H Company was almost four hundred yards distant from McCarthy's squad.

"Turn back, men! Turn back!" he cried at those troopers around him, waving vigorously, thrashing his arms in a vain attempt to command their attention. "We can make a stand with those men! Halt and turn! Back to the rocks!"

But it was already too late, no matter that Parnell and their four sergeants did the best they could. It made little difference how many of the retreating soldiers they grabbed hold of and dragged to a stop—once Arend or Reilly, Schneider or even John Conroy released a man, then that man was gone, continuing his retreat just that much faster. How Trimble had prayed that panic would not overwhelm H Company, prayed that this would be an orderly retreat to the rear until they found a defensible position . . . prayed that it didn't become a rout.

Despite the fact that he still had a half-dozen of these old files around him, Joel G. Trimble figured it was already too late. Already . . . it had become every man for himself.

*   *   *

Husis Owyeen sprinted after the fleeing soldiers.

His name was Wounded Head on account of a long-ago battle in buffalo country. This was not like fighting a real enemy. This was like chasing frightened buffalo in a stampede.

As wounded soldiers fell, warriors vied with one another to be the first to overrun them, finishing off the Shadows with their *kopluts,* sometimes a bullet. Then the warrior stripped the rifle from the dead soldier's hands, tore the cartridge belt from his waist . . . and ran on after the fleeing soldiers.

There were so many to fall victim to the *Nee-Me-Poo* that morning. Still, Wounded Head hadn't been quick enough to reach the fighting, fast enough to reach one of the wounded or the dead, to be the first to strip the enemy of his weapons.

Truth was, he'd had too much of the white man's whiskey to drink last night. Wounded Head could not be sure, but he fuzzily remembered stumbling toward the edge of camp, where he fell, passing out right where he landed. He had awakened to find his wife slapping him, yelling at him that No Feet brought word of the soldiers coming! Carrying their two-year-old son strapped in a shawl at her shoulders, she helped Wounded Head back to their lodge, where he searched for his old rifle—but neither of them had found it. So with a groggy, pounding head, the warrior had loped after the other fighting men long gone from camp, lots of gunfire still coming from White Bird Hill.

Not far from cemetery hill, where his people had long buried their dead, Wounded Head caught up with another warrior and asked him for one of his weapons, since the man carried a carbine in his hands and a pistol stuffed in his belt.

"I have used this already," he told Wounded Head, yanking the old, heavy, muzzleloading Walker Colt's revolver from his cartridge belt and handed it over.

All but one of its complement of black-powder charges and percussion caps were already used up.

The man shrugged as he started away. "I have fired it several times in our charge out of the bushes that began the soldiers' wild flight."

"Thank you," Wounded Head accepted the offer, hollering to the man's back.

A gun with one bullet was a little better than no gun at all.

Reining around the side of the hill, he spotted a Shadow ahead of him. Wounded Head saw no other warrior nearby. The soldier ran poorly, as if struggling with a sore ankle or an injured knee, lunging with each step so badly that Wounded Head's pony had no problem quickly gaining on him. The white man glanced back over his shoulder, hearing the warrior closing the gap.

When the soldier jerked to a halt, the flaps of his unbuttoned shirt flew open. The shirt underneath was smeared with mud. This much Wounded Head saw as the ashen-faced soldier dragged up his rifle and pointed it at him. But Wounded Head was faster with his heavy old pistol.

Pitching backward when the big bullet slammed into him, the white man landed on his back, his legs twitching as Wounded Head came up and dismounted, walking over to the soldier. A black hole between the Shadow's eyes seeped blood. Soon the eyes stopped fluttering, and the legs no longer quivered.

Kneeling, Wounded Head quickly laid his old Walker on the soldier's chest as a gift to this vanquished foe, then promptly set to work on the dead man's cartridge belt, shoving the leather strap free of the buckle. With some effort he managed to drag the belt from beneath the body. Remaining there on his knees, the warrior re-buckled it around his own waist, then snatched up the white man's gun. He had seen many of these carbines before, but never had he dreamed of having one of his own!

With his thumb rolling back the big hammer a second click, Wounded Head flipped up the trapdoor and found a loaded cartridge in the weapon's breech. With the palm of his left hand he re-seated the trapdoor, then stood. He bent and patted the old pistol, now empty of bullets.

Wounded Head left it for the dead soldier, exulting and giving thanks for this wonderful gift of the army carbine.

"Sergeant . . . look!"

Michael McCarthy turned when Private James Shay tapped on his shoulder and pointed to the rear.

He and his six were alone. Three hundred yards, perhaps more, separated them from the rest of H Company. Every last blessed one of those troops gradually moving away from McCarthy's fight. Their company splintering, breaking apart.

Then he spied two men on horseback coming to a halt at the top of a small hillock no more than two hundred yards along their backtrail. No trouble knowing who the big cuss was—that was Parnell. What a burden the man was to a horse!

And McCarthy thought he recognized the captain beside Parnell. They were waving wildly at him as they started their horses off that knoll, heading back toward his squad in the breastworks. The sergeant was about to rejoice when the pair of officers suddenly reined up only halfway there and stopped dead in their tracks. It appeared they dared venture no closer.

"Time to retreat, my weeds!" he bawled as he came off his knees and lunged toward their horses. McCarthy wasn't about to wait for any more of an order to retreat.

For the most part his squad had come to the rocks well-armed, prepared to hold out if the bloody horsemen made a seige of it. Besides their Springfield carbines and those .45-55 cartridges each of them had thimbled in their heavy ammo belts, not to mention the extra ammunition still rattling around in their saddlebags, every last one of the men McCarthy had hand-picked for this crucial mission was packing a side arm: his .45 single-action army Colt's revolver. While all of H Company's sergeants and most of the corporals wore their pistols on that march away from Fort Lapwai . . . none of the other enlisted men brought their revolvers into this fight, save for a trumpeter or two. A side arm was nothing more than extra weight many cavalrymen grumbled over and left behind at the first opportunity.

They had remained well-protected behind that rocky outcrop . . . at least until McCarthy got his men mounted and they were on their way toward Captain Trimble now. As the seven horsemen kicked their animals into a lope, the sergeant made out both Trimble and Parnell as they gestured and bawled at the soldiers streaming past the two of them. Suddenly he could hear fragments of those two officers ordering the troopers to return to the rocks McCarthy's squad had just abandoned.

"We can make a stand there!" the captain bellowed, his voice floating on the cool morning air littered with shreds of gray gunsmoke. "Back to the rocks with McCarthy, men! We can hold that high ground together!"

"Halt!" McCarthy shouted to his half-dozen, getting them

stopped eighty yards shy of the officers. "The cap'm's coming back to us! He's bringing them others back to the rocks to reinforce us!"

Wrenching his reins to the left, he spun his mount and raced back for the breastworks they had just abandoned. Leaping to the ground once more, the sergeant realized that mindless panic had chopped his squad in half. Only three had followed him back to the rocks. The rest were just then streaking past Trimble, on their way out of the canyon.

After every shot, McCarthy and his trio of corporals would anxiously glance over their shoulders to look for those reinforcements the captain and Parnell had tried flushing back to the rocks. But in less than five minutes, after firing no more than a dozen more shots from his Springfield, Sergeant Michael McCarthy realized no one was coming to join them. There wasn't a single man from H Company to be seen anywhere across that some 350 yards separating his squad from those who were retreating farther and farther toward the mouth of the canyon.

As his fingers went to the loops on his belt and searched for another cartridge, the sergeant was suddenly struck with just how few of them he had left. Quickly glancing at the belts worn by the others, McCarthy lumbered to his feet.

"Saddle up, you weeds!" he growled. "Make sure you got a cawtridge tucked under your trapdoor, for we're riding out while we still can!"

En masse the trio rose and lunged in among their horses with their sergeant. Reining their mounts around even before they had stuffed their mud-crusted boots into the hooded stirrups, the four of them ripped away at a gallop even as the cries of the warriors flooded over those breastworks the soldiers were just abandoning.

If he and his trio of veterans didn't make it across this open piece of ground, McCarthy knew they would be surrounded and overrun.

If he and the six didn't get back across the next three hundred yards to rejoin the rest of H Company . . .

"Joseph and Mary!" he cursed.

He and the rest were cut off already!

Chapter 38

June 17, 1877

Drawn by the gunfire, Isabella Benedict herded her daughter alongside her as they descended the canyon trail, mysteriously drawn toward the clamor of battle. She had to see, to know for certain that it would turn out to be the massacre she had predicted.

Her arms ached with the weight of the little one as they emerged from the brush at the mouth of the canyon. Here the air began to smell of sulphur. Gunsmoke, she thought. And gray-white tatters of it hung like torn lace curtains over the creek bottom where horsemen swirled. For the most part the soldiers were hidden from view: a knot of them here or there on the crest of the distant knoll. Then closer and closer she heard the hammer of hoofbeats, the grunts of huffing men—

Figures in blue suddenly boiled over the gentle swale right before her, most on horseback, but some labored up the trail on foot. Among them were some civilians. She thought she recognized a face or two among them. The first were approaching at a gallop when Isabella started to yell.

"Stop! Stop, please!" she begged. "Don't you know me? Give us your horse!"

One after another she pleaded with the soldiers as they bolted past her alone or in pairs, a few in small bunches of no more than four at a time. Not a one of them appeared to pay her any heed, much less slow their wide-eyed, heaving horses as they thundered into the narrowing canyon. She trudged up to the top of the slope the soldiers had just crossed.

Upon that crude crescent of a ridge not far from where she herself now stood, Mrs. Benedict could see no more than a third of the soldiers holding their position—some atop their mounts, covering the methodical retreat of the rest slowly backing up the slope on foot. Then of a sudden something strange and evil seemed to sweep over those diligently holding back the Nez Perce horsemen: they turned and started for her, seeking escape in the canyon as if all hope was lost.

It was like a flood, she thought, watching how the horses bounded past her with their loud, labored breathing, flecks of whitish foam grown gummy around their nostrils, yellowish bubbles lapping at their bits. And she was yelling again, trying to make one of the soldiers stop to help her daughters.

Stepping into the open, Isabella was forced to weave from side to side, pulling her oldest girl out of the way to left, then right, as they leaped from the path of the mindless retreat—crying out piteously to the unheeding soldiers.

"In the name of God, please stop for my children!"

At the last possible moment Mrs. Benedict lunged out of the way, that horse passing so close her cheek was stung with the hot foam flying from its lathered jaws.

"Damn, woman!" a soldier shouted at her as he raced past, his face clayish with fear, cheeks so pale below those liver-colored bags of fatigue hanging beneath his eyes.

"Whoa-a-a!"

The instant she turned, Mrs. Benedict confronted the wide nostrils of the horse a middle-aged civilian* struggled to bring to a halt—mere inches from her forehead.

"What the hell?" growled a young soldier† as he skidded to a halt beside the volunteer and leaped from his horse. He grabbed her upper arm and roughly shoved her to the side of the trail as more horsemen shot past.

"You'll get yourself kill't—"

"Please, sir! Your horse for me and my daughters."

Releasing his tight grip on her arm, the man turned to gaze

---

*William Coram
†Private John Schorr, F Company, First U.S. Cavalry

up at the civilian still mounted, his skittish horse prancing sideways as the retreat washed by them.

"There's loose horses comin', Schorr," the mounted volunteer grumbled as he peered back downtrail. "Catch one of 'em for the woman so we don't hafter ride double."

"You heard 'im, ma'am," the soldier said as he dragged his horse around and stuffed the reins into her hand.

In a crouch he leaped into the middle of the trail just when at least a half-dozen riderless horses were straining up the slope into the narrowing mouth of the canyon, following their four-legged kind in the mad retreat.

The moment the soldier dove and snagged the reins of one of those racing horses, he was yanked off his feet. But he dug in with his heels and managed to whip the animal's head around, forcing it to a halt.

"Lady! We ain't got all morning to get outta here!" he bawled at her as he dragged the fractious animal toward Isabella. The moment he halted, the soldier grabbed hold of the off-hand stirrup and held it steady for the woman.

"Here, hold her," Isabella ordered, handing her youngest to the soldier.

Having to drop the stirrup so that he could maintain his hold on the reins in his left hand, the soldier accepted the tot into the crook of his right arm as Mrs. Benedict clambered into the saddle. As soon as she settled, the man turned and passed the youngest child up to the civilian, where that man settled the girl in front of him, tying the toddler against his chest with Isabella's shawl.

The instant the soldier leaped back into his saddle, leaving the older of her daughters alone on the ground, Emmy began to wail, holding her arms up for her mother.

"I can't leave her!" Isabella shrieked with terror that she would be forced away without her child.

"We ain't going 'thout her!" the soldier hollered above the noise of snorting horses, cursing men, and gunfire gradually drawing closer and closer.

She watched him lean off the left side of his horse and hold down his long arm.

"Grab me!" he ordered.

The moment Emmy put her little hand up, the soldier latched hold of it and with a mighty heave swung the youngster onto the horse's rump behind him.

"Snug up here, child!" he commanded as he pulled her against his back. "An' hold on for your life!"

Mrs. Benedict watched her oldest daughter lock her blood-streaked arms around the soldier's waist and stuff them into the man's coat pockets.

"Ma'am—you hold on tight yourself and let the horse run fast as he'll go!"

And with no more warning than that, she watched both men bolt away with her two children.

Slapping the reins against the horse's neck and kicking it with her scuffed, muddy boots, Isabella thrashed the lathered, weary beast into an uneven lope. But from its very first steps she sensed something wrong with the saddle. With every uneven lunge it took in crossing the broken ground, the army saddle beneath her began to shift more and more from side to side until the cinch eventually gave way completely and catapulted Isabella into the brush at the side of the trail while the noisy, mindless retreat swept on past her.

Scratched, bruised, and bleeding, she lay there in the willow, catching her breath while she tenderly brushed a fingertip across the new gash a branch had opened in her cheek. Isabella rolled onto her hands and knees, slowly getting to her feet. Shaking her head groggily, she shoved her way out of the brush that refused to let her clothing go. And from the middle of the old wagon trail she watched the last few soldiers goad their horses farther and farther away, accompanied by that horse with its loose saddle slung under its belly: swaying crazily, swaying—

Aware that hoofbeats were approaching, Isabella lumbered around, her shoulder crying out in pain from her fall. She gazed back down the trail, hoping she could find another soldier, praying she could get the man to halt so she could climb up behind his saddle and flee the valley with him. Find her daughters . . .

But there were no more soldiers to race past her. Over there on the slope more than a quarter of a mile away to the west, the last handful were racing toward the mouth of the canyon. Already too far away to help. Thank God the girls were on their way to safety.

With all the soldiers gone into the canyon, the only horsemen stabbing up the trail in her direction were those red-skinned bastards.

Isabella opened her mouth to scream . . . but no sound came out.

The only horses coming at her carried warriors. Shrieking, grimacing warriors who had spotted her standing there in the open, helpless as could be.

She felt her heart go cold, certain one of the devil's whelps would recognize her for the store man's woman.

By the time Wounded Head reached the top of White Bird Hill, he could see how the others were right on the heels of the frightened soldiers, driving them like those docile cattle the white man had transplanted here to the land of the *Nee-Me-Poo.*

Proud of his new gun and cartridge belt, Wounded Head turned aside to join some others who were gathering up the loose soldier horses. As he leaned over to grab up the reins of one of the animals, Wounded Head heard a strange sound. Two others heard the noise too and came up to investigate.

It did not take long to find two wounded soldiers who had dragged themselves back into the brush. While Wounded Head stayed on his pony, the others stepped over to the groaning Shadows and bashed in their heads. The warriors stripped the dead men of their weapons and bullets, then started back for the village with Wounded Head and their horses.

They hadn't gone very far when some men farther down the slope called out Wounded Head's name, flagging their arms to get his attention.

"Look above you!" they cried.

He scanned the hillside; then his eyes spotted the figure lumbering up the trail that led out of the canyon. It wasn't a man, not hard to see that for the seafoam wave of a long dress making it extremely difficult for the woman's legs to flail step by clumsy step in her strenuous climb.

This confused Wounded Head: why had these white men brought along one of their women to the fight? The *Nee-Me-Poo* were far wiser than that! These Shadows were a simple-minded lot to needlessly put their women in danger just to have someone warm to sleep with on the war trail.

"Take my horses to camp," he asked of the others.

Then he started for the woman. The farther he followed her up the slope, the quicker he closed the gap between them. Suddenly one of her feet slipped and she tumbled into a clump of low willow.

The woman was just clambering out of the brush and grass at the side of the trail when Wounded Head reached her. She must have heard him coming, because the woman whirled around—her muddy, red face went white, her eyes filling with terror. Her mouth flew wide open as if to scream, but he was surprised when no sound came out. Her jaws moved, and her tongue wagged, but no sound.

Only tears streamed down her dirty face, making tiny tracks like claw marks on her grimy cheeks.

"I will not harm you," Wounded Head told her in his tongue.

She closed her mouth, staring at him dumbly, almost as if he had clubbed her on the side of her head.

Then he repeated that he would not hurt her and laid his new carbine across his thighs so that he could make signs with his hands—some signal or gesture that would tell her she did not have to fear him killing her.

Dragging a hand beneath her runny nose, the woman bobbed her head twice, as if she understood.

He held down his arm, offering his open hand. "Get up behind me." And he gestured with a sweep of that arm, patting the rump of the pony behind him. "Get up now, woman."

She reached out and grabbed his left forearm with both hands, then kicked her legs as he hoisted her onto the pony that shifted sideways in protest of the sudden additional weight.

Slowly turning the horse, Wounded Head started back down the trail with his prisoner. No telling how much she might be worth if the *Nee-Me-Poo* had to barter for the return of prisoners when making peace with the Shadows after this fighting. This frightened, blood-splattered, mud-coated white woman might be worth something after all. He was anxious to show her off to others. Not only had he earned himself a rifle and bullets, but he had earned himself a prisoner too!

"Wounded Head!"

He turned, saw the five women who were calling to him as his pony carried the two of them onto the creek bottom. They waved him over, so he reined the horse in their direction.

"What is this you have, Wounded Head?" an old woman sang out as he pulled back on the reins.

"See my prisoner! She is mine," he boasted, chest swelling. "And look at my new rifle—"

"What are you going to do with her?" another woman interrupted.

He was very confused. The five women pushed close around his pony, appearing angry with him. He thought they should be proud of him, envious of his new treasure.

"I—I will keep her," he sought to explain. "She will be mine as long as there is a war with the Shadows—"

"No, you can't keep her," a third old woman snapped at him.

Then the first ancient one declared, "That is something the Shadows do. We do not take prisoners of our enemies. We do not own slaves like other tribes. You must turn her loose."

Now he was really growing bewildered, "T-turn her—"

"Yes. Let her go!" grumbled another, much bigger and very round, balling her fists on her hips.

"She is mine to do with—"

"But she will only bring us trouble, Wounded Head," the second woman argued more softly. "Get rid of her now. Let her go back to the soldiers so they will not be any angrier with us for keeping their woman."

"Let her go?" he squeaked in dismay, wagging his head.

And he turned to peer over his shoulder at the woman, then gazed beyond her, across that slope leading up the canyon. For a moment he watched the last of the fleeing soldiers and those warriors in furious pursuit—the *Nee-Me-Poo* fighting men striving to make escape as hard as possible for the white men, striving to inflict even more loss on these soldiers come to attack their village.

"She will only bring us more trouble," the first woman protested. "Let her go so we can leave with our village when we travel to the buffalo country."

The big woman said, "That way the soldiers won't follow us looking to get their woman back."

"All right," he agreed reluctantly. With a sigh he turned slightly to shrug a gesture for the prisoner to get off.

But she did not understand at first. Only when the ancient one and the big woman stepped over to hold their arms up to her did the prisoner slide off the back of the pony. For a long moment the white woman just stood there as the women stepped back a bit, everyone staring intently at her—so much so that the white woman's eyes filled with fear again.

Wounded Head dismounted, landing right before her to hold out his hand so he could perform that gesture the Shadows put so much stock in. The white woman understood, took his hand, and they shook.

"Go," he said quietly and shooed her away. "Go now; go fast."

She turned and took some first, tentative steps. But she got only a few pony lengths before she stopped and looked back over her shoulder, as if afraid someone would shoot her in the back.

Instead, Wounded Head shooed her again, waving both hands. "Go!" he shouted loudly this time, hoping to scare her.

If this was what it took to save her life, to keep the soldiers from attacking again to get back their white woman . . . then he would scare her away, to make her run far and fast. If he could save his people from another soldier attack, then Wounded Head decided he would give his prisoner back her freedom.

Chapter 39

June 17, 1877

Captain David Perry hadn't seen such panic in a retreat since Gordon's Confederate raiders surprised the Union army's Eighth Corps in their blankets at Cedar Creek, back to October of '64.

Already Trimble's men were well up the canyon, scratching their way across the grassy, timbered slopes above him. Off to his right a ways was Parnell.

Good man, Perry thought as he fought his horse to keep it from rearing and losing its footing on a steep stretch of hillside. Parnell had persevered on Perry's left as long as he could after most had deserted the captain. There at the last, the Irish lieutenant had refused to retreat—standing like a huge, fleshy oak, barking orders at his immigrant soldiers. But in the end Parnell was left with no more than a double handful after the rest broke and ran. After losing command control, Parnell had little choice but to settle for his few hardcases, all of them covering the rest of the retreat from horseback.

What of Theller, though? Why, with the way the lieutenant's command had disintegrated so quickly and fled for their lives, Perry was sure Theller's men had to be far enough ahead of Parnell that he simply couldn't spot them anywhere on the slopes above. More than likely Theller's detachment was already close to Camas Prairie and on their way to the settlements in headlong retreat.

So with no sign of Theller, Perry was left with Trimble's and Parnell's outfits to make their way out with him. Trimble appeared to have a steady hand on things, holding those few men of his together more than four hundred yards ahead of Parnell. Strung out the way they were, Perry was nonetheless determined to make theirs an orderly retreat. So much ammunition had been wasted by the incompetent recruits—bullets fired at the sky, bullets burrowed into the ground—even more ammunition lost now in the saddlebags strapped to every one of the stampeded horses.

"Slow down!" he shouted at the troopers repeatedly, uselessly, as the horses flew past.

Off to his right Perry heard Parnell, that survivor of Balaclava, growl at the men of H Company who were spread out on the hillside that was leading them into the mouth of the canyon and escape. His great booming voice, every bit as imposing as his body, thundered over the frightened soldiers, "Form up, men! Form up and cover the bloody retreat!"

On his side of the withdrawal, Perry hollered, "Turn around and cover the file closers!"

Already his throat was raw from yelling above the snorting horses, the curses of the frightened men. He continued to lope his weary horse left, then right, from one side of the retreat to the other, shouting orders at small squads of men. But just as soon he managed to shame one group into turning about, the warriors rushed in to nip at their exposed flanks—and the soldiers would bolt like terrified quail. All across these hills, what had begun with some semblance of an orderly retreat had quickly deteriorated into nothing more than small groups of desperate men hacking their way out of certain death—

"Turn back or I'll shoot you for cowardice!" he cried without effect.

But he couldn't bring himself to shoot any of these men who gazed at him with their blank, dazed expressions, then dashed on past. Men whose eyes filled with such abject apology that they had been found wanting of courage under fire.

So as much as Perry and Parnell begged and pleaded, as much as either one of them threatened to shoot these men clearly deserting the battlefield, nothing slowed the frantic pace of this retreat.

Fighting off the numbing frustration to simply give up and

join in the headlong flight, the captain thought, *Dear Lord, for all of us now this has become a race for God . . . and the devil's taking the hindmost—*

His horse was wheeling an instant before Perry became aware of the smack of the bullet as it struck the big beast in the chest. It reared once as he clawed to stay on. And when it settled onto all fours, the front legs suddenly buckled and the captain was hurtled off. Landing on his back, stunned, Perry watched the horse rolling toward him. He would have his legs pinned if he didn't . . .

The captain rolled out of the way, stared at the dying animal as he rocked onto his knees, slowly becoming aware again of the rising noise as the war cries steadily drew closer and closer.

"Soldier!" he cried as four men beat their horses toward him, preparing to dash on by in their escape.

One of them slowed enough for Perry to reach out and grab the man's leg and stirrup.

"Colonel—leggo! For Chrissakes, leggo of me leg!"

"I'm climbing up behind you!"

As the wide-eyed soldier nodded once, it appeared he understood, and he reluctantly reached out with his arm to swing Perry up behind him on the horse's flanks.

After crossing no more than a few leagues, Perry shouted into the soldier's ear, "Halt, trooper!"

Upon stopping, they both turned to look over their shoulders at the slope behind them. Enough men were still scattered in disarray, the captain decided, that he should again attempt some sort of orderly retreat. Here—where it seemed the Indians were growing wary as most of the soldiers were succeeding in reaching the narrow mouth of the canyon. Because the enemy appeared to be hesitating in its pursuit, Perry calculated he might stand a chance of reclaiming control of these scattered remnants of H Company.

"Lookee there, Colonel!" the soldier in front of him shouted. He pointed as his horse side-shifted nervously with the approach of another handful of cavalrymen. "A horse for you, sir!"

Perry spotted the animal. A weary, lathered, riderless horse blindly following its own kind—the only one not burdened by a trooper as it clawed its way up the slope, coming straight for them.

"This is where I get off, soldier," Perry said as he pushed himself backward off the mount's broad flanks and struck the ground in time to dart toward that stream of horsemen.

Some troopers reined left while the rest pulled right the moment Perry stepped into the middle of the trail—then suddenly leaped forward in a desperate attempt to grab the reins of that riderless horse. The leather filled his palms.

He jerked the animal to a halt, and it spun them both around, nostrils flaring, staring at this two-legged creature that had interrupted its flight. When the horse came to a halt, Perry took that chance to loosen his two-handed grip on the reins and gaze down at one of his palms. A light film of red coated the flesh between the grimy seams of dirt and gunsmoke that had congealed within the long, deep, and distinctive wrinkles. Glancing back of the skirt and cantle on the McClellan, he spotted the troop designation on the saddle blanket.

F Company.

When he stuffed his left boot into the hooded stirrup and gripped the cantle with his right hand, Perry felt more sticky moisture. The saddle was smeared with a trail of blood. This was a dead man's horse. He shuddered.

Throwing his right leg over the cantle and settling onto the moist leather, the captain turned quickly to stare into the creek bottom. The dead man would still be lying somewhere below. As he spurred the animal into motion and turned away for the mouth of the canyon, Perry prayed the soldier would not have died in vain.

Loping sideways along the upper diagonal of that ridge leading into the narrowing canyon, once more the captain felt assured he could re-seize command of what men were still streaming up these slopes. After looking around and not finding Trimble anywhere in sight, Perry bellowed orders, shaming those who were still in hearing distance, reminding them that they were soldiers.

"Halt and re-form your lines!" he growled at the horsemen and the rest who were huffing toward him on foot. But he knew they wouldn't.

They were enlisted. Simple men. Uneducated for the most part. And many of them weren't even born in this nation. So how could they know, how could they ever feel the way he did about the West Point Code: "Duty, Honor, Country"?

So Perry waved his pistol, more a defiant gesture to the enemy who, it seemed, chose to remain below on the gentler part of the slope rather than continue their pursuit right behind the soldiers as the white men reached the steepest part of the ridge.

"You see that, boys!" a graying soldier shouted with a raspy throat as he lunged up on foot. Out of breath, he grabbed a younger trooper nearby and forced him to turn around. "See—them red-bellies ain't got the stomach to foller us all the way into the canyon!"

It was true, the enemy horsemen really were hesitating in their pursuit, allowing the soldiers to gain some ground on them as the white men made it into the canyon and started their climb along the foot of the high western ridge. Down there it had been like shooting fish in a barrel for the Nez Perce . . . but for now they don't show any desire to follow us into these close quarters—

"Form up, I told you!" Perry yelled, gesturing with that pistol arm, energized by the enemy's reluctance to push their advantage.

Of those who stopped and paid him heed, the captain was able to organize two squads—one composed of mounted men and the other made up of those who were on foot. This was going to be an exercise he hadn't used since those scraps in the Lava Beds during the Modoc War. One squad would lay down cover, firing at the enemy enough to hold back the Nez Perce, while the other squad retreated some fifty yards farther along the base of the ridge. That's where he had one of the old corporals stop his squad, turn them, and kneel so they could be more sure of their aim as they covered the retreat of Perry's detail.

On and on, rotating one squad after the other like a child's game of hopscotch . . . leapfrogging into the protection of the canyon, where the warriors grew all the more hesitant to follow. Yard by yard, minute by minute, these men with their powder-blackened faces, their eyes red-rimmed from lack of sleep and the sting of burnt gunpowder, their mouths compressed in lines of grim determination, their faces stony in acceptance of an honorable death while most of their companions had chosen life at all costs, fleeing like . . . like barnyard chickens when the turkey buzzards swoop overhead.

Halfway now, he told himself as he turned his squad and

started them back to where the corporal's men had stopped
and waited to lay down some cover. Perry gazed on up the
far ridgeline to their left, noticing the tattered strings of blue
that had once been his battalion. Up there now were horses
carrying soldiers and men on foot straggling up the last few
yards of the upper canyon, straining for its summit, where
they had waited for dawn that morning. Deep in the marrow
of him it felt as if they had been fighting these bastards all
day.

Far ahead, Perry spotted Trimble, still on his horse. A number of men were gathered around the captain, clearly under
the officer's command.

"Trimble!" Perry shouted, hopeful his voice would carry
up the wrinkles of the ridge. He listened to the word echo up
the ridge three times, then go flat.

They couldn't be that far away if he could recognize the
captain up there. Surely the man had to hear him call.

"Trimble! Return with your men! Return and cover our
retreat!"

For a moment the canyon fell silent: no gunfire and no wild
screeching from the enemy.

So he cried out again into the void, "Trimble—return with
your men to cover our retreat!"

Perry heard his voice echo, echo, and echo again on up the
folds of grassy slopes. certain that his orders had been heard
by Trimble, at least by those clustered around the captain of
H Company.

Then he watched as Trimble slowly turned; saw a handful
of the soldiers with the captain wave an arm just before Trimble and those men with him pivoted on their heels and followed the captain over the top of the canyon . . . disappearing
into the few trees scattered across the crest.

On their way for the settlements.

"Keep at it, Corporal," he commended the old soldier as
Perry took his squad on past the corporal's detail, still leapfrogging.

There just weren't that many targets for their men any
longer. Only a few of the warriors still dared to push their
ponies along the foot of the ridge now that the soldiers were
into the canyon. But booming volleys of rifle fire continued
to echo just below and to the east. The louder, lower-throated

boom of army carbines. Then the sporadic, discordant rattle
of smaller arms: Nez Perce repeaters.

Since he couldn't see that many of the enemy horsemen
anymore, because of that distant volley gunfire, Perry figured
someone was still having a scrap of it.

"Halt and hold!" he shouted to his squad as he dragged
back on the reins and wrenched the horse around.

As the soldiers were settling their mounts and bringing
their weapons into position, Perry glanced over his shoulder
at the top of the ridge, watching the last of Trimble's stragglers push into the tree line far above him at the summit.
And he wondered: from up there, surely they could see where
that other fighting was taking place.

It turned his marrow cold, forced to consider that rifle fire
echoing distantly from his left where he could not see any
warriors, nothing of any troopers.

And he suddenly wondered about Theller again, about that
frightened squad of F Company who had been the first to
scatter pell-mell in retreat. Were they on ahead of Trimble
in retreat?

Were Theller and his men already halfway gone to Mount
Idaho?

First Lieutenant Edward Russell Theller leaped from his saddle and tried pulling his horse up the steep hillside. It locked
its legs and would not budge.

Thick layers of foam crusted around the bit, at the edges
of the surcingle, and soaked the saddle blanket. Theller reluctantly admitted that the animal was every bit as done in
as he was. For a moment he glanced behind him . . . and
counted only seven of them. He didn't know where the rest
of his company had gone.

To the south he could still hear some sporadic gunfire. So
he wondered if he and the seven might be the first to get out
of the fight and this far up the canyon, thinking the rest would
be along momentarily.

As the first of those seven weary troopers and their snorting, panting horses halted around him, Theller turned and
gazed up the brush-choked slope. Sure was he that this was
the trail they had taken down to the creek bottom in the dim
light of dawn. This would be the best choice for their escape

from annihilation: return exactly the way they had advanced on the enemy.

And there was plenty enough of 'em. Just over the heads of those last two soldiers struggling to catch up, Theller spotted the first of the pursuing warriors on their ponies. Three, then another handful, and finally more than a dozen of them squeezing into the narrow mouth of this winding canyon. With one last look up the hillside, he despaired of finding any cover sufficient for his seven men to hide behind and hold off their pursuers. He scolded himself, forced to admit that they might well have reached the end of the line. No other way up the steep, grassy slope but to abandon their horses and claw their way up hand over hand.

Theller didn't remember it being this steep on the way down at first light. He was just about to give the order for the men to strip their animals of all extra cartridges, then kill the horses and form a barricade of the carcasses . . . when at the corner of his eye he spotted the brush-lined cleft dimpling the slope to their left.

Lunging a half-dozen steps farther up the slope, the lieutenant saw how the cleft quickly widened into a ravine. From where he stood, it sure as hell appeared that the ravine would make an easier go of their ascent to the summit.

If not, then the ravine would be as good a spot as any to hunker down and hold off this war party till more help came up the canyon from below.

"C'mon, men!" he yelled, waving them on.

After stuffing his hand into his saddle pocket and removing the last of his pistol cartridges, Theller slapped the lathered animal on the rump and sent it clattering back down the slope toward the onrushing enemy horsemen, parting the warriors.

"Grab your cartridges!" the lieutenant hollered as he waved them toward the brushy cleft. "Grab the last of your ammunition; then take cover in the ravine!"

The seventh man almost didn't make it. A bullet kicked up a clod of black earth at his feet, splitting his boot sole and knocking the soldier off-balance. Skidding onto his belly, the trooper crabbed the last three yards into the ravine to join the others. There he sat up, dragging one leg over the other thigh to inspect the bottom of his boot. The heel had been shot off, a narrow groove in the sole deep enough to expose the bottom of his grimy sock, which was starting to turn pink with oozy blood.

"Ferget your goddamned hoof!" one of the others bellowed as the warriors lunged off their ponies and immediately spread out behind the skimpy brush downslope.

In moments the soldiers could hear the Nez Perce creeping up on either side of the ravine.

Completely stunned at how quickly they had been surrounded, Theller gazed up at the shadows flitting along the top at either side of the ravine. He prayed they had enough brush in here so that his men would not be exposed if the warriors crawled up to the edge and began firing down—

A bullet slapped the man next to him, driving his head backward with an audible snap of his neck. After slamming back against the wall of the ravine, the soldier fell facedown, the entire back of his head a bloody, dirty, grass-choked pulp.

"Sell your lives dearly, men!" Theller rallied them. "Make every damned bullet count!"

Only as long as their cartridges held out—

At the ravine entrance another man pitched onto his back, writing in pain, dying noisily while Theller and the other five shot at anything that moved: a shadow, a sound, even a whisper of the warriors crawling up just beyond the mouth of the ravine.

Then another flopped at Theller's feet, clutching his shiny red neck in both hands, gurgling, gurgling . . .

Twisting about at the scraping noise, the lieutenant saw the barrel of a gun appear over the side of the ravine twenty feet away. He fired his pistol at it, kicking up enough dirt near the barrel that the warrior retracted his weapon.

Theller twisted around, hoping to find that they could work their way farther back into the ravine where he and the four would have better protection until reinforcements showed up. Maybe back in the ravine they would even discover a path that would lead them all the way to the summit of White Bird Hill by following the bottom of this deep erosion scar. And once up there they would drop over to the Camas Prairie, which would take them all the way into Grangeville and Mount Idaho—

But his heart sank as he realized this ravine was going nowhere. Less than fifteen feet from where he crouched against the wall, the ravine ended abruptly. A three-sided box. And the warriors were pressing hard, nailing down the last boards of their coffins.

He watched the skyline, shooting at anything that moved at the lip of the ravine, any tufts of grass or a branch that rustled while the red bastards screamed their bloody oaths.

Theller heard the men fall, one by one: some grunting, some yelping a high-pitched feral note of pain. And he could tell as they went that there were fewer and fewer of their Springfields booming. Much more noise from the warriors' Winchesters—

Three of them popped up in front of him suddenly as he brought up his pistol and snapped off a shot.

Watching the bullet's impact spin one of the warriors around and back from the entrance to the ravine, Theller was jerking the pistol toward its next target as he thumbed back the hammer—only to see the puff of smoke and tongue of fire burst from the muzzle of the next warrior's rifle. It was a Springfield carbine too.

The blow felt like the kick of a mule at first, hurtling him back against the end of the ravine. His legs started to lose all feeling, but he did his best to push himself up against the wall of grass and earth at the back of the ravine. Did his best to stand as he finished thumbing back the hammer, aimed it again, and pulled the trigger.

It clicked.

They were slipping toward him cautiously at a half-crouch as he frantically pulled the hammer back again, then aimed it at the first one who was grinning broadly at him.

His pistol clicked on a second dead chamber.

When the muzzle of another warrior's carbine spat flame, Theller felt himself shoved back into the end of the ravine so far that he was sure he was being buried by some massive, powerful fist. Propelled against the grassy wall, he sank slowly, his legs unable to support his weight any longer. The back of the ravine had become the end of the line for him.

Looking up, blinking through the sweat and dirt clouding his vision, he watched the fuzzy form take focus as it stepped closer. Lieutenant Theller stared at the warrior who held the muzzle of his soldier carbine just inches from his eyes, then fired a third . . . and final bullet.

Chapter 40

Season of *Hillal*
1877

After wiping out those eight soldiers in the brushy ravine, Yellow Wolf helped his friends strip the white men of their weapons and what few unused bullets they had left among them. The ground around the dead Shadows was littered with empty cartridge cases. Still, only one of the warriors had been slightly wounded in their ravine skirmish.

Some of his friends laughed at how these white men were such poor marksmen with their firearms!

Yellow Wolf stayed with the war party when they left the ravine, turning back down the slope toward the sound of renewed shooting. Evidently there were still more soldiers who had not yet made it to the mouth of the canyon. More enemies to kill somewhere below—more weapons to take and still more glory to make!

A half-mile down the ridge, Yellow Wolf topped a low crest to discover how most of the soldiers were racing from the valley by a route different from the one they had used in making their advance on the village. While the small group of soldiers he and the others had just wiped out in the ravine had been fleeing the battlefield at a point farther north along the base of the ridge, Yellow Wolf could now see how most of the white men were escaping along a more western route, clinging to the foot of the high bluff.

The rest of Yellow Wolf's friends were spreading out rapidly as they approached these last remnants of the enemy, charging their ponies in a broad phalanx toward that ragged blue line of soldiers angling across the steep hillside.

But . . . just then Yellow Wolf heard gunfire reverberate from the valley behind him. Had they been mistaken? Were there still some soldiers pinned down near the burial hill where for many, many generations the *Nee-Me-Poo* had laid their dead to a final rest? Yes, he spotted it then—a bit of gunsmoke puffing from a clump of brush and rocks. And farther on down the gentle hillside he could see several warriors firing back at the brush. They must have some of the Shadows pinned down!

With an exuberant whoop and jabs of his heels, Yellow Wolf set off to have himself some more fighting. He raced his pony straight for the rocks and skimpy brush where he had seen the puffs of smoke. Perhaps he could flush the white men into the open with his bravery run!

On the slope ahead two warriors suddenly stood, waving him off, shouting. But he could not hear their words for the pounding of his pony's hooves. They signaled their arms in warning, but already it was too late. Almost on top of the enemy, Yellow Wolf realized that the white men were hiding in two places on the hillside. While skirting around the rock barricade where he had spotted the first gunsmoke he had carelessly pointed his pony right for the second group of Shadows.

Just as he was starting to slip off the side of his pony to put the animal between him and the soldiers, one of the Shadows popped up from the brush, leveling his rifle at Yellow Wolf. Yanking hard on the pony's reins, the warrior vaulted off, landing hard. He rolled on his shoulders and was pulling the bow from the quiver at his back even while he clambered onto his feet.

The soldier's muzzle smoked. In that instant when he did not feel any pain, Yellow Wolf knew the white man's bullet had missed.

Immediately gripping the end of his bow in both hands, the warrior whirled the weapon through the air and hurled it against the side of the soldier's head. Stunned, the Shadow fell backward, but still his hands fumbled at the rifle's action.

Two more soldier heads popped up from the other rocks no more than five or six pony lengths away. As quickly, four other warriors were racing up to join him. One of them fired his rifle at the soldier Yellow Wolf had knocked down. The white man tried to rise on his elbow after he was shot, then collapsed and died without another sound.

Freeing a war cry from his raw throat, Yellow Wolf dashed straight for the boulders where he had seen the other two heads appear. As he neared the edge of a low depression where the pair had taken refuge, the young warrior attempted to slow himself. But his moccasins slipped on the wet grass and he went down, sprawling backward, continuing his slide over the edge of the depression, spinning toward the soldiers. He landed right in front of the white man who yanked his rifle down, aiming it at Yellow Wolf, then fired point-blank.

But the bullet smacked into the wall of the shallow depression beside Yellow Wolf's ear. Maybe the Shadow missed because he was so surprised to find the warrior falling in on his hiding place.

The moment that bullet slammed into the ground, the young warrior lunged out on instinct and seized the soldier's muzzle as he heard the approach of running feet. For long, desperate moments Yellow Wolf and the soldier wrestled for that rifle while the other white man in the depression struggled to feed a cartridge into his weapon. When that second soldier brought his reloaded rifle up to point it at Yellow Wolf, a shot rang out. Followed by a second.

At his feet both soldiers lay bleeding, dying within their nest of rocks and brush. As he knelt there above them, Yellow Wolf's heart was pounding like never before. Above him at the lip of the depression stood two *Nee-Me-Poo* friends. The muzzles of their rifles smoked. They had saved his life.

"There's another enemy!" someone shouted from behind them.

His two friends dove out of sight.

Twisting immediately, Yellow Wolf saw another soldier rising up within the nearby cluster of rocks, aiming his rifle right at him. Even by dropping to his belly, the soldier would still have a shot at him!

Bolting over the lip of the depression, Yellow Wolf flung himself to his feet and sprinted away, dodging side to side so it would not be easy for the white man to shoot him in the back. He heard a gunshot but dared not stop until another warrior called out his name.

"*Teeweawea* threw a rock at the soldier," Going Alone said. "It hit the Shadow on the head. Then we shot *him*."

"Come on!" cried Five Times Looking Up, standing on the far side of the depression. He was signaling frantically to Yellow Wolf and the others. "There are two more still alive and fighting in those trees down there!"

He looked down at the pale faces of the white men, then at the carbine near his foot. Now he had a soldier gun!

After stuffing his bow back into its quiver, Yellow Wolf dragged the cartridge belt from beneath one of the dead men, shoved a bullet in the captured carbine, then followed the rest who crept off to finish those last two Shadows who had not managed to escape the battlefield with the others.

There would be no prisoners this day.

"About bloody time you got here, Sergeant!" Parnell roared at Michael McCarthy as he and the one other soldier who had just survived their retreat from the breastworks came riding up. "Couldn't bring you any help," he explained, gesturing toward what few men had remained behind with him— only nine. "You see for yourself how badly this bloody retreat is going for us."

"For a time there," McCarthy huffed breathlessly, "didn't think I'd ever see your smiling face again, Lieutenant!"

"We'll hold these buggers back, by gawd," Parnell vowed. "But to do it I need you to take charge of the line, Sergeant."

"Yes, sir!"

"Hold this road if you can and block those red buggers from flanking us," the lieutenant ordered, quickly gazing up the ridge where the rest of the battalion was streaming. "I'll take the point of our advance. See what I can do to bring your outfit some help."

"Very good, sir," McCarthy agreed. Counting himself and Parnell, now there were twelve of them—a grimy, red-eyed, bone-weary, bloodied dozen. "We'll hold the line."

In moments the sergeant had his men spread out in good order across the gentle slope that rose against the high ridge flanking the valley on the west. Three yards and no more, he had given the order; that's how far apart they were to position themselves in a skirmish line as they slowly, slowly retreated. These ten soldiers were the last out of the valley. Make no mistake about that.

There simply was no more fighting, not any rifle fire, not a lick of noise coming from the creek bottom. Any soldier who was going to make it out had already gotten at least this far to join Parnell. The rest were . . . were—

Suddenly the warriors sprouted right out of the ground behind them and were throwing everything they had against his thin line.

From atop his weary, staggering horse the sergeant bawled at them, "This is where we hold the bastards back, men! This is where we save our hides . . . or this can be where we spill the last of our blood! There's no one else gonna help us now." And the raw taste of sentiment choked him a moment before he could speak again. "Now it's up to us!"

"It sure as hell ain't up to them thirty warriors!" Parnell bellowed at the other side of the road.

No, now there were forty of the savages—by the grace of Joseph and Mary! *Damn but there's bloody well at least fifty of them coming at us now!*

He was sure these other men had seen what he had witnessed below them on the slopes during their desperate retreat: how every wounded man, those either paralyzed with fear or so completely exhausted with fatigue, had been killed without resistance right before his eyes as the battalion pulled back.

So with no more soldiers left alive for all the warriors to fight down below, the red bastards were congregating, hurling themselves on the rear of the fleeing column. Even the bastards' war ponies had to be exhausted. Why, in the last desperate minutes since fleeing from the rocks McCarthy had seen one warrior's squaw bring her husband three changes of horses!

"Every march has them brave men what close the file, boys!" he shouted above the rising of the war cries as the warriors came rushing toward his few steady hands.

And he thanked his God that that was what Parnell had left him: these unflappable old files who hadn't bucked and run at the first shot of the fight earlier that morning. These were the ones who had remained steadfast until the very last. These were the men he could count on to fire slow and low. Around Sergeant Michael McCarthy at that moment were men who understood the final duty of true soldiers might well be to protect the retreat of the others . . . even unto the sacrifice of their own lives in the bargain.

Four times the hordes of screaming horsemen threw themselves against McCarthy's thin line of blue. And four times the old files held like an immovable rock wall. A soldier dropped here or there—winged or wounded—but the sergeant's line never broke.

Then just as he was thinking the warriors had pulled off so they could mass for a fifth charge, the horsemen surprised him by splitting and circling wide, racing high along the slope above the last man on his right flank, making for the rear of the fleeing column. A few of the enemy thundered past farther down the slope below them, their ponies lunging by the left end of his line.

"Time to go, boyos!" he shouted.

"But the Injuns are atween us and the column now, Sarge!" one of the men protested as the line stood and helped the wounded scramble to their feet.

Those few who still had horses remounted. And the rest who no longer had a horse to carry them out of this valley of death moved out among the riders, trudging up the hillside while their weary legs protested with the fiery burn of their superhuman efforts against this excruciating climb.

McCarthy heard the unmistakable sound the bullet's flight made at the very instant his horse shied, sidestepped, then almost went down before it gamely regained its legs. Directly in front of his right knee McCarthy watched the crimson glisten against the claybank's pale coat.

Loud voices instantly snapped his attention up the slope. The warriors who had swept around their right flank were doubling back and were pressing in on that upper end of McCarthy's line. Those men farthest up the slope were falling under the greatest pressure, unable to hold no more than moments before they bolted down the slope, some scattering onto the trail to race after the other outfits who had already fled, the remainder bunching up as they rejoined McCarthy's file closers.

"Halt and hold!" he cried at those now left him, sensing his horse shudder beneath him when he kicked it to start after those who would not stop. "Halt, men—and hold this line!"

But the animal would not move. He realized it was dying where it stood.

Down, down, down the slope came the horsemen, chasing the soldiers before them, rolling up the end of that thin blue skirmish line. When his horse shuddered again, whipping its head wildly, the sergeant could tell it was getting watery in the knees and about to go down. Leaping off before he was thrown aside or trapped beneath the animal as it sank, McCarthy saw how the left of his line had continued away, curving up the slope. Those men were already well past him on the trail, skirmishing with a few horsemen as they retreated.

Here he and a handful of men remained at the center of the line—which meant they were the last. Having scattered his right flank, the warriors were streaming down from the slope above. Other Nez Perce were blocking the trail with a line that angled around to shut off his hope of escape—a pulsing, screaming, horse-mounted barricade that stretched from the foot of the hill across to McCarthy's left, where it intersected his route of escape.

Turning on his heel there in the middle of the trail, the sergeant realized for the first time that he was without cartridges for his carbine. Dropping to a knee beside the horse, he yanked up the flap to his saddle pocket and stuffed a hand inside. Empty. And with the way the heavy carcass lay, he couldn't get to the other pocket—

As McCarthy stood, the danger immediately struck him. He was suddenly alone. Every other man was on his own and on the run, clawing up the slope.

The carbine in his hands did him no good now. He flung it aside, spun around in a crouch, and broke into a sprint, wheezing as his boots slipped on the damp grass.

Just ahead an Indian horseman appeared through the scrub brush. The sergeant lunged to a halt, prepared to fight with his bare hands if he had to—when he saw a second rider appear behind the first. An old soldier, one from his company—Private Fowler! Then McCarthy recognized the Indian horseman as one of the Nez Perce friendlies who had come along to scout for Colonel Perry.*

As the soldier and the tracker halted their horses on either side of him, at the same time the brazen warriors pulled wide and raced on past, the tracker held down his arm and helped McCarthy scramble up behind Charles E. Fowler. By the time

---

*Abraham Brooks

the three had started up the trail, the sergeant gazed up the slope to see how most of the warriors had bypassed his file closers, choosing instead to pursue the main column.

Within the next quarter of a mile, their two horses overtook some of McCarthy's men gone afoot, slowed as they helped the wounded retreat. Now there were seven of them struggling up the steep hillside together . . . when on the slope above him he spotted a detachment being brought back by Lieutenant Parnell.

In addition to First Sergeant Alexander M. Baird of F Company, Parnell had enlisted the service of six more men from H Company to return. They were deploying in good order to cover the rear of the retreat as McCarthy heaved himself off the back of Fowler's horse so he could catch up a riderless mount that was loping past, on its way up the road to rejoin its kind.

Sweet blessed Joseph and Mary! McCarthy thought as he looked over the dirty faces of those old soldiers who had returned down the hill. *Thank God in heaven Lieutenant Parnell brought these noncoms and enlisted weeds back! They're the only men who could hold fast under the heat of a fight!*

With the crack of a rifle, the sergeant wheeled to look over his shoulder—discovering more than a dozen warriors riding out of the valley and coming their way.

"Play yourselves out!" McCarthy hollered as Parnell approached. "We'll take our retreat slow! Two squads!"

"You heard the sergeant!" Baird yelled above the rising of the war cries. "Form up two squads!"

McCarthy took one and Baird led the other. Yard by yard, minute by minute, they backed up the ridge, moving from depression to depression, rock to rock, leapfrogging their way out of the jaws of certain death as one squad covered the retreat of the other—maintaining a foothold only until more than a dozen warriors swept around on their flanks and the squads had to pull back again.

"Hold your fire till you're sure of a target!" McCarthy ordered time and again. "Make sure your bullets kill!" He wondered how long these soldiers would have enough ammunition to turn back the Nez Perce pressure.

Step by step they struggled out of the valley, not losing a man as they held off the warriors, who didn't seem very anxious to get all that close to these steady hands. Once, the enemy horsemen even took enough time to halt and tighten their cinches—convincing the sergeant of just how reluctant the warriors had become to push into the Springfields' effective killing range.

Then the Nez Perce suddenly pressed their advantage again and attempted to sweep in on both sides, close enough that Parnell kept his pistol bucking, first to the left and then to the right. By the time the warriors pulled back from their fiercest assault, McCarthy had another horse shot from under him and was compelled to continue his retreat on foot while those few who remained with him were all mounted, though some were riding double on the weary horses.

None of them tarried long enough or turned back to take him up behind them. They had their own struggles to contend with the farther they stabbed into the canyon. Here and there warriors dogged them from both sides of the march, not only from higher vantage points on the slope but from the hillside below as well. None of Parnell's men had any time to notice that Sergeant Michael McCarthy was steadily falling farther and farther behind, simply because each of them was consumed with his own desperate flight.

Every muscle in his legs burned with torture. With each step they threatened to crumple beneath him as he trudged up the slope a yard at a time, halting to drag a breath into his fiery lungs, then drag his boot another step up the side of the hill. McCarthy stumbled again and again—spilling to his knees, ordering himself back onto his feet, where he willed his legs to take a step, then one more, and another . . .

The red bastards were gradually closing in, their ponies clattering nearer and nearer on both sides as Baird's and Parnell's men pulled farther and farther away from him. McCarthy's boots failed him again and he went down, spilling onto a hip so that when he landed in the grass he peered back down the trail to find just how close the horsemen were getting.

Close enough to use the revolver.

McCarthy dragged up the mule-ear on the holster as he rose onto his knees and yanked the pistol from his belt, lunging onto his feet. He heard them—damn well near enough they could club him if they chose to ride up behind him and knock his brains out.

The sergeant spun at the snort of their ponies, snapping off a wild shot as his feet sailed out from under him and he spilled off the side of the trail onto the dew-damp grass.

Tumbling, falling, spinning down the hill completely out of control until a clump of brush arrested his slide.

Michael McCarthy lay on his belly, holding his breath as the hoofbeats and war cries shot past ... slowly fading on their way up the slope.

Then the sergeant found himself alone.

Chapter 41

June 17, 1877

Somehow, David Perry had compelled enough men to halt and turn around that they managed to hold the Nez Perce at bay even as they made that terrible crawl up the rugged slopes of the ridge, struggling for the summit. Possessing the higher ground even provided the soldiers with their first advantage of the morning's fight.

Dividing his small force into two equal squads, the captain went at it by the book, leapfrogging his men as they covered one another's retreat up the grassy slope. They were all Perry had, now that Theller and then Trimble had both scurried out of the canyon and were fleeing headlong for the closest settlement. Higher and higher Perry moved his men; then just shy of the top he was able to catch a loose horse for himself.

And that's where one of the civilians suddenly popped up. The man suddenly emerged from a large stand of brush, leading a clearly jaded horse.

"Cap'n! Am I ever glad to see you!"

Perry raised his arm, halting his small command. "I supposed all of your militia had escaped the valley long ago."

"No, Cap'n," he said as he inched around his lathered horse so the soldiers could now see the blood crusted at the top of his left shoulder. "I was winged down there in the fight. Figger that's why I got a little too slow to keep up with Chapman and them others."

"What's your name?"

"Shearer, Cap'n. George Shearer."

"All right, Mr. Shearer: the more guns, the better. Throw in with my column if you choose—"

"Column?" Shearer scoffed, taking his free hand from his shoulder wound as he inched toward his stirrup. "If this here's all the men you got, it sure ain't no column!"

"The battalion was quite splintered."

Perry turned away from the civilian's harsh, judging glare and felt his chest seized by the sight of that valley. Warriors, warriors, warriors. But not another soldier—or civilian—anywhere on the slopes below.

"Let's proceed," he told them, setting out once more.

The moment his men gained the top of the ridge, Perry wanted to let them break out in a cheer, but he decided there was no time for celebration. Once the warrior horsemen reached the summit right on the army's tail, the weary Nez Perce ponies carried their riders in a renewal of their pressure on Perry's men. But despite charge after charge, his soldiers held. No matter how the warriors darted along both flanks, doing their best to encircle them, these last soldiers out of the canyon turned back every daring foray.

At the crest, Perry even caught sight of Trimble and his men one last time—far in the distance as they crossed over to the Camas Prairie. Then Trimble was gone.

All through their long, grueling ascent of the ridge, Perry had been keeping their hope alive, counting on reuniting the entire command once he reached the top, where Trimble and Theller surely would wait for the last survivors to scramble to the summit. But now those prayers were dashed as he watched Trimble disappear beyond the horizon.

For the longest time, Perry hadn't seen any soldiers below him on the slopes, deciding that Parnell was either ahead of Trimble or lay dead somewhere in the creek bottom. With Captain Trimble and Lieutenant Theller on their way to Mount Idaho, no one was left to form a junction with him as he started his survivors northeast along the high, grassy ridgeline.

Suddenly, one of the men riding in the advance turned around and shouted, "Colonel! By damn—it's Lieutenant Parnell!"

That news, especially the sight of Parnell's small detachment arrayed among the low trees ahead, lifted Perry's spirits as nothing else had in a long time. Amid the spontaneous cheers from both groups of muddy, powder-grimed men, Perry and Parnell saluted formally, then shook hands as only survivors of a battle could. Taking stock, the officers found that their combined forces now numbered no more than two dozen men.

"Have you seen Theller?" the captain asked breathlessly.

- Parnell shook his head. "Only saw Trimble hurrying off ahead of us. But I have no knowledge of Theller, Colonel."

"Then he must be ahead of Captain Trimble as I suspected," Perry surmised. "We're the last out, you and me."

"I was just about to cross this ravine, Colonel," Parnell declared, pointing ahead of them at the deep, brush-choked scar that sliced the top of White Bird Ridge. "I can't find any other way—"

Both of them jerked around at the same moment, watching in amazement at how many of the Nez Perce had just gained the top of the ridge themselves. Crying out their blood oaths anew, the enemy swarmed forward. For the first few minutes they chuffed along both flanks rather than hit the soldier line directly.

"Looks like we better get across while we can, Colonel!" Parnell roared.

"Agreed, Lieutenant. I'll take my men over, then set up on the other side to cover your retreat."

"Very good, sir," Parnell replied as he stepped away to form his men at the edge of the deep ravine.

It was a struggle for Perry's weary ten and George Shearer to slide down the steep banks, shove their way through the thick undergrowth at the bottom, then scramble up the far bank—but Perry drove them, prodded them, even though he knew that the sweetness of escape should damn well be goad enough.

No sooner were his men pulling themselves over the top of the ravine than Perry was among them, barking orders to deploy left and right so the ten could cover the retreat of Parnell's squad—

—but instead of holding the line, Perry's men bolted right behind Shearer, heedlessly scampering away.

"Stop, goddammit!" the captain bellowed in frustration. "I'll shoot deserters; by God in heaven I will!" Then he turned on his heel suddenly, finding the warriors making their charge on Parnell's outnumbered forces. "Lieutenant—it's now or never!"

Run or be swallowed.

Parnell immediately kicked his horse to one side, then the other, flushing his dozen men into the ravine before he himself jabbed his brass spurs against his obedient horse and sent it flying across the obstacle. Crashing onto the lip of the far side, the animal nearly collapsed under the extreme weight of its rider.

The moment the lieutenant landed among his men, Perry was already reining up behind them, ordering Parnell's detail to turn and cover their own retreat.

"Turn and fire, men! Turn and fire!"

Rather than scamper off like frightened field mice as the other squad had just done, these twelve men did turn their horses and face the enemy—some of the soldiers resolute, others just plain scared—firing two salvos at the Nez Perce when the horsemen neared the far side of the ravine Parnell's squad had just abandoned. In a noisy clatter of crying horses and screaming warriors the enemy reined up short and promptly retreated out of rifle range.

"Let's continue our retreat, Lieutenant," Perry advised as he reined his horse beside Parnell's mount.

"You take the advance, Colonel," Parnell offered, "and I'll have my men cover the rear."

"Whatever you do . . . see that your men don't get strung out, Lieutenant," the captain warned. "And don't dally behind. The way I reckon it, we've got a little better than four miles till we reach that ranch we passed on our way here. We can take cover there and hold them off . . . if we don't let them hack away at what few men we have left."

"Aye, Colonel!" Parnell roared enthusiastically. "It's a four-mile race now, sir . . . ain't it?"

"Joseph and Mary," he grumbled to himself as he dragged his aching legs down the shallow scar of erosion as it descended the grassy ridge toward a tiny creek in the middistance.* First Sergeant Michael McCarthy knew his exhausted legs wouldn't hold him, even if he tried to stand, much less run from the warriors who had to be everywhere around him.

Slow, slow, he reminded himself, wiggling like a snake so as not to disturb the brush as the narrow scar deepened into a ravine the lower he went. Reaching the sharp creek bank, the sergeant gently pushed himself over the edge and into the water. Because he now found himself exposed and in the

---

*Today's Magpie Gulch

open at the mouth of the coulee, McCarthy crawled downstream more than a hundred yards before reaching the cover of some overhanging willows. Breathing a sigh of relief, he slipped beneath the leafy branches and lay still in the icy water for the better part of a half hour as he listened, planning just how he was going to drag his hash out of the fire.

From time to time he heard a distant shot or two, along with a periodic shriek, always accompanied by war cries from the Nez Perce. He figured the warriors were finishing off the last of the wounded, yelping in fiendish joy when they discovered another hapless soul they could dispatch with glee and fury. Gazing through the leafy branches, the sergeant himself despaired of becoming another victim they would soon fall upon. For the most part the hills on either side of him were covered by nothing more than grass. He would make himself an easy target if he attempted to crawl back up the canyon to escape.

After he hadn't seen any sign of the enemy for a long time, McCarthy determined that he would belly-crawl back to where he had tumbled off the trail. If he could find enough brush on the way, he'd dare to struggle to the top of the canyon. If he couldn't, then McCarthy vowed he would lie in hiding right there until nightfall. He might well have to wait until dark anyway, he told himself: likely his legs wouldn't recover for hours, maybe not until the stars were out.

But first, he decided to take off his black slouch hat and set it aside. It might well give him away. And then he removed his dark blue tunic. It too might lead to his discovery. His dark gray undershirt more closely matched some of the rocks on the nearby slopes. He could only pray that he just might blend into the hillside. But he would drag the wool tunic along anyway—knowing he would need it once the sun had fallen.

More than an hour later McCarthy pulled himself into a clump of wild rosebushes and lay kneading a knotted muscle in his leg when he heard hoofbeats on the trail above him.

Holding his breath, he peered through the dense vegetation and spotted two ponies working their way down the slope. The warriors passed so close McCarthy swore he could have reached right out and touched the blanket draped over the back of one horse. In those terrifying seconds as they brushed past his hiding place, he steeled himself to fight to his last breath.

He simply couldn't believe that they didn't see him in the

wild roses. When the pair had passed him by, one of the warriors spoke in Chinook pidgin.

"Now we go shoot your horses."

As the riders continued by, unhurried, McCarthy was convinced the warrior spoke those words directly to him. If they were talking to one another, they would have spoken in Nez Perce. But the warrior used Chinook pidgin English: the common tongue of that region. It made McCarthy even more terrified that they were sure to turn around any moment and flush him from cover. But the pair continued on down the trail—when his attention was suddenly drawn by hoofbeats approaching at a fast clip.

Not all that far uphill rode a squaw on her pony. Behind her came a younger woman on horseback. They stopped on the slope directly above his bushes and shouted at the departing warriors. In Chinook the older woman cried out that she had spotted a soldier in the brush and wanted the men to return so they could kill the white man. He watched her point downhill at the very bushes concealing him, squawking her news to the warriors. The woman even described McCarthy's uniform, saying he must be a soldier and not a settler—then went on to describe the chevrons on the sleeves of McCarthy's blue tunic he was clutching in his hand.

Inch by inch, the sergeant pulled his legs sideways into the stream channel, submerging himself even deeper. Keeping only his head above the water, and it concealed in the thickest part of the rosebush, along with his right hand gripping a .45-caliber service revolver, McCarthy vowed to take one or two of them with him before . . . He would use a last bullet on himself rather than suffer the torture he was sure had marked the end of the wounded these warriors discovered in the valley.

Then the sergeant realized that he might never have enough resolve to press the muzzle to his temple and pull the trigger. Life was far too sweet for suicide.

Truth was, McCarthy told himself, he had already escaped death three times that morning.

Just as he was beginning to believe that the squaws had passed on by because they were unable to convince the young warriors to return, the sergeant heard hooves approaching with a clatter. From his bushes, McCarthy watched the two squaws descending the slope—but now they were joined by an old man on a horse. The three of them passed on by his bushes slowly, but when the trio had gone some fifty yards downstream they turned around and retraced their steps, inching by his hiding place again, carefully studying the brush.

As they leaned off their ponies and peered through the branches, McCarthy held his breath, amazed that none of the three could spot him. He saw their faces clearly as they searched the rosebush. And when the old man poked the muzzle of his smoothbore muzzleloader into the willow, that old weapon got so close to his nose that McCarthy figured he could reach right up and pull the Indian into the bushes with him. Slowly, silently inching his pistol into position, the sergeant prepared to shoot the curious old man, all the while trying to silence the loud drumming of his heart as each agonizing second ticked past.

At long last the three moved off down the trail, but just as he was about to breathe easier, McCarthy watched the older squaw doggedly turn back along the trail and stop above him again, giving the brush one last, intense scrutiny before she rejoined the other two and the trio finally disappeared around a hill to descend to the battlefield.

He waited some minutes to be sure the Indians were gone before he thought to pull out his pocket watch and see if all that time in the water had stopped it. The second hand still shuddered its way around the tiny face, and there was a reassuring *click-click* when he pressed it to his ear. Then McCarthy stared at the hands, dumbfounded.

Surely now it couldn't already be half past six o'clock in the evening! He simply could not recollect the sun passing overhead, climbing in the heavens during the fighting, falling from midsky during the fleeing. Looking up to locate the sun sulled over the eastern terminus of the canyon wall, the sergeant realized it had to be six-thirty in the morning.

Joseph and Mary!

Of a sudden, McCarthy recalled that he hadn't once pulled out his watch after Colonel Perry started them off the ridge and down the canyon for their attack on the village. In the fading starlight of the predawn gray he remembered seeing that it was just then four o'clock as the column moved out.

An excruciating drop into the canyon, followed by an eternity of fighting and dying, the whole ordeal crowned by this endless hell endured as he crawled for his life ... all that in less than three bloody hours!

Chapter 42

June 17, 1877

By the time Second Lieutenant William Russell Parnell reached the Henry C. Johnson ranch, some four miles from the top of the canyon, Captain Perry already had that squad of his men who had deserted him at the ravine positioned on a high, rocky escarpment just to the right of the abandoned house and barn. At the foot of the ridge a narrow stream cut its way between the rocks and the ranch buildings, spilling off the back side of the White Bird Divide and onto the Camas Prairie.

"Position your men on the firing line, Mr. Parnell," Perry ordered as the lieutenant rode in. "But I'll hold your detail in reserve should we face a frontal attack here."

The lieutenant sighed. "Look at these men, Colonel. They're all about at the end of their ropes. It's been a bloody time of it—what with the fighting in the valley, not to mention having to fight for every foot of this . . . this retreat."

With a nod of agreement Perry pulled his watch from a tunic pocket, glanced at the hands and face but a moment, then stuffed it away again. "Seven o'clock, Mr. Parnell. We don't have long to go now before sunset. I firmly believe we can defend our position until dark."

For an awkward, breathless moment Parnell studied the captain's face—suddenly unsure if Perry was merely having a joke at his expense . . . or if his superior might be losing control of himself. "C-colonel, it's seven o'clock in the *morning,* sir. Not the evening."

Turning to peer into Parnell's face, the captain blinked several times, then turned away to watch the timber beyond the house. Quietly he said, "Of course it is, Mr. Parnell. Seven o'clock in the *morning*."

Perry's mental state was just one more thing for Parnell to worry over now. This pitifully undermanned band of survivors might be able to hold back the enemy, he figured, but only as long as their ammunition held out.

When he excused himself from Perry, the lieutenant started down the left side of their line and asked every man to count his cartridges. Some had more, many had less—but by the time he had redistributed what these twenty-two men had in their britches and saddle pockets, each soldier ended up with some fifteen bullets for his carbine.

Reassuringly Parnell patted the small two-shot derringer he always carried in an inside pocket. If the time came, he could always kill Perry, then shoot himself. Better that than be taken alive by the savages. His skull crawled with the remembrance of those pitiable cries the wounded made when they were abandoned on the battlefield, the unearthly wails that made his skin crawl when the Nez Perce discovered each of the wounded soldiers, dispatching them one by one—

Lead began slapping against the rocks around them, singing and zinging while every soldier pitched himself onto the ground and took cover from the ricocheting bullets that were flying from both their front and along their right flank.

"Where they shooting from, Lieutenant?" wailed Private Charles E. Fowler as he and others frantically studied the ranch grounds below them.

Poking his head up cautiously, Parnell spotted puffs of muzzlesmoke from the enemy's weapons, many of which had to be cavalry carbines now. And it stood to reason that the Nez Perce would have plenty of ammunition too. In all likelihood, more firepower than these soldiers possessed.

One of the men pointed at the hillside about a hundred yards at their front. "The reds're above us, Colonel!"

"There's more over there!" cried Albert Myers.

Parnell spotted the motion off to their left. The Nez Perce had dismounted and were scurrying behind a fence line that angled away toward the timber and brush behind the ranch buildings. They were making for the hillside in an effort to flank the command, seize the horses, and have the soldiers surrounded with no avenue of escape. Thank God that company blacksmith had spotted them.

"They've got the upper hand, Colonel," Parnell growled at Perry as he peered at the knoll behind them, sensing just how trapped and vulnerable they were.

Perry nodded. "That bunch makes it up the back of that hill, they'll be right among our horses—and we'll be pinned down here."

"With respect, sir: I suggest we pull back immediately!"

"Pull back?"

"Retreat before it's too late," Parnell said sharply. "A strategic withdrawal. We don't fight a rear-guard action all the way into the settlements, we're gonna die here."

"That's more than six miles, Lieutenant," Perry argued.

But Parnell could tell that the captain was already relenting as lead steadily ricocheted from the rocks at their backs. "Colonel, we can die here together . . . or we can give these men a chance to fight their way back to the settlements. I beg you, sir: don't make 'em die like rats trapped in a grain shed!"

"Yes, you're right!" Perry agreed. "I'll mount my detail while you cover us."

Parnell drew his lips into a thin line of displeasure, about to register his complaint—then agreed as a good line officer should. Even though his men were again asked to protect Perry's detail—soldiers who had scampered off and abandoned them at the ravine—the lieutenant resolutely snapped a salute to his brow. "I'll form my men to protect your retreat, sir!"

The next time First Sergeant Michael McCarthy pulled his watch out, he found it was just past seven-thirty. Which meant he had been lying half-submerged in the narrow creek for more than an hour: listening to how the gunfire had died off, how the mountainside had grown so still without the comings and goings of horsemen or those squaws either.

He was starting to sense some relief until the wary, feral side of him warned that with the end of the battle, with the warriors having finished off those wounded soldiers down below in the creek bottom, it made perfect sense that the Nez Perce would start up the canyon in a concerted effort to locate even more wounded and dead white men . . . searching for every carbine, revolver, and bullet they could take off the bodies.

He didn't have long before they'd be coming.

Dragging his legs out of the creek and bellying himself onto the grassy bank there beneath the overhanging willow, the sergeant kneaded his muscles for a few minutes as his mind raced on what course to take. That time spent in the cold water had revived the cramped, overwrought muscles. He figured the legs might just carry him up the steep canyon wall. They had to.

But with the soaking he had given his boots, they had become heavy, waterlogged, and useless—what with the way the seams were coming apart. Rocking onto his back, he yanked them off one at a time and shoved them down into the water, where they sank to the creek bottom, out of sight. Then he crawled to the edge of the wild rosebushes and studied the hillside, especially the wagon road as it led down into the valley.

Taking in a deep breath, McCarthy burst out of hiding, dashing on his renewed legs to the next clump of brush thirty yards uphill. There he rested less than a minute, planning his next sprint in his soggy socks that threatened to trip him with every step across the grassy slope.

The sergeant hadn't gone more than a half-mile up the trail when he came across a large piece of bread, big enough to be the half-loaf rationed to every one of the cavalrymen back at Fort Lapwai. He scooped it up and slid into the bushes, his heart pounding as he greedily tore off a dry, crusty bite. Chewing, he suddenly remembered Trumpeter Jones passing his bread down to the white woman and her children as the column descended into the valley only hours ago.

He swallowed, peering from his hole in the bushes, looking up the trail, then down—wondering where that disheveled woman had disappeared. Why she had left the bread behind? Had she been taken prisoner and lost the loaf in a struggle with her captors?

He took a second huge bite, then stuffed the rest inside his damp, gray undershirt. Funny, how he could feel renewed by an hour in the creek, after no more than two bites of hard, stale bread. A soldier's fare: creek water, half-cooked white beans, and some crusty old bread.

But enough to make an old soldier feel pretty damned good about his chances!

Checking the trail below him, McCarthy emerged from hiding again and climbed almost straight up the hill toward the far section of trail, where he reached a large stand of leafy willow. The sergeant congratulated himself as he wheezed, catching his breath. Looking back down the canyon, he was gratified to see he had scrambled more than halfway to the summit.

Sweating heavily, his breath like liquid fire in his lungs, his legs quickly growing leaden and wobbly—Sergeant Michael McCarthy lunged from one clump of brush to another, following those hoofprints and boot scuffs scarring the side of the wagon road that was lifting him out of the valley, leading him up from the creek bottom, every step farther and farther away from the sudden death that had overtaken so many of the men who had been his friends.

In the taller, windblown grass at the crest of the ridge he dropped to his belly and peered back into the canyon. McCarthy lay there, painfully catching his breath, giving his legs and swollen feet a rest—not wanting to be discovered against the skyline now that he had reached the top. After a few minutes he spied the younger of the two squaws coming to a halt no more than fifty yards from where he had been lying in the creek.

The woman casually dismounted and pulled a buffalo robe from the back of her pony. Spreading it upon the grass, the young maiden lay back, her hands behind her head, staring at the sky above as her pony went to grazing nearby.

How strange this was, he thought—struck by this scene of such idyllic repose where minutes before on that very spot he had been prepared to sell his life dearly had she and the other two revealed him. She must now be in some deep reverie, he figured. Perhaps thinking wistfully on some young warrior who had captured her heart, reveling on his heroic exploits and victories of this bloody day.

Suddenly he imagined how this young woman might enjoy the pleasure of hacking him apart, joined by the older squaw and their aged companion with his muzzleloader. A tiny thread of relief flushed through him. He was beyond their reach now.

Nonetheless, McCarthy anxiously studied the rolling landscape across some 180 degrees of the compass. Somewhere out there was the rest of Perry's battalion. Off to the northwest he would find Grangeville or Mount Idaho.

But to ever get to the settlements he would have to stay hidden, alert his ears to every sound, and keep his eyes moving—for this ridge descending to the Camas Prairie would surely be crawling with warriors in pursuit of the fleeing soldiers. As he hung here halfway between the creek-bottom battlefield and the leaden sky overhead, somewhere between the enemy who wanted to butcher him and the soldiers who had abandoned him . . . Sergeant McCarthy found that he had never felt so alone.

One last time he gazed down from the canyonside, hoping against all reasonable hope to spot some other poor unfortunate like him making his escape from the bowels of that bloody battleground.

But the sergeant saw no one. Not a single living thing moving down there. How many had gotten out McCarthy could not know.

How many had been left behind . . . he did even not want to imagine.

The moment Perry's detachment was mounted and on their way around the brow of the hill, Lieutenant Parnell gave his squad the order to evacuate the Johnson ranch.

"Mount up!" he bawled. "Stay together! By God, whatever you do . . . stay together!"

His men were climbing into their saddles without any further prodding from him, the first of the soldiers reining their horses around and bolting away, right on the tails of the last of Perry's men as the captain disappeared into the timber northeast of the ranch, galloping hard along the base of the slope, making for the Mount Idaho Road.

Whirling on his heel as the last three soldiers kicked their horses into a gallop, Parnell's heart froze. He spun around again—this time in gut-churning panic—watching his detail racing away as his heart rose in his throat like a cold lump of stoker coal.

He was left behind . . . without a horse.

At that very moment his mount was running off riderless among the troopers he had just ordered away, galloping along with the men who were seeing only to their own welfare . . .

none of them realizing what had become of their lieutenant.

Of a sudden there was no more time to feel miserable for his predicament, no time to experience fury for those who had abandoned him in their flight—the warriors were shrieking in dismay as they realized their quarry was getting away. Off the hillside they came, tearing down the slope for the rocks where William Russell Parnell now stood alone. Wheeling around and huffing away at a trot, the lieutenant pulled up his revolver and flipped open the loading lever with his thumb, drew the hammer back to half-cock, and rapidly clicked the cylinder past the loading aperture, cartridge by empty cartridge. Every primer dimpled. Every shot fired.

Sensing despair overwhelming him, he shrieked at the blue backs of the retreating horsemen who were already a hundred yards away and gaining. With defeat about to overwhelm him, Parnell realized they couldn't possibly hear him.

Angrily he ejected the empty shells and jammed the useless pistol into the holster riding on his right hip. Immediately Parnell's fingers flew to the pocket sewn inside his tunic, reassured he still had that derringer.

Realizing he was not a man meant to run—built only to fight on horseback—the lieutenant clumsily rolled into a lope, straining to lumber faster as he heard the warriors and their own weary ponies approaching behind him.

Frantically patting the pockets at the front of his sky-blue britches while he lunged step by ungainly step, the large and fleshy Parnell felt no spare cartridges for the pistol. Only his bone-handled folding knife. It and the derringer were all he had to either defend himself . . . or take his own life at the end.

Then bullets were hissing past him, whining like angry summer hornets as the enemy horsemen rode into rifle range and began to shoot. On either side of him stood nothing but barren hillsides—nowhere to hide, to take cover and prepare for the final defense.

Just as his legs were about to give out, when his chest burned with such a heated intensity that he was certain it was about to be consumed with the excruciating pain of an iron poker stabbing its way through his lungs and heart—at the very moment he realized he was crippled with utter exhaustion—Parnell blinked in teary disbelief. Up the road ahead he saw a half-dozen soldiers racing back for him!

He choked on that lump in his throat, not completely sure the sight was real, and promptly stumbled. He nearly spilled but somehow caught himself before he pitched to his knees.

As the six horsemen approached, Parnell realized there were really only five soldiers and six horses. God bless!

"Reporting with a mount for you, Lieutenant!" shouted Corporal Frank L. Powers as he reined his horse up in a skid and yanked on the reins to the frightened, riderless mount.

Lunging to a halt among the horses as two of the soldiers fired into the oncoming warriors, the lieutenant pulled himself into the saddle with that last reserve of his strength. "Y-you came b-back . . ."

Powers grinned as all six of them wheeled and started away at a gallop. The old soldier said, "I looked around and didn't see sign of you, sir. Asked a couple of the boys, and none of us see'd you leave the ranch with us either. So I reported to the colonel that you was left behind. He sent me back with this squad to fetch you up, Lieutenant."

"G-god bless!" Parnell praised again in a breathless huff as they raced to rejoin the rear of Perry's detachment. "All my kingdom for a horse!"

Chapter 43

June 17, 1877

He hadn't eaten in almost four days, not a thing since Thursday morning. And chances were little Maggie Manuel hadn't either. Nothing more in their bellies than what moisture they managed to lick off the leaves back in the brush where the two of them had been hiding since early Friday morning after the youngster crawled into the brush with him, whimpering as she told how her mother and baby brother had been murdered by Joseph, one of the Nez Perce chiefs.

Just about the time Patrick Brice had hoisted six-year-old Maggie onto his back and was preparing to set off up White Bird Canyon toward Mount Idaho, the bottomground all around them came alive with Indians: warriors and women, children and ponies, everyone chattering as the Non-Treaty bands halted their march just south of the Manuel place and raised their buffalo-hide lodges beside the creek.

No longer were the two of them in danger of being spotted by any roving war parties. Now they were as good as surrounded by every Nez Perce who had sworn vengeance on the white man.

Over the last two days the camp had been consumed with celebration and singing, thumping on their drums and rejoicing in their victories—all of those revels lathered with a generous soak of whiskey. As he sat in the dark through each long night, clutching Maggie to his breast, Brice found it easy to vividly imagine that the Indians were jumping and cavorting around the scalps of those who had fallen to these blood-crazed warriors.

Maybe . . . the bastards had even discovered old man Popham and done him in. Patrick hadn't seen George since early that first night he heard Maggie's whimpers.

Brice's stomach had been snarling at him for the longest time, and the little girl had been sobbing continuously—still, she refrained from whining noisily with her agonized hunger. They had to stay quiet, he periodically reminded her. If the Nez Perce heard her and discovered them . . . they never would escape to the settlements, where Maggie could tell her story of how Joseph had killed her mother and baby brother.

But after so many days in hiding, with the unremitting strain of having the enemy camped all around them, made constantly aware that help was still more than fifteen agonizing miles away, the Irish immigrant realized his hunger had grown stronger than his immobilizing fear. Little Maggie required sustenance too. Over the hours the conviction grew stronger that he needed to take her somewhere she could begin to heal her heart and mind from all that she had seen happen to those loved ones murdered right before her eyes.

By dawn that Sunday he had steeled himself and prepared Maggie for their arduous ascent of the canyon, at the top of which they would cross over to the Camas Prairie. If they could only keep to the brush, Brice figured, the two of them would make their escape. But if they didn't find enough brush crawling up the ridge or if the warriors were constantly combing the countryside . . . then he'd have to convince Maggie they needed to spend another day lying in wait, hiding until the stars came out, when they could creep away and resume their climb under cover of darkness.

About the time the sky had begun to gray that morning of the seventeenth and he was preparing to set off from the Manuel place . . . the shooting and screaming began. Maggie had started shrieking too, so bad there at first that Patrick had to clamp his hand over the child's mouth, explaining to her sharply that if she kept up the caterwauling they'd be discovered and killed.

It felt like an eternity in limbo waiting for the gunfire to die off. Long hours they spent huddled together in the brush, listening as the gunfire eventually receded across the creek bottom, then reverberated up the canyon in waves, and ulti-

mately fell silent. For the longest time Brice had struggled
with himself over attempting the climb—fearing that his extreme hunger combined with his aching compassion for the
little girl would compel him to expose them both to danger.

Just past midday more than twenty warriors rode right past
their hiding place and dismounted in the Manuel yard nearby.
A few of the horsemen went inside the house, and others
entered the store. He figured they were probably searching
for something overlooked by previous raiders. But after turning their ponies out to graze in the knee-high grass, most of
the Nez Perce settled near the porch, where they cleaned
their firearms, smoked their pipes, and talked.

Patrick was sure they were boasting about the white folks
they had killed or raped—

Suddenly he saw a face he recognized. Brice wanted desperately to make sure before he did anything stupid, like allowing his immeasurable hunger to overtake his well-honed
horse sense. But the more he studied that middle-aged warrior, the more the Irishman was sure he had run across the
man before, perhaps up to Grangeville or Mount Idaho—
maybe even as far away as the mountain mining camps of
Florence or Elk City.

And if he recognized the Indian . . . maybe his luck would
rally and the Indian would remember him too.

"Maggie," he whispered into the girl's ear, cupping his
hand around his mouth at the side of her head, "I know that
Injun. Gonna give something a try. Ask 'im to let us go for
help—so we can get you some food, someone to look after
that broke arm."

Her sunken, hollow eyes lifted to concentrate on his face,
yet Maggie said nothing as she studied him. Eventually she
snuggled against Brice all the tighter, burying her cheek
against his breast. It was all the affirmation Brice needed. She
had agreed to put their lives on the line.

Weak and clumsy, Patrick struggled to stand, stumbling
sideways a little as he got to his feet with his little burden.
He shifted her onto his hipbone, so weary were his arms, then
shoved the limbs and branches aside with his right hand as
he began inching his way out of hiding.

The moment he emerged from the brush, that crowd of
Indians lounging in the grass shot to their feet, scrambling for
their weapons so they could train them on him, looks of sus-

picious bewilderment on their faces as they noticed the muddy, bloodied, half-starved waif he carried on his bony hip. The warriors fell quiet, extremely wary for the longest time as they watched his every move.

"Here we go, Maggie dear," he whispered and took another two steps toward the Nez Perce, whose dark eyes flicked apprehensively back and forth between the white man and those bushes behind Brice.

Patrick stopped—realizing the warriors feared there were more white men waiting in ambush. For a moment he was rooted to the spot, afraid they would shoot him because they suspected treachery. So the Irishman held up his right arm in what he prayed they would understand as a sign of peace.

Then, staring directly into that familiar warrior's eyes, Patrick Brice wagged his head and explained, "There ain't no more." He pointed to the brush where he had just emerged and shook his head again. "Just the two of us," tapping a finger against his chest, then pressing it against Maggie's breast.

After he took another scary step toward the warrior, Brice pleaded with him, "I-I ain't no soldier. Had no part in the f-fighting this morning."

The warriors spoke among themselves briefly, their eyes constantly on him and the brush, haughty and disbelieving.

Finally, as his heart was sinking and hope seemed all but gone, Patrick swallowed hard, summoning up the last of his courage, and begged, "I-if you're gonna kill me . . . all I ask you in the name of God's heaven . . . l-let the little g-girl go."

Black Feather was the only one on his feet when the white man suddenly appeared out of the brush with a small child in his arms.

Three of the warrior's companions sat on the ground nearby, smoking and talking about the fight they had had with the soldiers that morning. It had been a good fight. They had killed many of the *sua-pies*. Taken many rifles and pistols, a lot of bullets, from the dead men.

And they had chased the Shadows up the heights like they were whipped dogs an old squaw would chase out of camp. That is, until the last of the soldiers reached the Camas Prairie, fleeing for the town they came from, and the war chiefs commanded their young fighting men to stop.

"Let the soldiers go!" they cried to their warriors. "We have done these soldiers enough hurt! No Indian killed! Don't you see? Not one of us killed!"

So all four of them had been sharing this story or that from their fight with the soldiers when that lone Shadow stepped out of the brush at the edge of the meadow—startling them all.

Every one of them immediately jumped to his feet, all four of the warriors training their weapons on the white man, even while their eyes raked the brush behind him. There could be more—probably soldiers who had escaped the battlefield and would now take their revenge . . .

But a moment later, as his companions began to argue among themselves in anger, perhaps in fear, Black Feather began to think differently. This man was not dressed as a soldier. Instead, from the poor condition of the Shadow's clothing Black Feather took the white man to be one of those who scratched in the holes they dug in the mountains or perhaps even one of those who grew crops on a Camas Prairie farm.

Black Feather did not recognize this man as one of those well-known Shadows who missed no opportunity to cheat, beat, or kill any of the *Nee-Me-Poo*. Word was that Sun Necklace's war party had taken care of all of those treacherous Shadows—they had paid with their lives for their cruelty and thievery.

Besides, this shabby white man did not even carry a gun. And that poor little child—a girl just like Black Feather's own daughter—she wore only the thinnest of garments, was barefoot too . . . Black Feather remembered his daughter back in camp, and his heart ached for this little one. She had to be about the same age as his child.

". . . Camas Prairie . . . ," the Shadow said.

In the midst of all the words this white man was speaking to the warriors, the Shadow said a couple that Black Feather recognized of the foreign tongue.

"He wants to go to the Camas Prairie," Black Feather translated to the other three without taking his eyes off that little girl.

"What?" snorted Two Mornings, an older warrior. "We should kill him right now and check his pockets. Maybe he has some bullets, or whiskey—maybe some money in his pockets!"

"Yes!" Red Raven cried in agreement. "I will kill the Shadow myself!"

Whirling in angry desperation, Black Feather slammed down the muzzle of Red Raven's soldier carbine before he could shoot. "Don't!" he growled.

Red Raven wrenched his rifle away from Black Feather as the other two warriors crowded in on either side of Black Feather threateningly.

Confused, Two Mornings grumbled, "You must be fooling with my head, Black Feather! You don't want Red Raven to shoot the enemy?"

"No," he growled, his eyes narrowing on the others. "If you kill him, which of you is going to take care of that little girl?"

Black Feather waited for an answer from any of them, looking long into the eyes of each of his companions.

"Which one of you will take the little girl into your home?" he demanded, beginning to feel as if he had drained most of their anger, like an empty buffalo paunch they would slice open and empty on the prairie.

"Will you take her into your lodge, Two Mornings?" he asked. "If you kill the man, you will have to care for the little girl." Then Black Feather whirled on Red Raven. "And if you kill him, the child will be yours to keep. Do any of you want that?"

Two Mornings shrugged and said, "We can just leave her here—"

"No," Black Feather interrupted. "What is one Shadow to us? Aren't we better than the white men because we will let this one man go so he can take care of his little daughter? Aren't we better men that we don't make war on women and children like the Shadows do?"

"But I will only kill the man—"

Black Feather instantly wheeled on Red Raven and shoved him back a step, knocking aside the warrior's carbine again. "So if you kill the man, you will just as surely kill the little girl. Look at her arm! Look at her face to see how she hasn't eaten in many days! Yes, Red Raven: If you kill the man, you will surely murder this little girl. For all the rest of your days, I will heap the shame of that upon your shoulders!"

Red Raven quickly averted his eyes and a moment later turned aside. With his back to Black Feather, the warrior took his seat on the ground again and began to reload his pipe. Then Two Mornings and the third warrior sat to rejoin him.

"Let the Shadow go," Two Mornings sneered, with a wave of his hand, dismissing Black Feather without even looking up from his tobacco pouch. "Get both of them out of here now, before someone else shows up who will kill them for us."

Stepping right up to the white man, Black Feather stared a long moment into the Shadow's eyes. He tapped his hand against the man's chest, then gestured up the creek with that hand. Twice more he made the same sign to indicate the Shadow was to go, to make his escape up the canyon.

Finally Black Feather remembered the words. "Cah-mass. Go you Cah-mass."

"Camas Prairie," the Shadow gasped, his eyes beginning to flood with tears. The white man patted the little girl in his arms, looking into her face and spilling out a lot of words Black Feather could not understand.

But he nonetheless did comprehend the meaning of the look on the Shadow's face before the white man turned away and skirted around the ranch buildings, trudging wearily toward the canyon that would lead him over to the white settlements.

Black Feather watched them go, watched the Shadow's back grow smaller and smaller. And he watched the dirty, smudged face of that little girl as she peered back at him from over the white man's shoulder.

From the look in those sad eyes Black Feather knew she was showing him her gratitude the only way she could.

Chapter 44

June 17, 1877

T he animal beneath him wasn't near as strong as the mount he'd ridden into the valley of the White Bird early that morning, but Lieutenant William Parnell wasn't complaining one whit as he and his five rescuers caught up with those at the rear of Perry's ragged retreat.

When he saw the captain rein around and head back his way, Parnell considered telling Perry he had all but abandoned him . . . then thought better of it.

"Mr. Parnell!" Perry shouted when he brought his horse up there at the rear of those two dozen soldiers. "The Nez Perce are hard on our tails, aren't they?"

"Indeed they are!" And he licked his dry lips, wishing for a drink of water.

Perry glanced behind them a moment, then said, "Might as well await them here. Better terrain than the ground ahead of us."

"We'll make our stand here?" Parnell asked, his deep voice rising an octave. Feeling as if he had just escaped the frying pan only to fall right into the fire.

"Exactly." Then Perry pointed with a sweeping gesture. "Organize what men we have. Divide them by companies and put your men out as skirmishers."

Gulping with the realization of the danger his squad would face once more, Parnell asked, "You will remain in support of us with F Company?"

"I will," Perry promised. "No more than one hundred yards to your rear so I can come up as a reserve when things get hot."

"One—one hundred yards," Parnell repeated grimly, wanting so to express his misgivings. "Y-yes, sir."

In the end, the veteran did as he was ordered, deploying his men across an unusually broad front, explaining best he could to his dozen soldiers why he was spreading them so far apart: hoping to prevent the Nez Perce from flanking them on either end of their critically thin line again that day.

"The red bastards won't do it to us again, my boys!" he roared at them. "Hold the flanks. If you do anything else this day to save your hides . . . just don't fold on those bloody flanks!"

Then Parnell took his station at the center of that line, watching the Nez Perce approach across the prairie, noisy with the clatter of their hoofbeats, their shouts and war cries, their boastful cheers now that they had their outnumbered prey in the open. He knew the warriors had to be all the more arrogant and bursting with confidence after what bloody work they had accomplished in the creek bottom.

"Keep them off the ends of our line! Don't let them roll up our flanks!" he cautioned his men, shouting commands left, then right. "Aim low and hold your fire until I give the order!"

When the warriors were a hundred yards from the soldier line, they kicked their ponies into a hard gallop and fired their first shots from those captured soldier carbines.

"Fire by volley on my command!" Parnell roared. "Hold . . . hold . . . NOW!"

That first concerted explosion ripped through the onrushing warriors, knocking at least a half-dozen from their ponies. Horses reared and wheeled, pitching their riders into the air. Two of the animals hurtled to the ground, their legs thrashing.

"That's good!" Parnell cried, his voice crackling with joy. "Shoot low! Shoot low for their goddamned horses!"

"Lookit 'em, Lieutenant!" a man shouted on the right.

And then another soldier called out, "They're running away!"

"By damned, you turned 'em, boyos!" Parnell bellowed.

He waited a few more heartbeats to be sure that the warriors were indeed picking up their wounded and retreating out of rifle range before he gave the crucial order.

"Awright, you ugly buggers! Hear me to the right? Hear me on the left? Advance to the rear: slow, SLOW this time, goddammit! Rejoin in fours! In fours on the right! Let's do it pretty as can be, you bloody horse soldiers!"

They had started toward Perry, with Parnell and a couple of his old files keeping watch over their soldiers at the rear of the retreat, when the lieutenant saw the Nez Perce had regrouped and were advancing again.

"Here they come!" he shouted. "Right flank, by fours! Deploy on skirmish line! Play out! Play out!"

It was a pretty thing, he thought as those six men paraded out of that retreat column like they were a whole goddammed company on their own, prancing smartly across some grassy parade in dress uniform, all starched and puckered, sitting ramrod straight in front of high-ranking officers and ladies fair.

"Left flank! Spread out—spread out and make it wide!" he commanded. "Shoot low again, you buggers. What bullets you got left, you better kill one of those bastards with every cartridge!"

His twelve got spread out on both sides of him just as the full party of the Nez Perce came into view, arrayed in a wide formation.

"Hold your fire, boys. Just like we done before: hold your fire till my order!"

The enemy came on, riding as one, screaming and yelling—but not near as many as there had been in that last rush.

"Hold . . . hold . . . HOLD," he reminded his men, his own heart climbing to his throat so that he wondered if he was going to get that crucial word out when the moment arrived—

"FIRE!"

This time four horses reared and flung their riders to the ground. He saw that two more of their war ponies lay thrashing on the ground, two more that would never again carry a bloody goddamned warrior against them!

But this time the Nez Perce didn't simply drop back to regroup for another assault. Those who hadn't been knocked off their ponies immediately peeled away for Parnell's left flank in a desperate attempt to drive his skirmish line, his dozen brave men, toward the confines of Rocky Canyon, less than a mile away across the prairie.

"They wanna stampede your horses, boyos!" he warned them—knowing that if the Nez Perce got his men running in retreat, they wouldn't stop, and Perry's outfit couldn't help them. No—if these survivors of that fight down in the belly of the White Bird didn't hold here, then they would be running all the way to that narrow cleft in the Camas Prairie where these soldiers would be slaughtered like fish in a rain barrel.

"Hold that left flank and don't let 'em roll you up!"

These were good men, surely the steadiest of the lot. Even more grit to them than those twelve hanging with Perry. Time and again that Sunday morning, Parnell's dozen held the end of their line against overwhelming odds. Against a fifth charge they threw back their attackers. Then Parnell gave the command for an orderly retreat once more.

"Load your carbines and move out at a walk!" he bellowed, knowing they really needed no reminding by now.

Good soldiers, these. Covering the rear, and closing the file for lesser men. Goddamn, but he was proud to lead them!

Minutes later Parnell's men entered a marshy area at the edge of the prairie where the grass and reeds grew as tall as a man's shoulders—

Lord, if he didn't spy a head bobbing along through the waving stalks! Some lone soldier caught out there between his right flank and the Nez Perce horsemen who were dogging his squad's every step, waiting for an opportunity to pick off any stragglers, constantly harassing, forcing Parnell to turn around repeatedly and prepare to fire by volley before the warriors would immediately back off.

"Corporal!" he shouted to the closest soldier. "Take three men and move to the right! There's some lone bugger about to be cut off!"

The corporal saluted and dragged away three of his men, loping to the rear and the right, slogging their way over the soggy ground, piercing the tall grass and reeds, shouting every step of the way for the lone soldier to stop.

"Halt!" Parnell ordered the moment he spotted the Nez Perce preparing to make a charge on that solitary soldier and his rescue party. "Right oblique! By fours—and prepare to fire on my command!"

They came around smartly. All eight of them . . . only eight. But the way they brought up those carbines and held them at the ready . . . the Nez Perce weren't about to trifle with this bunch of hardcases any more that morning.

The rescue party lunged back out of the soggy marsh, emerging from the waving reeds with that soldier clutching the corporal's stirrup. Soaked to his armpits, caked with mud to his groin, the man lumbered to a halt at Parnell's knee. He saluted the lieutenant breathlessly.

"Hartman?" Parnell asked.

"Yessir. Private Aman Hartman, Lieutenant."

"Welcome back to H Company, son."

"N-never thort I'd get outta that swamp alive," the private admitted. "They was coming for me p-pretty hard, sir."

"Weren't you with Sergeant McCarthy at the rocks?"

"Sure was, sir. But I lost my horse below and everybody run off on me," Hartman gasped, still somewhat breathless. "Me an' 'nother was the only ones got out with the sarge. After I lost my mount, I come out on my own, sir."

"No others with you?"

Hartman shook his head. "No, sir. Dunno what happened to the sergeant. I figger he didn't make it out, since I never see'd him with them others what left me behind. When I lost my horse, the whole bunch of 'em got far ahead of me. But I kept a'coming."

"By damn if you didn't, Private."

"I been hearing your guns for some time," Hartman declared. "I was sore afraid—I stayed away from the gunfire till I see'd you soldiers. Then I come running through the bog. But them Injuns see'd me too."

"Stick with our line, Private," Parnell ordered. "We're on our way out of here."

"You can ride behind me," one of the corporal's rescue party offered, helping Hartman up behind him as Parnell started the bunch moving once more.

"Left by fours! In a walk: keep it slow!"

He wondered what time it was and gazed at the gloomy, cloudy sky. It felt as if they had been retreating for a week, crawling to the rear a hundred yards or so, then halting to form on a skirmish line. Sometimes they had to fire. But most times the Nez Perce stayed back once his men merely halted and prepared to unleash another volley.

They ground through the last of that retreat a quarter-mile by a quarter-mile, following the rear of Perry's squad across the prairie. It seemed the hours dragged by endlessly as he whipped his exhausted horse from flank to flank along their route of march, making sure his outriders kept a sharp eye peeled for any ambush the warriors might attempt.

Of a sudden, he noticed that for no apparent reason Perry's men had stopped ahead in full view, milling and jumping about.

Apprehension immediately flooded through him with a cold pain. Parnell shouted to his men, ordering them to pick up the pace, waving both sides of his skirmish line forward on the double so the flanks would not be left behind his center. Fear gripped his throat as if it were a muscular hand, scared that the Nez Perce had somehow swept around on one flank or another and gotten ahead of Perry's detachment to spring a trap on the colonel.

But when Parnell turned in the saddle, he found the warriors still behind them, coming on with deliberate speed. But . . . perhaps there was another jaw to the trap, these who remained behind and those who had closed the ambush in their front—

Then he heard cheering and laughter, realizing some of Perry's outfit were calling out to his soldiers as Parnell's skirmish line approached. Of a sudden, he saw that there among the blue-clad soldiers were more than twenty civilians.

"They're from Mount Idaho!" Perry was gushing when he reined his horse back to greet Parnell.

The lieutenant's heart sang as he twisted around, peering at their backtrail, finding that their pursuers were halting, turning away, disappearing at long last.

Giving up the chase after more than three hours. It was shortly before 9:00 A.M., and these soldiers had been gone from the settlements no more than twelve hours.

By now his men were dropping from their saddles, hopping around together like old school chums, pounding one another on the back and shouting fervent, heartfelt greetings to these civilian strangers not one of them knew. But they were friends this day!

By damn—every last one of these citizens come riding out from Mount Idaho were all good friends this terrifying, bloody day!

*   *   *

What a day it had been!

Yellow Wolf rejoiced with the others as they rode over the battlefield, yelping like coyote pups, searching for any of the enemy wounded who could not make it out of the creek bottom, looking for any firearms the Shadows had abandoned in their precipitous flight.

But they did not scalp the *sua-pies,* did not mutilate or strip the clothing from these soldiers. Those might be the custom of other tribes over east in buffalo country. But such was not a practice of the *Nee-Me-Poo.*

By late morning, the captured weapons had been brought to the village: something on the order of sixty-three carbines and perhaps half that many pistols. Along with the cartridge belts they had torn off the dead soldiers—these warriors were ready if the army should want any more fighting!

Considering how many soldiers had marched against them that morning, Yellow Wolf was amazed there were not more casualties among his people. Bow and Arrow Case had been wounded in the side during the early stages of the soldier retreat. Land Above had received a painful bullet wound in the stomach, but he was nonetheless expected to live. And all that had happened to Four Blankets was a minor cut on his wrist when he fell from his horse among some rocks as they pursued the fleeing soldiers. The fourth man* suffered only a broken bone from a bullet that pierced his leg.

Not one *Nee-Me-Poo* warrior had been killed!

Now the chiefs had the fate of three prisoners to deliberate. Robinson Minthon and Joe Albert—whose real name was *Elaskolatat*—were both agency Indians who had taken Christian names. The third, *Yuwishakaikt,* was a member of old Lawyer's Treaty band too, but he had never been baptized with water and given a white man name. It was he who explained to their captors that the three had come along with the soldiers solely to assure that the women and children were not harmed in the attack.

Frightened for his life, *Yuwishakaikt* did his best to convince the angry Non-Treaty warriors that he had been left back with the soldier horse-holders rather than engaging in the battle himself. And when the Shadows began their re-

---

*Historical accounts never recorded the name of this fourth casualty.

treat, he had hurried along with them until his pony gave out and he was forced to continue on foot. That's when the warriors caught up to him.

Much the same thing had happened to both Albert and Minthon during the frantic retreat of the terrified soldiers.

When the three were bound with rope and brought to the center of camp, Albert's father stepped forward. When the tensions with the soldiers had increased, the old man had chosen to remain among the Non-Treaty bands, the victors in this day's fight. Although the young man had come with the soldiers to attack the village, he spoke up for his son. And *Yuwishakaikt* had an uncle among the old warriors in the camp who spoke on behalf of his relation too.

Although Sun Necklace and the "Red Coats" wanted to kill these Treaty men and be done with it, most of the others felt that the decision should be left to the chiefs.

"This is not so easy a matter to decide," Yellow Wolf told his companions early that afternoon. "For *Nee-Me-Poo* to decide to kill *Nee-Me-Poo* is a bad thing. The Shadows kill their own kind all the time. But do we want to stoop so far that we become just as evil as they: That we could kill our own kind? To murder our own people simply because they have been led astray by the white man and his religion?"

Yellow Wolf decided it was important that he stand among those who would guard this trio of Treaty prisoners until morning . . . when the chiefs would decide their fate.

Chapter 45

June 17, 1877

———◦◦◦———

David Perry didn't quite know what to say to Captain Joel Graham Trimble when they finally reunited, face-to-face at last, in the tiny settlement of Grangeville after their disastrous fight on White Bird Creek. It was nearing ten o'clock in the morning when Perry and Parnell dismounted in front of Grange Hall with their two dozen men.

"Colonel Perry!"

The captain turned at the cheery call, stunned to find Trimble striding up as if nothing untoward had occurred during their retreat. Perry struggled to subdue his immediate impulse to seize Trimble by the throat and throttle the man within an inch of his life for abandoning the battlefield and the rest of the command.

"C-captain Trimble," he steadied his voice, one eye quivering. "You've been here for some time, I take it?"

"Yes, Colonel."

"I quite imagined you had." Perry fought to keep an even tone to the words he so carefully chose. "I spotted you and your men ahead of us, at the top of the ridge. I waved, attempting to call you back to assist us. I saw you and your men signal back to me . . . then turn and continue on your way—"

"N-no, I—I didn't see you at all, Colonel," Trimble asserted.

Perry could see the lie of it in Trimble's eyes. "A little

later, you couldn't help but see Lieutenant Parnell and me at the ravine on the divide—"

"Sir, I said I didn't see you," Trimble defended himself bravely, although his voice had taken on the air of a plea. "I would have come to your aid if I had. You must believe that, Colonel."

By then Perry had become aware of the number of men—officers, noncoms, and line soldiers—who had inched closer to listen in on their disagreement.

Clearing his throat, eyes narrowing, Perry grappled to keep a rein on his anger. "How many men did you bring with you in your retreat, Captain?"

Trimble wiped the back of his hand across his mouth. "I don't have a firm count, sir. I reached this settlement with some men from both companies."

Peering over Trimble's shoulder at those standing nearby, Perry asked, "Where is Theller? Perhaps he will know how many men we have—"

"Why . . . Lieutenant Theller hasn't shown up, Colonel," Trimble admitted, his brow furrowed with worry. "I thought he c-came out with you."

Perry turned immediately, gazing at their backtrail—somehow hoping against all logic that he would see Theller and more of the battalion coming up the rutted wagon road that would bring them into Grangeville. The welcome around him had been raucous, swollen with rejoicing, but now the air fell silent—only the pawing of weary horses, the scraping of cavalry boots on the ground. Perry ground his teeth together as he turned back to Trimble.

Don't ask him for an explanation here, the captain brooded as he gazed steadily at Trimble. *There's time enough for that later, when you don't have a war to fight and citizens to protect. Time enough to bring him up on charges of desertion in the face of enemy fire.*

"Who's in charge of these civilians?" Perry asked.

"A man named Crooks," Trimble answered. "Owns the biggest place, close by."

"Crooks?"

"That's me." An older man stepped up, presenting his hand.

Perry shook as Crooks introduced his two grown sons, both

standing at their father's shoulders. "How many riflemen can you muster, Mr. Crooks?"

The rancher spat out a stream of tobacco, then answered, "Twenty-five at the most. Lot more folks made it in to Mount Idaho."

"How many you figure are there?" Perry asked.

With a shrug, Crooks replied, "Don't rightly know, son. But I wouldn't doubt that Brown's got him more'n twice as many as what come in here."

"That's where I'm going," Perry announced, his decision made.

"Sir?" Parnell said as he stepped up. "You want me to form up the men to march on to Mount Idaho?"

For a moment the captain peered over the weary two dozen who had fallen out and were either already sleeping for the first time in more than two long days and nights or kindling some fires to heat coffee and rations. Their exhausted horses were cropping a nearby patch of grass.

"No, Lieutenant Parnell. You and Captain Trimble will stay here while I go on to Mount Idaho. Post some pickets on a perimeter to warn you of the approach of the hostiles. And keep your eyes peeled for any sign of Theller and his men."

"He's dead, sir," Parnell announced gravely.

That stung Perry, made him speechless for a moment. Then, clinging to a spider's thread of hope, he said, "Perhaps. But we don't know for sure."

"Anyone not outta there by now," Crooks growled, "they ain't coming out. 'Cept maybe hung over the back of a horse."

The captain's belly went cold with that image. Lord, didn't he know enough men had been killed that morning, bodies left behind on the battlefield for the Nez Perce to mutilate and scalp in their victorious glee.

"Mr. Parnell," he said, turning to the lieutenant, "before I leave, I want you to get me a count. Tally how many of both companies we do have here. How many made it out. I want to know before I see what fortifications they've undertaken at Mount Idaho."

Crooks stepped up closer and asked, "Are you figgering to drop back to Mount Idaho with your men?"

"If their defenses are stronger than what you've constructed here . . . then yes. I'll recommend all of you come with us when we leave."

"Me and my boys ain't leaving, son," Crooks declared evenly. "This here's our home and there ain't no Injuns gonna drive us off. We didn't ever steal nothing from 'em, so they better not come around here fixing to take anything away from us. Me and my boys ain't never hurt a one of 'em, but them sassy warriors come high-feathering it onto my place . . . I'm gonna kill ever' last one of 'em I can to protect what's mine."

There would be no sense in discussing withdrawal any further with Crooks, the captain decided. "Very well, sir. You've made up your mind."

"Made it up a long time ago, son," Crooks explained paternally. "This here's my home. We put down roots, my boys and me. We ain't going nowhere. I cain't speak for my sons, but as for me . . . I'll die before I let them Injuns run me off my land. Even for a day."

Perry saw Parnell returning.

"Colonel, I have your report," the lieutenant said as he walked up.

"Go ahead," Perry instructed.

"There are thirty-eight, sir. . . . I count a total of thirty-eight missing."

"Th-thirty-eight?" he repeated, just the echo of it punching him hard in the gut.

"Only two of the men present and accounted for are wounded," Parnell continued.

"Only two? Why s-so few?"

Parnell shook his head. "I don't know, Colonel. Only thing I can figure is that none of the other wounded made it out of that valley."

Turning on Trimble, Perry sensed his anger flaring. As evenly as he could, he told his fellow officer, "Captain, you are in charge while I am gone to Mount Idaho. Prepare camp here until I return with more news so I can write my report and get it off to Howard by messenger."

"As you order, Colonel."

Then Perry sighed as he turned away and stuffed his left boot into the stirrup. "And by all means, Captain . . . if the enemy shows up and you're forced to retreat . . . don't abandon any more of these men. And be mindful of your wounded."

"Y-you're certain you got the translation right?" Oliver O. Howard demanded of the agency interpreter. John Monteith had hurried over to Fort Lapwai that midafternoon.

A pair of the reservation scouts who had departed with Captain David Perry on Friday evening, the fifteenth, had just come racing in atop exhausted ponies here on Sunday afternoon. Even though he hadn't been able to understand their garbled, incoherent Nez Perce tongue while they awaited a translator, General Howard had no trouble comprehending the fear and despair in the tone of their voices, in the furtive look of their dark eyes, in their anxious wringing of hands.

"Yes, General," replied Perrin Whitman. "They say your soldiers have been defeated by their Non-Treaty brothers."

"Did—did these two stay till the end?"

Whitman turned back to Howard with the translation. "No. They admit they were some of the first out of the valley of White Bird Creek when the fighting started. But before they reached the top of the canyon, they could look back down upon the soldiers and see that your men were surrounded by warriors on horseback and under fierce pressure. I suppose any man might hope for the best . . . but the story these two tell doesn't give me much reason to believe that any of Colonel Perry's men made it—"

Sudden shouts and cries from the far side of the parade interrupted them all. Into view came two mounted soldiers, their horses so lathered and done in the animals were barely plodding along. Howard joined the others who rushed to the scene where the pair of cavalrymen halted and slid out of the saddle.

"General, sir," said Corporal Charles W. Fuller. "Company F. Both of us."

"We was wiped out, General," confessed the second man, Private John White.

"When was this?" Howard asked, his gall rising.

"Th-this morning," Fuller gulped. "At dawn, sir."

"All of Perry's men?" asked Captain William Boyle.

Fuller's eyes darted to those who pressed in upon him, eager for any shred of news. "N-no. Not all of them. Just F Company."

"You're the only two who got out alive?" Howard demanded.

"Only reason we got out was we run like hell soon as the trap was closing on us," White admitted.

Howard echoed, "A t-trap?"

The hair instantly stood on the back of the general's neck as he suddenly remembered the night of 16 June, when those two Nez Perce women showed up to noisily announce that Perry's command had been lured into a trap and all had been wiped out. How could she have known of disaster *before* the battle? How could that woman have foretold of a trap that would consume all of F Company?

"Are there others alive?" asked Lieutenant Peter Bomus.

Fuller shrugged. "Don't know, sir. We got out by the skin of our teeth and kept on a'coming."

"We figgered there was nothing gonna stop them savages," White asserted. "I decided the two of us owed it to everyone at the post to carry the news here so you could prepare your defenses, General."

"Prepare for attack!" arose the deafening cry as panic seized the bystanders.

Every man and what few women remained at the post huddled close around Howard and those two soldiers—murmuring, cursing, wailing in fear of the attack they were sure was to come.

"All right, let's get ourselves under control here! You listen to me and we'll be ready if we're attacked," Howard silenced their anxious voices. "Lieutenant Bomus, form a detail to stack cordwood around the Perry and FitzGerald house."

"Yes, General," the quartermaster replied, turning away.

Then Howard continued, "Now, quickly spread the word to all the rest here at the post: we'll use my headquarters in the Perry house as the rallying point when the Nez Perce decide to throw themselves against us."

Just past midday, Yellow Wolf was returning to the camp after watering his two ponies when he heard joyous voices crying out from the far end of the village. He trotted toward the clamor—a sliver of him fearing that while he had been away the chiefs had already decided the fate of their three captives.

So how his heart soared when he recognized some of those

mounted warriors slowly winding their way into the middle of camp, where they halted their long string of packhorses laden with buffalo hides.

"Rainbow!" he shouted above the tumult of the crowd.

"Yellow Wolf! Is that really you?" the one named *Wahchumyus,* Rainbow, asked as Yellow Wolf squeezed through the throng.

"Do you see how he has grown while we've been gone?" cried *Pahkatos Owyeen,* the one known as Five Wounds.

Reaching out his arm, Yellow Wolf grasped Rainbow's wrist. Behind him Five Wounds slid to the ground as the cheering continued. There was much happy pounding on one another's backs!

"What of this fighting?" Rainbow asked those around him.

"So much killing since you left for the buffalo country," Wounded Head explained.

"Three young men started by shedding white blood here on the Salmon," Two Moons related gravely as the crowd grew quiet.

So quickly was the joy of the hunters' homecoming gone, disappearing like a winter's breathsmoke. Over was this celebration for the return of those seven riders from the land of the buffalo far to the east.

"So now the soldiers have come?" Five Wounds inquired.

"Before breakfast this morning!" Yellow Wolf hollered. "But we killed many of the enemy and drove off the rest."

"The fools will know not to come against us again," growled the old Toohoolhoolzote.

Yellow Wolf watched the way Rainbow and Five Wounds turned to stare at the old chief. All seven of these hunters who had just returned to the land of the *Nee-Me-Poo* were veteran warriors. Their bravery and courage in the battle were unquestioned. They were not foolish, impulsive young men like Red Moccasin Tops and Shore Crossing. These were the finest warriors of the Wallowa band. And now they were home to fight in this first-time war against the Shadows.

"Do not be so quick to convince yourself you know what the white man will do," Rainbow warned the old chief.

"We did not need any of you in our fight this morning," Toohoolhoolzote sneered at the renowned warriors. "We took good care of the soldiers ourselves. And we will finish off the rest of them if they come back to attack us again."

"One thing is for sure," Five Wounds declared solemnly.
"The soldiers will not stop now."

Yellow Wolf grabbed Two Moons's wrist and asked in a
whisper, "What of the prisoners? Have the chiefs decided?"

"Prisoners?" Rainbow echoed, having overheard. "You
captured some of the soldiers?"

"No, we killed all the soldiers who were left behind on the
battlefield," Two Moons explained. "The prisoners are three
men from the reservation."

"Treaty men?"

"Yes," Yellow Wolf said. "They brought the soldiers to
find us."

"I must see them," Five Wounds said to the crowd.

The seven who had just returned from buffalo country soon
joined the chiefs and headmen in the debate over the fate of
those three turncoats. It took the rest of that afternoon, but
the council finally reached an agreement: they would free the
trio.

"But if you ever help the soldiers attack our camp," Two
Moons warned, "then we will catch you again, and whip you
with hazel switches."

Yellow Wolf was relieved, having believed the three would
be tortured unto death. In fact, when *Yuwishakaikt* asked for
an old horse so he could leave the camp, Yellow Wolf gave
him one of his to ride on the trip back to the reservation. A
woman gave one of her old travois horses to Joe Albert, and
the two Treaty men hurried away for Lapwai, although they
both had relations among the Non-Treaty peoples.

But the third, Robinson Minthon, declared he wanted to
stay with White Bird's band.

With the fate of those prisoners decided, the council*
turned to deliberating their next steps. Late that afternoon
the headmen admitted that the odds were very good that the
soldiers would return as soon as they had regrouped.

"But we do not have to fight them unless it is absolutely

---

*This great council deciding the life or death of the prisoners,
and what course to take next, was held just inside the north
boundary of the present-day township of White Bird, Idaho, on
the west side of "old" U.S. Highway 95, toward the battlefield
itself.

necessary." Chief White Bird spoke for many who were coun-
seling avoidance.

"Yes, we must do all that is possible to avoid killing." Joseph spoke up for the first time after so many days of self-
imposed silence.

"Then I propose that we cross the people to the far side
of the Salmon," Rainbow declared.

"The women and children can find good shelter from the
soldiers in the mountains," Five Wounds agreed.

Rainbow explained, "If the soldiers follow us across the
Salmon, then we will double back at any one of four or five
places and keep the river between us and the army."

"Yes!" Two Moons laughed heartily. "Everyone knows
how hard it is on the soldiers to cross a river! Ho, they will
fall farther and farther behind!"

"This is a good plan!" Toohoolhoolzote admitted. "We will
lead Cut-Off Arm on a splendid chase!"

"And when it comes time that we must fight," Rainbow
vowed solemnly, "we will choose our place . . . choose our
time. And finish the job you began this morning."

Chapter 46

June 18, 1877

BY TELEGRAPH

Bad Indians Again Raiding in The Hills.

DAKOTA.

Bad Indians in the Hills.
DEADWOOD, June 18.—On Friday last a small party of Indians made a dash on Montana ranch, nine miles from this city, and succeeded in running off considerable stock. A party of twenty miners bound for Big Horn from this point were fired upon by Indians about sixty miles out. One of the miners was wounded.

"Wood!" cried William Watson from the top of the stockade pickets they had buried in a trench surrounding the tiny cluster of buildings at Slate Creek. "John Wood! Get over here on the double!"

The paunch-bellied civilian came trotting up to the foot of

the logs erected as a fortress against possible attack by the Nez Perce. In the midmorning light, this middle-aged store-keeper who had sought shelter with so many other Salmon River settlers stared up at Watson standing at the center of some ten other men who were perched atop the wall. "What you want, Bill?"

"You got some fellas out here asking for you, John."

"Fellas? Who the hell's gonna be asking for—"

"Injuns," the old Confederate interrupted. When Watson saw he had struck the storekeeper dumb, he continued. "They knowed your name; said it pretty good too. Asked for John Wood."

"Likely wanna scalp you, Johnny!" sniped one of the others at the top of the wall. "Like they done to Benedict and Mason!"

"Hog droppings!" John Wood snorted. "That don't make a bit of sense. I ain't at all like Benedict or Mason. Always done right by them people."

One of those civilians standing beside Watson at the top of the wall said, "We can scare 'em, run 'em off, you want us to. Maybe even kill a few—you just go and say the word, Bill."

"No," Watson drawled thoughtfully, gazing down at the half-dozen warriors who had emerged from the timber below a flag of truce tied to a short stick, daring to cross the bare no-man's-land where they stopped near the foot of the new stockade Watson and the others had raised around this small settlement. "I figger if the Injuns was meaning to attack us, they'd done it already. There's gotta be a good reason this bunch is calling you out, John Wood."

The storekeeper nodded and went to the timbers at the middle of the wall, where the men could easily muscle a few heavy logs out of the way that would allow a man to pass out or a horse to be led in. With the help of another civilian, Wood shouldered one of the timbers aside and cautiously peered out at the six horsemen.

"I'm John Wood."

"John Wood," one of the warriors repeated with a thick pidgin accent as he inched his horse forward and stopped at the wall. "Owe you."

"You owe me?"

"Money," the Nez Perce explained without rancor, his accent heavy, yet every one of his words understandable to all those who held their breath, witnessing this strange meeting between enemies. "Owe you money, John Wood. Pay you money. Things get bad now. Pay you . . . then we go far from here."

"Y-you gonna pay me what you owe me?" Wood stammered, shaking his head in disbelief.

"If that don't beat all, John," Watson observed from the top of the wall while a Nez Perce woman came running up to stand beside Wood, peering from the slot between the timbers.

It was Tolo*, the Nez Perce woman who days ago had come on foot from the *Tepahlewam* encampment, after first racing to the mountain mining settlements to warn her white friends of the coming trouble.

Struggling to see out, she nudged Wood aside and poked her head through the opening in the timbers. "You bad, bad men!" she shouted in pidgin English.

The five horsemen behind the nearest rider inched closer, growling back at the woman in their native tongue.

"Bad men, kill my friends!" Tolo shrieked at them.

"You come back to your people," asked the lone horseman nearest the wall, speaking in English.

"No! I stay with my new friends. Not go with bad men kill my friends!"

"We not mean to kill the woman," apologized the lone horseman who peered down at Tolo's upturned face glaring at him there in the wall.

That seemed to baffle her. "Woman?"

"Man-well woman," the horseman admitted. "Warrior get drunk on whiskey. He kill her at the Man-well house. I sorry and sad he get drunk on whiskey—he kill her then."

"You killed Man-well woman?" Tolo sobbed as the horror of it struck her.

"Not me. Other warrior. Too much bad whiskey," the warrior repeated, wagging his head regretfully. "Good warrior no kill woman. Only whiskey kill woman." Then he called to the shopkeeper who stood behind Tolo in the crack between the logs, "How much, John Wood?"

---

*Sometimes rendered in the Nez Perce language as Tula

"You're the one called Stone,* ain'cha?"

The horseman nodded, holding out a small skin pouch. "Me. Stone, yes."

The shopkeeper wagged his head once as if trying to make sense of the incongruity of it all. "I don't rightly know how much. Suppose we say you owe me twenty dollars for ever'thing. How's that set with—"

"Twenty dollar," the warrior agreed and poured some coin into an empty palm he then held down to the crack in the stockade wall. "You take. Twenty dollar pay John Wood."

The civilian reached out cautiously and extracted two ten-dollar gold pieces from all those coins piled in the horseman's hand. Then the warrior poured the rest back into his small pouch and stuffed it inside his belt.

"We even now, John Wood?"

"Y-yes, we're even now, Stone."

"It's good," the horseman said. "Big trouble now. Maybe never see you again. Good-bye, John Wood."

And with that the warrior turned his back on the stockade and those white riflemen, rejoining the others, all six starting back for the timber.

"We can still get some of 'em, Bill!" a man hollered.

"NO!" Watson snapped sharply. "No shooting!"

He watched the bronze backs of those horsemen until they disappeared in the shadowy timber, then turned and watched John Wood shove the log back into place along the wall.

Wood gazed up at Watson, shrugging his shoulders. "Now I think I've see'd ever'thing, Bill. That Injun coming in here to pay me what he owes 'stead of fighting us."

"If that don't beat all, John," Watson agreed in wonder, thinking how their world had been turned on its head. "If that don't goddamned well beat all."

"One of the interpreters has come in, General!" announced an enlisted man as Howard lumbered through the doorway, brought out of his desk chair by the clatter of hoofbeats late that Monday afternoon, the eighteenth of June.

---

*A fictitious name I have arbitrarily given this actual historical character whose name has not been recorded for posterity; although there is no record of this warrior's name, this incident nonetheless did occur as I have written it.

It had been quite warm inside the Perry and FitzGerald house, so he was pulling his wool tunic over his damp dress shirt, hurriedly buttoning it as he threaded his way across the porch, sidestepping through the narrow opening the soldiers had left in the stacks of cordwood surrounding the building, and dropped down the steps to the parade as half-breed Joe Rabusco brought his horse over to Oliver Otis Howard and the three officers who hovered at his back.

"General," Rabusco said with his thick Indian accent.

"You were with Perry?"

"Yes," and the interpreter nodded dourly, sliding out of the saddle.

Howard wanted to seize the man by the lapels of his greasy canvas coat and immediately wring everything from him in one gush—but realized the interpreter's Indian blood made Rabusco taciturn, slow to bring to conversation.

"Did he send you to me?"

Rabusco nodded, stuffing his hand inside his shirt. From it he withdrew a crumpled packet of folded paper. "Soldier chief send me to you, carry this for Perry."

He snatched the wrinkled paper away as if it were nothing less than manna to a starving man. While he was opening the pages, Howard suddenly stopped to ask Rabusco, "When did you start away with this? Was the fight still going on? When did Colonel Perry write this?"

"Battle over, he write," the interpreter explained. "After dark last night." And he gazed up at the afternoon sky. "He write, give me this before moonrise. Before he go to his blankets."

Howard sighed, turned, and settled back on the porch steps, sitting heavily with the weight of what he knew he was about to learn. The post's three officers stepped up close. Others were coming as word spread of the courier's arrival from the scene of the recent fighting.

Then Otis's eyes began to crawl across the two crumpled pages.

DEAR GENERAL HOWARD.—I made the reconnaissance foreshadowed in my last letter. I made the attack at 4 A.M. on what was supposed to be only a portion of the main camp, and for the purpose of recapturing some of the large bands of stock taken from settlers in the vicinity of this place, and the possibility of dealing the Indians a telling blow. The camp proved to be the main camp of Joseph's and Whitebird's bands situated on the Salmon or White-bird river at the mouth of the latter. The fight resulted most disastrously to us, in fact scarcely exceeded by the magnitude of the Custer Mas[sacre] in proportion to the numbers engaged. As soon as the Indians made their shots tell, the men were completely demoralized. It was only by the most strenuous efforts of Col Parnell and myself in organizing a party of 22 men, that a single officer or man reached camp. The casualties, as far as I heard from "F" Co. 1 commissioned officer (Lt. Theller) and 22 enlisted men killed and missing, H company 15 enlisted men killed and missing. Some of the missing will I think come in to-night probably not many. Lt. Theller was killed on the field. The Indians fought us (Parnell and myself with our squad) to within 4 miles of Mt. Idaho and gave it up, on seeing that we would not be driven any farther except at our own gait.

We have been fighting and riding without sleep since leaving Lapwai. We saw about 125 Indians today and they are well armed, a great many of our guns and much ammunition must have fallen into their hands. I think it will require at least 500 men to whip them. All of my friendly Indians left for Lapwai before I got in and in consequence I have been much troubled to procure a messenger. I have promised him a fresh horse from Lapwai to Lewiston. Please see that he gets it. The messenger will return immediately if desired. Please send word to Mrs. Perry that I am safe. Am too tired to write.

Joe Rabusco can be of no further use to me. Please have him discharged. If the Indians emboldened by success return to Camas Prairie it would not be prudent to send the Pack Train. Neither should I like to escort it, [because I only have] the remnant of my two Companies.

The only thing I really need is ammunition as I can with your sanction purchase subsistence stores here.

Please break the news of her husband's death to Mrs.
Theller.

                         David Perry, Captain commanding
                         Fort Lapwai

Howard looked up at those waiting breathlessly around
him, their faces all masks of apprehension.

"Mrs. Theller," he said quietly as the gravity of his next
mission pierced him to the marrow. "Yes. I must tell her."

Standing, he passed Perry's letter to William Boyle. "See
that you place that on my desk I'm using inside the colonel's
home, Captain. Seems that Perry's suffered a terrible, terrible
defeat," he announced to the group around him, all of them
stunned into utter silence.

"General Howard," Boyle said, holding the letter. "Should
I see what I can do to get word over to Walla Walla and
hurry those reinforcements—"

But he interrupted the officer with a wave of his hand.
"We'll see to that in due time, Captain. But right now, I'm
going to pay a call on an officer's widow."

Howard tugged at the bottom of his dress tunic, smoothing
out those wrinkles that had formed as he sat on the steps,
reading that devastating news. She was the only officer's wife
at the post right then. The only one who had seen her husband off in the dark two nights ago.

Dear God, how he found this the worst part of leadership.
Starting away across the parade for the Theller house, his
mind turned on his own Lizzie Ann, on just who would tell
her or how she would learn that news a soldier's wife dreaded
every time her husband was out of sight and off on campaign.

The sun was shining brightly, the air still so warm this late
afternoon. *Damned unfair,* he thought. *Damned bloody unfair.*

His eyes spotted her stepping into the open doorway of
their tiny house, which stood across the parade from the post
commander's quarters. Her fingers tightly knotted themselves
around a clump of that shawl she clutched about her shoulders despite the extreme warmth of this day.

Then Otis realized he had slowed his pace, starting to drag
his feet, not eager in the slightest to perform this vital func-
tion of leadership. Then all that remained was but one step

that took a person up to the low porch of the small house. Howard stopped there before mounting that last obstacle, removed his black slouch hat with his good arm, and stuffed it beneath what was left of his right. He reminded himself to stand ramrod straight.

"Mrs. Theller."

"General, g-good afternoon. To what do I owe the pleasure of this call—"

"May I come in, Mrs. Theller?"

She looked beyond him of that moment, casting her eyes over his shoulder, perhaps scanning all the others who must still be gathered across the parade—that small crowd watching them both. Because of them and the gray of his face, she had to know now—what with the courier arriving, her watching him read Perry's letter there at the barricaded porch.

An officer's wife had to know.

Her eyes started to brim as she returned them to the general. Delia Theller suddenly lost her steely, army-stoic composure, her shoulders sagging the instant she began to sob, her knees starting to buckle when she shrieked, "Oh, my husband! My dear husband!"

Chapter 47

June 18, 1877

I sabella Benedict's heart hammered so loud, it was difficult for her to recognize that it wasn't the blood pounding in her ears but the distant thump of hoofbeats coming her way.

One horse. Only one. But it wasn't galloping, running her down as if the red bastard had spotted her. But then again . . . that horse wasn't walking slowly, carefully, quietly.

Her heart sailed into her throat as she remembered how she had heard hoofbeats coming while crawling up that trail out of the valley, when she clambered to her feet and turned, hoping she could convince another soldier to halt so she could climb up behind him—now that her children had been rescued—only to discover that the horses coming toward her carried warriors: their faces like a terrible nightmare of shrieking, grimacing fury. They had to know she was Sam's wife, had to know what Sam had done to those devil's whelps who had tried to steal from the store.

"Oh, Sam!" she wanted to whimper. "Where are you now?"

She cowered back in the brush and waist-high grass that covered the bottom of the slope at the edge of the trail descending the back side of the White Bird Divide. From here the wagon road led around the heights to Mount Idaho. Isabella's white-blond hair was clumped with mud, her sunburned face smeared with more mud and streaks of blood, tracked with furrows from her tears. It had been some time since she had cried. No tears left.

Making herself as small as she could back in the brush, Isabella reminded herself to keep thinking of Sam in the present. *Don't think of him as gone.* She had only seen the blood on that windowsill. Didn't ever come across his body. So he had to be alive. No matter all the Indians combing the country around their place when he disappeared . . . Sam just had to be alive.

If this horseman wasn't the one who had captured her on the other side of the divide, then let her go, Isabella was positive it had to be another warrior who would not be so kind. Chances were it was one of the most savage come searching for any survivors of the fight whom he could catch struggling back toward the settlements. This country had been swarming with the redskins across the last day and a half—ever since they had routed the soldiers, just as she had warned those officers.

The warriors had to be searching under every thicket, behind every rock, looking for survivors who were trying their best to catch up to the retreating army, heathens finishing off those they found one by one before moving on. Combing the canyon, sweeping over the heights, then spreading out across the Camas Prairie, the horsemen would eventually run across everyone who hadn't made it in to Grangeville or Mount Idaho by now.

"Thank God the girls are safe," she whispered under her breath as her chest went tight.

Clutching her long, mud-crusted dress tightly around her legs so that it would not get caught on the branches and briars, Isabella scooted on her belly, penetrating the thicket even deeper. She prayed the horseman would not find her—not now, after Sam had disappeared and she had seen her daughters to safety with the soldiers . . . now that she had climbed out of the White Bird Canyon all night long in the dark, inching from rock to tree, to clump of brush, on and on with nothing more than starshine and a tenuous thread of hope to guide her.

Not now! Don't get captured now!

It was so hard to hold her breath, but Isabella did just that, struggling not to make the tiniest sound as the horse came to a halt close by. From where she cowered inside the leafy brush she could see the animal's hooves, part of the front legs. Though she tried, she could see nothing of the rider.

But, she reminded her racing heart, this did not look to be the same horse that the warrior rode when he captured her.

"Damn you!" a male voice swore right over her.

Frightened out of her wits, Isabella looped her arms over the back of her head and pressed her face against the ground, doing everything she could to make herself smaller and unseen.

"Get out here, you son of a bitch! I said NOW!"

She couldn't breathe then. Some of the savages knew a little of the white man's cursing—so maybe they were trying to trick her. . . . Still, that didn't have the ring of an Indian mimicking the white man's speech.

"You heard me, redskin!" the voice growled. "Get out here before I put a bullet in you!"

"P-p-please," she whimpered, slowly dragging her arms off her head and rising to her knees. Isabella felt her face blanch to white with terror, knowing she had already used up about all the chances anyone could ask in making her dash to sanctuary.

As she slowly parted the branches of the thick brush encasing her, she suddenly saw the rider was a white man. His muddy, scuffed boots and those grease-stained canvas britches.

"C'mon, I tell you!"

"I-I am."

The horseman jerked his horse backward in surprise, training his rifle squarely on that figure slowly emerging from the trailside brush when he suddenly exclaimed, "Jesus!"

"Dear God, you're a w-white man!" she gushed with relief as she fell on her knees, collapsing completely there on the grass, rolling onto her belly while weeping tears of deliverance.

"Mrs. Benedict?" the rider asked as he eased down the hammer of his carbine and flung himself out of the saddle. When he knelt beside her, propping the gun across one leg, and reached out with both hands to grip her shoulders and raise her off the ground, the man asked, "It really you, Isabella Benedict?"

She choked off a sob, gazing up into his face, reading something familiar in the eyes, something soft and reassuring. Realizing for sure this was not some warrior dressed in a dead man's clothing. This was one of her own. For a moment more

Isabella tried to utter something to him, her lips moving, but unable to make a sound.

"D-don't you know me, Mrs. Benedict?"

She did—honestly she did—but her tortured mind could not remember his name, where she had known him to be from, so all she could do for the moment was wail in complete and utter relief and let the tears gush while she dragged her legs under her and let him help her to her feet. He tenderly held her quaking shoulders there by the brush, staring intently into Isabella's face as the new tears made tiny furrows down the mud and blood crusted on her cheeks.

"My name's Robie, Mrs. Benedict," he reminded her in a whisper as quiet as could be, holding her face with both hands so close to his that she had to gaze right into his eyes. "You 'member me, don't you? Joe Robie, ma'am."

"Joe . . . Joe Robie," Isabella echoed. "Whatever are you doing out here?"

"When them soldiers come in to Mount Idaho," he explained gently as she pressed her cheek against his shoulder, trembling, "I heard a few of 'em saying they had to leave you behin't in the retreat. So I come looking for you."

"Why, why come for me?"

He cleared his throat self-consciously as he embraced her there in the shelter of his strong arms. And when he could finally speak, he confessed, "I-I long admired you, Mrs. Benedict. Wanted to make sure no harm come to you."

Then she suddenly remembered and started to pull away, embarrassed to be held by him. "My Sam? Anyone seen my Samuel?"

He twitched a little with the sudden sound of her husband's name. "No, no, ma'am. Not anyone I know of seen him come in. But I'm sure we'll find him."

Robie let her push herself away from him; then he slowly dropped the arms that had sheltered her. "For now, you come with me back to Mount Idaho. You'll ride behin't me."

Robie quickly settled himself in the saddle, then pushed out the empty stirrup with his left boot while reaching down with his left arm. "Here, Mrs. Benedict. C'mon up behin't me."

She grabbed for his wrist with one hand, seized the cantle in her right, then stuffed her left boot into the stirrup and hoisted herself behind the saddle, stuffing the torn dress and muddy petticoats beneath her across the horse's rump.

"Hold onto me," he instructed, wrapping one of her arms around his waist as he took up the reins in the other hand. "If'n we run across any of the sonsabitches, you hol't on, ma'am."

She laid her cheek against Joe Robie's back as he put the horse into a lope. Sensing his warmth after such cold, such loneliness and cold. How she wanted to hold Sam again, to feel safe in his arms, to feel his warmth the way she could sense this man's animal warmth coming through his canvas coat.

"Hold on," he had told her. And hold on she would—even though she had seen the blood where her Samuel had crawled out of the window and knew he wouldn't stand a chance out there in the woods against all of them.

So Isabella did hold on tight to Joe Robie . . . even as she felt herself letting go of the last remnant of hope that she would ever again see her Samuel alive.

Patrick Brice started his journey with little Maggie Manuel, heading across the battlefield and into White Bird Canyon, not knowing when they might stumble into more of the Nez Perce warriors. It wasn't a question of if. No, more a question of when.

After all their days without food, lying in hiding, compelled by terror to ignore the hunger pangs in his belly, the Irishman gazed up the grassy slopes to the top of the far ridge, his heart sinking. He knew the chances were slim that he would ever have enough strength to make that climb, to carry little Maggie out of harm's way and back to the safety of the settlements.

After hurrying away from those warriors at the Manuel ranch, Brice found his strength flagging faster and faster after each frequent stop to catch his breath. At first he was halting every half-mile or so, setting Maggie down while he lay back, listening intently for danger as she huddled against him. Then the distance he could force out of his legs began to shrink to something less than a quarter-mile between stops.

That trip crossing the broken ground where the soldiers and the Indians had fought was especially grueling, not only in terms of what it took out of them physically but more so in terms of what they endured emotionally.

"Look there, Mr. Brice," Maggie announced at his ear, where he held her piggyback.

He followed the direction her little splinted arm pointed and saw the contorted body of a soldier, his outstretched arms and legs raised, frozen in death as if he were imploring the sky. Maybe begging God to take him far, far from here.

The Almighty had done just that, Patrick reflected.

"There's another one too," Maggie said, pointing to the other side a few moments later. "See? There's lots of 'em now."

That much was the Lord's truth. They were trudging through a garden of the dead scattered across the blood-drenched grass.

"We ain't in trouble no more now, Mr. Brice," she said once as they neared the foot of a tall, rounded knoll.

"How you figure that, Maggie dear?" he asked as he set her down and they made themselves small against some low brush, so as to be out of sight should any warriors make an appearance.

"The Injuns are gone now. They left the dead soldiers be. Them Injuns ain't coming back now," she explained in her quict, tiny voice how it made perfect sense to her. "We're safe now."

Oh, to have the innocence of this sweet, little child, he thought. *To believe in the simplicity of events rather than the complexity and downright messiness of life.*

Later, as they were approaching a figure dressed in soldier blue, a man standing beside a huge bush at the edge of a copse of black cottonwood saplings, Maggie said, "Maybe he can tell us the easiest way to get out of the canyon."

Brice's heart leaped: to think that this soldier might help give them direction, if not be a companion to help carry Maggie up to the Camas Prairie.

But as they got closer, he could see that the figure was not standing straight up as a man would if that soldier realized they were coming. Instead, the figure was bent slightly over the bushes. And when they stopped within a few yards, Patrick saw how the sharp brambles snagged in the man's tunic and britches to hold the soldier upright. He was as dead as last winter's potatoes. Eyes wide open as if having just witnessed something of such horror, eyes possessed of that dull glaze of long-ago death.

"He's dead too," Maggie said so matter-of-factly that it yanked Brice right out of his reverie.

He lunged ahead, his legs weary and in need of another stop, but he dared not. At least not anywhere near that dead man who was all but standing there, arms wrapped around that bramble bush, waiting for someone to come along and save him.

Too late now.

When Patrick set her down at last, his legs shuddered from fatigue and he collapsed back against the ground. He laid his arm over his eyes, thinking he would steal a few minutes of sleep and feel brand-new as they started off the battlefield and into the canyon itself.

"Mr. Brice," she called, shaking him gently with her good hand.

He woke up, looked at her face, then down at the hand, and finally up that arm at the bloodstains on her sleeve where the arrow had pinned her.

"Maggie dear," he said apologetically, knowing he had fallen asleep.

"There's another one right over there." She pointed in the direction they were heading.

"Dead one?"

Nodding, Maggie said, "I ain't ever seen a man without the top of his head."

Swallowing with apprehension, he clambered to his feet and held out his hand, hoping she would walk beside him for a while. Angling off, Brice didn't want to take her close to the body that sat partly propped up against a boulder. Only close enough for him to see that she was right. Maggie must have gone over to investigate while he was asleep, Brice decided.

The top of the soldier's head was cleaved off in a pulpy mess. His brain was exposed, torn; some of it oozed down the side of the crushed skull. The sight spurred him into the mouth of the canyon.

As that Sunday afternoon aged and evening came down, Brice struggled up the side of the grassy slope, following the soldiers' trail, staying with the imprints of all those boots and iron-shod hooves. After a while, he told himself he couldn't bear to look up at the top of the ridge anymore, since it made his heart faint to see just how long it was taking them. So he vowed to keep his eyes only on the trail just ahead of him. Step by step as twilight fell, when he didn't have to worry about seeing the faraway top of the prairie above them. It was too dark to see anything that far away.

Every hundred yards or so, he set Maggie down and they would rest a few minutes. But he did not allow himself to lie down anymore. He knew he would fall asleep and then he would awaken right there in the morning—if the Indians hadn't found him before sunup. Better to force himself to stay awake. On through the dark, up, up, up . . . until he realized his legs were no longer climbing. Now he was carrying little Maggie over ground more level than the ordeal of the last few hours.

The quarter-moon had risen late that night of the seventeenth, so late that Patrick wondered if it wasn't long past midnight when he realized a part of the starry sky ahead was blotted out by a black shape. Large, angular, squat against the horizon where the rest of the skyline was bright with a jumble of stars.

He wanted to hope. Even more, he wanted to tell Maggie. But more than anything he wanted to shout for joy, because that had to be a house. Black as it was, with nary a candle or a lamp lit in the window—by damn, it just had to be a house!

Stumbling into the yard, Brice recognized these buildings that stood near the head of Rocky Canyon. "It's the Harris place, Maggie dear," he gasped with relief.

"We saved now?"

He dropped wearily to one knee, and she slipped off his back. "Not yet. Soon. C'mon with me."

Patrick took the tiny hand in his and led her up to the house. Every door, every window, had been smashed. Plain as paint the warriors had been here to loot it of all worth carrying off. Cold as they were, with the way the wind had come up after dark, the place was welcome shelter from the ravages of the night. Chances were, he convinced himself, the warriors had already been here. Likely wouldn't return.

"We stay here, Mr. Brice?"

"Just the place for us tonight," he answered.

After settling her on one of the small tick mattresses the Indians hadn't slashed too badly, Patrick searched in the dark for a candle or a lamp. He finally located a candle, and with it spreading a warm, flickering light he continued his search.

Behind a pantry sideboard he located some foodstuffs the Nez Perce had ignored. A few loaves of bread and a small slab of bacon, along with some tea and a little sugar. It made for a right fine supper after he got a fire started and Maggie huddled up close to its warmth.

While water for the tea was heating and he had strips of the bacon sizzling on a cast-iron griddle over the flames, Brice took his candle on another search. When he came back to the fireplace he had an old dry-goods crate in one hand and some leather harness draped over his shoulder. After feeding himself and the girl, the Irishman knocked off one of the crate's four sides, then rigged the straps around this makeshift "chair" so that he could carry it on his back like a pack-basket, with little Maggie perched inside.

"Look what I made for you," he said proudly as he turned it around to show the child, discovering that she had fallen asleep there beside the fire, her plate emptied, half of her warm tea gone.

Brice covered Maggie with a torn section of burlap sacking, since the Indians hadn't left a blanket in the place; then he banked the fire and curled up beside her.

By the time he awoke gritty-eyed and cotton-mouthed, Brice found the fire had burned itself out and the sky outside was renewing itself for another day.

"Come along now, Maggie," he coaxed her gently after she had herself some breakfast and returned from the outhouse at the side of the yard. "Time for us to hit the trail again."

"We gonna get to town today?"

"Yes, Maggie dear. We'll be there before another night."

When he knelt, he had her sit down inside the crate, holding onto the two sides where her head and shoulders protruded from their tops; then he stood, clutching the harness straps over his shoulders.

Brice felt renewed, just like this day. What a wonder a little food and some sleep had done him. He felt as if he could walk with her strapped to him all day if he had to, which is just what they did. Mile after mile, they plodded around the edge of the hills, skirting the prairie and staying high enough on the timbered slopes, avoiding the road to the settlements for fear of the Indians. Stopping only for rest and water and to let Maggie slip off for some privacy in the bushes.

But he grew concerned as the sun quickly slipped off behind them that afternoon and the light began to fade. A little scared they would have to spend another night out in the cold after he had promised her—

Brice smelled woodsmoke. He stopped dead in his tracks, realizing it could be anyone's fire, even a war party's. Did he have the heart to beg for Maggie's life again and not beg for his own?

The closer he got, the stronger became that sweet fragrance in his nostrils. Then he heard voices . . . and a familiar song bursting from some man's melodious throat, a heartfelt melody sung with such fondness and warmth that Patrick knew this had to be a place farthest from the Nez Perce War there ever could be.

Out of the twilight he thought he recognized some of the storefronts, then made out the barricade of logs, rocks, and hundredweight flour sacks down at the end of the town's long street.

"Who goes there?" a voice demanded out of the inky dark.

"P-Patrick . . . Patrick Brice!" he cried, tears pooling in his eyes, starting to stream down his dirty cheeks.

"By God . . . he says he's Patrick Brice!" The voice was flung at others noisily shuffling up to the barricades.

"Who was that, Mr. Brice?" Maggie asked in her tiny voice near his ear.

"I don't know his name." He choked on a sob as a half-dozen men pushed through the wall of wagons and barrels erected across Mount Idaho's narrow street and continued toward the barricade lit with flickering lamps. "All I know for sure is that we're back among friends, Maggie dear. We're back among friends."

Chapter 48

June 19, 1877

BY TELEGRAPH

An Indian War.

WASHINGTON, June 19.—General Sherman has received from General McDowell at San Francisco, the following dispatch from General Howard at Fort Lapwai, Washington territory, of the 16th instant: The Indians began by murdering a white man in revenge for a murder of his, killing three others at the same time. They have begun a war upon the people near Mount Idaho. Captain Perry has started with two companies for them. Other troops are being brought forward as fast as possible. Give me authority for twenty-five Indian scouts. Think we shall make short work of it.

Signed, HOWARD.

General McDowell adds: I had already informed Howard of your direction that the division has all the Indian scouts that can be allowed.

These rubber miner's boots flopped and flapped with every step as he trudged over the broken, brushy country, but First Sergeant Michael McCarthy was grateful to God that he had found them when he did.

When they had set out from Fort Lapwai, the soles of his cavalry boots were already scraped thin as parchment, hardly worth riding in, much less when he had been forced to go afoot like an infantry doughboy the way he was. After lying so long in that stream, the stitching had come apart, and he left the all-but-useless boots behind to continue his escape. Mile after painful, tender-footed mile, the first sergeant had trudged up the canyon and over to Camas Prairie in nothing more than a pair of grimy stockings that eventually became nothing more than tatters flopping around his ankles.

Then he had stumbled across an abandoned cache of supplies, which included these rubber boots. No weapons, no bullets, and no food . . . but damn if these boots weren't just about the sweetest discovery he had ever made!

His journey to the settlements had taken McCarthy a lot longer than he had planned for the simple reason that he got himself lost more than once. By avoiding the wagon road and staying far off that trail left by Perry's retreating survivors, McCarthy hoped to avoid any unexpected encounters with Nez Perce war parties. Three times he had gotten himself turned about and covered a lot of miles headed in the wrong direction.

Then he would notice something about the sun and the path it was taking—rising of a morning or sinking of an afternoon—realizing that he had eaten up valuable time and strength pushing away from the settlements instead of pressing on for the bivouac Colonel Perry was sure to make once the Indians let off the pressure on their rear guard.

And now with the bright sun rising this Tuesday, the nineteenth of June, McCarthy trudged on in his noisy boots, skirting along the timbered hillsides, his eyes scanning the vast, rolling sweep that was the Camas Prairie. That's when he spotted the few small buildings on the horizon.

It ended up taking him more than two hours to reach the place, what with those clumsy boots and the weary state of his legs. He hadn't much strength left to go on—nothing more than water for better than a day now—but still figured he was bound to reach the settlements before he dropped from hunger. At the edge of the tree line he stopped, licking his lips unconsciously as he looked the place over, wondering if he should take a chance since the ranch seemed deserted.

Just as he was emerging from the timber, the sergeant spotted two horsemen loping toward the place from beyond the ranch. He ducked back into the shadows and watched until he recognized them for white men.

His throat was hoarse with disuse when he called out to them, lunging their way in those ungainly rubber boots, bursting from the timber as the two horsemen reined up in the yard. Instantly they both pointed their weapons at him. McCarthy started to laugh. Crazy, gut-busting, tear-rolling laughter.

"I ain't no god-blasted Injun!" he roared at them, sensing the relief wash over him like a warm flood as he lumbered toward the house where the two had stopped.

"By Christ!" one of the pair exclaimed. "It is a soldier."

"Y-you seen any more soldiers?" McCarthy asked as he lunged to a halt and squinted up at the two astonished horsemen.

Nodding, the second man said, "Yep—them what made it out of the fight."

Then the first man explained, "They're hunkered down over at Grangeville."

"C-can you get me there?" McCarthy begged, dragging the back of his muddy hand across his mouth.

"Sure, we can get you there," the second man declared. "Doubt the Injuns left a horse here, though—so you're gonna have to ride double with us."

"C'mon," the first civilian instructed, offering his hand and an empty stirrup. "You start the ride up here with me."

McCarthy stepped around the rear of the settler's big horse, reaching the back of the saddle, where he peered at the saddle pocket the instant the thought struck him just behind his belt buckle. "B-by the way, mister . . . you got any rations in there? Anything to eat?"

Then the pair dug out a half-loaf of bread and a handful of dried bacon, watching in amazement how the sergeant wolfed it all down greedily in less time than it took to drag those vittles out of their saddlebags.

"You ain't got no more, do you?" he begged, swiping the back of his hand across the lower half of his hairy face.

The first man shrugged. "You just ate all we brung out for the whole damned day, soldier."

McCarthy grinned lopsidedly and held up his hand, jabbing his foot into the offered stirrup. "All right then. If you ain't got no more food . . . I s'pose it's 'bout time to take me on in to them soldiers at Grangeville."

This was their country.

From birth the *Nee-Me-Poo* knew all the rivers and streams, knew where to ford at what seasons. So it was that the leaders chose to cross to the south side of the Salmon at Horseshoe Bend, where the swollen waters slowed as the river curved around a jutting thumb of land. It was here to the south of White Bird Creek they migrated the day after driving off the army. Then, just after sunrise the next morning, the women began to gather their children, the old ones, and all their possessions on the north bank.

Since the Non-Treaty bands were able to locate only one of the white man's canoes, the women and some of the older men had constructed rafts and bullboats for their perilous journey across the river. For much of the previous day they were busy chopping sturdy lengths of green willow, while others laid out their buffalo hides, hair side up, on the grassy bank. They crisscrossed the limber poles over the hides, then drew poles and hide up together to form a bowl-shaped vessel. Two more willow saplings were then lashed completely around the outside of the bullboat to form the lip of the bowl that would hold all the inside supports in place.

By the time the sun was making its appearance over the heights to the east, the first of these floating bowls were being led into the current by a few of the young men riding the strongest of the war ponies. In addition, two strong swimmers accompanied each boat for its dangerous journey, then were ferried back to the north shore by those on horseback. Inside the vessels the women had placed their lodge covers, kitchen kettles, and the rest of their family possessions. Atop some of the heaping piles of baggage rode the small children in their woven basket hats, even the very old who were too weak to sit astride the horses that would be driven into the river only when everyone else had completed the crossing.

Man, woman, and child went about their duties, knowing what was now at stake. The chiefs had not elected to escape far to the west for the Imnaha. Nor had they decided to go to the land of Joseph's Wallowa band. Instead, the chiefs merely wanted to put the river between them and the soldiers they knew would come again, making another try at driving the *Nee-Me-Poo* onto the reservation where no free man should be forced to live.

It was decided that when the soldiers came—and everyone knew they would—the bands would simply re-cross the Salmon and make for the Clearwater to the northeast. So all their efforts that morning would serve only as a delaying tactic by these People of the Coyote. From the youngest who could understand to those few ancient ones so frail they had to be carried in another's arms and laid in the bullboats, every person realized that back there at the *Lahmotta* camp on White Bird Creek their lives had irrevocably changed for all time to come.

No more would they be left in peace to wander their long-held homelands in that ages-old circle of the seasons. By the same token, they would not be forced to live as paupers and farmers on the reservation with the Treaty bands. The *Nee-Me-Poo* were going to have to forge a new life for themselves now—if not in their homeland ... then they would seek out a new country.

"*Teeweawea,*" Ollokot called out to that trusted older warrior when the last bullboat was on its way across the roiling surface of the Salmon.

Yellow Wolf joined the many warriors, fighting men both young and old, all of them moving over to listen in on the conversation.

Laying his hand upon *Teeweawea*'s shoulder, Ollokot told that veteran of the buffalo country, "I want you to pick from among our men to go with you: choose three-times-ten."

"What do you wish us to do? Take the horses and cattle across the river?"

"No," Ollokot replied. "The rest of us will do that and protect the camp. Instead, I want you and your party to do something very crucial for our survival—you must stay back and watch for soldiers."

The veteran warrior nodded with a grin. "We'll ride back to *Tepahlewam* and keep watch for soldiers coming across the Camas Prairie in pursuit of our village."

"Send a runner with any news," Ollokot suggested. "And we will let your courier know where our camp is moving."

Teeweawea turned, regarding the crowd of eager warriors elbowing one another there in the first ranks—mostly young men who no longer lived with their families in lodges, men who slept beneath blanket bowers with other young fighters. Yellow Wolf stared intently at *Teeweawea,* praying the older man would sense the intensity of his gaze, desperately willing the veteran to choose him for this vital mission.

Slowly, one by one, the first ten were chosen from those close around Yellow Wolf. Then *Teeweawea* turned away slightly as he stepped on around the circle, continuing to choose those who would ride with him on this scout. When the veteran passed right by Yellow Wolf, the young warrior's heart sank to the ground and turned hollow with growing despair. The leader went on to choose three more from the crowd of expectant men.

Then *Teeweawea* surprised them all by suddenly wheeling around, a big smile across his face. The instant his eyes landed on the young man, the veteran announced, "Yellow Wolf—you will ride with us too!"

His heart soared! His blood surged, pounding loudly in his ears! How he wanted to shriek with joy, now that he had truly been accepted as a warrior of his people!

Before long the thirty followed their leader away from the Salmon. Like Yellow Wolf, most every one of these scouts gazed back over his shoulder at those families and friends who were already across the river, their village slowly moving west into the heights, marching away from the army. As he watched, those men left behind were beginning to drive their great herds* into the water.

How it made Yellow Wolf's breast swell, knowing that he was one of the few who now stood between the *Nee-Me-Poo,* a free people . . . and those soldiers who would be coming to snuff out the last vestiges of their liberty.

These men loping north across the White Bird battle-ground, climbing into the canyon, and making for the Camas Prairie were prepared to lay down their lives when the Shadows came to avenge their disastrous defeat on this bloody ground. For it would never be a question of *if* the soldiers would come.

Only a matter of when.

*   *   *

---

*Reputed to be something on the order of 2,500 to 3,500 head of horses

Last evening when Patrick Brice was first surrounded and welcomed by those citizens who had already streamed to the safety of Mount Idaho, he was surprised to find that George Popham wasn't there among the crowd who clamored to hear his story.

Throughout that night and into the next day, the Irish miner brooded on what was to become of all this, just what was to happen now to the mines and to the farms, what was to become of these tiny settlements under seige now that the Indians had gone wild and back to the blanket. And he feared most for the old man.

But by the next afternoon Popham finally emerged from the timber at the edge of the settlement and hailed the citizens who stood watch at the Mount Idaho barricades.

"I gave you up for dead, old man!" Brice hollered above the pandemonium that erupted now, just as it had each time someone who had been assumed a casualty walked in big as life.

"Never thought I'd see you alive neither!" Popham cheered as they hammered each other on the back, both men reveling in their desperate relief and this joyous reunion.

"I brought Maggie in yestiddy," Patrick confided.

The old man's eyes grew moist; then he asked, "Jennet and the baby—they was already here when you come in?"

Brice's heart went cold behind his breastbone. "Maggie . . . why, she told me the Injuns kill't her mamma and li'l brother."

"Naw," Popham replied gruffly, sawing his head back and forth the way a man would who refused to believe some shocking news just told him. "They cain't be dead. I know for my own self she got out alive—"

"Maggie said she saw 'em both," Brice explained gently as he looped an arm over the grieving father's shoulder and led him away from the crowd celebrating Popham's arrival. "Saw 'em after—"

"Maggie saw 'em . . . dead?"

Brice nodded, sensing the muscles tense across the old man's shoulders. "Maggie hid outside when the Injuns come back around, but told me she watched Joseph hisself kill her mamma. Later on when the Injuns was gone, Maggie went back in the house, to where the bastards left the bodies . . . where she watched 'em kill your daughter and grandson. But

Maggie said she didn't find the . . . didn't find neither of your kin."

Popham dragged a grimy hand across the lower half of his face, rustling the heavy stubble of a graying beard, snorting back the dribble at the end of his nose. "Then I gotta figger there's still a chance Jennet's alive, the baby too."

"George," Patrick cautioned, "maybe it ain't such a good notion to count on that—"

Fiercely grabbing Brice's shirt, Popham growled, "Maggie said herself she didn't see no sign of 'em when she went back inside. You told me that. So their bodies wasn't in the house when the red bastards burned it to the ground."

"B-burned the house?"

"Yeah. The Nez Perce torched it, every last stick of lumber."

Bewildered, Brice declared, "B-but the house was still standing when I left with Maggie."

"Must've happened after you took off with her," Popham admitted. "I stayed till there was nothing left but cinders and smoke. When you and me got separated, I vowed to stay in one place. Figured I was safer that way, rather'n moving around and getting caught. But once John and Jennet's house went up in flame, I figgered there was no reason left for me to hang around—since them sonsabitches had took everything they wanted and burned down the rest. It was likely safe for me to slip away."

"I never saw no trace of Mrs. Manuel or the baby," Brice confessed with a wag of his head. "Not no sign when we started for here."

"Neither did I," Popham said grimly. "That's why I'm gonna figure Maggie got it wrong—the little dear. That's why I'm gonna believe that Jennet and the boy are still alive . . . out there somewhere."

"We'll go look—you, me, and some others too—soon as we get some more soldiers brave enough to ride back over to the White Bird," Brice vowed.

Laying his big, dirt-crusted hand on the Irishman's bony shoulder, Popham declared, "They're alive, son. I know in my gut Jennet and her boy are still alive."

Epilogue

Fort Lapwai
June 19, 1877

Dear Mamma,

We have lived through so much since I wrote last time that it seems months. It has all been so horrible, I should like to tell you about it and not write. Doctor has not come back yet, but probably will on Thursday. You know how I mourned over his having to go, and he did not want to go at all, and now I am so thankful, I don't know what to do. He, of course, would have left here with Colonel Perry's command, had he been home on Friday night, and that poor little band we will never see alive again. I can't write you how everything is going on here. I only hope, if we all live through it, sometime to tell you, but this Indian War is many times a more extensive affair than any one imagined.

The Non-Treaty Nez Perces, to a man, joined Joseph's forces, and he is being constantly reinforced by bands from other tribes that are encouraged by the success he has already met with. Colonel Perry went to Mount Idaho to reach those settlers. More than thirty had been murdered before he started, including quite a number of children and women. When Colonel Perry's troops (not a hundred men and two officers—all that could be possibly found in reach) got there, the Indians were gone and were supposed to be retreating towards the buffalo country by a certain pass. Colonel Perry hoped to catch them while they were crossing a river. They were supposed to be about eighty under Joseph and White Bird. On Sunday, by forced marches, they came up with what they thought was a detachment of Indians, and the fight began. It was such a hot day, and we waited here for the news with heartaches. It is only about fifty miles from us. Yesterday morning, at daybreak, the news came. More than half the command is dead and missing. Poor Mr. Theller is dead. The wounded were left on the field. Colonel Perry with twenty men had gotten back to Mount Idaho.

The poor little laundress, who has also lost her husband, has been staying in our house ever since her husband left, as she was afraid in her own quarters outside the garrison. Can you imagine how terrible it is for us women at Lapwai with all this horrible Indian war around us, and with these two women, who have lost their husbands, constantly before our eyes, and we not knowing who will be the next sufferer. They are the first, but they will not be the last.

I hope and pray my dear, old John will be spared to me and not sacrificed to those red devils for a country that isn't worth it.

Your loving daughter,
Emily F.

Afterword

What a treacherous and thorny road I've chosen to walk by attempting to write my usual historical afterword to a story that is far from over!

I hope those of you who have written me over the years wondering when I was going to get around to including a book on the Nez Perce War in this Plainsmen Series are not dismayed that this book ended right after the first battle. You're going to get not only one, but three volumes!

The story is simply too complicated, the characters far too numerous, the locales too distant for me to cover in one book. For years now I had counted on doing this story in two novels. The first would take us from the murders and White Bird Canyon through the Battle of the Big Hole in Montana Territory. Then the second book would carry us from that point through to the eventual surrender at the Bear's Paw and exile to the hot country of Indian Territory.

But a funny thing happened on the way. History and historical characters have a compelling means of making themselves known to me, and hence to you. Yes, I could have written one big academic text as others have done, complete with the cultural and historical background on the tribe. But I chose to do what I do best: tell this story by dropping us right down into the middle of the frying pan when things were coming to a boil.

I'll trust that in the end my factual telling of this all too human a story will prove to be more compelling than all those academic textbooks put together!

Before I go any further, there are a few people I want to thank for their generous and unselfish help in seeing me down the road with this first of three volumes about the Nez Perce War.

At the outset, I should express my gratitude to my long time friend and National Park Service historian, *Jerome A. Greene.* A couple years back Jerry helped open the door for me at the Spalding site. In a conversation on another matter regarding Nelson Miles's Yellowstone campaigns, I found out Jerry was working on a long-term, exhaustive study of the Nez Perce War. We kept in touch from time to time, often discussing my perceptions of that war's historical characters. He was a tremendous resource to me in that regard.

Last spring it came time for me to visit the sites where the story took place one last time. And on this trip I wanted to get my hands on Jerry's materials being guarded in the basement at the Spalding Nez Perce site.

Robert Chenowith, curator at the site, graciously welcomed me into their archives (even though he admitted he doesn't read historical fiction!). Bob introduced me to *Linda Paisano,* a wonderful Indian lady who serves as the museum technician, as well as *Rob Applegate,* who was experiencing his first day on the job as the site librarian.

Rob and Linda got me set up in a quiet room just off the locked archives vault, where I could come and go with the huge boxes of Jerry's research. I was like a kid in a candy store. While I was digging through the boxes, Bob Chenowith came in with his personal copy of the uncorrected proofs to Jerry's newest book, his forthcoming volume on the Nez Perce War, to be published in the spring of 1999 through a joint effort by the National Park Service and the Montana Historical Society.

Before I go any further with this historical wrap-up, I want to remind you of the proper pronunciation of *Nez Perce.* Although that name was given to the *Nee-Me-Poo* people by the obscure French voyageurs working for the British fur trading companies (just as the French designated the Lakota people by the foreign word *Sioux*), it should not be pronounced with some Americanized "French" twist to the words: "Nay Per-say."

Nor should it be spoken as "Nez Per-say," even though in some academic volumes you will often come across *Perce* written with a diacritical accent mark over the last e in the word. And some folks make the mistake of pronouncing the first word correctly—"Nez"—then mispronounce the second word by giving it its English translation: "Pierce." Also incorrect.

Instead, the common usage among both those *Nee-Me-Poo* I have met in my travels and those whites who live in Nez Perce country gives us the following proper pronunciation:

"Nez Purse."

Let me push on by agreeing with Jerry Green in saying this is a story of friendship forgotten and trust betrayed. I will take a leap further by saying that the forgotten friendship and betrayed trust occurred on both sides. While the wave of political correctness sweeping our country would emphasize broken treaties and betrayal on a grander, more global, scale . . . I focus in on the dissolution of longtime friendships and the destruction of trust happening on a more personal level— between individuals on both sides in those final months before the outbreak of hostilities.

Simply put, the Nez Perce bands saw their trust in the white man shattered, and many of the white settlers along the Salmon and across Camas Prairie saw their relationship with the Nez Perce brutally crushed right before their eyes.

Beyond the fact that there was treachery and deceit on both sides—enough to ignite one of the most tragic conflicts in our country's history—I believe any more of an attempt to place blame on one group or another is nothing more than an attempt by the historians to split very fine hairs.

It is quite amazing to me that so many historians state that there is no accounting for what happened with those first bloody murders of innocent whites at the hands of a few drunk warriors.

I think I understand perfectly.

Across some twenty years, more and more white men flooded into Nez Perce country until there were three or four whites to every Indian. While a majority of the newcomers did not seize the land for themselves or mine gold on Nez Perce ground or steal horses or cattle from the tribe . . . while most of those who simply crowded in where they didn't belong weren't the sort to rape the Nez Perce women, weren't

the kind who would beat or even murder a Nez Perce man
... there nonetheless were the greedy few who found a land
of opportunity where little restraint had to be exercised in
dealing with the Nez Perce. After all, the Indians were an
inferior subclass, a heathen populace who weren't using the
earth, making it fruitful, as our Christian God had commanded of us many thousands of years before.

Against this backdrop of deceit, greed, and downright evil,
it was only natural that resentments grew, tallies of wrongs
were kept, and strong emotions simmered just below the surface. So you want to tell me that there's no accounting for
what happened in June of 1877?

It was payback time, in a big way. The tragedy of it was
that when it came time to pay the piper, most of those killed,
raped, or robbed were innocent of having done anything
against their murderers in specific, much less against the Nez
Perce tribe as a whole.

I'll wager that most of you folks who have some speaking
acquaintance with this war didn't know about those first murders the three young men committed or about the fourteen
other murders and rapes committed by Sun Necklace's second revenge raid. Truth is, most people have never really
cared to learn anything about the complexity of what happened between the settlers and the war parties bent on spilling white blood. Instead, too many folk have chosen to
believe that the army came to attack the Indians at White
Bird Canyon because those Indians had refused to go onto
the reservation after the Nez Perce had guaranteed they
would.

So it has been that the majority of people, even those with
some knowledge of the Nez Perce War, are convinced the
story is entirely one of black and white, a classic tale where
the soldiers repeatedly harassed, attacked, and killed the Nez
Perce at White Bird, again on the Cottonwood, then on the
Clearwater, and finally traipsed after them into Montana to
surprise the tribe at the Big Hole, Camas Meadows, and
Canyon Creek, then ultimately brought the war to an end at
the Bear's Paw Mountains—a few miles short of sanctuary in
Canada.

While this concept of how the war began and was prose-
cuted may be currently in vogue, and most certainly what we
would call politically correct, it is *wrong*. Ignorance of the real

story does neither side any justice in this tragedy, much less serve the historical record.

Speaking of the historical record, the crucial May sessions between General Howard and the Non-Treaty chiefs at Fort Lapwai are rendered from more than Howard's writings. I also drew from the recollections of some of the chiefs who attended the councils and in later years took exception with Cut-Off Arm's version of the dialogue between the principals, which he published soon after the war in *Nez Perce Joseph*. It's only natural that both sides in a passionate dispute would have serious differences over what occurred, if not what was actually said in the heat of argument.

Thirty-four years later, an aging Yellow Bull (whose name was actually Sun Necklace at the time of the 1877 war) claimed Toohoolhoolzote's words in that council confrontation were less severe than Howard rendered them. Other Nez Perce joined in to claim Howard used rude and inconsiderate language, occasionally telling Toohoolhoolzote to "shut up" and even pushing the old *tewat* angrily at one point.

I can understand how such raw tensions might have flared during those heated discussions. Both Howard and Toohoolhoolzote were men with unshakable convictions. It's easy to see how the old shaman could goad the soldier chief into something rash, just as easy as it is to see Howard unable to resist his natural impulse to berate or even shove the stubborn "heathen."

Oliver Otis Howard had come west under a cloud of suspicion from a scandal concerning his mismanagement of funds at the Freedmen's Bureau, not of his own doing. Although he would later be cleared of those charges before assuming his command in the Northwest, it is also true that Howard never weathered criticism well. He would smart from the indignities of those charges for the rest of his life. Perhaps those still-oozing wounds, if not his own thin-skinned nature, might well have contributed to his inability to deal more evenhandedly with the Nez Perce when his patience was tested.

Despite the way the chiefs found Howard treating them, it remains part of the historical record that *after* the council at Lapwai when Howard ordered the Non-Treaty bands onto the reservation or he would have to send his soldiers after them, but *prior* to the murders on the Salmon and Camas Prairie, Joseph reportedly told a friendly settler, "But you know they won't kill us, for General Howard and [Agent] Monteith are Christians."

A belief more tragic than it is ironic. Tragic in that a few chiefs like Joseph still believed that the white man would unflinchingly adhere to their own Christian beliefs and not make war on the Nez Perce. Ironic in that it seemed the Indian agents of the West—at least those who were not robbing their wards blind through graft and greed—were so consumed with preparing their Indians for a life everlasting in heaven that they ended up making the Indians' existence a veritable hell on earth!

For decades the Nez Perce had suffered indignities without any hope of redress. With every season they became more confused about the world they were compelled to live in—a world where the white man made not only the rules about the land but also the rules about what the Nez Perce could believe regarding the supernatural. In this world, and in the next, the Non-Treaty bands must have felt themselves set adrift in a roiling sea of despair and frustration that simmered—but never quite boiled over.

Not until June of 1877.

After so many years—so many rapes and robberies, so many land swindles and crooked whiskey men, so many murders of the Nez Perce without any of the murderers coming to justice—exactly what was the spark that finally set off the powder keg? Was the outbreak of the Nez Perce War really caused by something so simple as the wounding of one young warrior's cocky pride?

To judge by an exhaustive reading of the contemporary records, it appears to be no more complex than that. The story I've written of just how this young warrior, Shore Crossing, came to be the spark is compiled from all the various, and sometimes conflicting, accounts. Most of those who left some record on this part of the story don't mention that Shore Crossing was married or that even though he was married, he was nonetheless still quite taken with another young woman.

What the accounts do agree upon is that the *tel-lik-leen,* or the martial parade, performed at *Tepahlewam* by the young men was a chance to strut and preen before the eligible young women. Most of the historical record goes on to state that during this parade through camp the pony Shore Crossing and Red Moccasin Tops were riding accidentally, perhaps brazenly, stepped upon a canvas where an old woman had laid her roots to dry. Furthermore, most of the accounts are consistent in stating that the old woman's husband, Yellow Grizzly Bear, sharply berated Shore Crossing for his rude clumsiness—even unto chiding the young man that he had no right to parade with the warriors because he himself had not avenged the death of his father at the hands of Larry Ott.

For more of the story I had to scratch deeper and deeper into the records, eventually finding out that Shore Crossing might well have been scolded again, even ridiculed before other young men and women at a traditional dance that very evening in the Split Rocks camp. And I discovered that the one who embarrassed Shore Crossing—a young warrior named Red Grizzly Bear (is it nothing more than coincidence that his name is so similar to Yellow Grizzly Bear?)—might well have been the older brother of the young woman Shore Crossing had been seeking to impress. An obscure story about their confrontation at the dance indicates that Red Grizzly Bear challenged all those who had not avenged the deaths of their relatives.

The story almost appears sophomoric at this juncture—something that might happen between some teenagers at a school dance, what with the blustering and bullying, the name-calling and wounded pride. Almost like an amusing tale ripped from the hallways of any modern-day high school . . . were it not for the tragic consequences of that challenge issued by both the old man, Yellow Grizzly Bear, as well as the young warrior named Red Grizzly Bear.

This part of the outbreak story is awash with discrepancies, and a great deal of personal opinion as well.

The author of one of the landmark books on the Nez Perce, Alvin M. Josephy, Jr., appears to me to have set himself up as an apologist for the cruelty, murders, and depredations committed by the war parties in the early days of the conflict. At the most, he attempts to justify the bloody retribution taken on innocent white settlers, and at the very least Josephy does his best to deflect the blame from falling where it should by stating that—according to what he calls "tribal legend"—Shore Crossing did not drink alcohol. For this claim Josephy has taken not only the word of the tribe's unofficial white historian, L. V. McWhorter, but also the testimony of a more recent tribal elder, Otis Halfmoon, who repeated the very same Nez Perce oral lore. `

Weighed against are the many accounts given by other Nez Perce stating that Shore Crossing was, in fact, drinking the night before he rode off on that first raid. Three of those accounts come from very reliable sources: Young Joseph, Sun Necklace/Yellow Bull, and Two Moons.

We know that there was a great deal of whiskey in that camp, brought in by unscrupulous white traders out of Grangeville, Mount Idaho, or even as far away as Lewiston. And these reliable accounts declare that the warriors young and old did indeed partake of the whiskey over those days immediately prior to the outbreak. Even Jerry Greene, the Nez Perce War's newest historian, writes that the three young warriors were "fortified with liquor" when they raced off for the Salmon River settlements.

So it appears to me that Josephy's story becomes nothing more than a politically correct apology for brutal, bloody atrocities committed against innocents, because the truth of the matter is that Shore Crossing not only lost more of his good sense the more he drank but also found his courage to commit cold-blooded murder at the bottom of a cup of whiskey.

It's a matter of the historical record that there was considerable whiskey trading going on with the Nez Perce in that day, a story replete with the varied troubles that whiskey was causing in the region. We know that long before the Nez Perce War, members of the tribe understood how Joe Craig, half-breed son of former mountain man William Craig, often abused his Nez Perce wife when he was in his cups. Likewise, Samuel Newell, son of mountain man Robert "Doc" Newell, was in and out of trouble with white officials as one of the "troublesome half-breeds" repeatedly indicted for "disposing of whiskey to an Indian of the Nez Perce nation."

Make no mistake: the sale of liquor to the tribe became a constant source of trouble in the months preceding the outbreak. Not only did it cause turmoil for such notorious whiskey traders as Samuel Benedict and Harry Mason, but also the trade in alcohol had been escalating every year around the time of the Camas Prairie gathering. Dancing, horse-racing, getting drunk on the white man's liquor—these activities all went together, summer after summer, making for a potent brew that would eventually spell disaster.

Isn't it strange that after Larry Ott murdered Eagle Robe, Shore Crossing's father, the settler very conveniently seems to have been absent from home when the three warriors came calling? Here's where we find differing accounts concerning just what happened to the man. Some of the contemporary reports circulating among the Nez Perce at the time reported that Ott learned of the nasty temperament of the *Tepahle-wam* gathering and grew scared. Sensing that he was going to be the target of a reprisal, Ott promptly ran off to the nearby mountain mining town of Florence. It was there that Yellow Wolf reported Ott put on "Chinamen clothes and worked with the Chinamen washing gold."

Contrary to this bit of tribal lore is the fact that Ott's name appeared on the roll of volunteers mustered at the Slate Creek barricades, joining sixteen civilians who came down from the Florence mines. So did Larry Ott first flee his homestead on the Salmon and reach safety in the mountain mining town? Then when he was reinforced with the strength of numbers did he journey back to the Salmon River to reinforce the settlements with the miners?

The name of this forty-two-year-old Philadelphian on the muster roll at Slate Creek is written in a neat script. Could it have been written by someone else? Perhaps one of the women if Ott could not write it himself?

Ott's flash-fire murder of Eagle Robe indicates that he was unquestionably of the ruffian type often found on the frontier. His very presence on this tiny bit of land beside the Salmon River gives rise to the speculation that he had been a miner who failed to make a strike or—more likely—that he might even have been an extreme "undesirable" who was run out of the rip-roaring mining camps of Lewiston, Florence, or Elk City.

A man living alone on that narrow strip of land bordering the river where the murder took place sure leads me to believe he was *persona non grata* among even the most violent element on that Idaho frontier. In the final analysis, it's not hard to understand why Ott's casual killing of Eagle Robe is generally regarded as the match that ignited the fuse already priming the powder keg that eventually exploded into the Nez Perce War.

One by one over the past few years I read those books

listed in the bibliography that appears near the end of this afterword. With each new volume I found one or more details of the story that differed in some minor, obscure way from what I had read before. It didn't take long before I realized that the published accounts of what occurred with Shore Crossing at the *Tepahlewam* gathering, as well as many of the complex of details in what happened to the Salmon River settlers, were imprecise and very often in disagreement with one another. More likely than not, the various stories recounted slightly different chronologies.

From the very beginning of this Indian Wars saga that began with my writing *Sioux Dawn,* I have been confronted with the necessity of making decisions and arriving at conclusions that the historians aren't forced to reach. In a work of nonfiction, the academic writer can present the various opinions, options really, of what might have happened, offering his reader several different scenarios.

But I've never had it so easy. I can't plausibly write a character across two or more story lines. My character can't be in two places at once, nor can there be two time lines or conflicting chronologies for my stories.

In short, I have to come to an informed decision on what happened to who and when it happened, then stick to it without any equivocating. So despite all the conflicts I found in more than three dozen sources used to write this story—even among some of the most respected of historians—I had to write the story that my own instincts told me actually happened.

Remember that fact when, or if, you ever pick up one of the books I recommend for further reading on the Nez Perce War. Which means we must be perfectly clear on this: From among all the conflicting clutter of the firsthand contemporary records and secondhand historical accounts I had to weave a story not of what *might* have happened. Instead, you've just read the story of what I believe actually *did* happen. Remember what I told you in the introduction before you even started this novel. Every incident happened when and where and how I have written it.

Conflicts? Sure there were. Let's examine one of the thornier ones.

In the days following the first murders, Idaho district attorney J. W. Poe alleged that Hattie, the older Chamberlin daughter, had been killed as the mother was forced to watch, "by having its head placed between the knees of a powerful Indian and crushed to death." So history records that Mrs. Chamberlin and her younger daughter survived. Just how they survived their terrible ordeal at the hand of the drunk, enraged warriors, and in what state, we can only surmise. But Bruce Hampton, author of *Children of Grace*, leaves me with the impression that the older daughter survived, when my reading of the accounts indicates that the younger one lived— the daughter who was found beneath her dead father's legs, her tongue nearly severed, either from a knife wound or from a fall.

And in all my reading it appeared that there is some continuing dispute as to the number of whites killed during the outbreak of murders on both the Salmon and the Camas Prairie. But, here again, I had to write the story that history itself dictated. I couldn't have it both ways. When the contemporary accounts indicated that a settler was murdered, my story tells of that killing—when, where, and how it happened. There are no two ways about it in this novel. Eighteen whites lost their lives in the uprising.

After his first report that thirty settlers had been killed, Howard whittled back his tally to fourteen. Around the same time, Arthur "Ad" Chapman placed the number at twenty-two. Later, on 26 June, Howard finally wrote division headquarters: "The number of murders thus far are seventeen (17), one woman, two children and fourteen men." To that list would be added the name of Joe Moore, who lingered (as much as three months according to historian Mark H. Brown) before he succumbed. So eighteen is the number used by historians of the National Park Service.

Beyond those bloody murders and the brutal rapes, the raiding left widespread destruction. The tall columns of smoke Captain David Perry and his cavalry spotted in the distance as they crossed the Camas Prairie proved to be only the tip of the iceberg. Houses, barns, outbuildings, and stacks of first cuttings of hay—anything that the warriors could put to the torch—were set afire. What buildings weren't burned they plundered. What wasn't taken was destroyed and left in ruin. Horses and cattle were stolen. What sheep and hogs were not driven back to the *Tepahlewam* camp and from there to the White Bird Canyon were slaughtered and left behind at the looted ranches, their carcasses bloating among the piles of ash and rubble.

I would be remiss if I didn't mention the discrepancy between some of the sources regarding Mrs. Benedict's four-year-old daughter. Two of the writers attempted to give the girl a broken arm when it was actually six-year-old Maggie Manuel who suffered the broken arm in her fall from the horse while fleeing with her father, John Manuel. In addition, one of the modern-day sources reports that the Benedict girl was even named Maggie too!

It seems perfectly clear to me that the historian got his girls confused—conveniently turning Maggie Manuel into Maggie Benedict.

Another source reported that the Benedict daughter had a fractured skull. Did this historian mix her up with the older of the Chamberlin girls, who had her skull crushed? Appears there's more than enough confusion to go around concerning these poor little girls.

Oh, and a brief word of caution concerning the elder of the two Benedict daughters. Because no record exists (at least any source I can locate in any of the archives or the literature on this account), I have arbitrarily given the Benedict girl a first name—Emmy—in hopes that the two young girls (Manuel and Benedict) are kept entirely separate in the reader's mind.

When considering all the innocents caught up in this outbreak, how tragic and pitiable is the aftermath of what happened to Helen Walsh and Elizabeth Osborn once they rejoined their white frontier society. Because they had been gang-raped by a war party in front of their own small children, both were too ashamed to show themselves in public for a long time following their rescue. What unspeakable horror was committed against them they themselves never divulged. Yet there's enough testimony to convince historians that the women were repeatedly brutalized by the warriors, a horrific trauma those on the Indian frontier in that day called "a fate worse than death."

So it's very intriguing to note that in all the published accounts she gave over the months to come Helen Walsh claimed that she and Elizabeth Osborn were treated kindly by the war party. Mrs. Walsh wrote: "[The Nez Perce warriors] told us that they did not want to kill us; that we could go to Slate Creek or Lewiston without fear." But First Sergeant Michael McCarthy, who saw them at Slate Creek a week later, stated that the women would not show themselves, did not venture out of the self-imposed prison they made of a small cabin. He surmised it was because of their overwhelming shame.

Another settler declared that the two women had "received treatment that was but little better than death," leaving no doubt what either of these accounts really meant. Rape was far from being an unknown allegation during the first few days of the outbreak, but if these two women were abused in this manner, then Mrs. Walsh and Mrs. Osborn both took their terrible secret to the grave. Friends and neighbors never pressed either survivor for a public admission—a small blessing those folk could bestow upon two women who had somehow survived torture and terror.

For me the rape of these two women brings up the nagging question that appears to be all too easy for others to dismiss but difficult for me to fathom: why did the warriors on both raids murder some of those they caught, while letting others go without harm? What accounts for this most curious and unexplainable fact?

At their core, the raids along the Salmon were clearly reprisals against only a few of those whites who had settled along a part of the river where the land was ill-suited to much of anything. Remember, this was a valley without attraction except for its wild and seductive beauty: there was no gold in the gravel bars along the Salmon as there was in the nearby mountains; the steep hills rising abruptly from the river's edge did not lend themselves to agriculture in any shape or form. So except for the storekeepers, why did these settlers put down roots there?

In his *The Flight of the Nez Perce,* author Mark H. Brown posits a claim that the hollows of the Salmon near the mouth of White Bird Creek became a "Hole-in-the-Wall" country for those hard-core "undesireables" banished from Lewiston, as well as Florence and other mining camps (as we already pointed out in the case of what led Larry Ott to be in the valley). Evidence for this is that they attempted to grow a few crops on some poor ground instead of prospecting in the mountains. Such "banished" characters couldn't simply leave Idaho and go to Montana, where a decade before vigilantes had already proved very ably that they were not about to put up with ruffians and scofflaws in their mining camps. So Brown goes on to declare that this area of the Salmon was home to "far more than a normal proportion of tough characters."

Pardon me? Are we really to believe that these family men—Samuel Benedict, Jurden Henry Elfers, Harry Mason, Benjamin Norton, John Chamberlin, and others—were outcasts banished from the roughest element of frontier society? Can you actually picture any of these citizens as historian Brown depicts them? Could he seriously believe that these were such hardened characters that they were unable to live in the crudest of wild societies operating in those mining camps?

Bullshit. What kind of politically correct claptrap is that, to declare that the men who were murdered had it coming because they were the outcasts, the dregs, of even the worst of frontier society?

If these few settlers and "store men" were guilty of anything, it was nothing more than being guilty of greed, along with a healthy dose of stupidity. What do I mean by that? you might ask. Guilty of greed for selling or trading whiskey to the Nez Perce and guilty of utter stupidity for not realizing that the sale of that whiskey could come back around to bite them in the ass at some future point in time. After all, an undisputed fact of life for these folk who carved out a place for themselves on the western frontier was that, as author Brown states, "drunken Indians have always been known to be noisy and ugly."

Standing on the heights and gazing down at the valley of the White Bird Canyon, I was immediately struck with how the Nez Perce managed to cram their herds of some twenty-five to thirty-five hundred (or more!) horses in so confining a place. It boggles my mind when I look down upon the village site from the new Highway 95 or from White Bird Hill or even from Perry's "command post" itself! Yet the Non-Treaty bands would wrangle those horses across rivers, over mountain chains, driving the herds through more than a thousand miles of wilderness in the flight to come. In crossing and re-crossing the ground where this war started I grow all the more awestruck at this monumental feat.

Many of the accounts vary on just what happened in those

moments while Ollokot and Two Moons waited with their warriors as the six peace delegates made their way under a flag of truce toward the first, small group of soldiers. Civilian Ad Chapman—who had a cold, then hot, relationship with the Nez Perce—fired those first two shots without any provocation. Why? Especially when most every source, except Chapman, of course, stated the peace party was carrying a white flag.

Did Chapman actually feel such hatred for the tribe that he decided to start the battle single-handedly? In his own heart did he fear that Perry's soldiers and the Indians would end up talking peace and there would be no fight? Was he really afraid the warriors would flee back to the camp and the entire village would escape across the Salmon just as he and the other civilians had warned Captain Perry? Or, in the end, was Chapman just so arrogant that he thought he was only doing what was needed to open the fight?

What's surprising is that no one, not even Perry himself, ever confronted Chapman on that score, even though some thirty-three dead men lay abandoned back in White Bird Canyon because of what Chapman had started. No one ever called the civilian to task for the fact that what he did meant there would be no turning back. Not for many months, not for many, many miles of drama, tragedy, and heroism.

In growing acquainted with every facet of this short battle I was fascinated with the legend of the "Red Coats." Why did those three young warriors wear those blankets? Was it to conspicuously show the other men or perhaps the young women that the three of them were that much braver than all the other warriors? Or was it a visible appeal to their *wyakin,* their own personal spirit helpers, to watch over them in the coming fight? One thing was certain in this story: what soldiers survived to make it out of that valley did indeed remember those "red coats" and the damage they inflicted.

So why did Perry's soldiers lose this fight—without making an attempt to regroup, to enjoin and hold against the enemy, much less countercharge the warriors? Most historians agree that those two companies of the First U.S. Cavalry suffered from mediocre leadership, despite the fact that they outnumbered Ollokot's and Two Moons's fighting men. Compounding this lack of decisive commanders, the loss of one or both trumpeters only exacerbated the officers' inability to direct and control their men.

Much of the blame must be laid at the feet of David Perry. Unlike some Indian Wars officers who chose to ignore the intelligence brought them by their civilian or Indian scouts, Perry considered what the Mount Idaho citizens had to warn him about . . . then chose to believe that the Nez Perce would indeed attempt to escape across the Salmon River. This meant he reasoned that he could believe the assessment of those civilians like Ad Chapman who had a long history of contact with the tribe when they claimed that the warriors would turn tail and run if confronted by the soldiers.

Would you have done any differently? If you had been in Perry's boots, dismounting on that ground at sunset outside Grangeville, listening to the opinions of those citizens who had daily contact with the Nez Perce . . . would you have decided to take a different approach?

With history as hindsight, we can now state that Perry might have chosen to send some of his Treaty scouts to the White Bird village to request a parley with the chiefs, a council during which he could demand to have the murderers turned over to him while he escorted the rest of the bands onto the reservation. But . . . he did not.

Perry was swayed by the "volunteers" who had his ear at that moment, volunteers who said they knew the true heart of the Nez Perce. The very same volunteers who would abandon his battalion almost from the first shot.

The debate has raged for years: centering on Perry's abilities or lack thereof; on the necessity of sacrificing one-fourth of your command when you send horse-holders to the rear; on the truth or fallacy in the actual number of warriors Ollokot led into battle; on the fact that many of the soldiers were raw recruits; on the dearth of training for both the soldiers and their horses; on the poor condition of their weapons . . . and on and on.

It's much the same debate that has raged over other battles when the army was found wanting and got itself whipped. There will always be those who step forward attempting to find some reason for a stunning defeat other than the fact that the army was simply beaten.

At White Bird, Ollokot's outnumbered warriors pressed their advantage and succeeded in frightening both the civilians and soldiers into turning tail on their weary horses. So let me quiet much of the debate, point by point:

1.) Perry's leadership in the fight would be assailed in the months to come—so much so that the captain requested, and was given, a court of inquiry to answer charges brought against him by Captain Trimble and others. After several days of hearings and testimony critical of Perry from Sergeant Michael McCarthy and very few others, the court did not find against him in his execution of the battle or the retreat. My belief remains that Trimble began the groundswell of sentiment against Perry when he realized just how culpable he would himself be for his own precipitous flight from the valley. Trimble was, after all, the first to the top of the ridge—and the first to finish the race to Grangeville! Trimble escaped, fled, ran . . . leaving far better men to close the file and cover the rear of his retreat. Trimble abandoned thirty-three far, far better soldiers in the valley of the White Bird that Sunday morning.

2.) Even after Perry's company commanders, Theller and Trimble, sent their horse-holders to the rear, it's an undeniable fact that the soldiers still outnumbered the Nez Perce.

3.) After more than a hundred years, there is no longer any dispute about the number of warriors who made it into that fight with the soldiers. Most of the "fighting men" were either too hungover or passed out and in no way capable of defending the village when Theller's detail appeared on the slopes of White Bird Hill. So, I want you to consider just what might have happened to those who did survive the Battle of White Bird if there hadn't been so much of the white man's whiskey in that camp. There is no doubt in my mind that had there been less whiskey, or none at all, more warriors would have been able to mount their ponies and ride into the fray, meaning more of Perry's command would have been killed. In fact, there is enough evidence to believe that Perry's cavalry might well have been annihilated to the last man.

4.) Despite all the apologists wanting to make hay over the fact that an appreciable number of Perry's men were untested recruits, you must remember one undeniable fact: for the most part, the majority of Ollokot's and Two Moons's warriors were even more untried in battle than those green recruits!

5.) Not long after the fight, Sergeant McCarthy wrote: "Many of the guns choked with broken shells, the guns being rusty and foul." Sounds all too familiar after reading about the fatal experiences of those five doomed companies who followed George Armstrong Custer into the valley of the Little Bighorn, doesn't it? I might be able to believe that the raw recruits, not given much of an opportunity to practice with their weapons, left their carbines to grow rusty, to become fouled and unusable . . . were it not for the fact that in both the case of Custer's defeat and the debacle at White Bird Canyon those guns were retrieved from the battlefield and put to good service that very day as well as in the months to come by the victorious Indian warriors!

Make no mistake that I take my stand on just what happened to Perry's command that Sunday morning. It was a simple case of a combination of small, otherwise insignificant, factors that when brought together overwhelmed the abilities of the army commanders.

Under any circumstances, the loss of not only one, but *both*, of Perry's trumpets made it virtually impossible for the captain to issue orders under battlefield conditions.

In the days and weeks to come, the Mount Idaho volunteers would suffer severe criticism for abandoning their position at the far end of the left flank—almost from the first shots! In fact, the first volunteers to flee the fight reached Mount Idaho by 9:00 A.M.! That's when Loyal P. Brown began writing his first dispatch to General Howard.

When those volunteers abandoned the fight, this exposed Theller's left to a brisk fire. At first it took only two or three of Theller's men to waver, turn, and leave the line—following the retreating civilians. And once the first few soldiers turned to flee the fight, once enough soldiers refused to heed the orders of their noncoms or their mediocre commanding officers ... the trickle became a tidal wave.

In his recollections, that courageous, if not impetuous, Sergeant McCarthy went on to summarize the shortcomings of the command:

> *We were in no fit condition to go to White Bird on the night of the 16th. We had been in the saddle nearly 24 hours and men and horses were tired and in bad shape for a fight. To cap the matter, we were marched into a deep canyon and to a country strange to us, and familiar to the enemy. If there was any plan of attack, I never heard of it. The troops were formed in line and about a third advanced in squads and the remainder very soon afterwards retreated in column up a ridge and out of the canyon. The detached advance squads, each acting independently and extended over considerable ground, were attacked in detail and scattered and scarcely any escaped out of the canyon ... Many of these men could have been saved if the retreat of the main column had not been so rapid.*

I don't think any of you will argue with me that Ollokot's fifty or sixty Nez Perce horsemen, outnumbered even as they left their village behind, acquitted themselves most admirably in that first battle ever fought between their people and the U.S. Army.

Now if any of you have an opinion on the mystery of how Jonah Hayes's wife knew of this fight even before it began, if you have some idea how she knew of the "massacre" the night *before* Perry led his men into White Bird Canyon and why she would describe a "trap" being laid for the soldiers *before* the fact ... I'd sure like to hear from you! Very simply, for me this is one of the two most enduring mysteries of this entire outbreak of hostilities.

And while we're on the subject of these Nez Perce women, consider for a moment the courage, what was nothing less than unvarnished heroism, it took for the older woman named *Tulekats Chickchamit* to leave the emotion-charged gathering at the traditional campsite of *Tepahlewam* and make a long, looping ride south over the divide, down the White Bird, reaching the Salmon River settlement of Slate

Creek, where she reported those first murders that had occurred along White Bird Creek itself. Many of the refugees huddled among the few buildings at Slate Creek realized the miners in the nearby hills should be warned of the outbreak and the appeal should be made for those miners to come over to the Salmon, where they could help reinforce the community's defenses.

· But when the white men looked sheepishly at one another, not one of them would volunteer for that twenty-six-mile wilderness ride to Florence. Eventually, the defenders agreed to offer five dollars apiece to the Indian woman, who was a noted gambler, if she would carry their message to the miners.

She completed that difficult ride to the white stronghold of Florence . . . and that's where a colorful bit of folklore was given birth. Like Portugee Phillips more than ten years before her, arriving at Fort Laramie in the midst of a winter blizzard, when *Tulekats* dismounted among a gathering of curious miners her horse collapsed beside her, dead of exhaustion.

If you include Larry Ott in their number, seventeen white miners crossed over the divide on what was called the Nut Basin Road to reach the tiny settlement of Slate Creek, led by *Tulekats*. And when not one but two small bands of warriors showed up at the Slate Creek stockade under a white flag to settle their accounts with trader John Wood before they departed for the buffalo country, *Tulekats* made her way to the walls, where she berated the men of her tribe for killing her friends—saving her harshest scorn for when she chastised them for murdering white women and children.

I'm saddened, but not surprised, to report that neither the settlers nor the Florence miners ever paid *Tulekats* what they had promised her for that daring ride. Eventually, however, this brave woman was rewarded for her courage in the face of her people's fury when her name—once it had been corrupted to *Tolo* over time—was given to that forty-acre lake six miles southwest of Grangeville, the lake on *Tepahlewam* where her people had traditionally gathered for generations. Upon her death, Tolo was buried nearby in Rocky Canyon. It was there that the American Legion Auxiliary erected a memorial to her in 1939.

In years after the Nez Perce conflict, First Sergeant Michael McCarthy became quite vocal in what complaints he had to lodge against Captain David Perry. McCarthy had kept a diary on the campaign,* a record of his escape from the battle-field, which he expanded upon years later. In reading his critical testimony against Perry, along with his unflinching support of Captain Joel G. Trimble, I pause to wonder if McCarthy's memory isn't tinged with rancor at Perry for ever leading the command into the canyon in the first place.

It took two decades after his miraculous escape, but in 1897 the courageous Michael McCarthy finally received the Medal of Honor for his bravery in the face of enemy fire at White Bird Canyon. The citation—though marred with minor errors—reads:

> *Was detailed with six men to hold a commanding position, and held it with great gallantry until the troops fell back. He then fought his way through the Indians, rejoined a portion of his command, and continued to fight in retreat. He had two horses shot [out from] under him, and was captured, but escaped and reported for duty after 3 days' hiding and wandering in the mountains.*

Second Lieutenant William Russell Parnell also received a Medal of Honor for his courage in combat at White Bird Canyon.† In addition, he was awarded a brevet of colonel for his distinguished gallantry in action.

Lew Day, the courier who started from Mount Idaho for Fort Lapwai with news of the first attacks but didn't get very far beyond Cottonwood House when he was jumped, and Joe Moore, the Nortons' hired man, together held back the Nez Perce, preventing them from rushing in to finish the last of those survivors huddled under the wagons or behind the carcasses of their dead horses. Day lingered with his wounds until the morning following their rescue (although Mark Brown says he lived six days). And Joe Moore tenaciously clung to life an agonizing six weeks before he died (Brown claims Moore lasted three months).

I sensed an undeniably strong presence as I stood before

---

*Michael McCarthy Papers, Manuscript Division, Library of Congress, Washington, D.C.
†*The Medal of Honor of the United States Army* (Washington: Government Printing Office, 1948), p. 230

the graves of these two men in that small, out-of-the-way cemetery tucked at a far edge of the tiny community called Mount Idaho, a feeling of standing in the presence of genuine, honest-to-goodness heroes. As I slowly moved from one grave marker or headstone to another in that quiet, shady cemetery, I found many of them memorials to those unfortunates caught in the cross-fire of a conflict that made little sense. With the sunlight slanting through the trees, stirring the remnants of the ground fog left by last night's rain, I stayed longer than I had intended—just listening.

Not all the heroes are buried there.

Delia Theller had been the only officer's wife still at Fort Lapwai when Perry's command marched away at dusk that fifteenth day of June. Tragic that Edward Theller should be the only officer killed with his men less than thirty-six hours later.

Once General Howard led his reinforcements into the bottom of White Bird Canyon and temporarily buried the lieutenant with the other dead, Mrs. Theller penned heartwrenching letters to the newspaper editors throughout central and northern Idaho. Realizing that the Nez Perce might take in some captured goods to trade off for ammunition, supplies, or whiskey to some storekeeper in the region, she offered to pay a reward for the return of any personal item that had been taken off her husband's body by the warriors who had killed him, items the lieutenant had carried with him when he kissed her farewell and marched away from Fort Lapwai into history: his watch, rings, cabinet photos, or any papers that might serve as mementos.

Hers is a part of the story that will bridge over to the second volume of this Nez Perce War tragedy.

That Irish miner named Patrick Brice had seen enough of war against the Nez Perce. Because of his uncanny release from the warriors, unsubstantiated rumors and various discrepancies would whirl around the man for close to a hundred years. Some of the early writers, Loyal P. Brown included, incorrectly recorded his name as Patrick *Price*. This mistake was carried over to modern days when writer Mark H. Brown likewise referred to him as Price.

Even L. V. McWhorter called him *Frederick* Brice! McWhorter, a great supporter of the Non-Treaty Nez Perce, was one of the first to give credence to the fanciful tale that Brice had saved himself when confronted with the warriors in

White Bird Canyon by exposing his chest to show the tattoo of a Catholic crucifix. The rumor had it that the Nez Percé were so awed by the powerful medicine of this tattoo that they immediately gave Brice and Maggie Manuel their freedom. Yet it's strange that not one of the Indian informants McWhorter used to research his books (including the man who gave the authoritative Nez Perce account of that meeting with Brice, Black Feather himself) remembered anything of any marks on the white man's breast—no painting, no symbols, no tattoo!

Why would these members of the Non-Treaty bands, warriors who had rejected the white man's religion, suddenly give any special significance to the white man's crucifix?

Stranger still, Brice himself never mentioned anything of a tattoo in his account, nor does he say anything about the basis of a second, and even more fanciful, rumor popularized by McWhorter and a few others: that Patrick Brice secured his freedom from the warriors by vowing to return to the Indian camp once he had delivered little Maggie to safety.

In her book, *Saga of Chief Joseph,* General Howard's daughter perpetuates this myth regarding the courageous Irishman. It seems that after Brice had reached Mount Idaho with the small girl and rested a day, ". . . he went back to the Indian camp where he presented himself as a hostage, supposedly to Chief Joseph, who magnanimously sent him on his way unharmed."

But this story would not enjoy its real heyday until after the turn of the century, when Charles Stuart Moody wrote an article titled "The Bravest Deed I Ever Knew" for the March 1911 issue of *Century Magazine.* In it Moody explained how Brice had hammered out a deal with the Nez Perce to return to the White Bird camp after he had taken the child to safety in the settlements. Moody explains that the Irishman offered the warriors to "work their will upon him" when he returned. This ludicrous tale ended with Moody declaring that Brice returned to the valley, just as he had promised Black Feather, and was promptly granted his freedom because the warriors were so deeply impressed with not only his courage but mainly the fact that he had kept his word!

A few of you might be wondering about the enduring mystery of whatever happened to Jennet Manuel, just where she and her young son disappeared to after daughter Maggie told

Brice she watched Chief Joseph stab her mother in the house, where the Irishman was unable to find the bodies later on. When reunited in Mount Idaho, Jennet Manuel's father, George Popham, told Brice that the house had burned to the ground. . . .

No, I think I'll stop right there. Going to leave that matter until the next volume, when I'll address the conflicting accounts of her disappearance simply because of the reports that continued to drift in concerning a disheveled blond-haired white woman spotted among the Non-Treaty bands as they pushed south through the Bitterroot Valley, making their way to the Big Hole.

The high level of confidence the warriors—indeed, every man, woman, and child in the Non-Treaty bands—gained with the army's debacle at White Bird Canyon would assure that the Nez Perce War would not be a short-lived campaign. The *Nee-Me-Poo* would go on to fight at Cottonwood and Clearwater, then escape to Montana Territory via the Lolo Pass. Their great victory on the White Bird—just like the victory of the Lakota and Cheyenne on the Greasy Grass the year before—gave the Non-Treaty bands the unmitigated confidence that they would eventually triumph in their struggle, gave them unbridled hope that if they could not return to life as it had been in their own land, then they could not be stopped on their migration to the Old Woman's Country.

Their sweet victory at White Bird Canyon would soon grow bitter in their mouths. Time and again over the coming months, fate would tease the Nez Perce, ultimately making fools of them for believing in what they had accomplished against Perry's soldiers.

Forlorn Hope, John D. McDermott's book on the murders and the outbreak, is nothing less than the cornerstone to this historical novel. My story would not have been written were it not for Jack's trailblazing research. Back when he first encountered the Nez Perce War, the history books dealt with the White Bird fight in no more than a page or two. And when any of the sources mentioned the court of inquiry Perry requested to clear his name, none of the authors dealt with that court's deliberations or its findings. But Jack does, and the testimony is illuminating—material I was able to incorporate into the narrative of my story.

If you do further reading from the bibliography that follows, be forewarned. Most of the sources contradicted one another on the murders, raids, and depredations—always conflict in the number of victims, locations, who was involved from the bands, etc. Clearly, someone had to sift through everything available in each of the archives and make sense of all the characters and their individual dramas. That was just the sort of detailed job for a man the likes of Jack McDermott, who loves scratching around in the dark corners of archives for what others have missed!

Realize that my novel of what really happened in the outbreak of the Nez Perce War could not have been written without Jack's pioneering work on those opening days of the tragedy. If his monumental efforts in *Forlorn Hope* prove one thing, it is that the first works by Josephy, Beale, and Mark H. Brown hadn't exhausted the study of the Nez Perce War. Instead, their efforts were only the opening chapters of a story still being written.

With what Jack McDermott and Jerry Greene have done to shed light on the shadowy places, bringing more details into focus, we are now able to view what has been an incomplete picture left by the earlier historians. I firmly believe we are close to knowing *all* that really happened in those early days of what became a tragic struggle to maintain a way of life, what I hope will eventually be seen as a heroic saga on both sides of the conflict.

To read more about these first days of the war, I recommend you get your hands on the following volumes:

An Army Doctor's Wife on the Frontier—Letters from Alaska and the Far West, 1874–1878, by Emily FitzGerald (edited by Abe Laufe)

Battle Drums and Geysers, by Orvin H. and Lorraine Bonney

Chief Joseph Country, by Bill Gulick

Chief Joseph—The Biography of a Great Indian, by Chester Anders Fee

Chief Joseph's Allies, by Clifford E. Trafzer and Richard D. Scheuerman

Chief Joseph's Own Story, edited by Donald McRae

Chief Joseph's People and Their War, by Alvin M. Josephy, Jr.

Chief Lawyer of the Nez Perce Indians, 1796–1876, by Clifford M. Drury

Children of Grace—The Nez Perce War of 1877, by Bruce Hampton

Famous Indian Chiefs I Have Known, by O. O. Howard

The Flight of the Nez Perce, by Mark H. Brown

Following the Nez Perce Trail—A Guide to the Nee-Me-Poo National Historic Trail with Eyewitness Accounts, by Cheryl Wilfong

Forlorn Hope—The Battle of White Bird Canyon and the Beginning of the Nez Perce War, by John D. McDermott

The Great Escape—The Nez Perce War in Words and Pictures, by Pascal Tchakmakian

Hawks and Doves in the Nez Perce War of 1877—Personal Recollections of Eugene Tallmadge Wilson, edited by Eugene Edward Wilson

Hear Me, My Chiefs!, by L. V. McWhorter

Howard's Campaign Against the Nez Perce Indians, by Thomas Sutherland

I Will Fight No More Forever, by Merrill D. Beal

In Pursuit of the Nez Perce, compiled and edited by Linwood Laughy

Indian Wars of the Pacific Northwest, by Ray Hoard Grassley

The Last Stand of the Nez Perce—Destruction of a People, by Harvey Chalmers II

Let Me Be Free—The Nez Perce Tragedy, by David Lavender

A Little Bit of Wisdom—Conversations with a Nez Perce Elder, by Horace Axtell and Margo Aragon

The Long Flight—A History of the Nez Perce War, by Harrison Lane

Massacres of the Mountains—A History of the Indian Wars of the Far West, by J. P. Dunn

My Life and Experiences Among Our Hostile Indians, by Oliver O. Howard

The Nez Perce Indians and the Opening of the Northwest, by Alvin M. Josephy, Jr.

Nez Perce Joseph, by Oliver Otis Howard

The Nez Perce Tribesmen of the Columbia Plateau, by Frances Haines

Northwestern Fights and Fighters, by Cyrus Townsend Brady

The Patriot Chiefs—A Chronicle of American Indian Leadership, by Alvin M. Josephy, Jr.

Phil Sheridan and His Army, by Paul Andrew Hutton

Red Eagles of the Northwest, by Frances Haines

Saga of Chief Joseph, by Helen Addison Howard

Sword and Olive Branch—Oliver Otis Howard, by John A. Carpenter

Tales of the Nez Perce, by Donald M. Hines

Thunder in the Mountains, by Ronald K. Fisher

The U.S. Army and the Nee-Me-Poo Crisis of 1877: Historic Sites Associated with the Nez Perce War, by Jerome A. Greene

U.S. Army Uniforms and Equipment, 1889, with foreword by Jerome A. Greene

War Cries on Horseback—The Story of the Indian Wars of the Great Plains, by Stephen Longstreet

Yellow Wolf: His Own Story, by L. V. McWhorter

For those of you who thought you knew the whole story before—much of which was probably a sanitized and politically correct version of history—I'll wager you should have laid this book down long before now!

As I draw near to closing, I also want to thank the good folks of the town of Grangeville, which served as my base camp for nearly a week of research, as well as tiny communities up and down the east bank of the Salmon River. Everywhere I turned in my travels, the people I ran across were eager to help me find one site or another in my explorations of the real story of the Nez Perce War.

Should you ever find yourself in west-central Idaho, you can visit the historical scenes of my story with a little detective work on your part and the maps at the front of this book. But I imagine most folks will be satisfied with taking the self-guided auto tour that descends White Bird Hill down the switchbacks of a narrow two-lane road to the battleground rather than viewing the canyon from the top of the new highway that never makes its way into the valley. Better yet, you can begin your journey into the past right in the little community of White Bird itself, taking the short drive to the battlefield following in the hoofprints of Ollokot's warriors that Sunday morning as they raced out to confront Theller's detail and Chapman's civilians.

There's a small spot at the west side of the winding road where there's room enough for two cars to park, where you can step through a gate and follow a steep, little-used trail up the heights to the soldiers' position. But let this serve as a warning to all but the hardiest of you: this will be a strenuous hike up from the valley floor. Take your time. Along the way you can stop and enjoy the view in all directions. Your first halt might be once you reach the volunteers' position. Catch your breath there before continuing on to Theller's hill, then higher still to Trimble's ridge. And finally you will be rewarded when you have gasped your way all the way to the top of the battlefield, finally standing where McCarthy's men held out as long as they deemed they could against overwhelming numbers.

From this perspective, you'll witness everything: from the valley floor to the top of the ridge, able to see firsthand how the battle unfolded. You will be standing on ground where the ghosts still walk.

Not far up the canyon, erected right beside the twisting two-lane blacktop that leads you to the top of White Bird Hill, in fact, you'll pass by a lone concrete memorial shaft that marks the spot where Sergeant Patrick Gunn of Company F held his private duel with an unnamed Nez Perce warrior. A handful of soldiers in retreat turned around to gaze over their shoulders, watching this gray-headed veteran in the middle of his fourth enlistment as he spilled from his horse, wounded.

Yet the sergeant scrambled to his knees, dragging his pistol from its holster as a single warrior closed in and dismounted his weary war pony.

Struggling to his feet—so say the survivors who witnessed this duel from the slopes above—Sergeant Gunn fired at his lone adversary. The approaching warrior fired back, darting from one clump of brush to another. For the next few minutes, as the retreating soldiers watched, that lone Nez Perce closed in and the two enemies fought their very private duel . . . until the soldier ultimately fell beside the bush growing near the present-day marker.

It was Sergeant Gunn's body that Patrick Brice and Maggie Manuel found standing nearly upright, suspended in the thorns of the bramble bush, as they hurried across the battlefield and up the heights. Because he stood almost erect against the bush, they initially believed his corpse was a warrior about to attack. In the day to come, that upright positioning of Patrick Gunn's body would even fool Howard's troops (come to bury the dead) that the corpse was really an Indian still lurking about to ambush the unsuspecting burial details.

I choose to believe that the victorious Nez Perce warrior who ultimately killed Gunn in this very personal, very courageous duel consciously decided not to leave the soldier lying on the battlefield. Instead, I believe the warrior sought to honor his worthy opponent by placing the sergeant's body against the bramble bush. Standing: the way a proven, honorable warrior would confront his enemies.

Back up there at the high ground within McCarthy's rocks, I began jotting down my thoughts for this afterword as the rain-laden clouds crept in.

But it is here, beside this solitary memorial to a lone cavalry sergeant, that I finish my thoughts on this first fight between the army and the Nez Perce.

Here I stand in awe, once again hoping that in some small way what I have written will honor the last great sacrifice made by those brave souls who still walk this hallowed ground.

—Terry C. Johnston
White Bird Battlefield